About the Authors

Bronwyn Scott is the author of over seventy books. Her 2018 novella, *Dancing with the Duke's Heir,* was a *RITA* finalist. She loves history and is always looking forward to the next story. She also enjoys talking with other writers and readers about books they like and the writing process. Readers can connect via Bluesky @bronwynscott.bsky.social

Christine Merrill wanted to be a writer for as long as she can remember. During a stint as a stay-at-home mother, she decided it was time to 'write that book.' She could set her own hours and would never have to wear tights to work! It was a slow start, but she slogged onward, and seven years later, she got the thrill of seeing her first book hit the shelves. Christine lives in Wisconsin with her family. Visit her website at: christine-merrill.com

The Grinch Who Stole Her Heart

BRONWYN SCOTT

CHRISTINE MERRILL

MILLS & BOON

First Published in Great Britain 2025
by Mills & Boon, an imprint of HarperCollins*Publishers* Ltd
1 London Bridge Street, London, SE1 9GF

www.harpercollins.co.uk

HarperCollins*Publishers*
Macken House, 39/40 Mayor Street Upper,
Dublin 1, D01 C9W8, Ireland

ISBN: 978-0-263-41923-8

FSC
www.fsc.org
MIX
Paper | Supporting responsible forestry
FSC™ C007454

This book contains FSC™ certified paper and other controlled sources to ensure responsible forest management.

For more information visit: www.harpercollins.co.uk/green

Printed and Bound in the UK using 100% Renewable Electricity at CPI Group (UK) Ltd, Croydon, CR0 4YY

DANCING WITH THE DUKE'S HEIR

BRONWYN SCOTT

For Drum and Daphne and the girls.
Thanks for opening your house to us and all the good meals over the past years. You are all great fun!

Chapter One

Thursday, 24th December 1818, Christmas Eve

Christmas. Again. The fourth without his father, without his brother. Vale Penrith drew a deep breath and stepped down from the warm carriage into the bracing cold of winter, the soles of his boots crunching on the crisp, thin layer of newly falling snow. *Lumi*, the Sami people of Lapland, his latest anthropological study, would call it. Perhaps later it would turn to *viti*, powdery snow, or if they were less lucky, *iljanne*—snow that was only a thin layer atop ice. Vale cast a glance towards the grey clouds, sending a prayer skywards. He just had to get through the next twelve days. At least, he wasn't doing it alone.

Vale reached into the carriage, offering a hand

to his mother. Margot Penrith descended, a fragile, beautiful snow queen, delicate and elegant, swathed in expensive furs. The look in her pale blue eyes mirrored the thoughts of his mind: they weren't supposed to be here. Not like this, a broken family of two mourning the loss of their other halves: a beloved husband, an adored brother; a widow and an unlooked-for heir. He'd never thought to be at Brockmore as the heir to his uncle's legacy, a legacy he felt ill suited to assume. He was a politician by conscience when the occasion demanded it, an anthropologist by choice. He was *not* a duke.

He took his mother's arm and together they climbed the entry stairs to the imposing double doors already swagged with greenery. An invitation to some, Vale supposed. A note of caution to others like himself. Either way the message of the greenery was the same: Christmas began the moment one passed beyond these doors. Guests could expect the Duke and Duchess of Brockmore to engage the holiday fully. His aunt and uncle did nothing by halves.

Inside, the hall was warm. The sound of happy voices drifted from the drawing room along with welcoming scents of spiced tea and fresh baked cakes. The butler had barely taken their coats and furs when Uncle Marcus appeared, silver hair thick, clothes immaculate, his carriage hale and perfect as he strode forward, his arms held out wide, a broad smile on his face, his voice booming in welcome. He took Vale's mother in a full embrace. 'Margot, my dear sister-in-law! You're here and just in time. We'll start the greening in an hour or so. Alicia will be so glad you made it. One never knows with the roads this time of year.' He turned to Vale, studying him for a moment, the keen blue Brockmore eyes sweeping him from top to bottom in approval. 'My boy, it is good to see you,' he said simply before wrapping him in his arms. Vale hugged him back. For just a minute, he wasn't the heir, but simply a beloved nephew and this man was not the mighty Brockmore, powerful duke, but his uncle, his father's older brother, a living link to the man he'd lost. And Vale savoured it.

Aunt Alicia materialised beside him, tall and regal in a fashionable gown of dark blue, just as Vale remembered her. She looped her arm through his mother's, taking the delicate Margot under her hostess's wing and ushering her into the heart of the party in Brockmore's famed blue receiving room, already drawing her in with chatter and news of the guests. Uncle Marcus clapped a firm hand on his shoulder. 'Come, there's some people I want you to meet.'

Brockmore toured him about the room. He met the golden, blue-eyed Aubrey Kenelm, heir to the Marquess of Durham, the poised brunette, Lady Anne Lowell, daughter of the Earl of Blackton, whom the Duke introduced with a certain sparkle in his eye. That sparkle sent a *frisson* of caution through Vale. His uncle was notorious for his matchmaking at these parties. He had no wish to be his uncle's next project. Vale nodded politely to each woman, careful not to be too polite to Lady Anne, while smiling warmly at her subdued companion, Marianne Pletcher, who by nature of her situation posed no danger to him as a potential match.

These were the sorts of people he expected to meet. They were the sorts who ran in his uncle's circles. Well-bred, well-moneyed people with marital hopes. But, he noted, there was another set of guests that populated the drawing room—in fact, made up the majority of the guests in attendance. There was Miss Rose Burnham, a decidedly pretty girl of good family whose father had fallen on hard times, leaving her with nothing than her looks as a dowry; Matthew Eaton, son of the local baron, who never quite made it up to London but was charming and handsome despite the lack of any other true prospects to offer. With the exception of Kenelm and Lady Anne, these were *not* the typical guests one usually encountered at Brockmore. Finally, his uncle brought him to a man of later middle years sitting by himself in the corner.

The man rose to greet them, his uncle putting a hand on the man's shoulder in affection. 'Silas Arthur, Lord Truesdale, this is my nephew, Vale Penrith.'

Vale watched the man's tired eyes register with recognition. 'Ah, Penrith. The heir.' Vale was coming to hate the title, a constant symbol of all that had transpired in order for that label to come to him.

They made small talk briefly before his uncle excused them, his voice quiet at his ear as they moved away. 'Silas lost his wife two years ago.' Uncle Marcus squeezed his shoulder, drawing Vale's gaze. 'You are not the only one here who mourns.' There was a fleeting sadness in his uncle's gaze, a reminder that his uncle had lost a brother the same way he'd lost R.J. when his father had died. And yet, one would never know except in these unguarded moments. He envied his uncle that ability to go on. He had not mastered that quality yet. Perhaps he didn't want to. Perhaps he wanted the clock to stop on the twenty-first of April 1814, then both his father and R.J. would still be alive.

His uncle steered him towards the small cluster of gentlemen at the fireplace, the momentary sadness gone from his gaze. 'You'll want to get to know the other young men,' he instructed. 'They're all very nice. I think you will enjoy Kenelm and Eaton, especially. Others will be joining us before long.' He winked and gave him a final clap on the back. 'Be happy, Vale.' His eyes sparked with mischief. 'Don't think I don't know you'd prefer to stay hidden away in London in your library with your anthropology, trying to ignore the world. Life goes on whether you want it to or not. You might as well enjoy it. Consider it my Christmas gift to you.'

Not just to him, Vale thought as Kenelm moved over to make room for him in their circle at the fireplace. It explained the mix of guests; the lonely widower in the corner, the pretty, desperate debutante, the country-bound baron's son who for all his potential would never escape the country without a boost from a high-placed mentor. The list went on. His uncle's gift to them was a chance: a chance to marry well if you were Rose Burnham, a chance to rebuild your life if you were Lord Truesdale; a chance to rise beyond the limits of the countryside on the merits of your own wit if you were Matthew Eaton. A chance to be happy and alive, if you were Vale Penrith and you'd been dead inside already for nearly four years.

At the entrance to the drawing room, his uncle clapped his hands, demanding attention. 'Everyone! A moment, please!' He waited for the room to silence. Aunt Alicia took her place next to her husband, smiling her own greeting. 'We want to welcome you to Brockmore for the holidays. We have festivities planned from skating parties to a gingerbread fair, and masquerade ball for Twelfth Night. It will be a Christmastide to remember!' Swift murmurs of excitement undulated around the room. Brockmore called for silence once more. 'The footmen have returned with the boughs, freshly cut from Brockmore pine. Let the greening commence! Let Christmas begin!'

Applause and cheers went up, filling the drawing room. Beside Vale, Aubrey Kenelm was good naturedly stripping out of his coat, ready to work. 'The ladies will need us for the heavy lifting.' He grinned and nudged Matthew Eaton with his elbow as if they were the best of friends even though they'd only met an hour ago. He grabbed Vale's arm with his other hand. 'Come on. I'll take the doorways, you and Matthew take the staircase.' Just like that, Vale found himself in charge of draping the banister with no chance to slink off to his room to unpack his books. He had a report to write for the board of the British Museum concerning Lapland and the mysteries of the north. His uncle was right. He'd rather be tucked away in his library where no one could bother him instead of being in the thick of the festivities. But it was too late to turn back now. The museum report would have to wait.

Just another half an inch and she'd have it. She couldn't turn back now, not when she was nearly there. Lady Viola Hawthorne stretched on the tips of her toes atop a ladder in Brockmore's hall, a mistletoe ball hanging from her fingers as she reached for the fire-polished crystal drop hanging from the chandelier's centre. Almost… there…

The ladder swayed precariously as she adjusted her position. A good sixteen feet below her a crowd of young people greening the hall began to gather around the base of the ladder, intrigued by her antics. On her periphery, she caught sight of a tall figure moving rapidly down the stairs. She felt firmer hands on the ladder a moment later, followed by an even firmer admonition. 'Come down at once! Do you want to break your neck?' She didn't dare look to see who it was below her or she'd lose her nerve. Did the Scold really think she hadn't already come to the same conclusion? She'd simply chosen to ignore the danger. Playing it cautious didn't fit her plans. Cautious girls weren't expelled from house parties.

Lady Viola laughed, loud and brave. 'Never!'

The Scold's reproach served to spur her on, urging her up on to one toe like a ballerina, her gown drawn tight against her breasts as she stretched upwards, her hem lifting to reveal her ankles and quite a bit more. One could indeed be enormously scandalous atop a ladder, which was precisely what she intended, precisely *why* she'd worn silk stockings, red garters and nothing more beneath her gown. But at the moment, she cared less what the local lads might sneak a peek at and more about the challenge at hand. She was fully extended. There wasn't a fraction of an inch left to be had. Unless…

She couldn't be closer to the chandelier, but the chandelier could be closer to her. Viola's fingertips could just reach the nearest arm, just enough to give it a push. She set the great chandelier to swaying, a little at first and then more when it gained momentum, but not too much. It was delicate work. She didn't want the chandelier to mow her down like a wrecking ball. Now, all she had to do was time the in-swing, and… *Voila!*

'Got it!' she exclaimed, hooking the mistletoe on to the dangling crystal drop as the chandelier made its third pass.

The guests beneath her broke into applause and cheers, all except one—her disapproving ladder holder. Never mind him. She had no time for spoilsports. She climbed halfway down, stopping to sweep her adoring audience a gallant bow, before launching herself. 'Catch me!'

She let go of the ladder and fell. There was a collective gasp, a moment's chaos, others rushing forward to steady the ladder and then she was in his arms: strong arms, angry arms. He was not nearly as amused by her finale as everyone else. His blue eyes were thunderous when he set her down. 'You little fool! Have you no care? Do you value yourself so cheaply as to throw your life away over a tawdry trick? Or the lives of your fellow guests? You put them at risk as well. What do you suppose happens to them if the ladder falls, or the chandelier crashes without warning?' He did not bother to lower his voice and his tone froze the levity she'd conjured.

'Who the hell are you to tell me what I can and cannot do?' She looked him up and down, from steely blue eyes to long legs, her hands on hips in outrage. How dare he publicly reprimand her as if she were a naughty child? Worse than that, how dare he steal *her* attention?

'I'm Vale Penrith, Brockmore's nephew. This is my home as much as it is my uncle's. I will not see it used as a staging grounds for imprudent behaviour.'

The heir. Oh, well done. This was a record even for her. She'd been here less than two hours and she'd managed to give Brockmore's heir a peek up her skirts. This would not do. She knew a moment of uncharacteristic panic. Her parents, when they arrived, would be furious *if* they found out. True, she wanted them furious enough to send her home, away from the dangers of matchmaking, but not too furious—if they thought they could use a scandal to compromise someone as enticing as Brockmore's heir to the altar, her plans would have backfired in the extreme. The altar was what she was trying to avoid.

Diversion! She needed something to top the ladder escapade, something everyone would talk about instead. She flashed a challenge at tall, imposing Penrith with his angry eyes and strong arms before turning to the others. 'We're standing under a mistletoe ball and you all know what that means!' Viola pulled the nearest young man to her, Matthew Eaton, and kissed him hard on the mouth, a glorious, open-mouthed kiss that lingered long enough for everyone to take note. This was no chaste peck on the cheek, or a polite, dry buss on the lips.

Viola stepped back and raised her arms in pronouncement. 'The first kiss of Christmas!' The guests whooped with delight. Just like that, she had the crowd back. She tossed Penrith a victorious grin over her shoulder, but he was already gone, back up the stairs to fasten the last of the bows on the garland at maddeningly even, precise intervals, thanks, no doubt, to the measuring stick he probably carried in his…head.

Chapter Two

Whoever said rank had its privileges didn't have to go in to dinner with Vale Penrith and all of his perfection. He stood before her in the drawing room punctually at seven o'clock with a bow and the offer of his arm, immaculately turned out in dark evening clothes and crisp white linen, cravat impeccably tied and accented with a ruby stick pin in the dead centre. He probably had a mental measuring stick for that, too. Even his hair, a dark blond and arguably his only break with convention since it was surprisingly longer than most men's, was tied back in a black ribbon, also perfect. Not a literal hair out of place.

She wanted to mess him up. Just a little. Perhaps pull a stray hair loose, or bump that stick pin a fraction so it was off centre. Or maybe she wanted to do something more devastating like spill her red wine on his white shirt at dinner. Except now she couldn't because of the 'hall incident'. He would think a little spilled wine was her idea of revenge instead of an out-and-out rebellion against his perfection. No, wine would look petty. She'd have to think of something else.

All she could do for the present was take his arm and try to behave as blandly as he, as if they hadn't sparred earlier in the hall, as if one of them—not her—hadn't attempted to belittle the other in public. Surely, if he could pretend the hall incident had not happened, she could manage it, too. On the surface, at least. She was willing to *pretend.* She wasn't willing to forget.

They joined the parade into supper, the third couple behind the Duke and her mother and the Duchess and her father. Anne Lowell and Aubrey Kenelm were behind her. There was that to be thankful for at least. She'd have Kenelm on her other side to break up the monotony of conversing with Penrith. Good heavens, what *would* they talk about for two hours? If ladder safety in halls was of primary importance, she could imagine his concerns over the dangers of dining; The safety of knives, perhaps? The perils of open-flame candles and hot wax? They stepped into the dining room and all thought of conversation fled. Brockmore knew how to serve a supper and it was breathtaking in its subtle luxury.

Viola was used to opulence. Her father, the Duke of Calton, had wealth aplenty, but even a familiarity with luxury did not dim the elegance of Brockmore's formal dining room decked with all the pomp demanded of a ducal Christmas Eve dinner. The long, polished table featured three eight-armed candelabra done in heavy silver and set at intervals down the length of the table, the thick white tapers shining their light on thin-stemmed crystal goblets and beautiful china plates trimmed with a cranberry and gold rim.

The room even *smelled* lovely, like winter and Christmas combined, thanks to arrangements of rosemary and bay placed artfully about the room. While she'd been climbing atop the ladder in the hall in a blatant display of festivity, risking life and limb for a kissing bough, someone had seen to a discreet greening of the dining room. Probably some of the older ladies.

Subtle was not something Viola aspired to, but in this instance she approved. Her gown complemented the setting ideally in style and in tone. She was even glad her mother had insisted she wear the ivory gown with the elaborately worked net slip and its complicated draping, the overskirt edged in a detailed lace. Even the hem of the net over-slip was done in a heavier, pointed lace to give it weight. The gown was exquisite, the kind of fashion only a duke's daughter could afford.

Wearing such an advertisement always made her wary, however. Her mother suggested gowns for a reason. Viola cast a sideways glance at Penrith as he held out her chair, seeing him through her parents' desperate eyes: tall, perhaps handsome in their estimation, the candlelight favouring him, showing off the sharp planes of his face, the high cheekbones with their slight, aristocratic hollows beneath, the long straight slant of his nose. But that didn't change the fact he had the personality of a stump, or that marriage was for ever.

Just the thought of 'for ever' made her shudder. For ever with a stump? Well, that was absolutely *unthinkable* no matter how much money he had. It validated for her all the reasons she had for avoiding marriage so heartily. She would not give her life over to the whim of a man. It would mean the end of her dreams: of travelling the Continent, of studying music in Vienna, where she heard a woman could enjoy greater freedoms. To her, marriage was nothing more than a woman's enslavement. Enslavement to a *stump*.

Viola sat, careful of her skirts, and gave Penrith a polite smile for his efforts. She didn't dare anything more, not without raising her parents' hopes. Girls who won the hands of ducal heirs were *not* expelled from parties. She could imagine what was going through her parents' minds. She had no doubt they were covertly watching, and rejoicing. Their daughter had gone into dinner with Brockmore's heir, a most fortuitous event. One they could not have controlled, but certainly had hoped for.

Viola knew very well the only reason they'd been invited was because they'd *begged* Brockmore for the invitation. She was twenty-one and, in their estimation, running out of options, after having run off the most eligible men of the ton for the last three years. Dukes' daughters were never in dearth of suitors. Viola surveyed the table, taking stock of the guests assembled all in one place at one time, and took note. There were a lot of desperate people here. She did not count herself among them. She was not desperate for marriage. She was desperate for freedom.

Things were turning out *exactly* as she'd planned three years ago when she'd made her debut. Another year of living outrageously, and she'd be considered unmarriageable. She could get on with her life and not worry about the encumbrances of a husband and keeping up appearances. If she could get politely 'excused' from the party by New Year's she could be back home celebrating Twelfth Night with her friends in the village, performing her new musical composition.

'Lady Viola,' Penrith's baritone murmured on her left as partridge soup was placed in front of them. Brockmore had chosen to serve the meal *à la Russe*. 'So, you're the girl who swings from chandeliers.' The frosty disapproval was still there in the hyperbole.

'Yes,' She graced him with a wide, teasing smile, letting her eyes spark with a little flirtation because it would annoy him no end. 'And you're the man who brought her in to dinner. How do *you* feel about that?' It was probably quite disturbing to him that all of his perfection should be linked to such a madcap even for the span of a dinner. Disturbing or not, he gave no sign of it.

He gave a neutral shrug. She suspected he did a lot of that—embracing neutrality. It saved from having opinions, feelings. 'It is out of my control. The social gods preordain who takes who in to dinner.'

His reaction was disappointing. He was infuriatingly proper, infuriatingly unflappable. Infuriatingly *empty*. At least silly men had *something* in their heads even if it was inane. That decided it. She would get a rise out of him before dinner was over. It would be payback for the hall. 'Are you sure? Isn't it "who takes whom"?'

Something flickered in his blue eyes, his voice striving to convey patience while not being condescending, a battle his tone only partially won. 'I am sure. "Who" is used for subjects, and "whom" is used for objects. Furthermore, "whom" is reserved for use in subordinate clauses in most cases.' Oh, he did not like her. His disdain was evident.

She gave a sly smile and fluttered her eyelashes in her best impression of a simpering debutante. 'That is *most* scintillating, indeed. Perhaps it is *I* who am in the company of a celebrity. I had no idea someone actually *listened* to grammar lessons.'

'*You* are mocking me, Lady Viola. Please do not.' He wiped his mouth quite decisively with his napkin, signalling he was done with his soup and ready to have it removed, perhaps a metaphor for what he'd like to do with her. Or maybe she gave herself too much credit. Wanting to have her removed assumed she'd got to him.

He surprised her, leaning close to her ear, his voice low as if imparting intimacies, which was how it would look to the rest of the table. The table would be wrong. There was nothing intimate or even friendly about his words. 'I know all about you. I know what they call you in town—London's Shocking Beauty. While I'm sure you endeavour to live up to the epitaph, if you want to get a rise out of me, you'll have to do more than question my use of English grammar. I have far weightier considerations to spend my time on than forward young women who risk themselves needlessly on high ladders in order to give the local lads a peek up their skirts.'

'*I* was hanging mistletoe!' Viola hissed defensively, furious he'd seen through her so easily. 'How dare you make it into something lurid.'

'*I* didn't,' he replied blandly, leaning back so the footman could set down the second course, a hot raised pie of winter game that smelled divine. 'You did that all on your own when you decided to climb the ladder, or perhaps even as early as this morning when you decided to forgo wearing certain undergarments.' He gave her a piercing look that would have withered a less intrepid soul. It nearly worked anyway.

'So you did look?' She infused a sense of victory into her whispered response, but there was little victory. She could protest all she liked, but somehow he *knew* she'd known very well how she looked on the ladder, that it had been artfully arranged.

'How could I not? I had to balance the ladder, it required I assume a certain posture. Had there been another way, rest assured I would have taken it. Your red-ribboned garters hold no charm for me.'

Viola felt her cheeks burn. He was calling her 'easy' and he wasn't done yet. 'It was a cheap trick you pulled today. I was not impressed. Foolhardy risk never impresses me.'

'And stiff propriety doesn't impress me.' She shot the innuendo back hotly, her temper getting the better of discretion. She wanted to shock him, to say something outrageous. 'How dare you sit there and scold me for having a little fun. It's the holidays and the Puritans have been out of style for centuries now, in case you didn't know. It's no wonder you've been invited, no wonder you need your uncle's help in finding a wife. No one would have a prig like you in their beds without the title and the money.'

For a moment his eyes blazed, a brilliant sapphire flame that was extinguished as quickly as it had been lit, so quickly it might have been only a trick of the candlelight. A cool, triumphant smile took his mouth and for an instant it occurred to her how truly handsome he could be if he would only try. He leaned close again and she smelled the vanilla-bay undertones of his soap—a winter scent for a wintry man. 'I think the question is, who got a rise out of whom? Now, if you'll excuse me?' He turned away, devoting himself to Anne Lowell as the Duchess of Brockmore initiated the turn of the table, leaving her beaten at her own game. She had meant to annoy him, but just the opposite had occurred.

The pie smelled delicious. Unfortunately, Penrith's comment ruined it. Damn him. Game pie was one of her favourites. Viola gave it a petulant stab with her fork. Fine. She didn't want his stuffy company anyway. He could talk to Anne Lowell about grammar all night if he preferred and who knew? Maybe Anne Lowell was well born enough to know her duty and listen.

With a huff, Viola threw herself into flirting outrageously with Kenelm on her left and engaging him in a personal conversation that left no doubt she found his company preferable to Penrith's. She was Viola Hawthorne, London's Shocking Beauty, the life of the party, not some cheap trick, but when it came time to remove the game pie, hers was still untouched.

That did it. It was no longer enough to try to get a dinner rise from him. He'd scolded her twice now *and* he'd ruined her favourite dish. This was not over, not by a long shot. Whether Penrith knew it or not, he'd just declared war.

Chapter Three

'Lady Viola, I need your help,' Lady Anne Lowell whispered in rushed undertones as they took their seats in the chapel for Brockmore's midnight service. 'I need you to do something for me.' Anne's hushed excitement was at odds with the serenity of their surroundings, candles illuminating the rich stained-glass windows that lined either side of the little church as midnight approached.

Intrigued, Viola leaned towards Anne, making sure her mother couldn't hear. 'What is it?' Anything to cause a little trouble.

'I need you to distract Penrith.' Anne leaned near, offering words of encouragement, trying to avoid the censorious glance of her cousin, Marianne, who sat beside her on the aisle. 'It shouldn't be difficult. I am only asking because you seem to be the logical choice. He was interested in you at dinner. Your heads were close together.'

Viola stifled a snort. If Anne only knew what had been said. Her friend might be less impressed with her abilities to 'distract' Penrith. 'Distract him? Whatever for? I don't know that Penrith finds me very compelling.'

'*Whoever* for,' Anne corrected. 'For me.'

Viola raised an eyebrow in enquiry, not quite sure she understood Anne's concern. 'You've only been seated by each other for a single dinner. It's hardly a proposal.'

'Don't you see it?' Anne argued swiftly. 'Conventional wisdom suggests Brockmore wants to find him a wife. He's thirty and its time for him to set up his nursery in earnest, especially after all the bad Brockmore luck these past four years. He really dare not wait.' She blushed and looked down modestly at her hands. 'I suspect that's why I'm here. In fact, I know it. My father and Brockmore have it all worked out.'

'You're to be the virgin sacrifice?' Viola said frankly, tossing Penrith a more assessing glance past Anne's shoulder, considering Penrith's suitability for Anne. 'I suppose he's handsome enough.' Penrith would be considered a catch by many, just not by her.

'He's certainly rich enough.' Anne answered practically, 'but I'm not interested.' She looked at her hands again, preparing to dissemble. 'I have fixed my attentions elsewhere, some time ago,' she confessed shyly before adding, 'with Kenelm. Please?'

Viola's instincts were on alert now. She gave Anne a sly look, taking in Anne with a new level of respect. Perhaps she wasn't such a virgin sacrifice, after all, like so many other young women too afraid to stand up for what they wanted. 'You and Kenelm? You know each other from before?' Perhaps more than knew each other if she considered Anne's words. Anne blushed again and Viola waited for the secret to come out. The vicar was ascending the steps to the pulpit. She hoped Anne would hurry or else she'd have to wait until the service was over.

'You can't tell anyone. Nothing is official. His father…' Anne's voice dropped off decorously, a sure signal there were secrets for the probing if Viola was willing. 'Will you do it for me?'

'If I do,' Viola said slowly, 'you have to do something for me.' An idea was taking shape as her gaze darted past Anne once more to the pew across the aisle.

'Yes, anything!' Anne breathed in relief as the vicar opened his Bible and shuffled the pages of his sermon in the pulpit. 'What shall it be?'

Viola grinned. 'Anything. Just like you said. Anything I need, any time I need it. No questions asked. Do we have a deal?' But of course they did. Anne wouldn't have asked otherwise. It was settled. She would distract Penrith. Now the question was how to do it?

The vicar began to speak, welcoming them to Brockmore. He had a deep, sonorous but commanding voice, very pleasing to listen to, and Viola did listen. For a while. Viola fingered the pearl pendant at her neck, running her hand over the smooth nacre ball as she thought—sermons were good for that, plenty of time to be alone with one's thoughts. She had some of her best ideas in church, like the time she'd come up with the plot to ride a horse into a tavern dressed as the Ghost of Cawdor Castle in a blue-velvet gown to protest the innkeeper's poor quality of meat. That had been at a relative's in Nairn. She'd not been invited back, but she had heard the innkeeper's menu improved after that.

Ghosts wouldn't work with Penrith. He would be a challenge, perhaps her greatest challenge up until now. Somewhere in the middle of the Christmas story, after Caesar Augustus had sent out his decree, and before an angel of the Lord appeared to shepherds, she came up with a plan. She'd start with getting Penrith's attention. Once she had it, she'd make him betray himself: She'd drive him wild. He'd like it, but he'd hate himself for it afterwards.

Her gaze slid to Penrith. He sat straight and tall, the candlelight doing the planes of his profile all nature of favours. It was a pity really, that a man who had so much going for him was so empty. It raised the question: how did a man with so much promise become so empty? Were some people simply born with no interest in the world around them? With no passion for living? Had he never felt a flicker for anything, good English grammar excluded?

Her mother elbowed her and gave her a reproachful look. Around her, everyone had stood up to sing ‘While Shepherds Watched their Flocks by Night’, decidedly *not* one of her favourite Christmas hymns. She didn’t mind tonight. She was too busy plotting. She could use her arrangement with Anne to put herself in Penrith’s path, while furthering her own agenda, which was twofold: ruin Penrith’s control *and* get excused from the party. This was working out splendidly. Even though it was early days yet, she felt confident she could check this house party off as a ‘success’. She’d escape again with no husband in tow.

The vicar’s pretty service concluded not long after the hymn, Baby Jesus safely swaddled in his manger and the angels returned to heaven as Brockmore’s congregation rose once more and sang ‘Adeste Fidelis’, a hymn far more to her liking with its robust chorus, the ending punctuated by the first peal of the Christmas bells.

The bells. Her favourite part of Christmas Eve.

The small crowd of guests filed outside, hushed and respectful of the occasion, to hear the bells ring in the night. Viola closed her eyes and drew a deep breath of cold night air. This was one of her favourite moments of the year, perhaps *the* best moment of the year. She gave herself over to it—the deep pealing timbre of the bells, the ice of the falling snow on her face, the warmth of her body wrapped in the folds of her fur-lined cloak. She knew what peace on earth was. It was this. It was now. Throughout the year she tried to recreate this moment, recreate the intense peace of it, where she set aside her frantic, fast-paced life of frivolity, and she was never successful. This moment alone was unique among all the moments that peopled her year.

If she listened carefully, she could hear the bells in the village adding their song to the night. Did anyone else feel it—the beauty of the moment? It didn't matter. She did and she held on to it, eyes shut tight until the last peal faded away, knowing full well when her eyes opened the moment would be gone. She would be Viola Hawthorne, London's Shocking Beauty, again. But only for one more year.

A little spark of realisation flickered. This was the last year she had to maintain her reputation. After this Season, she'd be a candidate for the shelf—out three Seasons and no husband in sight. She could get on with her dreams. This time next year, everything would change. Her parents would have despaired and been all too happy to send their wayward daughter to Vienna, where she'd be out of sight, out of mind. And she'd be happy to be there.

She wrapped her arms about herself in a little hug just before she opened her eyes and whispered, 'Happy Christmas to me.'

Around her, groups formed as people drifted towards Brockmore Manor, where, no doubt, hot drinks were waiting on cue to send people off to bed. The fallen snow had become thick enough to make Brockmore's sleigh viable, a sleek red and gold affair with front and back seats for four. Brockmore himself was at the ribbons with two smart blacks jingling in harness. She watched Penrith hand in his beautifully fragile mother and his aunt who was followed by the sad-looking, older man, Lord Truesdale. Penrith took the space in the front seat beside his uncle, but not before he'd tucked warm robes about the passengers and bent attentively to hear something his mother said, squeezing her hand, a fleeting smile on his lips. The moment was surprisingly tender. She almost wished she hadn't seen Penrith like that, so attentive, so caring. It went against the idea he was an empty shell. He *did* feel something, *could* feel something, at least in small increments. What else could he feel if he'd let himself? What could she *make* him feel?

He wished he hadn't seen her like that—Viola Hawthorne outside the chapel tonight, her head tilted slightly towards the sky, eyes closed in approbation, snowflakes dusting her face, dancing on her eyelashes before dissolving. Vale stripped out of his coats, alone in his room. He'd given his valet the night off to enjoy the holiday below stairs. He undid the cuffs of his shirt, put the links in a small dish on the bureau and discarded his shirt. He should have looked away, but she'd appeared *serene*, nothing at all like the vixen who'd sat beside him at dinner.

He was being whimsical now. He had to stop before he started comparing her to an angel, which she most assuredly wasn't. He'd seen her true nature today, twice in fact: atop a ladder, ankles exposed and more, and then again at dinner, the display of her cutting wit. She had not minced any words when it came to how she'd felt about him; an unmarriageable prig. Ouch.

His gaze lingered on the bureau mirror and the bare-chested man in the reflection. He studied his face, searching for signs of his supposed priggishness. Was that what he'd become? He was quieter, he supposed. There hadn't been that much to celebrate, these past years. But quietude wasn't priggishness. It was…restraint, respect, discipline. Only, he hadn't been all that restrained at dinner. He'd given back equal measure. He braced his hands on the bureau and hung his head, recalling his angry words. He'd accused her of being a cheap trick, not exactly the most gentlemanly of remarks. Well, perhaps he'd given her some proof there about the unmarriageable part. Great. Now, he was a prig and sharp-tongued to boot.

He turned away from the mirror and finished getting ready for bed in earnest. He was disgusted with himself. Not entirely for how he'd behaved—Lady Viola *had* been in need of a scolding—he was more disgusted with his reaction, which struck him as rather petty. Why did he put so much stock in the opinions of a girl who had no sense of decorum? If ever there were opinions that *didn't* matter, they were hers.

Chapter Four

Saturday, 26th December 1818, Boxing Day

He'd escaped them! His uncle's guests were insatiable when it came to holiday festivity. He was not. He'd had his fill of looking cheery. Vale breathed a relieved sigh and sank into a wing-backed chair of softest leather in front of the fire in the Brockmore library, but his eyes still darted nervously about the room, landing on dark corners and the heavy folds of curtains at the windows where someone might hide, just in case he wasn't the only one to take refuge here. Not that anyone else would want to. *They* were all having a marvellous time.

After two days of Christmas, that was how he viewed the guests: *them* and *him*. Two distinct groups. Oh, he liked his uncle's guests well enough. Kenelm and Eaton and the other young men were good fun. They'd had some good billiards games after the ladies had retired for the night. But, by Jove, Vale needed a break. After a late Christmas Eve service, there had followed a Christmas Day full of games and feasting, as well as another church service and gift-giving to the children of the estate. This was followed by yet more good cheer as they assembled baskets for his uncle's tenants this morning and tramped through the snow to deliver them this afternoon. He was socially exhausted. He hadn't been around this many people for this long in years. All the politeness and pretence that he was enjoying himself positively wore him out.

It didn't help that *she* was everywhere, she being Viola Hawthorne. When he was in a room, he heard her laughter, noticed her gowns for reasons he couldn't quite name, caught the sound of her voice, the movement of her body always in motion, always at the centre of the party. He had the sensation it was her energy that fuelled the high spirits as much as it was his aunt's exquisite planning. If rooms weren't brighter when she was in them, they were certainly louder.

The clock on the mantel, a beautifully carved wooden affair from the Black Forest a German diplomat had given his uncle years ago, showed three o'clock. Boxing Day was nearly over. Just four hours until dinner and then some of the holiday cheer would ease. He hoped. The clock ticked, the sound loud in the glorious quiet. His papers and notes lay on the long reading table that ran the centre of the room, waiting for him. He'd not touched them since he'd arrived. There'd been no time. His aunt and uncle had kept him and every guest busy, moving them skilfully from activity to activity.

Vale closed his eyes. In just a moment he'd get up and see to them. There was the new translation of a Lapland history that had just arrived before he left. He was eager to read it in the hopes it would help his latest research and he had the report to get to if he wanted sponsors for the expedition by next year. But not yet. It was nice to sit here by the fire, in the stillness and just be with himself, just for a moment…

He must have dozed. It was suddenly five o'clock and someone was at the table looking through his papers. A female someone. Vale sat up. Not just any female someone, but the one guest he wanted to avoid most. 'Don't touch those. I have them in particular order.' Not entirely true, but he didn't want them messed up and who knew what *she* might do with them.

'Are these the "weightier matters" you referred to the other night?' She glanced up, but kept reading through them in complete disobedience with his request. 'A history of the Sami? Whoever they are.'

'They live in Lapland. I'm compiling a report and I hope to launch a northbound expedition next year if I can get the backing. The north is the new frontier these days,' he explained in his defense.

She feigned a yawn. 'Boring.' She rose from the table, hips swaying as she strolled the perimeter of the room, her hand running idly over the spines of books. She turned her head and tossed the words over her shoulder. 'Especially when there are more entertaining diversions at hand.'

The tease was implied in the lilt of her voice, the spark of her eyes—eyes that were always sparking. He hadn't seen them without a spark these past two days. 'Are you supposed to be that diversion?' he replied sharply, moving from the comfort of his chair to the table to straighten his papers.

'I might be.' She laughed and stopped her perambulations in front of the sideboard holding his uncle's brandy. She lifted the stopper from the crystal decanter and sniffed. 'Ah, that's good. Would you like a drink?' She poured a glass before he could respond and then arched an eyebrow at him in query, waiting. What was she waiting for? Clearly not his answer since she'd already poured.

'I was going to say no, but I'll take a drink so it doesn't go to waste.'

Lady Viola smiled wickedly. 'It won't go to waste. I never pour precipitously when there's good brandy at stake.'

It took him a moment to grasp her meaning. She held up the glass, gently sloshing the contents. 'This one's mine. *Votre Sante.*' She took a long swallow, head tilted back, eyes closed, the long column of her neck exposed as she savoured the brandy, not unlike he'd seen her outside the church on Christmas Eve. 'Sweet heaven, that tastes even better than it smells.' She fixed him with a smile. 'Are you sure you won't have some?'

He ignored the request, still processing what she'd done; she'd drank his uncle's brandy! 'What are you doing in here? The party is…' He didn't know exactly where the party was at present. He waved a hand in the general direction of the door. 'Elsewhere.'

'Actually, I came looking for you.' She took a smug sip of her brandy, holding her glass in one hand with the easy negligence of an expert. She held out a slip of folded paper. 'In the spirit of holiday giving and selflessness, we've all drawn secret admirers, or whatever you want to call them. We're not to tell anyone who's on our slips. We are to get to know our person, without being obvious, select a meaningful gift for them and give it to them on New Year's Day when all is revealed. *I* think it sounds fun.' She threw the last out as a challenge, already assuming that he hated the idea. *He* hated that she was right.

It sounded terribly social. He left the slip of paper on the table. He'd look at it later. 'Thank you.' He infused the words with a sense of finality—her task was complete. She was free to go. He sat down at the table, making all the signs of a man getting down to work. Surely she wasn't obtuse enough to miss the signals. Surely she'd take the hint and depart.

She didn't. She went back to strolling the shelves of books and for some reason he couldn't look away from the sway of her hips in the purple day dress flecked with spots of dark gold. The design of the gown was nothing out of the ordinary—long sleeved with a slight puff at the shoulder, a modest round neckline— yet her movements made the standard gown come alive. Of course they did. This was the woman who'd climbed a ladder and let everyone glimpse her ankles and more. Her body was a tool, an instrument for attraction.

What else can she do with it? came the wicked thought before he could push it away. He would not dignify that with a response. No doubt it was what she wanted him to think—perhaps not even him specifically, but what she wanted any man to think.

'I wouldn't want to keep you from the party,' he offered politely.

'You're not.' She smiled to match his politeness. 'Everyone's in their rooms resting and changing for dinner.' Yes, damn it, she was right. Everyone would keep to themselves until seven when they began to make their way downstairs to congregate before dinner. A horrible thought occurred to him. Surely she didn't mean to spend the next two hours in the library *with* him?

'Perhaps there's somewhere else you'd rather be? I don't need you to keep me company.' He gestured to the papers laid out before him. 'I have work, I'd be poor company anyway.'

'Has it occurred to you that I'm precisely where I want to be?'

'No, it hasn't. Frankly, Lady Viola, you don't strike me as a library kind of girl.'

'Tsk, tsk. I thought you were a smarter man than that. Of course I like libraries.' She arched her eyebrow and bit her lip playfully. 'You should have known better, Penrith, there are ladders, after all.' With that, she leapt on one of the great, long ladders that bracketed the floor-to-ceiling shelves and pushed off with one foot, sailing the length of the wall. She laughed then, a sound that was full bodied and loud, the sound of a woman enjoying herself.

'Lady Viola, please!' Vale cautioned sharply, taken aback by the forthright loudness of her outburst. 'Someone might hear.' It occurred to him rather belatedly how this might look, the two of them together, a woman's laughter, all during the quiet time when everyone was supposed to be changing. To be caught would be absolutely compromising.

Lady Viola jumped off the ladder, mocking laughter in each word. 'That would be scandalous! Two people in a library with nothing for chaperons except books. Shocking indeed!' She walked behind him, trailing her fingers across his shoulders. Her touch sent an unlooked-for frisson of awareness through him. 'I wonder, Penrith, are you afraid of being caught, or…' she bent to his ear, the scent of her, all plum and bergamot, sending another spear of awareness through him '…is it the being alone with me you fear?'

It was the audacity that aroused him against his preferences. He'd never been touched so boldly by a woman before outside the bedchamber. Certainly, there'd been lovers but they'd kept their forwardness confined to the proper place and time, which was not the middle of the afternoon in a library where they might be discovered at any moment by almost anyone.

'After all, there is always the question of what might I do?' She was on his lap now, her arms about his neck, a knowing smile on her red lips as she sat him side-saddle, her bottom wiggling as she made herself comfortable, her comfort coming into contact with his discomfort in the process. 'I see you've already thought of what I might do. Perhaps you *are* more man than monolith.' She put her forehead to his, her voice soft, invitingly intimate. 'What is it that you think I might do to you? What do you *want* me to do to you? I know what a man likes.'

Lucifer's tight, aching balls, London's Shocking Beauty was a temptress nonpareil. How did a duke's daughter 'know what a man liked'? Never mind. That was not especially salient at the moment. He could not partake of this particular temptation no matter how his body roused. She was not for him and she was *definitely* not for the future of Brockmore. But she could be whether he liked it or not if he didn't get her off his lap soon, before someone walked in. There was a serious sense of urgency in that regard. The threat of discovery was real. 'If you do not remove yourself from my lap, Lady Viola, by the time I count to five, I will stand up and you will be dumped on the floor.' He offered the warning bluntly.

She trailed a finger down the curve of his jaw. 'You can stand up any time you'd like. All you have to do is pay the forfeit.'

'What might that be?' He had no idea why he was bothering to humour her. She would only see it as a way to prolong this dangerous game.

'A Christmas kiss, of course,' she whispered her *dare*. He should do it; kiss her hard and fast in this chair, call her bluff and maybe scare some sense into her about the sort of man she toyed with. He was no green village boy or a prig as she accused. Just because he was discreet in his dealings as a gentleman should be didn't mean he was unfamiliar with the arts of passion.

'One,' he began. Kissing her was too risky here, his more logical side asserted. There was no mistletoe ball to excuse the behaviour. 'Two.' She was not budging. Instead, she shifted closer, her hip now firmly against his groin. 'Three,' he ground out evenly. He would not give her the satisfaction of counting faster. If he did that, she'd know he was trying to escape, trying to run. It would only suggest he was indeed 'afraid' of her. 'Four.' She gave him a witching smile, her only warning before her mouth covered his, taking his lips in an open-mouthed kiss. A little sigh of pleasure purled softly from her throat as she worked his mouth with her tongue, her body pressed up against his, as she gave herself over to the kiss.

He was aware of all of her in those long moments: the plum bergamot smell of her, the softness of her breasts pressed to his chest, the feel of her in his mouth, her hands in his hair, pulling it loose from its ribbon. He was aware of himself, too; of the tightness ebbing from his body, of his escalating arousal that went far beyond a simple, physical erection, his want overriding his good sense, his mind forgetting the risks. How long had it been since he'd let himself get carried away just for the sake of being carried away? He was cognisant of his mouth answering hers, his hands cupping her face, framing it, in order to drink every ounce of pleasure from her lips before it was too late. Even so, it was done too soon.

She slid off his lap and straightened her skirts, looking suddenly prim and very proper as if *she* hadn't tried to seduce *him*. 'If you'll excuse me? I have to go change for dinner.' She gave him another witching smile. 'I knew you had it in you. You're a man, after all, Penrith.' But she was wrong, he was all rock; hard rock.

He didn't even remember the slip of paper until well after she'd gone and his body had restored itself to order. Vale reached for it with a sigh. He was not interested in getting to know someone else and, if he knew his aunt and uncle, he'd bet money the name on his slip was the name of some respectable lady whom they wanted to put forward as a marriage candidate.

Vale unfolded the paper and stared. The words, 'Lady Viola Hawthorne' were neatly written in his aunt's elegant cursive. The holiday spirit, if there was such a thing, was certainly a contrary one. Here was the one person he'd least likely wanted to draw and evidence that his aunt hadn't engineered it. His aunt and uncle would not find the likes of Viola Hawthorne a suitable future duchess. Well, if there was some good in all of this, it was that he wouldn't have to think too hard about her gift. He'd get her a bottle of his uncle's brandy and call it square. It could have been worse, he supposed. She could have drawn his name and who knew where that would have led? Well, actually, he knew. All the better it had worked out this way instead.

Chapter Five

Sunday, 27th December 1818
—skating party on the lake

He was still thinking about those kisses the next day, proof that his foray through the snow to the frozen lake with the other guests for skating was a failed attempt to cool thoughts of hot kisses with the crisp winter air. Vale had held out hope that a turn or two around the lake would succeed where cold air had failed, but he'd found no success in exercise either.

Who could concentrate on ice skating when there were stolen kisses in a library to think about? Kisses so disturbing he'd lain awake most of the night analysing them in a variety of detail; his mind contemplating every aspect from his shockingly lusty and immediate response to the feel of her on his lap, in his arms, pressed against him. It was the immediacy of his response that bothered him most. He'd *enjoyed* kisses from a woman whose behaviour he found appalling in the extreme. Was that truly the target of his aversion? Perhaps it was not *her* passion, but *his* reaction that he found appalling.

What had he been thinking to respond like that? Perhaps he hadn't been thinking at all. For a few moments his carefully constructed armour of polite aloofness had been down and he'd forgotten to be the man he'd become in the wake of R.J.'s death. For a moment, the self he'd tamped down all those years ago—the self that knew the thrill of a fast horse and the excitement of the hunt, and revelled in them, had managed to break free. Probably not the best idea. He'd tamped that self down for a reason—two of them. The heir to Brockmore couldn't go kissing forward girls any time he felt like it and the man he'd once been was tired of hurting, tired of feeling, because to feel good, one had to know how to feel badly. He was tired of sorrow.

Boots crunched on the snow and he turned towards the sound as his uncle came to stand with him. 'You should be out there skating.' His uncle nodded towards the frozen lake, filled with house guests enjoying themselves. 'You still have your skates on. It's good you've been out already, but hopefully not for the last time today. I remember when you were younger, nine or ten, maybe. You and R.J. use to love to skate. Your father and I took you out every day when you'd visit in the winter. The two of you would race from end to end trying to outdo each other. Those were good times when the house was full of children.' His uncle looked at him and smiled. 'The house will be full of children again one day. I look forward to that.' This line of conversation was not subtle at all. Vale smiled politely in response. The Silver Fox was losing his touch.

'I know many men prefer women in the spring, with all the pretty fashions and light fabrics, but I'm a winter man.' His uncle's eyes crinkled at the corners as his gaze returned to the ice. 'I think women are lovely in furs and coats, their cheeks pinched with a touch of colour from wind and cold.' Anne Lowell skated by, arm and arm with her cousin, her colour high, the epitome of his uncle's description. 'What do you think of her, Blackton's daughter?' Oh, his uncle was not subtle at all.

'Anne Lowell?' Vale struggled to get his thoughts on track. He'd been searching the ice for a whirlwind in a maroon coat. 'I haven't thought much of her at all. We've only had conversation at dinner.' Opening with the truth seemed to be a good strategy as long as he didn't have to go into the reasons why he'd not devoted any thought to the pretty Lady Anne. Whatever thoughts he'd given time to had been directed towards a dark-haired minx with violet eyes.

'Perhaps you should,' his uncle said amiably, but Vale knew better than to be fooled. His uncle had the soul of a matchmaker and—how did one put it?—a certain arrogance when it came to believing he knew best what suited others. It was a well-earned arrogance and not without support. He and his aunt had brokered many successful marriages in their three decades of entertaining and he was in no way finished pushing his latest match. 'Lady Anne is attractive, from a good family, well dowered, although you don't need it, her father is politically connected and she's personally accomplished. You'll get to hear her sing at one of our musical evenings. Intelligent, too. She'd be interested in your cultural work. There'd be no running out of things to say at the breakfast table.' He chuckled the way a long-married man does when imparting knowledge to a bachelor yet to take the plunge.

Vale nodded. 'I am sure Lady Anne is a paragon.'

'She is and true paragons are not thick on the ground.' He nodded towards a figure Vale recognised too well. Viola was out on the ice, spinning in circles with Eaton's little sister who had come over for the day. 'Consider the Duke of Calton's daughter.' His uncle shook his head in general disapproval, watching Viola spin with the younger girl. 'She should have been taken in hand long before this. With her fortune and her family connections, there's no good reason she's not married by now, except poor parenting.' It was hard to know if his uncle disapproved of Viola specifically or if his larger objection was with her circumstances. 'They've let her grow wild and wild she has stayed.' His uncle gave him a meaningful but inscrutable look. 'It will take an extraordinary match to an extraordinary man to save her now.'

'A little spirit is an admirable quality,' Vale began, startled by the surge of defensiveness he felt on Viola's behalf. Since when did he feel the need to champion her?

'Most definitely,' his uncle agreed readily. 'But she's taken it beyond "a little spirit". I am not oblivious to what that "little spirit" has got up to since her arrival. I know about her escapade in the hall. I've noticed how she garners all the attention in a room when there's a game to play. There's the right kind of attention a lady should attract and then there's the sort *she* attracts. A gentleman knows the difference. Calton will have trouble getting her off his hands if he waits much longer, duke or not.' His uncle continued knowingly, 'Men will flirt with girls like her, but they won't risk the family line by marrying them. A smart man takes a wife like Anne Lowell, every time.'

Dear lord, his uncle was tenacious! Vale had forgotten, or maybe he'd simply not known, never having had that tenacity turned his direction. Vale knew very well who the 'smart man' was in that allusion. 'I don't think it's an issue of Anne Lowell's qualities.' How did he tell his uncle he didn't need a match made for him? He'd make his own. *When* the time came.

His uncle blew out a frosty breath in the silence and his voice dropped. 'Then what is it a matter of? Don't tell me you're not ready. You're thirty and you've had time to adjust to your circumstances.' In other words, to accept his duty as Brockmore's heir to beget an heir or two of his own. 'Do you do find Lady Anne to be flawed in some way?'

'Of course not. She's all you claim, but my preference is to find my own bride at my own time.'

That did not sit well with his uncle. He raised a grey brow. 'You're the heir, my boy. Whether you like it or not, your time is not your own. Don't wait too long. Your aunt and I aren't getting any younger. If the events of the past four years have shown me anything it's that we're all mortal. We can be called home to our maker at any second. R.J., your father, the Princess Charlotte, notwithstanding. Coronets and kingdoms didn't protect them and they won't protect us either.' He clapped Vale on the shoulder. 'I'm a selfish man in the final analysis. I'd like to see Brockmore full of youth once more before I go, full of laughter and hope. I want to meet my reward knowing my legacy will continue, that my life's work has not been spent in vain.' He gave Vale a long stare. 'You, dear nephew, *are* my life's work.'

Vale swallowed against the rising emotion in his throat. His uncle's appeal was a potent one, logically and sentimentally. He owed a good marriage to the family as much as he owed it to himself, even if the idea of 'good' varied depending on who was asked. Clearly, his uncle equated the idea of a sound marriage with bloodlines and accomplishments. Vale held other ideas about what might be involved—affection, mutual respect among them. But how to respond without provoking an argument or setting himself against his beloved uncle when he hadn't quite sorted through how to let those emotions out for himself? How did he have an emotionally satisfying marriage if he didn't allow himself to give his own emotions free rein?

A flurry of maroon and fur flew past, skates

close to the edge of the shore, a gloved hand grabbing for his at the last moment, pulling him on to the ice. 'Come on, there's something I want to show you!' Vale let momentum take him, let it drag him away from his uncle's well-intended matchmaking. Far better to be skating than to be arguing. The rescue could not have been better timed. Had she been watching him?

Viola had him firmly by the hand, leading him across the ice at a fiend's pace. They wove in and out among the other more sedate skaters, her laughter floating back to him. 'You can do better than this! I saw you out on the ice earlier.'

He answered her scold with a burst of speed, dropping her hand as something primal surged in him to prove his superiority in this small way. He could go much faster. He pushed with one foot, flying forward, finding the rhythm of his youth. He sailed past Viola, the blades of his skates whispering their dare on the ice. He knew she was with him. He could hear her own blades take up the reckless pace. The party fell behind them, fading with the shore, the island in the centre of the lake looming closer.

It was his chance to lead and he took her around the leeward curve of the island to the far side, where the island was naturally protected from the wind before coming to a full stop, breathless and exhilarated. He bent down, hands on knees, gathering his breath between gulps of laughter.

Viola skated up beside him a few seconds later, letting out a whoop of delight that was swallowed up in the winter silence. 'That was magnificent! You're a champion racer, Penrith.' The accolade warmed him unexpectedly, like he'd won a silver cup.

She flopped down in the snow at the edge of the lake, falling backwards like a snow angel. There he went again, thinking of her as an angel. Why did his brain insist on doing that when his body knew she was the very devil? She sat up in the little snow drift, the hood of her coat falling back to reveal her dark hair, glistening with errant drops of melted snow. 'Care to join me?'

'I already have. I'm here, aren't I?' His sense of self-preservation warned him to stay upright. If he gave in to the urge to plop in the snow beside her, who knew what might happen? What did he *hope* would happen? Another kiss? Did he want her to kiss him again or did *he* want to do the kissing this time? Wait. *He* wanted to kiss Viola Hawthorne? The discoveries were unending. Earlier he'd been moved to defend her, now he wanted to kiss her? He needed to stop surprising himself like this. If there was to be any more kissing, it would be easier if she kissed him. Then, he could play the victim. He could tell himself he had no control over *her* actions.

Just the thought of taking that route smacked of cowardice. He was not the sort of man who waited for a woman to make the first move. In all of his relationships, he was the one in charge. But if he kissed her, that would change everything about their association. He'd have to stop being appalled by her behaviour and concentrate on his. He'd have to decide what came next. What *did* come next with a woman like her? A woman who was so secure in her emotions, her sexuality? A certain thrill bubbled up inside him before he could tamp it down—the age-old thrill of the hunt.

She leaned back on her gloved hands, looking entirely comfortable in the snow drift, and cocked her head to gaze up at him, 'Suit yourself.'

'Did it suit you to pull me on to the lake?' He doubted there'd been anything to actually come and see.

She shrugged. 'It appeared to suit *you*. You seemed in need of rescuing. There was something about the look on your face, *and* the look on your uncle's, both of you were being so politely determined with each other.' She shrugged. 'Call it intuition, if you want.'

'I suppose a rescue *was* in order,' Vale offered,

attempting neutrality and failing. He was finding it impossible to look at her without his gaze falling to her lips, without his thoughts going back to yesterday's interlude.

'What were you discussing so intently?' She was audacious even without trying. No decent lady of his acquaintance would probe so indelicately into a gentleman's business. His uncle's words came back to him. *There's no good reason she's not married by now, except poor parenting.*

'That's not any of your business.' Vale began to skate a figure eight, anything to distract him from looking at her, from thinking of her.

'I will make it my business. Shall I guess?' she persisted. She tipped her head skyward, showing off the long column of her neck. Perhaps she knew full well the pretty picture she made with her dark hair and maroon coat against the stark whiteness of the snow. He didn't want to find it picturesque, but he did. His body did. Even in the cold, he was rousing. She would have his secrets out of him in no time at this rate.

Chapter Six

She would have his secrets or die trying, Viola vowed. It would be part of her larger victory, part of her mission to break Vale Penrith's impenetrable shell. Even if she hadn't decided to take on the challenge, she'd still be morally obligated to probe a bit. The 'perfect' gift was on the line, after all, and she needed some ideas.

Viola slipped a hand into her coat pocket, her gloved fingers closing over the slip of paper from Brockmore's game yesterday. She'd drawn Penrith—something of a blessing and a curse. Well, she'd sort of drawn him. She'd actually traded Anne for him. She'd originally drawn Kenelm and Anne had drawn Penrith, which made Viola think the game might have been rigged.

Viola began to think out loud, confident she would guess the source of the argument. Was

Penrith arrogant enough to think men were such a mystery to women? Besides, she had an advantage thanks to Anne's information.

'Was it about money? Men always discuss money and it leaves them in poor spirits. But Brockmore has plenty. So, no, I do not think it was money.' She tapped a gloved finger against her chin. 'Love, perhaps?' She tossed him a coy look, only to be disappointed by the shake of his head. She gave him a pout. 'Not love, Penrith? Marriage, then?'

'Are they mutually exclusive?'

His words caught her off guard. She'd not been prepared for the revelation.

Viola's eyes narrowed in contemplation. 'It's really a case of the possible against the probable. Love *is* possible in marriage, merely not probable, not the way the *ton* does it anyway.' She fixed him with a violet stare. She was on to something. He hadn't denied her guess. 'So, it *was* marriage that had you and your uncle at odds?'

'It's still *not* your business. Marriage is a private arrangement,' Penrith protested, but he was starting to crack. He *wanted* to tell someone. She could see it in the way his gaze flitted away from her, how he couldn't meet her eyes. He was hiding something.

'Then make it my business. Tell me. You look

like you need a friend.' She teased the temptation in him, 'Who's to know? We're on the other side of the island, nothing around us but winter. We might as well be the only two people in the world.' She patted the snow again and took a calculated risk. 'Sit down and tell me why you don't want to marry Anne Lowell.'

His blades skidded to a halt, his body plopping down beside her. 'How did you know?' There was fleeting panic in his eyes. 'My uncle hasn't announced it, has he?'

She laughed. 'No. It's just obvious. Brockmore brought her here for you. I'm the only other one here with a pedigree worthy of you and he certainly doesn't want you to marry me.'

Penrith shrugged his broad shoulders in assent. 'I suppose you're right on that account.'

That stung. *She* could point out how unmarriageable she was, but that didn't mean he could. The hurt in her wanted some revenge. 'Anne doesn't want to marry you either. She told me so Christmas Eve.' Viola leaned in conspiratorially. 'She has her sights set on Kenelm and he on her, only his father resists.'

'Well, good. Then she and I are in agreement.' Penrith remained disappointingly unruffled by the news. 'If she and Kenelm have affection for one another, I hope they will be able to marry.'

'Don't tell me, *you* believe in love?' What had

he said earlier? That love and marriage needn't be mutually exclusive? Was that what he believed? She wouldn't have guessed.

'And you don't? You think they have to be separate?' He was not afraid to challenge her and she was enjoying it. She didn't *want* to enjoy it, that hadn't been part of her plan. She *didn't* want to like him, didn't want to be looking up into his serious blue eyes and thinking about the straight length of his nose, or the high curve of his cheekbones. She certainly didn't want to be thinking about his mouth on hers, or how his body had felt at her touch, all hard muscle and strength coming alive beneath her fingertips when they kissed, and oh heavens how the man could kiss!

'Look around. How many marriages do you see that incorporate both? Conventional wisdom says I'm right. You'll see. Even your marriage will prove it.' She meant to taunt him with her words, meant to put him on the defensive so she could stop liking him. He'd say something conservative and old-fashioned and she'd remember he was a borderline prig. *Who just happened to kiss like a rake.*

'What about yours? Will yours somehow be different?' It was not said unkindly. He had not taken the bait.

Viola tossed her head, letting her eyes flash with daring to match the audacity of her words. 'I'm not getting married.'

'Why ever not?'

'Why aren't you going to marry Anne Lowell?'

'That doesn't mean I don't want to marry, I just don't want to marry her,' Penrith argued. 'I want to pick my bride. I want there to be something between us besides duty. Don't you want that?'

'I've already established I don't think it exists, not up in the rarefied air you and I breathe, anyway,' Viola shot back. This conversation was not going as she planned. She was supposed to be ferreting out his secrets. But she felt like the one being exposed. She opted for the most shocking revelation in her verbal arsenal. 'I can have that "something else" without marriage. I don't need to marry a man for the pleasure of his bed. After all, men don't marry for it. They seek pleasure outside of marriage and before marriage. Why shouldn't a woman?' Viola grinned. It was clear from the frown on his face that she'd succeeded in irritating him.

Penrith stood abruptly and with an extraordinary amount of grace considering he wore skates. 'To be discussing this with you carries a hint of the absurd. I think it best we end the conversation here.' He dusted the snow off his caped greatcoat with sharp swipes, his agitated gestures a further sign of his unrest.

Viola rose, too fast to be graceful. 'Why? Because I spoke of conjugal relations? Because a woman shouldn't claim as much freedom as a man? No one expects *you* to come to the marriage bed untried. Why should society expect a woman to? I mean, that doesn't work mathematically, does it? It's entirely illogical. Who are the men going to sharpen their prowess on if women can't join them?'

She meant to shock him at his priggish core and maybe she had, but it was his turn to do the shocking. He fixed his solemn blue eyes on her, his voice sternly quiet. 'Why should anyone have to practise at all? Why can't intimacy be discovered together between two people over time? Why should a man's intimacy be reduced to the seeking of cheap pleasures? For that matter, why should the choice to marry be reduced to those same cheap pleasures? Is that all marriage is to you, Lady Viola? An opportunity for intercourse? When I said something more, I meant something more than what you refer to. Quite a bit more, in fact.'

For a moment she was speechless. What sort of man talked like that? Thought like that? No man she knew. A wicked thought occurred to her. 'Are you a virgin, Penrith?' she whispered in part-awe, part-disbelief. He couldn't be. He was thirty years old and he didn't kiss like any virgin she knew. And yet, she had to wonder, with romantic sentiments like that…

'No, but that is yet another item that is none of your business.'

'Don't you think your stance is a little hypocritical?' Viola pressed, ignoring his jab at her invasion of privacy. They were standing close together now on the ice, their argument having decreased the space between them.

'I think society is the hypocrite. Perhaps *it* shouldn't equate manliness with a man's reputation regarding the quality of his bed sport.' His eyes had gone the shade of midnight sapphires, his pupils wide. He was aroused, too, and the recognition was heady knowledge. Perhaps his idea of flirtation was spouting homilies on sexual moral code. It was working.

'Do you have such a reputation, Penrith?' Her voice was breathless. This discussion had moved from the broader scope of sexual politics to personal ones and the shift was intoxicating. It conjured up hot speculation. What would it be like to be in bed with a man who believed as he did? Not just bed, he'd made it clear bed alone was not enough for his finer appetites, but in bed with all that he suggested should be present. She was starting to burn.

'I hear it is, if we're being honest.' His voice was pure gravel now. 'When I bed a woman, it is because she means something to me.' That was the absolute best line she'd ever heard, the best advertisement of the prowess he claimed not to care for. What woman would refuse such an invitation? Not her. Her curiosity was searing her alive. She wanted to know what Vale Penrith could do to a woman, to *her*.

Viola whet her lips. The glimpse of the man beneath the shell was tantalising, to have a marriage that was not the enslavement she railed against. What if she could have a marriage like that with a man like this? A man who wanted more from marriage than a trading of titles and wealth? Would that be enough to change her mind? *What if*? Would her dreams be safe with a such a man?

Oh, no. There were no 'what ifs'. She didn't allow for them. Curiosity was meant to be satisfied. She'd never met a man she couldn't charm into compliance, virtues and ethics notwithstanding. Penrith was still a man no matter what philosophies he ascribed to and that meant he should be just about ready to capitulate. She was not the only inferno here. He was aroused and spouting lines that put Casanova to shame. It was time to move in for the kill.

Her gloved hands gripped the front of his coat

as she tilted her face up, lips parted, wet and glistening in invitation. 'I've never met a man like you, Vale.'

His eyes, dark and half-lidded, dropped to her mouth, his hands covered hers, his grip firm. She let a little sigh escape her. His mouth lowered. A kiss was inevitable. She let her eyes close. In three, two…

'No, I don't think I will kiss you.' The firm hands pushed her away, sending her sliding gently backwards on her skates. For a moment she was stunned. He was rejecting her! *He was rejecting her?* For the first time ever, a man didn't want what she was offering. She hardly knew what to do. Failure was not an option she'd considered and yet here it was.

Penrith gave her a curt nod of his head, his shell firmly intact. 'And, I don't recall giving you leave to use my first name. Forgive me, I must return to the party.'

Vale Penrith skated away—before he was missed, before anyone found them together and suspected he actually had claimed the kiss he'd refused, before she could exact immediate revenge for her rejection. That was twice now he'd played her, turning her game on its head. But she'd learned something valuable today. She'd been wrong. Penrith wasn't a prig, after all. He was an idealist. A romantic, even. How novel.

Viola kicked the snow with the toe of her skate. Hadn't given her leave to use his first name? Hah. They'd be on more than a first-name basis before New Year's. He'd be screaming her name to high heaven before she was done.

Chapter Seven

Evening, Monday, 28th December 1818

Raucous yells and boisterous whoops met Vale halfway down the hall leading to the billiards room. It was after midnight. What could possibly be going on? The sound of feminine laughter—laughter he was coming to recognise too well—rose above the rest and Vale found himself hurrying down the corridor out of intrigue, interest and perhaps a little fear—what had she got up to now? Why did he care? They'd parted poorly yesterday on the lake. They owed each other nothing.

Why hadn't she gone to bed like the rest of the guests? There'd been music and wassailing in the music room after dinner, the guests merry but tired after another day filled with non-stop activity. There'd been a special beverage, too—one with rum and other flavours he couldn't identify. He'd imbibed carefully, although others had partaken quite liberally. It was supposed to be good for the vocal cords. Vale thought the drink was likely better for the ears, making the listener more tolerant of whatever 'special' talents were on display.

Surprisingly, those talents hadn't included Viola. She had sat the evening musicale out, letting the other ladies take centre stage, although she'd got plenty of attention just sitting there. She'd worn an enticing red dress and had stationed herself on an ottoman. It did him no credit to have noticed. She had beaux swanning around her on all sides. Martindale and Throckton coming and going on one side, Eaton and Kenelm on the other, even though Kenelm's eyes never left Anne.

Whatever she may have lacked in attention, she was making up for now. The sight of her in that red dress, bent provocatively over a billiard cue, the curve of her derrière displayed, the swell of breasts pressed tight against the low-cut bodice confirmed that rather empirically. All of her 'charms' were on exhibit. Vale felt a bolt of jealousy shoot through him. Her red dress had him seeing green. How dare she flirt with the others the way she'd flirted with him? Did she kiss them, too? Did she dissemble with them the way she had with him at the lake, sharing her unorthodox views? Did her eyes promise them the passion they'd promised him? *Passion you'd rejected*, he had to remind himself. He'd passed on her dubious charms. He had no right to claim them now or to prevent others from claiming them.

Viola sank a ball into the corner pocket and then repositioned herself for another shot, nudging Throckton with her hip to do it. She tossed Throckton a teasing smile and sank another shot, and then another to rowdy applause. She'd nearly cleared the table and the gentlemen were egging her on. He was starting to think 'gentlemen' might be a loosely applied appellation. Martindale was here, Throckton, the aristocrat's bastard, Eaton and Kenelm. With the exception of Kenelm, none of them were of serious rank. Of them all, Kenelm ought to have known better than to let this get out of hand. It was more telling as to who was absent. Lord Truesdale and Captain Milborne would have added some sobriety to the gathering.

'I'm down to two balls, gentlemen.' Viola delivered the allusion in a smoky, whisky-laced voice. The gathering laughed.

Eaton matched her in wit and innuendo. 'I think it's more like six, unless you count Penrith over there in the doorway. Then you've got eight. I'd say that's a handful.'

She straightened and reached for the chalking cube, eyes landing on him. 'Penrith, won't you come in and join us? You're just in time. Martindale has bet me a kiss I can't clear the table. If I sink this last shot, I can kiss anyone in the room. If I lose, I have to kiss him.' Jealousy dug him hard in the ribs at the thought of her kissing Martindale. Across the table, Martindale traded knowing smiles with her and Vale wondered if he already knew what it was like to taste her lips. He wondered, too, if Viola preferred Percival Martindale's kisses to his. It was not well done of him. She could kiss the whole damn party if she wanted to. He just didn't want her to want to.

Viola twisted the chalk, her gaze never leaving his, daring him to stay. She managed to make the gesture provocative before she brought the cue to her cherry-red lips and blew. Good lord, he was going to go hard right here in the billiards room in front of the company. When she flirted, her eyes went straight through a man. That gaze made him feel like the only man in the world even when the room was full of men whose company she obviously preferred to his.

He ought to leave now. Before something happened—something always happened when Viola was around. Being here was *not* in his best interest. Being here was, in fact, the perfect miserable ending to what had not been a good day. This afternoon, his uncle had chastised him, politely, of course, but the scolding had been obvious. He'd skipped all of the day's activities today and most of yesterday after the skating. Uncle Marcus had been 'concerned' about his untimely and lengthy disappearance with Lady Viola at yesterday's skating party, followed by his abrupt departure. He'd absented himself from the skaters' luncheon altogether and only reappeared at dinner that night and this one.

'Makes it look as if you'd had a quarrel of some significance. Have you? Is that the impression you want to create?' had been his uncle's words, which were followed by a lecture on the merits of Anne Lowell and a few not-so-subtle reminders about the character of Lady Viola, not that he'd needed any warnings. He'd seen her 'character' first hand. And yet he couldn't bring himself to cede the room and leave her to the likes of Eaton and Martindale and whatever after-hours entertainment they got up to in his uncle's billiards room. But here he stood, his attentions riveted by a red dress and a pair of flashing eyes.

Viola strolled the perimeter of the table, hips swaying as she surveyed the baize. She bent and stood, moved on, bent and stood again, repeating the movements a few more times. He shouldn't let himself be interested in such tawdry play, but Vale felt his gaze studying the table and assessing her chances—or rather Martindale's chances. The shot was tricky but not impossible if one played a significant amount of billiards and had some experience with banking and splitting. Still, he arrived at the conclusion she was going to lose. Even if he suspended belief for a moment, Vale couldn't imagine Viola had that kind of experience. When would she have acquired it? Surely even Calton's negligent parenting hadn't allowed for such a skill to develop. Maybe she wanted to lose.

She bent and let out a breath, ready to settle. A hush fell over the room, everyone suddenly intent on the shot as if a championship rested on this and not a mere kiss. Throckton's voice broke into the silence. 'Lady Viola, I think you'd have a better shot if you moved just a bit to the left, like this.' His hands were at her waist, his body angling intimately over hers as he guided the cue. Vale felt his blood boil. How dare Throckton take such liberties, how dare she allow it?

'That's cheating,' Martindale growled.

'That's hedging his bets,' Eaton put in good-naturedly. 'If she makes the shot, perhaps she'll want to reward him.' Martindale shot him a hard look. 'What?' Eaton laughed. 'I thought maybe you were saving your kisses for Lady Beatrice Landry, anyway.' That earned him another searing look. He held up his hands in surrender. 'I'll kiss you then, Martindale, if you're so desperate.'

Vale found himself suppressing a chuckle and another stab of envy. This time, not over Viola, but over the easy comradery between the gentlemen. He'd not joked with friends like that for what seemed a lifetime.

'Are you ready, Lady Viola?' Throckton had his mouth at her ear, his body over her like a stallion covering a mare. 'Shall we take the shot together?'

She laughed, shaking off Throckton. 'I'll make my own shots, thank you.' She drew back the cue and struck true, the cue ball splitting the pair. The first ball had speed and the closer pocket. It dropped with ease. The second ball had further to go. It slowed as it neared the pocket. Vale found himself holding his breath. It paused at the pocket, coming to a near stop, teetering on the pocket and then dropping with the last of its momentum.

'Gentlemen, I win.' Viola laid down her cue stick and held her arms wide. Someone put a brandy glass in her hand. 'To my victory!' She took a long drink while the others cheered. 'Now, to my prize.'

She looked around the room, giving each gentleman the consideration of her eyes. 'I've already had you, Eaton,' she joked, passing over him. 'Under the mistletoe, I recall. I'm not likely to forget it. That leaves Martindale, whom I must eliminate—it is whom, isn't it, Penrith?' She gave a throaty laugh. 'After all, it makes no sense to win a bet and then kiss the same person you would have kissed if you lost,' she teased Martindale with a smile. 'That leaves me with three.' Vale tensed. He did not want her to announce she'd already 'had' him. Eaton's kiss had been public. Everyone knew. But their kisses had been entirely private and he wanted to keep them that way.

She set down her brandy glass, eyes narrowing in a look that sent a *frisson* of anticipation down his spine. It was positively predatory. He knew what she would say before the words were out of her mouth. 'I choose Penrith.'

There was a general manly outcry of disapproval. She silenced it with a smile. 'Gentlemen, he needs it most.'

Fabulous. Now he was a charity case. She swayed towards him, hips rocking beneath the folds of her red dress, eyes glistening. Somewhere in the house a clock chimed one—it was far past time someone showed a sense of decency. What would happen if one of these gentlemen told his uncle what had transpired and that he'd participated? That they'd all witnessed him kissing Lady Viola, that he'd let her drink brandy and play midnight billiards, one unmarried woman alone with five men. This would all be his fault. He'd be the one to pay. He took Viola by the arm. 'There will be no kissing. Let me escort you to your room.'

'Come on, Penrith, we're just playing,' Throckton argued on Viola's behalf.

'Playtime's over. We should all get to bed.' He'd only meant to be stern, but he recognised his poor choice of words immediately and she didn't hesitate to turn them on him.

'All of us?' Viola purred, tossing a smoky glance over her shoulder at the others. 'That's a mighty big...*bed* you've got then, Penrith.' She lifted a shoulder in a negligent shrug. 'I'm game if you are.' The others laughed. Loudly. The whole house would hear them at this rate. Vale was angry now. He could feel his temper running hot in his blood, feel his frustration rising. Why did she insist on challenging him at every turn? Every word? Why did *he* insist on being her champion when she clearly didn't want one?

He glared at her, she smiled back, undaunted with eyes flashing. The tension ratcheted another notch, the other gentlemen exchanged uncomfortable looks. Kenelm cleared his throat. 'I think I'll head up. Eaton, are you coming?' Matthew Eaton agreed with astonishing alacrity and far too much enthusiasm to be natural. Throckton and Martindale muttered about getting a nightcap in the library. Throckton stopped as they passed Viola. 'Did you want to join us, Vi?' Vale didn't miss the challenging glance Throckton threw his way or the excessive familiarity. It was insulting, really. An aristocrat's illegitimate son equating himself with a duke's daughter. She might allow it, but Vale wouldn't.

He spoke before Viola could even think of accepting one more indecent offer this evening, the grip on her arm tight, in full anticipation of a bolt. '*Lady* Viola is staying with me.'

Throckton hesitated, looking as if he would like to try out that assumption. Vale added, 'I don't think Lady Beatrice would appreciate hearing about your evening escapades.' There was no sense in mincing words. He meant it as a threat and he wanted Throckton to take it as one, without any ambiguity. Throckton moved on.

Vale waited until the group was out of sight. He kept his voice low, his words barely more than a growl as he rounded on her. 'What in heaven's name do you think you're doing?'

Chapter Eight

'I'm waiting,' Viola replied, eyes wide in feigned innocence. 'I thought you were taking me to bed.'

'Stop it.' The words were a growl. He was angry and it was a ferocious sight. Most angry men she knew blustered. Like her father. Angry men yelled and made horrible but ultimately toothless threats. Occasionally they threw something priceless at the fireplace and regretted it later. Not Penrith. His body went still and hard, his eyes glittering, determined slits as his mind and body worked to keep the boiling anger in check. She heard the effort in the gravel of his voice. She heard the breaking in it, too. She nearly had him, just as she had nearly had him at the lake. That was when he usually slipped away, put himself beyond her reach emotionally and physically. He was proving to be a wily opponent, a man who would not allow himself to be manipulated, a strong man.

Viola twisted her arm, trying to step back, but he wouldn't let her go. 'Stop what?' She was pushing him hard now. She knew how much he hated the feigned innocence, hated being called to bluntness.

'This game, all the games. What do you think happens if word of tonight gets out?'

'I get sent home? Oh, do you think someone might tell your uncle I was playing billiards and drinking his brandy? I do hope so.' She let her sarcasm needle him. She kept pushing. 'Wouldn't that be a shame? I'd get to go home and be with my friends instead of here, being trotted out by parents who are desperate to get me off their hands. They can hardly wait to hand me over to a husband and let me be his problem. I've been a trial to them since the day I was born.' Since the day her mother had nearly died giving birth to the only child her poor body could sustain. She shrugged and slanted her gaze in Penrith's direction. 'It would have been different, of course, if I'd been born with a penis. Then the jeopardy I put my mother in would have been acceptable. Instead, the risk was disappointing, as I have been every day since.'

He let her go, the tension in him coiled tight. 'So that's why you do it? To shame them?'

'Hardly. My rebellion isn't quite that juvenile.' She tossed her head and poured another brandy. 'It's simple. I don't want to be here. I'd rather be at home and the fastest way to get there is to be expelled from the party.'

'I don't believe that. This is not an isolated incident. It's a long-standing behaviour.'

'Next you'll be saying I do it to get attention, to feel better about myself.' She pointed the glass at him, her words starting to slur slightly so that her 'S's came with 'H's. 'You, sir, know nothing about me. If you did, you would know this is a rebellion against the female enslavement also known as marriage, where a woman submits to a man's pleasure in order to preserve her own financial security. But you don't me know at all. So, I'd appreciate it if you kept your assumptions to yourself.'

When he said nothing, she gave a giggle. 'Now I've gone and shocked you.'

Dear sweet heavens, she was a drunk philosopher! She had shocked him, but not in the way she thought. It was the vulnerability behind her rant that him speechless. She would regret that in the morning. She would not like anyone seeing her so exposed, especially not him. 'That's it, you've had enough. Give me that.' He was on her in two strides, wrenching the brandy out of her hand, liquid sloshing on the carpet. He did it more for her than for him. What did he care how much she drank or said? But she made him pay for the intrusion.

'And maybe *you* haven't had *enough*.' She wound her arms about his neck, trapping him against her. 'I'm not so drunk, that I've forgotten you owe me a kiss. I won that billiards game and I get a kiss from whomever I want.' She had her hands in his hair, pulling it loose from its ribbon. 'Why do you grow your hair so long?' She was starting to feel warm and tingly, the world was tilting just a bit and it was fuzzy on the edges, soft. The softness felt good and disconcerting all at once. But Vale Penrith was a solid anchor. As long as she clung to him, everything would be all right. Vale would never let her fall. He was too much of a gentleman, no matter what he thought of her.

'Do you know what I wanted to do to you the first night I saw you? I wanted to mess you up. I wanted to untie your cravat, I wanted to pull your hair out of that black-silk bow. I wanted to spill wine on your shirt.' She had her mouth inches from his. 'I still want to. You're so damn perfect and such a good kisser.' She was beyond warm now, uncomfortably so. She was hot and wet and she wanted him to be hot and wet, too. She kissed him then, hard and fierce, but his mouth would not be enough, not tonight when she was burning. She slipped a hand low between their bodies, finding the intersection between his legs and stroking up, up over the hard length of him, her hand closing over the tip of him where it jutted against his trousers, giving him away entirely. He might be angry, but it hadn't stopped his desire. 'Seems like we might not make it to bed, after all.'

Lady Viola Hawthorne had her hand on his member—his *fully* aroused member. He ought to put a stop to this, but he knew as soon as the thought crossed his heated mind he wasn't going to do a damn thing about it. He'd tried to fight fire the traditional way—with water. He'd tried to douse her enthusiasm with scoldings and warnings. But clearly to no avail.

Now it was time to fight fire with fire and call her bluff. She wanted to play the temptress? So be it. He was in charge here. He'd let her see how a man responded. He took the kiss away from her, his mind and body more than ready to take charge, more than ready to break free of the artificial constraints he'd acquired to hold them in check. He gave his want free rein, his mouth devouring hers in a hard kiss, proof that actions had consequences: *her* actions, *his* consequences.

And yet, it was her hand on him, driving him mad; mad enough to push her up against the billiards table, mad enough to lift her, to settle her bottom on the bumper of the table. He felt her thighs part, her legs gripping him, holding him close as her hand stroked, her other hand working the fastenings of his trousers. She was excited, *he'd* excited her, this minx of a temptress. It was heady knowledge to know he could arouse *this* woman who liked to hold all the cards.

'Let me bring you off, Vale. Right here.' Ah, those words! It was a rare woman who knew how much dirty talk could turn a man on, even a gentleman, or perhaps *especially* a gentleman. Her voice was all naughty smoke, the slur of brandy gone, pushed aside by the rush of excitement and arousal. He might have let her do it, too, if he hadn't understood her better. He knew what drove her: control. Not attention. She liked to control situations, to control others. But she would not control him. He wouldn't allow it.

'You first,' he growled, pushing her back on to the table, sliding her skirts up to reveal… nothing. Was it possible to get any harder? Vale swallowed. 'You aren't wearing anything.' No petticoats, no pantalettes, *nothing*.

'Undergarments are such a bother.' She gave a coy smile, her tongue running over red lips, giving every impression of a woman not yet ready to relinquish control. He answered with a wicked grin. If he wanted control he'd have to take it. It was to be a siege then, a long, slow assault on the citadel of her womanhood. His thumb feathered the entrance of her core and he felt her shudder, then she whispered the most provocative words he'd ever heard, 'Use your damn mouth, Vale.'

He knelt then, cupping her buttocks with his hands and drawing her forward to the edge of the table with a hard slide. He did not mean to take her easily. It would be a rough siege. She would pay first before he gave her pleasure. He put his mouth to her core, blowing warm breath across her damp curls, listening to the ululation of her sighs as she melted into the caress of his mouth. But it was a prelude only. He had more in mind than a gentle climax. He would not let her get off that easily.

He began to lick, to suck, teasing her with the nip of his teeth, and she began to rise. Her hands searched for purchase on the flat of the table. Finding none, they anchored in his hair, tugging as her sighs turned to pants, her breath coming in ragged inhalations, her body arching, her mons pressing hard against his mouth asking for more, pushing him to his own limits even as he pushed her.

She was all wetness when she broke, her legs tight around him, holding him to her as she let the pleasure take her. Perhaps she feared he would leave her before she could claim it. But he hadn't the power or the desire to think of leaving her. Watching, feeling, the completeness of her climax was far more intoxicating than any beverage his aunt served. She lay back on the table, gasping, her skirts askew, her hair tumbling about her shoulders, her eyes…her eyes. They brought Vale to a halt. They weren't flashing. They weren't full of fire and mischief. He'd never seen them like this, violet and calm. They were full of peace. He wondered how long that would last.

She sat up, dark hair falling about her, and her eyes began to move, began to flash even before she spoke in her smoky voice. Her hands were at his shoulders, shoving him gently towards a chair. 'Sit. Now, it's your turn and I mean to have my wicked way with you, Vale Penrith.'

He should protest. This had gone far enough. This bordered on a sensual, physical feast far different than his usual sexual venues, but he could not resist. Perhaps he didn't want to resist. Vale was in the chair, his legs wide for her before he could mount a reasonable offence. She tugged at his trousers, sliding them over his hips until she had full access to him.

She took him in hand and he felt himself harden, strain against the cylinder walls of her fingers. Had anything ever felt as good and irrationally so? Why did this minx of a woman rouse him to such heights? These were questions for another time. His brain could only focus on the purposeful glide of her hand, stroking him from tip to base with a rhythm designed to tantalise, driving him to the edge of pleasure and then pulling him back from the brink—something his body both celebrated and resented, his mind torn between wanting to claim the pleasure and prevent its achievement. To claim it meant to end this, to prevent it meant to prolong the exquisite dilemma of her hand.

Her other hand moved to cup him beneath. She squeezed and he groaned. She laughed up at him, her eyes dark. 'Tell me if you like this.' She put her mouth to him, her lips taking the place of her hand. He would explode. Right now. It was the only certainty in his world as her mouth worked him, laving his tip with her treacherous tongue, licking the pearl that beaded there as if she tasted the finest cuisine. Had any woman ever shown him such attention? Or such enjoyment of the act? Treating it as something more than a perfunctory action that had to be performed? That in itself was a heady elixir, so heady, that Vale felt his body tense and gather. She was pushing him to the brink of pleasure again and this time it would be different. He knew instinctively this time he'd go over that edge. He was groaning out of hand now in hard rasping sobs that gave no illusion of control. She'd stripped him of all semblance of order, stripped him down to his most primal, and he relished it. His body arched beneath her mouth, thrusting into her one last time. She moved, taking him in hand, and he spent, in hard, pulsing spurts.

'Dear lord,' he managed in a hoarse voice he barely recognised as his own.

Viola rose and put her fingers to her mouth, sucking each one by one. He could not pull his eyes away from her. He was going to be hard again after only a moment ago feeling as if the very life had been drained out of him. Her eyes slanted like a cat's as she licked the last one. 'You, my lord, taste like victory.' He reached for her, but she moved away, turning her back to him as she sashayed towards the door. 'Hmm. Some say victory is sweet, but I'd say it's salty. Yes, definitely salty.'

Chapter Nine

She'd gone and turned their exchange of intimate oral pleasures into a game of one-upmanship. A game! Damn it! That was the only reason he didn't run down the hall and drag her back into the billiards room by her hair—his pride wouldn't allow it. And of course, there was the fact that to do so would wake the entire house—something else his pride wouldn't allow. It was bad enough he had to witness his own folly. He didn't need the entire house party to see him chasing after London's Shocking Beauty.

Vale raked his hands through his hair and leaned back in the chair. What a disaster! This was not like him at all. He was always so careful, not just with *affaires* and avoiding the traps of matchmaking mamas, but with himself. He worked hard to keep his emotions in check, his passions restrained, let out only in the proper time and place with the proper sort of woman for those activities; a lovely member of the *demi-monde* or perhaps a wealthy merchant's discreet widow. But a woman known for her notorious accumulation of near-scandal?

Viola Hawthorne could not be *less* his type. She craved attention where he craved obscurity, she was a flagrant flirt where he sought solitude, a daredevil where he clung to the safe and the pragmatic. She was a woman to whom scandal hoped to attach itself, but never quite managed to stick. Scandal didn't dare to even breathe in the direction of Brockmore's heir. He knew her reputation for trouble and her incredible luck in extricating herself from exile. Any one of her antics would have seen any other young woman promptly shuttled out of society's sight, never to return. Yet no one dared to challenge Viola Hawthorne's right to move in society while doing whatever she pleased, with whomever she pleased.

Whomever she pleased. He didn't want to think about that. To do so, he'd have to admit she shared tonight's pleasure with others. Why was it so wrong to want to be her only experience with such pleasure? It wasn't his first time with those pleasures, although it might have been the *best* time, especially if she hadn't flounced out afterwards declaring him salty as if it had been a mere lark to put her mouth between his thighs and swallow him whole. Vale groaned. He was getting hard again at the thought. He needed to do up his trousers before someone walked in and thought he'd been pleasuring himself, which was almost worse than someone knowing Viola had pleasured him—the idea that a duke's heir had to make do with his fist.

Vale fumbled with his trousers. He should have left the room and left her to her fate. He should have let her kiss Throckton. Now, he just felt foolish. He'd let himself go, let himself engage in an act that he reserved for a special few and certainly in more private settings than a billiards table, and she'd encouraged him. How ironic, when he'd been seeking the same from her, to teach *her* a lesson about poking sleeping dragons, to show her that outrageous overtures had consequences.

But she'd not been the only one learning that catechism. She'd called his bluff just as he called hers, and she'd raised the stakes: *use your damn mouth, Vale.* She'd been ready for him and now he was reeling. At least he could be assured she wouldn't tell anyone if the vitriol behind her earlier rant could be believed. Marriage was the last thing on Viola Hawthorne's agenda, something she'd reminded him of on two occasions now.

The best thing he could do was put the evening behind him and move on.

Truly, he tried to do just that. Vale threw himself in to the party spirit the next day, joining the large group of guests going down to the village for the Brockmore version of a Frost Fair and Gingerbread exhibit. The day was overcast, but without wind, which made walking about the village tolerable if one was properly bundled. The Brockmore guests made a gay addition to the fair; the men in their caped greatcoats and wool mufflers, the ladies with their coats and muffs, although Vale noticed more than one lady had forgone her muff in order to tuck a hand through a gentleman's arm instead.

'The party is shaping up nicely.' His uncle fell into step beside him and followed the direction of his eyes to where Miss Pletcher and Lord Truesdale walked apart from the group. 'I had fancied Truesdale for your mother, but it seems Miss Pletcher and he have found common ground.'

'Mother?' The announcement took Vale by surprise. He'd not expected his uncle's matchmaking efforts to extend to her. 'But Father…' He couldn't quite put the thought into words. Surely his uncle, of all people, wouldn't want his mother to remarry, to replace his own brother.

'Your father has been dead for four years. Not

her. Not you. She has a lot of living left, another thirty years, God willing. That's nearly a third of her life. Why should she spend it alone, or as only a spectator to other people's lives? Why shouldn't she start again?' his uncle prompted gently. Put that way, Vale didn't have an adequate response. Yes, indeed, why should she not?

His uncle nodded towards Truesdale. 'He and Miss Pletcher have made that decision.'

'After only five days?' Vale was sceptical. 'Is it even wise to make a life-altering decision in such a short time? They can hardly expect to fall in love in a handful of days.'

'And yet they have. Love does not run by our clocks, Vale. Silas insists on it.' His uncle spoke fondly of his old friend. 'They came to us separately. Miss Pletcher spoke with Alicia yesterday afternoon and Silas spoke to me last night. He was like a young man again, full of a bridegroom's eager worries over pleasing a cherished bride and providing for her.' His uncle smiled wistfully.

'Of course, he is more than capable of providing Miss Pletcher with every comfort. He even talked of children, of wanting to have a second family with her. Silas doesn't think fifty-eight is too old to be a father. Perhaps it isn't when one's bride is twenty-seven and more than able to give him two or three children if they're determined.' His uncle sighed. 'Talking with Silas reminds me that love can find us when we least expect it and with whom we least expect it. To think my old friend has found it with a woman thirty years younger than he is amazing proof of that.' He chuckled, then added slyly, 'We were up quite late in the library talking it over.'

Vale was on full alert now. If his uncle had been in the library, he would have encountered Throckton and company looking for a nightcap. They stopped at a booth to look at intricately frosted gingerbread men, fresh from the oven and still warm. 'I think five days of close quarters is plenty of time to take someone's measure,' his uncle went on as he selected a gingerbread to eat. 'Kenelm and Lady Anne have taken a shine to one another, although I understand some of that polish was already there. At least I can help pave the way with Kenelm's father. Miss Burnham and Matthew Eaton have done well together. I have hopes there. I wasn't sure how that would work out, so far it's been promising. Mmm. This is good gingerbread. Are you sure you won't have any?' Vale shook his head. His stomach had tightened at the mention of the library. He was sure the Silver Fox was working towards something that involved him.

'Love's a funny thing, Vale. Your aunt and I didn't plan the party as a specific venue for matchmaking, not like our summer parties, but we had our intuitions about who might suit if given a chance to discover one another. We had hopes for you, too, although you seem to have gone a different direction, which is fine. I won't force you to marry where I want, as long as you know what you're getting into. Marriage makes up too much of a man's life to be a miserable venture.'

He paused here and Vale waited. It was hard to process that last bit and he sensed the shoe hadn't dropped yet. 'I heard there was a bit of a contretemps in the billiards room last night.'

Lucifer's balls! There it was. Vale felt as though he was back in school again and one of the boys had tattled to the headmaster about private business. 'Throckton should keep his mouth shut, we aren't boys. Besides, he started it with his ridiculous wager long before I arrived at the scene.' Vale winced. That last line hardly supported the former claim. Not schoolboys indeed.

His uncle shrugged and wiped his hands free of gingerbread crumbs. 'Apparently, you finished it.' Had finished and been finished.

'I only meant to come to her aid,' Vale offered in defence. It was true as far as it went.

'An admirable sentiment if it was any other girl. But she's one chit that doesn't need help. She's always *exactly* where she wants to be:

swinging chandeliers, climbing ladders, billiards rooms after midnight,' his uncle chided, looking at him askance. 'Lately, with you.' His uncle didn't miss a thing. Damned if Vale knew how his uncle did that. In a house full of people, his uncle knew precisely where everyone was at all times.

'Dinners hardly count.' Vale tried to shrug it off. 'The social gods control that.'

His uncle seemed to ponder the remark for a moment before shaking his head. 'And skating parties? Long disappearances on multiple occasions where neither of you can be accounted for? Wicked wagers in billiards rooms? Do the social gods ordain that as well?' He wondered what his uncle would say if he knew his nephew had drawn her name for the secret-admirer game as well? Social gods or not, it seemed fate had decided to throw the two of them together.

'Step in here with me, Vale. I need to speak with the owner.' His uncle opened the door to a small shop set just off the village green. The bell overhead jingled as his uncle finished his confusing lecture, the second in two days on the subject of Viola Hawthorne. 'If she's the one you've chosen, then we'll talk. I'm not saying she can't be redeemed, I'm only saying it would be a challenge. Certainly, marriage to a duke's heir would go a long way to making her acceptable and we would do our part. Perhaps she's decided it's the only avenue left to her now if she wants to remain in society. On the other hand, I don't want to see you manipulated into a situation not of your choosing. Lady Viola is dangerous, Vale, if you don't know what you're doing.' That was the burning question, wasn't it? What was he doing with Viola Hawthorne? What *did* he want from her? He hadn't had time to think.

'I don't want to marry her,' Vale began automatically. She certainly didn't want to marry *him*. His uncle's voice cut through his thoughts.

'Then stay off my billiards table, my boy.' His uncle clapped him on the shoulder, raising his voice in jovial tones as the shopkeeper approached. 'Mr. Williams, I've come to look at the new stock you promised me. This is my nephew, he'll want a taste, too.'

The 'store' was devoted solely to spirits, Vale discovered as the shopkeeper set out two glasses on the counter. It was an ingenious idea—a shop that carried Madeira from Portugal, ouzo from Greece, French brandies, and other more exotic drinks like the Italian monks' Vin Santo. The shopkeeper even boasted a small supply of absinthe. There wasn't just one variety of each, but several.

The shopkeeper poured glasses of an amber

liquid. 'This is what you came for, Your Grace, the Vin Santo.'

'Holy wine?' His uncle held his glass up to the light.

'You'll think so, too, once you taste it.' The shopkeeper produced a plate of gingerbread and plum cake. 'Taste it with these. I call it the Christmas wine, perfect with our holiday treats. Can you imagine how it would taste alongside a mince pie?' He turned to Vale. 'It's a Tuscan dessert wine, been served in Italy since the Middle Ages. I finally got some in. The one you're drinking now is rarer, it's been aged for ten years. Most of what I got in has been aged for five. Still, very good.'

Vale nodded and took a thoughtful sip, letting the liquid roll over his tongue. At the first taste, the dry sweetness of the Vin Santo connected to Viola, his brain registering: 'Viola would love this.' The thought made no sense, other than he'd seen her drink brandy, but his gut knew—she would like this. It was like her: different, unique. He took another sip, instinctively knowing Vin Santo was not to be rushed. A small glass could last a man a long time, much like Viola herself. Too much at once would go to a man's head.

His uncle nodded his approval. 'It is good, everything you said it would be, Williams, and perfect for dinner tonight. The five-year-old will be fine. Have it sent up to the house.'

'And I'll take a bottle of the ten-year-old,' Vale put in spontaneously. 'Make that two bottles. I'm quite taken with it. You can send them with my uncle's order.' He'd just found Viola's New Year's gift and it was perfect.

That feeling of elation over finding a perfect gift lasted all of three minutes until he stepped outside and realised what he'd done: he'd bought alcohol for a woman! He couldn't possibly give the bottles to her in front of everyone. Who gave alcohol to a young woman? Apparently he did and he hadn't even blinked an eye at it until now when it was too late. Even worse, he'd set himself up to have to give it to her *privately* if he gave it to her at all. Added to that, he'd selected a very personal gift that only had meaning between the two of them.

What was becoming of him? This was hardly behaviour he would have engaged in five days ago and it wasn't an isolated incident—there'd been the kissing in the library when he should have dumped her off his lap but didn't; the bit on the backside of the island, a place he never should have taken an unmarried girl; and the exchange of intimate pleasures on the billiards table. *None* of these were things he would have engaged in, left to his own devices. Which meant it could only be her. She was the new variable.

He was changing since he met Viola. The choices he'd made four years ago to keep himself apart from society—something he could not always manage physically, but had succeeded in managing emotionally—no longer seemed enough. His body, his mind, were hungry. They wanted to connect and it was no longer enough to stimulate them through research; reading and writing about other people. They wanted to connect to *someone*. Why had they chosen Viola Hawthorne? She was like choosing fire over the frying pan. Certainly, there were better candidates for socially re-engaging, to ease back into it all with. But there was no halfway with Viola. Was that all he wanted from her, an awakening? Or something more?

His uncle had hinted twice now that he was not against Viola Hawthorne, merely her circumstances. What had not been clear the first time had become abundantly clear today in retrospect. His uncle was not warning him away from Viola, but warning him to know his own mind before proceeding. That might be easier said than done.

His uncle's questions today had prompted many more on his part. Why had she chosen to flirt with him? Had she indeed decided, as his uncle suggested, a duke's heir was her only way back to respectability—which assumed she wanted respectability—something Vale didn't believe she was seeking, not after last night's revelations—or was it all merely a game to her, one more scandal to add to her collection? He liked to think there was something more between them, but if there was, what would he do about it?

Whoa. That was setting the Christmas sleigh before the horse. Before anything else was accomplished, he needed to determine what Viola was about. 'Uncle, if you'll excuse me? I'd like to catch up with the others.' Vale made his excuses, his gaze already searching the Frost Fair market for his target. He had shopping to do and someone he needed to do it with. What better strategy for picking out a gift for his secret admirer than to see what she liked first hand? Who knew what else he might learn?

Chapter Ten

Viola's hand stilled over the loaf of gingerbread she was selecting, her chatter ceasing, her body freezing in place as she became aware of him. Vale was behind her. Not just merely behind her in a passing crush of people, but *approaching* her.

'There you are, Lady Viola. I've been looking for you.' Vale's voice was at her ear. Not just approaching her, then, but *seeking* her. He smelled good, the sharp scent of winter set against the sweet aromas of the booths. She'd not expected to see him. He'd been angry last night when she'd left him; angry at her and angry at himself.

He wasn't angry now. In fact, he seemed positively friendly and that gave her pause. What could he possibly want? 'If you're looking for a billiards game, I'm busy.' She tried the old strategy of going after him, trying to ruffle him.

'I'm not looking for a game, I'm looking for a shopping partner.' The strategy hadn't worked, although one could argue it never had. Except maybe last night. But even then, those results hadn't exactly protected her. If anything, they'd made her vulnerable. She'd wanted to break him last night and maybe she had momentarily, but the price had been high. He wasn't the only one who'd broken and, this morning, she was still picking up the pieces of that choice. While she was doing that, he was making decisions. 'We'll take that gingerbread,' he directed the waiting vendor. 'Wrap it up for us.'

Then he was leading her off to the next booth, and the next, looking at brightly coloured hair ribbons, carved toys and sweets. Oh, the sweets! There were so many: liquorice drops, peppermints, the gingerbread decorations, artistically frosted biscuits in different shapes, sugared almonds and plums, warm, roasted chestnuts to hold in your hand.

'I think the sweets might be my favourite part of the fair,' Viola said, accepting a paper cone of chestnuts from a vendor. She'd already eaten most of the gingerbread men she'd purchased. Vale tried to pay for the chestnuts, but she was faster. 'I've got my own money,' she scolded Vale, handing over the coins.

But even that didn't faze him today. It merely made him curious, another tactical error on her part, which just went to prove she was still reeling from last night. She'd not expected to enjoy last night quite as much as she had, nor had she been prepared to lose herself as deeply. For all her parting claims of victory, she had not been in control.

'Do you have to be so stubborn about everything?' His hand was at her back, guiding her through the crowd, his voice low at her ear, where she liked it best. Everything he said was just for her. Just for them. Just *between* them, His words were private, as was so much else about him.

'Yes, I do,' she answered almost defiantly.

One of the most difficult realisations about last night was that she'd been wrong about him. He wasn't a shell as she'd originally thought. He was private; his thoughts, his passions, all of them were carefully hidden away from public display and only a privileged few were allowed to see them, to participate in them. Last night, for a brief time, she'd been one of those elite.

'Whatever for?' They stopped in front of a pasty booth for fresh, hot meat pies. This time, when Vale asked for two, she let him pay.

'Because if I'm not, I'll be eaten alive,' she answered honestly, simply. They'd found a place to stand and eat the pies without being jostled by the crowd, but Vale didn't eat. He stared at her, pie forgotten.

'By whom?'

'My parents, society, every gentleman that comes to call. I'd be devoured if I didn't, married off at nineteen and tucked away in someone's country estate. I thought I made that clear last night.' Didn't he see? Everything she did was to protect herself. She'd hoped for better from him. She despised men who couldn't fathom the idea that she might not want to marry them, might not want to give them control over the rest of her life. She didn't want to despise Vale, which was a quiet revelation all its own. Standing here in the snow, it was inexplicably vital he understand her.

Vale lowered his voice. 'I understood the "from" part perfectly the first time. You protect yourself *from* marriage, but *for* what? I think that one word makes all the difference. Prepositions count, my dear.'

'There you go with the grammar again.' She laughed, hoping to dissuade the direction of the conversation. Vale didn't laugh. He merely waited until she had no choice but to say, 'I'm saving myself *for* me, so that once I'm free of all this…' she waved a gloved hand towards the crowd '… I can get on with what I really want.'

'And what is that?' The question was asked sincerely and it nearly undid her. Did she answer it? She'd never told anyone before, never been *asked* before, not even by her parents. Most conversations didn't get this far, she didn't let them. Usually by now she'd have done or said something outrageous to derail any line of personal questioning. But here she was in the middle of a holiday fair, surrounded by others, being asked to answer the one question that drove her.

She met his gaze. She wasn't London's Shocking Beauty for nothing. If she could climb ladders and hang mistletoe balls from chandeliers, she could answer one simple question. 'I want to travel and to study my music.' She took a defiant bite of her pie. There. She'd said it. Now she waited, waited for him to laugh, or to declare her goal impossible. He did neither. He merely smiled and began to eat.

'Was that so hard?'

She favoured him with a considering glance. It was time to turn the tables. 'You tell me. What you are saving yourself for?'

'Who says I'm saving myself for anything?' He furrowed his brow.

'I do,' she answered smartly. 'If stubbornness is my armour, privacy is yours. You keep yourself hidden away for a reason. It's only fair you tell me what it is.'

He began to move, ushering her out of their space and back into the stream of people shuffling past booths. 'Wouldn't it be more fun if you guessed?'

She gave a short laugh, part-frustration, part because she'd come to know him so well in the last few days. The response was so typically him. He was being evasive, protecting his privacy to the last. They'd stopped in front of a booth selling children's wooden toys and he changed the subject, picking up a boat. 'I used to have one of these.' He smiled and it lit up his entire face, making the serious man look winsome and boyish. To her dismay, Viola felt her stomach flutter. 'My brother and I used to sail them on the shores of my uncle's lake when we visited in the summer.'

'You have a brother?' She was too engaged in learning something about him to think about her response, she only wanted him to keep talking, to keep sharing, to break down some of privacy's wall.

'Had a brother.' He abruptly put down the boat and walked away. She followed, rushing a little to keep up with his long strides. He was suddenly in a hurry.

Had. Yes, right. She'd been foolish not to remember. The great Brockmore tragedy. She knew about it. Everyone did. No one mentioned it. The uncle's brother and brother's son had been killed simultaneously in a sailing incident. She'd forgotten there'd been a brother, too. What had it been? Four years ago? 'I'm sorry, I didn't mean to bring it up,' Viola apologised, but only because she wanted him back, the smiling, laughing version of Vale Penrith who was charming her so effortlessly today at a village fair. She had not meant to chase that man away.

'Are you?' He shot her a sideways glance. 'You've been intent on plumbing my depths since this game has started. Now you have and you want to run from it.' His voice was ice-hard and he was apart from her: no more low tones at her ear, no more hand at her back.

'I don't want to run from it. It seems that you're the one doing the running,' Viola replied sharply. 'Tell me about your brother. Tell me anything.' She was running now to keep up with him. He was trying to drive her off physically, emotionally. The harder he tried, the harder she pushed. She was close to his secret, close to understanding the core of him. She might not get another chance. 'What was his favourite colour? What was the name of his boat? Your boat?' She grabbed for his arm, stopping him. 'Tell me *something*, Vale!'

He whirled on her then with enough force to send the hem of his greatcoat swirling against his boots. 'Talking about my brother is not a game, it is not part of this.'

'Game? Who says this is a game?' Viola snapped, her breath coming in frosty gasps.

'You do.' His eyes were blazing, cobalt coals, his voice an angry growl. 'Everything is a game to the Shocking Beauty. Even duke's heirs.' The vehemence of his reproach scalded her. In that moment she hated the title she'd worked so hard to create, to truly earn. He pulled away from her, dusting off his coat sleeve where she'd gripped him as if he wanted to be rid of her touch. 'Excuse me.' His tone was as cold as the air. He pulled away and was gone, his broad shoulders disappearing in the crowd before she could answer.

She wanted to shout it wasn't true at his retreating back, that he wasn't a game, not any more. Perhaps it was best she didn't. It made her too vulnerable. The words were new and they surprised even her. Was that truly what she thought? What had happened to getting expelled from the party? What had happened to 'home by New Year's'? How had this pursuit of Vale Penrith morphed from being a game to support Anne Lowell's covert courtship of Kenelm to something far more serious? It was no longer a chore to sit beside Vale at dinner. It was no longer an effort to seek him out, but a pleasure. Her eyes went to him even in a crowd, as they were doing now. She caught sight of him in the crowd, emerging fifty feet ahead of her, beside Percival Martindale at a booth further down the aisle. Maybe she should go after him and apologise, make him see that she was capable of more than a game. That she was more than what the title reduced her to. But her pride prevented it. Why couldn't he see that all on his own?

'Let him go for now.' A friendly, almost fatherly voice at her shoulder stopped her. A firm hand took her arm and led her in the opposite direction. Brockmore. Damn it all.

They walked in silence, the Duke nodding to acquaintances as they moved to the outer edges of the fair. He stopped at a stand selling hot cider and took two steaming mugs, finding them a place to stand where they could watch the Brockmore chef, Pierre Salois, conduct his gingerbread house demonstration. Under other circumstances, she would have appreciated the feat and the patience it took. At the moment, she was all tense awareness of the powerful man beside her. What did *he* want? More importantly, what did he know and would it ruin her?

'Are you enjoying the party, Lady Viola?' He passed her a mug. Viola wasn't fooled. Cider was a nice way to dress up the pretence of wanting conversation with her. What did he want? To remove her from the scene? To keeping her as far from Vale as possible?

'The party is excellent.' Viola answered coolly. 'But I hardly think that's what you want to talk with me about.' She fixed the Duke with a stare, opting not to be intimidated, hard as it was. Brockmore was an imposing man, but he was just a man, after all. She'd been managing men for years.

The Duke laughed. 'Save your wiles, Lady Viola, for men who will be affected by them. I'm far too old and far too astute to be taken in by such manipulations, no matter how pretty the face who wields them. Like recognises like, my dear.' It was friendly as warnings went, but it was still a warning. She heard the steel beneath the chuckle. 'Lady Viola, it's time you and I had a talk. About my nephew.'

Chapter Eleven

Ominous words indeed, but Viola didn't back down. If Brockmore expected her to drop her eyes and demurely apologise for overstepping herself he'd be disappointed. 'Is this the point where you tell me to stay away from him? If so, let me save you the effort. I do not want him, not in the way you mean.' She tried for neutral nonchalance, the words harder to say than she'd expected. She did not want to denounce Vale, it felt disloyal. She felt like a fraud.

Brockmore chuckled. 'If you want plain speaking, Lady Viola, you shall have it. I've not come to threaten you. I'm not that sort of man. I'm here to guide you, maybe even help you.'

Viola stared, nonplussed. Compliance was always more frightening than conflict. Brockmore laughed. 'I see I have surprised you, which is no mean feat if the rumours about you are true. Surprise is usually *your* business. How do you like the shoe being on the other foot?' Brockmore sipped his cider. 'I know you and my nephew have had some clandestine meetings.' He held up a stalling hand. 'No need to protest. I don't require either good form or explanation. My nephew is a grown man with a mind of his own. He's made it clear he is not interested in Anne Lowell. It must be no secret she was brought here for him to consider.' Brockmore sighed. 'But the young have different opinions about who suits whom.'

Viola tensed. Surely, he wasn't leading up to the idea of a match between them? 'I don't wish to marry, no matter what my parents have told you.'

Brockmore seemed to ponder her response. He nodded. 'Fine. I just don't want to see my nephew hurt in the process, or dragged into scandal. Whatever you do, it must be circumspect. I demand discretion. I demand you be honest with him.' He paused here, his gaze far away, his words halting as he gathered his thoughts. 'My nephew has been dead inside for quite a while. I hoped this party would help him rediscover a passion for living.' He looked at her. 'I think it has. *You* have. But what happens when the party's over? I would not want to lose him again because someone was careless with his heart.'

The sentiment touched her. 'You must love him very much to worry. But as you said, he's a grown man.' She felt an uncomfortable kinship with the regal duke in those moments, standing at the fair with their cider mugs talking about a man for whom they both had feelings. 'I will be as careful as I can with him,' Viola whispered.

The Duke nodded. 'See that you are. Vale is precious to me, even though he can take care of himself.' He cleared his throat. 'There is also the matter of your parents.' Her newly recovered stomach sank again. 'They will be disappointed if there's no match. He's a duke's heir. You're a duke's daughter. It makes sense to them. They will push. I do not want to see either of you compromised into a marriage neither wants. Nor do I want to see my hand forced.' He lowered his voice. 'I am aware you've indulged in certain, ah, shall we say, "behaviour" since your arrival. Others might be willing to attribute this behaviour to the high spirits of the holiday season. However, I do not think your parents are among those tolerant souls. They will use that behaviour to get you both to the altar.'

Viola felt her cheeks heat. 'Shall I stay away from him, then?' Compliance or conflict, the message was the same: stay away from Vale. The Silver Fox was wily.

Brockmore smiled. ‘You’re being *advised*, nothing more. What you do is up to you. I will help all I can, for my nephew’s sake. And for your sake. I know you don’t want to be here.’ Damn it all, the man really did know everything. ‘I am generous to those who support me. I’d like to be generous to you, Lady Viola. For all of your wild antics, you strike me as person very much in need of a friend.’ He gave her a bow and stepped apart from her. ‘Enjoy your cider, I have other guests to see to.’ Other guests to ‘advise’, he meant. Viola pitied them. Brockmore had a way of getting what he wanted. ‘Anne wants Kenelm,’ Viola called after him. If he was going to hassle Anne Lowell next, he might as well have the truth.

He turned back and gave her a slight incline of his head. ‘Yes, my dear, I know that, too. Just as I know what you did on my billiards table last night.’

Touché. Her cheeks burned. Round one to Brockmore. But what had the Silver Fox won? He had not threatened her. She’d expected blackmail along the lines of ‘stay away from Vale or I’ll expel you from the party’. But there had been none of that. Neither had there been compliance with her parents—'you've dallied with my nephew, now marry him.'

She watched Pierre Salois apply icing to the sides of the gingerbread mansion to created elegant long windows complete with panes resembling the ones at Brockmore. What did the Duke's counsel mean? Did Brockmore find her unsuitable for Vale? If so, why not threaten her? Send her away? If she was acceptable, why not side with her parents and force a match? The third option was that he'd meant it; she and Vale were free to follow their own path, discreetly, of course. He wanted no scandal and no broken hearts. Was he an ally or an enemy? Or was there middle ground? The conversation would have been less curious if she knew. It also raised the question of what was she doing with Vale now?

It seemed her motives had changed. She still wasn't looking for a match, still had no desire to marry. But she no longer wanted to leave the party. Yet, now that caution had been introduced, it would be torturous to be near Vale and not be able to act on that. Public sightings were out of the question. That meant no more feel of his hand at her back. No more rumble of his voice at her ear. No more dinner conversation. She was sure the Duchess would find a reason to rearrange the table after this, as part of the Duke's plan to 'help' her, whatever that truly entailed as enemy or ally. She still wasn't sure. Cheers to the Duke. He'd managed to present her with quite the Sisyphean dilemma. She took another sip of her cider. She was already thirsty.

She stayed 'thirsty' through the dinner, an excellent affair of French-style Cornish game hen for the sixth day of Christmas despite the meal's finale, a dry, sweet, dessert wine Brockmore proudly introduced as Vin Santo, a holy wine from Tuscany. Lord, that was good stuff. Just a sip or two was enough to satisfy, or at least it would have been if Vale had sat beside her. Her instincts had been right. The Duchess had reset the table seating.

Ostensibly, it was because the house party was halfway through. But Viola thought she knew better. If it was any consolation, Vale had been as surprised as she. He'd taken Lady Beatrice into dinner instead. Viola had gone in with her father, a nod to keeping her on a leash, she was sure. She couldn't get up to any trouble with her father on one side and Lord Truesdale on her other side. Thank goodness. She was secretly grateful for the arrangement. Her mother had been waiting for her after the fair, glowing, in fact. Brockmore's instincts had been right, too. 'Vale's attentions,' as her mother put it, 'had been duly noted.' On a related note, her mother had gushed the news St. George's was available the second weekend in April if they moved quickly enough, followed by did she think Brockmore would be open to a shorter engagement? Viola had not been tactful in her response and much of her joy had gone out of the evening, her thoughts preoccupied. She not only had to explain things to Vale, now she had to warn him.

Around her everyone was in good spirits after a day spent out of doors at the fair. There was plenty of conversation through dinner and afterwards, but Viola had no desire to linger for cards and music after dinner, especially when Vale didn't emerge with the other gentlemen after port. She waited a decent interval before pleading a slight headache and making her escape with the help of Anne Lowell. With Anne on her arm, acting as an escort, no one could doubt her intentions of going straight to bed, least of all Brockmore or her parents. They were the only parties she was truly interested in convincing.

Anne had barely left for her own room—which Viola didn't think for a moment she'd stay in—and Viola was off, conducting a swift, methodical search for Vale. She had to explain. She couldn't leave things as they were from the fair. He'd glanced her way once this evening at dinner and she'd been forced to look away, but not before she'd seen his eyes go to stone. She knew he believed her to be nothing but a game-player and she would not tolerate being thought a liar.

But Vale was proving to be elusive. He wasn't in any of his usual hiding places; the library was empty, it was too early for late-night billiards. She even went daringly to his bedroom. He wasn't there either. Thankfully, neither was his valet. That would have been hard to explain and Brockmore would have been sure to find out about it. She frowned to herself. If he was in the Duke's office or in one of the sitting rooms, she would be out of luck with no chance of getting him alone. The rooms were far too public, too accessible to the Duke.

She wandered through the darker recesses of the house where the party didn't reach: quiet sitting rooms, perhaps used privately by the Duchess, reading rooms, a room devoted solely, it appeared, to playing chess. A long hall loomed, lined on one side by windows, portraits on the opposing wall. She strolled down the corridor, her feet picking up speed when she caught sight of a figure at the opposite end. Her breath caught in her throat. She'd found him.

She'd found him. Vale knew it even before she announced her presence. He heard the determined rustle of skirts invading his sanctuary, the quick speed of feet once she'd spotted him.

No one else would come looking. But she would. Viola was unpredictable that way. She'd fought with him at the fair. She'd avoided his gaze at dinner and now she was searching for him.

'What do you want?' He drew a weary breath. He was tired of her games. At least that's what he told himself. But something flickered in him at the prospect that she'd come, even as his common sense warned him this was just another layer of her games to get under his skin and nothing more.

'I want to explain myself.' Her voice was a furtive whisper and he thought she might be nervous for once. She looked down at her hands, laced together and squeezed tightly at her waist. She *was* nervous. That was unexpected. It seemed nothing ruffled her. She had his full attention now. 'And to warn you. There is danger afoot.'

'Danger? Sounds intriguing.' He patted the space beside him on the square, padded bench set in front of the portraits. 'Come, sit, tell me.'

She shook her head. 'I don't dare stay that long. My parents.' Her conversation was a collection of half-started, unfinished sentences. 'I fear they want to push for an alliance between us. Our association has been noted by them, and by your uncle, but for different reasons, I think.'

He chuckled. 'You're being obtuse. But I

know what you mean about my uncle. He spoke with me today, too. I'm not sure he's pushing a match or warning me away from it, or just wants discretion.'

'Discretion. It is up to us to figure out what we want,' Viola affirmed. 'It's why I couldn't look at you at dinner, it's why the seating chart was rearranged. Your uncle believes he's "helping" by keeping us apart in public. But you looked so hurt, so angry tonight. I couldn't allow that. I didn't want you thinking I had toyed with you.'

He let her words rush out. He fixed his attention on the smallest among them. *We.* A small word with big connotations. 'Is there a "we", Viola? I confess to being unsure,' Vale enquired. 'If there is a "we" that is for us alone to decide. I don't like the idea of my uncle interfering, even if it is meant with good intentions. I am no man's puppet.' How like his uncle. He had meddled anyway, despite Vale's own assurances.

'I'm more worried about my parents than your uncle. My mother came to me tonight. She even has a date picked out and she can be tenacious.'

Vale gave a wry chuckle. 'So, that's where you get it. Like mother, like daughter.'

'It's not funny, Vale,' she protested in genuine horror. 'You have to take them seriously. My father is a duke.'

'I know about dukes.' Vale reached for her

hand with a laugh. She was too close not to touch. He pulled her down on the seat beside him. He'd missed her beside him at dinner, fight at the fair or not. He'd come to terms with it hours ago. It wasn't her fault he didn't want to talk about the accident. That was his own problem. 'We haven't been caught yet. Besides, what would anyone catch us doing? Looking at portraits? Hardly an altar-level offence.' It was interesting how truly worried she was.

'Don't you see? It's because you'd be doing it with *me*. You can look at portraits with Rose Burnham, or Anne Lowell, and no one will mind. But my reputation precedes me.'

'And you regret that?' he asked quietly, not wanting to push away the moment. This conversation was far different than any they'd had. Their previous conversations had been peppered with challenges, pitting them against each other. This one they were in together. She was vulnerable tonight, worried not only about herself, but about him. He saw it in her eyes and heard it in her words.

'The means justify the ends. Next year, it will all be worth it. My parents will be so tired of me, so embarrassed by me, they'll be all too happy to send me to Vienna. Out of sight. Out of mind. They can forget all about their errant daughter.'

'Unless they marry you to a duke's heir first,' Vale supplied.

'Yes.' Her response was vehement. 'That's why I'm worried.'

A thought occurred to him. 'You really want to study music? I seem to recall you didn't play at the musical.'

'My music isn't for drawing rooms and debutantes.' Of course not. He knew instinctively that for her, it would be part of her soul, that part of herself that shouldn't be paraded out needlessly. He understood that. His grief, his family's tragedy, wasn't for drawing rooms either and yet it had ended up there. It was still there, four years later, every time he walked into a room. He carried the tale with him as assuredly as he carried the title 'the heir'. For society and for himself, the two could not be separated.

'We're not that different, then.' Vale ran his thumb over the back of her hand. 'We both have titles we don't want. I never wanted to be the heir.' When he'd first met Viola, he thought that was the difference between them and their labels. She aspired to hers, he'd thought, and he wanted to be rid of his. He'd give anything not to be the heir.

'I guessed as much today.' Her voice was softer, its edge gone. She did not, thankfully, press for more. Instead she sat beside him and stared with him at the portraits, apparently willing to forgo the risk of being caught unchaperoned in his presence. Which begged the question, would it be so bad if they were caught? He could feel the warmth of her body, smell the subtle fragrance of her. There was peace in his world, until she went and ruined it.

'So, that's your father? Robert Penrith?' she said quietly. 'He looks like you, the same hair, the same eyes, the same chin.' Damn her. She wasn't going to let him off easy. 'Did your brother look like him, too?' There was no picture of R.J., of course. He wasn't the heir while his father was alive and they'd died together.

'Yes. The Brockmore genes run strong.' He swallowed. Maybe that compensated for the fact that the Brockmore ability to sire children seemed compromised either through biology or tragedy.

'It was four years ago?' She pressed, her fingers lacing through his. 'Will you tell me about it?'

It made no sense to tell her, this woman he barely knew and up until now hadn't possibly even liked. It gave credence to his uncle's words that love had its own clock, that maybe a handful of days was long enough to know someone's true measure. Maybe it was the darkness, maybe it was the warm press of her hand in the cold corridor, or maybe his need couldn't be bottled up any longer. He'd never told anyone. But he told her, one of the most notorious women in London, a woman who didn't want scandal, but courted it anyway all for the sake of her own freedom. Maybe *his* freedom needed to tell her.

'They'd gone out on a yacht. The day was clear, the water calm. There was no reason not to. It was early spring. But the yacht's steam engine exploded without warning. They never stood a chance.' His voice broke. 'They never had a chance to fight, to save themselves.' To say goodbye, to make peace with their fate. He felt the tears come. One of them rolled down his cheek. But it was dark, so he let it.

'How awful.' Viola's voice was quiet and stunned. Her grip on his hand tightened and he knew: She *understood* what no one else had grasped: The root of his grief lay in the nature of the death, not in death itself.

His voice was a series of croaks punctuated with breaks as the words struggled to get free. 'They didn't get to meet death on their own terms. They woke up that morning and had breakfast. They read the newspapers and told jokes. My mother had left for her charity work before my father could tell her goodbye. She wasn't in the house when he left and then he never came back.' That was the piece that ate at his mother's heart to this day. She'd been in a hurry to leave that morning with promises to catch up with them that night. She'd never dreamed she wouldn't get to keep that promise. 'I had breakfast with them. They'd asked me to come with them. But I had plans to go to Tattersall's with a friend to look at horses I didn't need.' What if he had gone? Would he have seen the boiler malfunction? Could he have stopped it before it was too late? He shook his head. There were too many tears to worry about wiping them away. 'It was an ordinary day. We were all supposed to have dinner together. Nothing extraordinary was supposed to happen.' He was gripping her hand too tightly now, struggling to keep himself together.

He waited for the platitudes to come: *you were lucky, if you'd gone, you'd be dead too. At least they didn't feel a thing. They'd died not knowing pain.* He'd heard all that at the funeral and from countless people in the weeks following who'd come to offer their condolences. But Viola said nothing. It was what she did next that pushed him over the edge.

Slowly, she took his head in her hands, her own head pressed to his, foreheads meeting. 'Thank you.' There was profound sincerity in her gaze and it moved him. Had he ever received such genuine compassion before? He could not pretend any more. He was falling for her. He closed his eyes and let it happen. He *wanted* to fall. He didn't want to fight the emotions being with another raised in him. Instead, he gave them full rein. He wanted to drink her in, the scent of her in his nostrils, the touch of her fingers at his face. At her touch, a wall inside him began to crumble, slowly, becoming an avalanche of jubilant emotion and thought: he was alive! And whole. For the first time, he wanted to celebrate that instead of apologise for it and he wanted to celebrate it with her, right here, right now.

'I want you, Viola.'

She whispered her smoky offering, 'Then take me. Tonight, I'm yours.'

Chapter Twelve

Viola drew a shaky breath. This was no brandy-fuelled game of Truth or Consequences on the billiards table. This was Vale Penrith unleashed and it was devastating to behold. She had never had a lover with his confidence. She did not have to lead tonight. She couldn't wrest the lead from him if she tried, even if she'd wanted to. But she didn't want to. Sisyphus be damned. She would not go to bed thirsty tonight. The slow burn that had licked at her all night began to build. She *wanted* him to be in charge.

He moved into her, taking her mouth in a lingering kiss as if he could drink his fill from her. Vale gave a low groan, hungry and primal. Yet for all of its growing roughness, this was not one of their usual kisses; there was no competition to hide the passion behind and pretend it was something else. The passion was naked tonight. They'd be out in the open in more ways than the literal.

His hands cupped the rounds of her bottom, drawing her on to his lap, pressing her full against him, taking her core where he wanted it, flush against the hard root of him, core pressed to core. His hands slid up the silk of her bodice, taking her breasts in their palms, thumbs stroking the fabric over her nipples until they were taut and straining, further proof that this seduction was all his. His hands were back at her bottom, this time sliding beneath her skirts and taking a firm grip. She moved against him, pressing hard against his stiffness. Then he flipped her.

In a lightning move, she was beneath him, looking up at blue eyes and loose hair. Gone was the restrained aristocrat, replaced by primal man and raw desire. One hand worked the fastenings of his trousers with exquisite dexterity and thankful speed.

What had started with a slow kiss, had quickly sped up in tempo to match their need. They were frantic now, having teased themselves to the edge of madness with kisses and cupping. Viola gripped his shirt, pulling him down to her, wanting the weight of his body on her, wanting to feel the press of muscle, the contour of manly planes. 'You will be the death of me, Viola.' He was already panting.

'I will be the life of you,' she answered, meeting his eyes, feeling his phallus take up position at her entrance. But who would be the saving of her? If last night had cost her something, how much more would tonight take from her? And yet, in the moment, the price of her desire was not too much. It never occurred to her to turn back from this, from him.

Viola rose up, letting the tip of his phallus brush against her, teasing him as he teased her with a hint of the wetness and heat that waited within. Then he was in. She gasped, feeling the slide of him, long and full, *filling* her, and she was complete just for a moment before he retreated. She groaned her displeasure, her thighs gripping him in a plea to return. He slid deep again and she clutched him to her. There was a brief bout of competition, each of them struggling to gain the upper hand and then deciding they were better together than against. She picked up the rhythm of his thrusts with her hips, her back arching. All she wanted was him, all her body was focused on him, focused on *them* driving towards pleasure together. This was new frontier, never had she been *partnered* so exquisitely, matched so well.

Vale's body was all hard heat above her, the

muscles of his arms straining with effort as they bracketed her head, his hair falling forward, framing the primal emotions of his face as he thrust into her, and yet for all the pleasure this act brought him, *her* pleasure was his concern. He *wanted* them to come together, all his effort was concentrated on that aim and now hers was, too.

Her breaths came ragged and irregular. 'Almost,' she gasped, only to inhale sharply as his next thrust came into her hard and fast, the quickening of his pace indicating they were nearly there. Once more, twice, and then completion. He had her in his arms, holding her tight against him, their bodies locked together as it took them in all its shattering brilliance.

He held her for a long time afterwards, wrapping her in the cocoon of his arms, his body still joined with hers, neither of them moving. She didn't want to recover, not if it meant him leaving her. Perhaps this was why people were so adamant about making love in beds as opposed to portrait galleries; so they didn't have to move afterwards. How was she supposed to get up and *walk* back to her room after this? She barely had the strength to sit up, and where she'd find the strength to have him disengage was a mystery to her.

Perhaps they could just stay here until she'd

fully processed what had happened. She'd just made love with Vale Penrith. Not 'had sex with'. To describe what had just transpired as merely a physical act was nowhere near adequate. This had not been like any of the other times—all two of them. One had been a dare, the other had been a wager. While not entirely unsatisfying in their own ways, neither had held the promise of this.

Vale shifted his weight. He would leave her soon. She begged him with her eyes to stay a little longer. He smiled down at her, content to do her bidding. 'I've never seen you looking so content.' Viola returned the smile with a sleepy one of her own. She was feeling drowsy and lazy. If he offered to carry her to her room, she wouldn't say no.

'I've never seen you look so beautiful before,' Vale murmured.

'My hair is a mess, my clothes are wrinkled. You call that beautiful?' She was shamelessly fishing for a compliment.

'Yes, I would.' Vale dropped his eyes, gathering his thoughts. She braced herself, willing him not to speak, for fear that words would ruin these moments. Time would do that all by itself shortly. They couldn't stay this way.

She reached her arms up and twined them about his neck, stopping his words with soft kisses, her words interspersed. 'I've never done anything like this before.' The words seemed inadequate. Would he know she didn't mean the physicality of making love out in open?

Vale grinned. '*We've* never done anything like this.'

'We.' It was where their conversation had started. The sound of that single word thrilled her as much as it frightened her. What did 'we' mean? More of this soul-searching lovemaking? For how long? She gave him a smile and a gentle push. It was time to go. Before one of them said too much.

How she made it to her room would always remain somewhat foggy. One moment she'd been lying on the gallery bench, the next she'd found the fortitude to wander the halls back to her room, somehow avoiding guests. But fog was preferable to the clarity that came once she was abed, alone. *What had she done*?

She'd never pushed herself so close to the edge of her doom. Taking a lover was always scandalous. Taking Vale Penrith, the heir to Brockmore, as a lover was downright dangerous. He was not some randy squire's son who was looking for a hayloft affair to pass the winter. Neither was he a baron's second son having a fling before he took up his commission on the Continent. Those men posed no real danger to her. That wasn't true of Vale. The danger he had posed to her tonight hadn't been the mere danger of discovery by others, although that risk was certainly present. There was no denying Vale represented the establishment she'd fought so hard against—loveless marriage, enforced motherhood to as many children as a husband wanted, all in exchange for financial security. Surely a woman was entitled to more than that? Surely she was entitled to as much freedom as a man to choose the life she wanted? The Shocking Beauty had been her protection against the establishment and her protest.

But perhaps the other danger was greater. In one night, she had risked throwing all her hard work—every scandal, every flirtation, every wager—away. What if Vale went to his uncle and told him what had happened? What if Vale insisted they marry out of honour? It was almost enough to make her cringe beneath her bedsheets. To be a duchess was a horrible fate; a woman buried alive under daily menus, seating charts and social calls. But to be his? That did not bring the requisite shudder it had brought last week when Anne had proposed her ploy. Some traitorous part of her wondered if the trade-off would be worth it to be the woman who went to bed with him every night. If the days were torture, at least the nights would be exquisite consolation.

And your dreams? her conscience challenged. What happened to them? The wife of Brockmore's heir couldn't hare off to the Continent and study music or travel about at her leisure with no destination in mind. She would need to be feathering her nest, taking her place in society, birthing an heir. Vale would want a child as soon as possible. More than one. An idea, that tonight, she didn't find terribly unpleasant—a frightening realisation all its own. Since when did she think about children?

She was letting her thoughts run away with her. There was always the chance Vale would say nothing. A very good chance, too. Why would he want to put himself in a position to *have* to marry *her* when there were more suitable, more biddable girls to become the future Duchess of Brockmore? There was no logic in it and Vale was, if anything, logical. What he wasn't was empty. She'd been wrong Christmas Eve, to assume he was nothing more than a pretty shell. He was merely private. Tonight, he'd let her into that private world for a small, intoxicating glimpse and she wanted more, against all odds. Viola had taken challenges before, but the stakes had never been this high. How ironic that the greatest threats to oneself often came from within.

* * *

'You're not out risking life and limb?' Kenelm slapped Vale on the back jovially as he surveyed the racecourse with the other spectators. Guests were taking advantage of the powdery snow that had fallen last night resulting in the perfect sledding conditions. The more intrepid guests had made a 'horse' race of sorts out of it, with the gentlemen acting as horses pulling ladies on sleds in a race around the improvised course.

'No, this sort of thing isn't for me.' Vale smiled congenially. 'Nor you either, I take it?'

'No, I'm letting Eaton pull Anne.' Kenelm's gaze drifted to the starting line where Anne's dark hair and cardinal-red coat showed bright against the snow. The easy-going Kenelm sobered. 'To throw the Silver Fox off the scent, so to speak. Don't want to be too obvious.'

'Why not?' Vale couldn't resist asking. 'You mean to marry her. Perhaps being obvious is the best way to declare your intentions, perhaps even to make it impossible for anyone to object.'

Kenelm elbowed him good naturedly. 'A chip off the old block, aren't you? Already stepping into your uncle's matchmaking shoes.'

'My apologies,' Vale began. 'I didn't mean to presume.'

Kenelm shrugged. 'Presume away. Perhaps you're right. Perhaps Anne and I should stop slinking around. A man who is willing to hide the woman he claims to love sends the message he's not willing to commit to her. Why should anyone take him seriously if he doesn't take *himself* seriously?' He pondered that for a moment, eyes riveted on Anne. 'I think you may have something there, Penrith. Thank you.'

Great. He'd solved Kenelm's dilemma, but was nowhere nearer to solving his own: What to do about Viola Hawthorne? He'd slept like a log last night, much to his surprise. He hadn't lain awake wallowing in regret or in retrospection, two activities that usually ate up quite a bit of his nights. Instead, he'd fallen asleep promptly and deeply. He'd slept the entire night. If he'd dreamed of her, he didn't remember.

Could she possibly understand what a watershed last night had been? Last night, he'd shown a lover more of himself than he ever had before, shared with her more. And now he didn't know what to do or what that meant. Did he simply go about his day as if it hadn't happened? Did he watch the races and go up to the library and work on his report? Come down to dinner and take Lady Beatrice in without a glance Viola's direction? That seemed to make a mockery of last night. It had been a watershed for her, too. They'd both transcended game playing. Now they were in new territory. Now, there was 'we', a stunning realisation for a man who'd spent four years alone for all intents and purposes, and he was willing to embrace it.

Vale watched the racers with half an eye to the entertainment, already composing in his head a very important note and thinking through his options. It was too bad he couldn't take his own advice to Kenelm. But he could take the opposite. He needed a covert strategy to give he and Viola time to sort through what 'we' meant without outside pressure. That would require playing a double-layered game where he ignored Viola in public to appease his uncle, but lavished all his attention on her in private. The idea held merit. Anticipation could be a seductive tool. He was already looking forward to the rest of the party. He dared not think beyond that.

Chapter Thirteen

Thursday, 31st December 1818,
New Year's Eve—Hogmanay

Anticipation was indeed a potent aphrodisiac, especially when it was turned his direction, a *most* unexpected development. Vale thought of the note tucked in the pocket of his evening coat, hiding a secret smile.

He'd planned to send a provocative note of his own, but Viola had beaten him to it. She'd sent the note during the 'last meal of the year'—a Scottish-themed feast complete with neeps and tatties and a bit of haggis, which had tasted decently enough if one didn't think about the ingredients. It was easy enough to ignore the idea of eating intestines when he had Viola's evening to occupy his thoughts and Viola herself.

He'd never had a woman take the lead in his passionate encounters before and the novelty was a heady one.

Vale stole a furtive glance at his pocket watch. An hour until midnight. Time was starting to drag. He'd played the anticipation game before, but not as the recipient. Usually it was him doing the teasing, a role he enjoyed. He'd thought teasing to be the most delectable part of the game, but he'd been wrong. *Being* tantalised was, especially when the role of tease belonged to the incredibly inventive Viola Hawthorne. *Come to me at midnight. I will be waiting.*

Fifty-five minutes. Vale glanced around the ballroom, looking for her. Where was she? She'd been striking this evening in a gold gown, her dark hair piled high, her eyes sparkling, her laughter everywhere as they played favourite holiday games. She'd been inexhaustible, the life of the party. But now, everyone's attention riveted on the excellent bagpiper his uncle had brought in for the evening as part of his effort to celebrate Hogmanay in honour of his Scottish guest. This would be the calm before the party picked up again at midnight with the First Foot, and dancing, Scottish reels, no doubt, although he wouldn't be around to see them. Everyone would be too busy to notice one quiet man wasn't present. But they might miss her. He did wonder how Viola would sneak away unnoticed.

A flash of burnished gold at the door moved on his periphery. Viola! He turned slowly, careful not to alert anyone. She paused at the ballroom door, catching his eye with a wide, wicked smile full of promise. She pressed a finger to her lips in playful warning before mouthing the unmistakable words, 'my room'. Then she was gone, making her escape into the empty hallway. *To get ready for him.* Just the thought sent a bolt of white-hot desire through him. She was preparing herself for him, taking down her hair, loosening her gown. Vale crossed and re-crossed his legs, shifting his position on the little folding chair, trying to dislodge his growing arousal. It would be difficult to explain why 'Amazing Grace' gave him an erection.

Three classic tunes later, the concert concluded. It was time to make his move. He'd sat in the back precisely for this reason. The audience's enthusiastic standing ovation was the perfect cover for slipping away. He was in the hall in no time, checking his watch. Five minutes before midnight, five minutes to reach Viola's room. The further he got from the ballroom, the faster he walked until he was nearly running.

He'd not touched her at all yesterday and he was starting to burn.

Her room was unlocked and he stepped inside, out of breath and aroused, a condition that seemed inevitable. If he hadn't arrived in such a state, he would have been rendered into it at the sight of what waited for him: Viola garbed in a dressing gown of red silk, limbs arranged in a provocative curve in the centre of the big, canopied bed, the lines of her body limned in the seductive light of candles, her dark hair down over one shoulder, long and luxurious, a veritable Circe waiting for her Odysseus. 'Happy New Year, Vale.' Her smoky voice reached him from the turned-down bed.

She rose, eyes on him as her bare feet padded across the floor in slow, purposeful strides, stopping several feet from him, her hand working the satin belt of her robe loose. 'Tonight, I want you to see me naked. And I want to see you.' She slipped the gown from her shoulders and his mouth went dry. Somewhere in the house a clock began to strike midnight. He couldn't think of a better way to ring in the New Year.

She licked her lips and let him look before she stepped close and took his hand, putting it on her breast. He squeezed, caressed. She closed her eyes and exhaled a soft moan. He loved this about her, how she not only embraced her own passion, she *engaged* it. 'I want you, Viola.' His voice was already hoarse. 'I've thought of nothing else all day.'

She kissed him. 'Not yet. Tonight is not to be rushed.' She pushed his coat of his shoulders and worked his cravat loose, his waistcoat, his shirt. 'Everyone is busy celebrating,' she promised. She ran her hands over his chest.'You're beautiful, Vale, so exquisitely made.' Her appreciation was as heady as her touch. She skimmed his flat nipples with her nails and he threw back his head, exhaling deeply at the eroticism of her touch. Then she was gone, stepping back from him and sitting down in a chair near the bed, her legs spread wide in provocative invitation, her eyes glittering. 'Take off your trousers, Vale. One of us is overdressed and it's not me.'

He held her gaze, no mean feat, and worked the fastenings in a tease of his own. He took his time sliding the trousers over his hips, letting the candlelight reveal him part by part until his trousers were off. A coy smile lit her face. 'You are magnificent, so vertically…male. So…mine.' She slipped a hand between her legs, stroking the wetness there. 'Do you see what you do to me?'

Vale swallowed hard. 'Careful, Viola, or you'll have me spending before I can give you pleasure.' He desperately wanted to replace her hand with his mouth.

'Are you going to stand there and watch or do something about it?' she issued the invitation.

He knelt before her, his hands gripping her thighs, his voice a growl. 'Damn right I'm going to do something about it.'

Viola slid down in the chair, unable to help herself. It was happening again. She was losing control and it was all his fault. She'd half-hoped the other two times had been merely circumstantial; the first time driven by the heat of anger, the second time in the portrait gallery inspired by emotion. Perhaps this time, she'd discover he was only a man, fallible in passion as a man is fallible in much else. But she'd been wrong. Her hands tangled in his hair as she begged his mouth for mercy, as she moaned his name and climaxed halfway out of her chair. He helped her the rest of the way, pulling her into his arms and laying her on the floor beside the fire, his long body stretched out beside her. The bed was going to go to waste.

Vale Penrith was one hell of a lover. Not all of her was disappointed by this revelation. But it did complicate matters. She'd chosen him over returning home. She no longer thought of wanting to get expelled from the party. She only thought instead of how to stay, how to avoid getting caught and still have what she wanted—and that was this gorgeous secret of a man lying beside her, the firelight his only cover.

'My parents would be thrilled if they knew. They'd force your hand and, if that failed, they'd force your uncle's,' she murmured, running a hand along the muscled curve of his hip.

Vale chuckled. 'You make that sound like a bad thing.' He smiled and reached out to wind a dark curl about his finger.

She rose up on one arm and faced him squarely, alarmed by the nonchalance of his response. 'It *is* a bad thing, Vale. A *horrible* thing. You don't want to marry me and I don't want to marry you. It would ruin everything. You have your Lapland expedition, I have my travels in Europe, my music.' Men forgot all nature of things when they were gripped by passion.

A slow fire started to burn in his eyes. 'And this thing between us? Is that a *bad* thing, too?' The conversation was starting to get dangerously near to topics she didn't want to discuss, topics she didn't have an answer for.

Pleasure was the best distractor she knew. She reached for him, taking him in her hand. 'This between us is not a bad thing, Vale, it's the getting caught that's bad.' She slanted him a hot look. 'I have a confession to make.'

He raised a dark eyebrow. 'What might that be?'

'It's New Year's Day now, technically.' She

shifted closer to him, letting her breasts brush his chest. 'I can reveal my secret admirer. It's you. Anne Lowell traded me your name for Kenelm's.' She ran her tongue over her lips, watching the angry flames in his eyes give way to more passionate fires. She kissed his lips, the base of his throat, the centre of his chest, making the journey to his navel. She blew against it. 'I have a present for you and I have to give it to you right now.' She kissed the length of his phallus, moving to the tender tip of him, and felt him shudder. She released a sigh of relief: danger averted. She was safe for now.

She was, in fact, safe for three hours. But she was fast learning Vale Penrith was tenacious, even without trying. The fire had died and he moved them to the bed, drawing the covers up over them and cradling her against him. She could feel him starting to rouse where her buttocks met his groin in spoon fashion. 'There's an old New Year's tradition that says whomever you kiss at midnight, you'll end the year with,' Vale murmured against her hair, springing the trap just when she thought she might fall asleep unless he had ideas of taking her from behind.

'Don't, Vale,' she warned with drowsy caution. The allusion to the tradition was just another angle on the earlier question and she had no answer. To discuss the future, would be to fight and she didn't want that tonight. Perhaps it was selfish, but she just wanted to be in his arms, to be in his private world as long as she could. 'If you want to worry about something useful, worry about tomorrow. Tonight was mine. Tomorrow it's your job to find a way for us to be together.'

'Hmm.' Vale sighed. 'Is that a challenge? Shall we make this a competition?' He chuckled in the dark, a warm sound at her ear. 'I'm just thinking how ironic it is that the first half of the party I hadn't wanted to be here and now for the last half, I am dreading it being over.'

'Then don't think on it.' She turned in his arms and kissed him. Conversation was getting dangerous again. 'The future will take care of itself.' But who would take care of him? Of her? When had she started to care about the answer to that?

Chapter Fourteen

Vale did better than take care of the next day. He took care of the next four. Viola found her days settling into a decadent pattern. Each morning began with a gift, delivered discreetly through her maid, whom Viola assured him was trustworthy. New Year's Day, it had been a small bottle of the Vin Santo she'd enjoyed—and something only Vale would have access to. It made her smile to think of Vale presenting her with wine. The Vale he'd been would never have dared it. But the Vale he was becoming had a wicked side.

The Vin Santo had been the beginning of their double life. In the drawing room that morning when the secret admirers had been revealed in much merriment, Vale had presented her with a 'decent gift' of gingerbread, a pretty box of all her favourites from the frost market. But she knew what paired well with gingerbread—the Vin Santo that remained beside her bed upstairs. It was a tantalising prospect that kept her on the edge of anticipation all day, waiting for night. He was good at tantalising. How had she ever thought he was an empty shell?

He flirted with her when no one was looking, bringing a blush to her cheeks when his eyes met hers, his gaze a hot reminder of what they'd done with their 'holy wine' the night before. Turned out, navels made good sipping cups. Interestingly, it also turned out that Vale knew the Brockmore house better than anyone. On Saturday afternoon, while the others were engaged in the Brockmore Winter Games down at the lake, he lured her to a small unused practice room at the back of the third floor. 'All of my boyhood explorations are paying off.' He laughed as she kissed him to show her appreciation.

'It's perfect, but are you sure no one will miss you?'

Vale had merely grinned, his hands at her waist in a proprietary gesture she was coming to love. She was his when he touched her like that, so easily, so naturally. 'I told my uncle I needed to work, that I'm behind on my report.'

She gave him a sly stare, eliciting a laugh. 'Don't look at me like that, Vi. I *am* behind on it and I *do* need to work on it. I'm just not working on it now. It's not a lie. It's…subterfuge.'

'You'd rather be with me than working on your report? I will consider that progress, all things considered. So, what shall we do first?' It was said teasingly, but there was sombreness that followed, their gazes falling together on the old piano and she suspected he might have chosen this room on purpose.

'Will you play for me?'

The request touched her. She knew him well enough by now to know that he understood the intimacy of his request rivalled the intimacies they'd already shared. Playing for him was another way of being naked before him, of being exposed. Viola nodded slowly and walked to the piano bench. She sat, closed her eyes, her hands resting just over the keys as she contemplated the piece. She'd play the Bach for him, the 'well-tempered clavichord', with its nuances; surging *crescendos* and quiet *pianissimos*, a piece that spoke to intensity and mood.

She risked a glimpse at Vale as she neared the end only to find that he'd never looked away. His eyes were riveted on her, as if he could see into her very soul or because her soul was so nakedly on display. And he *liked* what he saw. There was awe in that gaze. She finished and gave him a tremulous smile. Now that he'd seen her, *truly* seen her, what would he think?

He didn't offer accolades as he strode towards the bench and offered his hand to help her rise, and she was glad for it. People had tried to classify her playing before with words—stunning in some cases, overwhelming in others. Some had even called it 'different' simply because a young woman didn't play such pieces or play them with such passion. A young woman should limit herself to polite pastorales. But Vale offered her the words she'd offered him. 'Thank you. I think I understand now, as much as someone can understand another, anyway.'

'Now, it's your turn. Tell me about Lapland.' She wrapped her arms about his neck. 'Do the Sami have interesting sexual rituals?'

He laughed down at her and she was relieved to see some of the awe fade, his eyes starting to sparkle. 'I don't know about that, but they do have female goddesses like Maderakka. She gives humans their bodies and she has dominion over all the women of the tribe.' He paused in thought, remembering. 'And dominion over boys until they become men, if I remember correctly.'

'Ha! Everyone starts life as a woman then.' Viola grinned smugly. 'I think I like the Sami. Very liberated in their thinking.'

'I supposed you could look at it that way.'

Vale led her to the fire and she sat down on the floor, tucking her skirts around her and taking in the pleasant warmth. 'They also believe the deceased and the living are merely two halves of the same family.'

'The dead are always with us? I like that, too,' Viola said softly. She feathered his cheek with her touch. 'I can see why that appeals to you. There's no need to say goodbye. What else appeals? I want to know everything.' She wanted to draw him out, wanted to see his soul.

He showed it to her, there before the fire that afternoon, pouring out tale after tale of a people who lived simply with nature, in a world unbothered by cities and so much of the needless complexity that governed life as they both knew it. 'To be sure,' Vale said, wrapping up his exposition, 'they have their own rules, their own organisation, but it seems much purer to me, more straight forward than London and dukedoms.' He gave a thoughtful sideways glance and she pushed aside the warning in her head that this was becoming a courtship in truth.

This was becoming too real. In her honest moments, she had to acknowledge she wanted Vale in ways that superseded the physical. It was true of Vale, too. He wanted her in ways no one else had. Surely, Vale understood that what had begun in earnest at the stroke of midnight on

New Year's would end on the stroke of midnight on the Twelfth Night? But what if he didn't? What if Vale thought this was more than affair? Why didn't that thought frighten her? Why did she no longer see the risk in that?

A girl could only change a man like Vale Penrith so much. But her mind started to play the 'what if' game. What would she do if he started to think of this as more than a casual holiday affair? What if *she* did? Perhaps she already was. The idea was already hovering on the fringes of thought and it stayed there as the days passed along with the growing realisation of exactly how careful they had to be.

In public, they allowed themselves no words, no errant touches, no glances. Viola no longer thought of wanting to go home; the absence of interaction became a foreplay of its own, an adult version of the 'opposite game' played by children, where what one said meant the reverse. When Vale told Miss Philippa Canningvale how lovely she looked in her green velvet before the Victor's Supper after the games, Viola knew who the compliment was really for.

Vale's secret room became their sanctuary, the one place they felt safe in being together and they stole away as often as they could; sometimes for stolen kisses, other times just to be in one another's company. She'd sit at the piano while Vale worked on his report. He'd moved all of his work here, out of the library. She had her music books here as well and those little touches seemed to make the room theirs in truth, and the domestic fantasy spun by a 'place of their own' was potent indeed. Was there a way to have this? To have her music and Vale?

Their efforts made Viola wonder if they weren't the only ones playing various games under the cover of politeness. What other courtships were going on beneath her nose? There was no arguing that the party was changing. In the days after New Year's the atmosphere shifted, underscored by a new tension. Men were disappearing for intervals to meet with Brockmore in his office. Women were in close tête-à-têtes with the Duchess, hands tightly folded in their laps as important discussions took place. Even if Brockmore insisted this party had not been a matchmaking event, it seemed many of the guests had taken up that thread anyway and matches were resulting.

There were also those who became less careful. Miss Pletcher and Lord Truesdale treated everyone to an announcement of their engagement at the Victor's dinner after the Winter Games. Kenelm and Anne were quite obviously together now, sitting beside one another at every event. At the box supper on Sunday before the village theatrical on Monday, Anne bid an insane amount of money on Kenelm's dinner. Viola had felt a twinge of jealousy, wishing she could have bid on Vale's dinner. She consoled herself with the practicality of it—she wouldn't have had time to eat anyway. She was one of the leads in the play and there would be 'dessert' later.

They were running out of 'laters', though. It was the first thought Viola woke up to on Tuesday. Monday night had been heavenly, right here in this room, all rosy candlelight and pleasure. Dessert indeed. There'd been more gingerbread, and more Vin Santo, some of which they'd drunk, some of which they'd lapped from each other's bodies. He'd even brought her roses as if she were a fine Drury Lane actress worthy of acclaim. They'd found things to do with the rose petals, too. Very soft, rose petals were. She smiled and stretched, trying to hold on to the night and its memories, trying to shake the feeling that something was amiss. But her intuition wouldn't let her.

Her maid entered with a tray of chocolate and a roll. 'Here you are, Lady Viola.' She set the tray down and began bustling around the room, picking up discarded clothing and costume pieces from last night. Viola sat up. Her maid was never quite this brusque. There were usually questions about the previous night: how was dinner? How was your fellow? Sally was the only one who knew about Vale. She didn't know everything, of course, but she'd been ferrying the morning notes.

'How is everyone, Sally? I can't help but feel something is not right this morning. Has something happened?'

Sally stopped fussing with the clothes. She dropped the items in her hands and turned, her face crumpling. 'My lady, your parents have requested an interview with His Grace this morning.'

Viola felt her stomach grow cold. 'Why?' How could they know? She and Vale had been careful. The Twelfth Night ball was this evening. They'd been so close.

'I thought you'd want to know.' Sally was trembling. Viola stood up and began to pace. She could not give in to panic. She had to think. The Shocking Beauty never let others dictate her actions. She wasn't going to start now. For now, she had to assume the worst: that her parents knew about the *affaire* and were attempting to force Vale's hand.

Oh, God. *Vale.* She clutched the window sill, her knuckles white with realisation. This was worse than any scandal she'd ever sought to create. Those scandals had actually been helpful tools. Not like this where a scandal would bring down another person.

She knew how the morning would play out. Brockmore would call Vale to the study and tell him. What would Vale's reaction be? She feared it would be anger. He would feel betrayed if it happened this way. He'd think she'd used him all along, that she'd been covertly in on her parents' ploy to snag a duke for their daughter, that all of her protests to the contrary were for show. How could a marriage even survive if it was started under a cloud of such doubt and mistrust? There'd be no hope for the beauty they'd shared over the past week and that tore at her heart. She couldn't bear to lose those moments, to have them ruined by matchmaking contretemps.

Who could she go to in order to stop this? Viola considered her options; she could go to the Duke and plead her case, but she was unsure of his response. Their conversation at the Frost Fair had indicated he had empathy for her, but it had also indicated that he was not opposed to her spending time with his nephew. Did that mean he'd sanction a match if he thought it suited his nephew even if it didn't suit her? No, the Duke was too big of a risk. There was Vale. She could go to him right now and explain everything, but he might opt for the honourable route. Hadn't he indicated as much? He wanted to talk about a future, refusing to see the drawbacks to that future. A duke-to-be like him could not be saddled with a girl like her. But she'd put him off. She was regretting that. How could they talk of the future now without those plans being tainted by outside interference? No, she could not go to Vale. She had to solve this on her own.

Viola looked out over the white and black expanse of the winter landscape, the Brockmore lawns deep with snow, but the lanes were black, wet and clear. *Roads* were passable. A coach could travel. An idea began to form. It was not an easy one. But what choice did she have if she meant to protect Vale? And herself? And their dreams? Vale couldn't marry her by force or by want if she wasn't here. It was time to go home and get on with her plans.

The old Viola would have seen the benefit to this turn of events. The scandal of walking out on the Duke of Brockmore and his nephew would be too great. Her parents would be too glad to let her go. They'd pack her off to Vienna willingly now, just as she'd wanted all along. The old Viola would say this was coming along as planned. But the new Viola, the woman she'd become with Vale, wanted none of it. Viola pushed her maid aside. 'Sally, quickly, get my cranberry travelling ensemble out. We must pack as fast as we can. Send for the coach as quietly as possible and then bring me some paper.' She would leave, but not without saying goodbye. Perhaps the letter could be her absolution.

It wasn't until she started to write did she realise how deeply she'd fallen. At last, she'd found love. She'd never thought to find it and she'd certainly never thought it would hurt this much to give up the man she'd found it with. Perhaps in time Vale would understand, or perhaps he'd simply be relieved. She would never know. She'd be a continent away in Vienna, playing her heart out, or what was left of it.

Chapter Fifteen

'Where is she?' Vale burst into his uncle's office without permission, not caring that he'd trampled over the butler to get here. He cared only that Viola was gone. Her trunks were missing, her room was starkly clean, the bed made, the clothes picked up, so different from the tumbled sheets and rumpled garments that had littered the floor last night. Something sick and cold had taken up residence in his stomach at the realisation. This was *not* how it was supposed to end. He didn't know how it was supposed to end, but this was not it.

His uncle looked up, something alert passing behind his sharp eyes. 'I have guests.' He nodded to indicate Matthew Eaton and his newly arrived parents who had driven over for the

Twelfth Night ball and quite possibly to meet Rose Burnham, their future daughter-in-law.

'If you would all excuse us. I need to speak with my uncle. There seems to have been a misunderstanding.' Vale sent an apologetic glance at Eaton. He liked Eaton. He didn't want to ruin any betrothal talks, but this was important. If Viola was gone, he wanted to know why.

His uncle waited until the room was empty to scold him. 'You've cleared *my* office, Vale. Now, what is all this about Lady Viola?'

'This!' Vale shoved the note at him, impatient. Time was of the essence, especially if he meant to go after her and bring her back. 'I want to know what happened. Why did you do this after all the subtle encouragement? You never condemned her,' Vale challenged.

His uncle glanced at the clock, ignoring the accusation. 'It's been a busy morning, Vale. Her parents were here two hours ago, as soon as it was decently possible. We had breakfast together.' His distaste over the interview was evident in his tone. His uncle did not care for Calton and his wife. 'They want a marriage between you and Viola on the suspicion you've been spending clandestine time together. They say you've compromised their daughter.' He winked. 'If it's any consolation, I don't think they know about your secret room on the third floor or the billiards table, or New Year's. I think they're bluffing with their "suspicions".' Some time later when he was not panicked, he'd want to know how his uncle knew. But not today. Today, he was only concerned about finding Viola.

'You had nothing to do with it?' Vale pressed.

His uncle shook his head, suddenly serious. 'I've been in here all morning, meeting with guests. I was unaware Lady Viola departed earlier this morning. If she did indeed leave, she did so of her own volition. I had no hand in it, nor is it something I would have wanted. I told her parents I would not force your hand, that in light of no witnesses to any indiscretion and only their hearsay to go on, this was a matter for the two of you to decide.' He paused. 'I hope that was appropriate? I wanted to respect your wishes to do your own bride choosing, Vale.'

His uncle's sincere support calmed his anger to a manageable simmer. 'I am sorry I accused you.' Vale slumped into a chair. 'She left to protect me, to protect us. She didn't want any great sacrifices made.' That was the more difficult piece to decipher. Had she done it altruistically or had she decided to take advantage of the drama and make her escape out of self-preservation and the lure of Vienna? Was all of this really just about her in the end?

'What does your heart tell you, my boy?' his

uncle put in quietly when he'd finished airing his thoughts.

'I've never known anyone like her,' Vale answered truthfully, words forming from ideas he'd only dared try out in the privacy of his mind.

'She's beautiful and outrageous, quite a departure from London's usual offering,' his uncle said. 'I can see the appeal, especially when you've been living like a monk.'

'I have *not* been living like a monk,' Vale protested. 'She's more than her reputation, Uncle. She's funny and insightful. She listens when I talk. I'm more than an heir to her, more than a man who carries a tragedy with him.' The attributes were tripping over themselves as they poured out. How had he ever thought her appalling? 'She's talented. Have you ever heard her play? She's inspired and passionate. She's *alive*. For the first time since R.J. and my father died, I want to be alive, too. I want to be alive *with* her.' But did she want to be alive with him? Could he bear it if he went after her and she refused?

'Does she know any of this?' his uncle prompted, his eyes mysteriously glassy. 'Have you given her a reason to stay?'

'No. I tried. She didn't want to talk about a future. She says marriage is a trap,' Vale began. That's what had him reeling now. Did she still feel that way? Was marriage to *him* a trap to her?

He wanted to go after her, because it was what he wanted. But he also wanted to give her what *she* wanted and if that was freedom, he wanted her to have that, too, even if it hurt him.

His uncle leaned forward over the desk. 'Then try again, Vale. You know, your aunt refused me the first time I proposed. And the second. She said I was too arrogant.' His uncle smiled. 'She was likely right. But her refusal humbled me. It made me see that it wasn't about *her* getting to marry *me*. The real bargain was that *I* was getting to marry *her*. Once I figured that out, nothing was going to stop me from winning her.' He was silent for a moment. 'You're good for each other, Vale. She's calmer when she's with you. And you've come alive these last days. You're more like yourself than you've been in years. If she's the one who can bring you back to happiness, you have to risk claiming her.'

Even if she chooses Vienna, was the unspoken risk. Vale was out of his seat. He'd had his conclusion before talking with his uncle, but now he was centred. The conversation had given the shattered pieces of his plan direction. 'I'll need my horse. It's going to be a cold ride.' He folded the note and put it in his pocket.

Twenty minutes later, Vale swung up on his horse, a strong Cleveland Bay with winter shoes for icy roads. He gave his uncle a nod, not wanting him to see how much his words had resonated with the doubt in him. 'I'll bring her home.' He'd found a woman to love, the woman he wanted to spend his life with. She was not going to get away from him, especially when he had a plan that would give her, give *them*, everything they wanted. There was no turning back from the future now, whatever it held.

She should go back. It wasn't the first time Viola had entertained the thought since the coach had set out. But there was no logic for it. She couldn't plead the weather. The coach was luxurious, the interior warm and supplied with all possible comforts, from blankets to warm bricks and a basket of food. Neither could she plead that she'd made a mistake. Vienna was within her grasp. This was the opportunity of a lifetime. One she'd worked towards for years. Why would she go back? And for a man? Hadn't she spent her adult life avoiding entanglements like this? No woman should ever be held back by a man. It was the height of irony that she of all people would be considering that now. So, Viola kept going. Mile after mile.

There was no reason to turn back except a tall, handsome man, with blue eyes and a secret smile, who had made her no promises. *That was your fault*. Her conscience was relentless. *What would you have done if he had?* How many times had she tortured herself, mentally replaying that moment New Year's Eve when he'd talked of tradition and ending the year with the one you started it with? What if she'd allowed him to spin out his fantasy instead of silencing him with a kiss?

Logic came to her rescue. Maybe it wouldn't have mattered. He had his work, his Lapland expedition. Additionally, Vale Penrith was going to inherit Brockmore. He needed a suitable mate by his side. Only the accident of her birth recommended her as that mate. She'd ruined herself long ago. She'd never regretted becoming the Shocking Beauty until she'd met Vale.

There was a rap on the ceiling from outside. The coachman wanted her attention. Viola opened the window. It was starting to snow again. 'There's a rider coming up behind us, my lady. He's signalling for us to stop. Shall I?' The roads had been deserted all day. Her driver was likely worried about highwaymen. Who else would be out in the weather? Viola looked behind her at the approaching rider. On second thought, why would a *highwayman* be out in this weather if there was no guaranteed quarry? Only a man on a mission would choose to be out. She squinted, her pulse starting to race. Or a man in love. 'Stop. He means us no harm,' Viola gave the order, trying to collect herself. Vale Penrith had come for her.

Chapter Sixteen

She stepped out of the carriage to meet him, using the cold air to steady herself. 'Out for an afternoon ride?' She didn't want to appear too desperate, or too glad to see him until she was sure why he'd come.

But Vale had no such compunction. He swung off his horse, his emotions an obvious storm of turmoil on his face. 'You left.' He was mad, this man who had hidden every emotion until she'd broken through. Now, he wore this one all too plainly.

Viola swallowed. 'I left a note explaining why. It's for the best, Vale. I will cost you too much.' She'd not thought she'd see him again. It was almost too much right now to see him, so tall, so confident and commanding. 'I didn't want you to think I'd had any part in my parents' plots.'

'I know you better than that. I thought you knew me better than that, too, that I would be unlikely to believe such a thing of you after all we've shared.' He advanced towards her, boots crunching on the snow. 'When I went to your room and saw that note, it undid me. I didn't know where you'd gone or why. Or what I had done to drive you away.'

She tried to break in. She couldn't have him taking all the blame. She was the one who had run. But he shook his head, a cue for her not to interrupt. 'I know what happened. I spoke with my uncle about your parents. But I won't let them ruin our decisions. I should have settled this with you before now. I gave you nothing to believe in, Vi, no promises, nothing to weigh against your dream.'

No, not nothing. How could he think that? 'Vale, I…' She tried to override his words, tried to tell him leaving had been a mistake. She should have come to him no matter what the price. She pressed a cold hand to his lips. 'You gave me nothing? Is that what you think? You gave me too much. You saw beyond the scandal, beyond the façade. You didn't care how ruined I was and you understood why I had done it.'

He had her bare hand in his gloved one, kissing each freezing finger, warming it with his breath. 'I never thought of you as ruined,

Viola. Just the opposite. You are so much more than me, more alive, more courageous. Nothing daunts you.' His confession came in fast words. 'I should have told you. I should have shown you that you don't have to choose between me and your dreams. We can have it all. I will see to it.'

'You tried to. I put you off. I didn't want to hear it. I'm not as courageous as you think, Vale. I was too afraid.'

He squeezed her hand. 'I'm afraid, too, Viola. I'm afraid of going back to Brockmore Manor without you, afraid of going on without you. You make me feel alive, Viola. Not just in bed.' He tapped a finger to his head. 'In my mind.' He tapped his heart. 'In my soul.' He paused, letting out a frost-laden breath. 'And I'm afraid right now of what you'll say, when I ask you this. I want to marry you. Do you want to marry me? I promise it won't be a trap.'

She'd never thought a proposal would happen this way, here in the snow beside a coach on the edge of a road, just the two of them. She'd always imagined it as a very dry occasion, with paperwork and her future husband walking out of the study with her father and a smug smile on his face as he contemplated the enormous dowry he'd just signed for. She wasn't a commodity to Vale. The realisation caught her off guard. He wasn't a commodity to her either which was why she had questions, too. ‘What about Lapland and the Sami? That work is important to you. I can’t ask you to give it up.’

‘I don’t recall you asking.’ Vale’s eyes were serious. ‘I won’t ask you to give up Vienna.’

‘But how?’ The words were nice, but she didn’t understand how that was possible.

Vale smiled. ‘Have you ever heard of a honeymoon? Vienna is beautiful in the spring.’

‘And the Sami?’ She would not have only her happiness upheld.

‘The next spring. It will take at least a year to organise the expedition and I can do that from Vienna.’

‘You have it all worked out.’ The tension was starting to leave her.

‘I had plenty of time to think it all through on the ride.’

Vale’s smile widened and it gave her confidence. ‘Now, all I need is for you to say yes.’

‘Two years. That will be a very long honeymoon,’ she teased, contemplating the question.

‘I’ll take that as a yes.’ He drew her to him and kissed her, a long, lingering kiss that had her wishing they were closer to home. ‘Be warned, Viola, I intend for that honeymoon to last longer than two years, more like the rest of my life.’

‘What next, then, Vale?’ It was one thing to

dream of the future, it was another to live it, step by step.

'We go back to Brockmore and we dance, and on the way, we just might try out the coach's hospitality.' He held open the door and helped her up.

'I think life with you will be an adventure. I hear you have a penchant for all sorts of unusual locations.' Viola laughed, already reaching for him as the door shut behind him.

'You're the adventure, Viola. *My* adventure,' he assured her as she pulled him down the leather seats.

She giggled. 'Together, we'll be unstoppable.'

'I plan on it.'

She laughed against his shoulder. Of course he did. Vale Penrith was that sort of man. It was a good thing she always had plenty of surprises up her sleeve, because once one got past his outer layer, he was a vast wilderness she'd get to map and she wouldn't have it any other way.

Epilogue

The Twelfth Night ball might have been the most lavish entertainment the Duchess had ever thrown. The ballroom was swathed in velvets of deep, rich blues and violets, shot with silver. White winter roses in vases populated the niches of the room, letting off a light fragrant floral smell among the forest scents of pine. Not all of the green had been taken down and the ballroom held the last remnants of the holiday season.

The Duke and Duchess had led out the first dance, a surprising waltz, or not so surprising if one considered how many matches had been made over the past twelve days. What better than a waltz, a dance of love, to start the last festivity of the party? Everyone wore masks, but no one was under the impression they were dancing with a stranger.

'You've outdone yourself, Alicia.' Marcus pressed a kiss to his wife's hand. She looked stunning tonight in a dark violet gown, diamonds in her hair, at her ears and about her neck, his very own star in a dark sky.

Alicia laughed. 'It's you who've outdone yourself. We weren't even trying to make matches!'

'Silas and Marianne,' the Duke said as the couples sailed by. 'Rose and Matthew, and Throckton and Lady Beatrice—a most excellent match, it will be the making of that young man. He has talent, all he needs is a bit of confidence.'

'Those are triumphs indeed,' the Duchess agreed smilingly, 'though not as astonishing, I have to say, as Miss Canningvale's, if it comes off.'

'You are in the right of it there, my dear,' the Duke replied, eyeing his dear niece Verity's rather outrageous friend Philippa Canningvale circling by in the arms of Captain Milborne. 'You had a word with the chit, regarding the nature of the Captain's condition? Those headaches of his, the uncontrollable tempers…'

'The Captain himself has left Philippa under no illusions,' Alicia replied. 'She says she admires him more for his honesty.'

'A rare enough quality.' Marcus sighed heavily. 'And as for that pair,' he said, eyeing Drummond MacIntosh sailing by with Joanna Forsythe in his arms, 'thanks to them, I shall have to be brutally honest myself with Wellington when we meet in a few days, and I can't say I'm looking forward to it. Twice now, he's begged the favour of having one of his men here at Brockmore and twice the outcome has been very far from what he intended. Are you really set upon becoming a patroness of this school those two are talking about?'

'Yes, I am. I think it a marvellous idea. It will be in the Highlands, too, such a romantic place, a perfect setting for a couple so clearly in love,' Alicia said, eyeing the pair indulgently. 'They could be quite alone in the room, for all they are aware of the rest of us. Do you remember that feeling, Marcus?'

'My love, I only have to look into your eyes to feel the very same way. If only it were the same for everyone here,' Marcus said with a sigh, nodding towards the corner where Margot Penrith sat alone. Not for long, though. Viola's mother was on her way over to chat. They had a wedding to plan between them. That would give Margot purpose for the immediate future and, with luck, grandchildren shortly afterwards. Marcus hoped perhaps her soul was on the mend. In time, maybe she'd find someone. He'd keep looking. It was what Robert would have wanted.

Alicia patted his arm. 'We did well, especially

where Vale was concerned.' She leaned in close. 'Tell me, Marcus, did you have that planned all along?'

Marcus chuckled and feigned innocence. 'How could I have? I had Lady Anne Lowell here for him.'

'For him or for Kenelm? I think it might have been a ruse. I know you too well, my dear.'

'I should think so, after all these years. Love is a remarkable thing, is it not, Alicia? Do you recall our last Midsummer Ball, how meticulously we planned the matches?'

Alicia chuckled. 'And though many matches were made, I don't think any of them were the ones we had in mind,' she said, smiling reminiscently. 'Now this party, where we had not a single match in mind, yet love has blossomed between the most seemingly disparate couples. A most remarkable and unpredictable thing indeed, my dear.'

'It is fifty years this spring we have been married. Can you believe it?'

Alicia sighed, shaking her head. 'It feels like fifty days, my darling. Where has the time gone?'

Marcus smiled. Life had been mostly…extraordinarily…good. Vale danced by with Viola. There would be youth at Brockmore again, soon. It would be a blessing to see it. Life was good.

He'd been luckier than most and he wanted to share that luck with others especially when it came to love.

'Does it matter, Alicia? As long as there's tomorrow and you're there to share it, that's all that matters to me.'

* * * * *

A REGENCY CHRISTMAS CAROL

CHRISTINE MERRILL

With thanks and apologies to Charles Dickens.
And a question. Why did the spirits do it 'all in one night' when Marley is so specific about needing three? That's always confused me.

CHAPTER ONE

December 1811

BARBARA Lampett ran down the lane at the edge of the village of Fiddleton, feeling the crunch of icy mud beneath her feet and the stitch in her side from the cold air in her lungs. Lately it seemed that she was always running after something or other. She wondered if the lack of decorum on her part was the first sign of a life spun out of control.

It was really no fault of her own. Had she the choice, she'd have been in a seat by the parlour fire, staring out at the changing weather and pitying those forced to go about in it. But Father paid little heed to his own discomfort when he was in one of his moods, much less that of others.

And she could hardly expect her mother to go. Mother's volatile nature would add warmth to the day, but it would do nothing to cool her father's zeal. Nor was Mother young and strong enough to face the crowd that surrounded him when he spoke, or to extricate him from the hubbub he created.

The new mill lay almost two miles from the centre of the village. It was too short a distance to harness a carriage, but longer than a pleasant walk—especially on such a chill December day as this. Barbara found some consolation that the ground was frozen. She had decided to forgo pattens in favour of speed, but she did not wish to ruin the soft boots she wore by walking through mud.

And much mud there would have been if not for the cold. Ground that had once been green and lush was now worn down to the soil, with the comings and goings of wagons and goods, and the tramp of growing mobs that came to protest at the gates of the new buildings of Mr Joseph Stratford.

A crowd gathered here now. Another of the demonstrations that had been occurring almost daily thanks to her father's speeches. Mixed amongst the angry weavers were the curious townsfolk. They did not seem to care either way for the plight of the workers, but they enjoyed a good row and came to the gatherings as a form of entertainment.

There was a sudden blast of wind and she wrapped her shawl more tightly about her, unable to fight the feeling of dread that came with the exhilaration. While it pleased her to see the people attracted to her father's words, the path he was leading them down was a dangerous one and his actions dangerously unwise. With each passing day he seemed to grow more reckless, speaking from the heart and not the head. He could not seem to understand what his comments would do to the local populous.

But she could feel them, caught in the crowd as she was, buffeted by the bodies of angry and fearful men. There was a growing energy in the mob. Some day a chance word or a particularly virulent speech would push them too far. Then they would boil over into real violence.

When the wind blew from the east you could still smell the burned-out wreckage of the old mill, where so many of these men had been employed. That owner had paid dearly for his plans at renovation, seeing his livelihood destroyed and his family threatened until he had given up and quit the area. That had left the protestors with no work at all, and even angrier than they had been before.

It seemed the new master would be cagier. When he'd built his new mill, like the pig in the old story, he had used bricks. It loomed before her, a blight on the horizon. Every element was an insult to the community and proof that the person who had built it lacked sensitivity for his neighbours. It was large and squat and altogether too new. He had not built in the wreckage of Mackay's Mill, which might have given the people hope of a return to normality. Instead he'd placed it closer to the grand old house where he currently lived. It was not exactly in the front park of the manor, but plainly on the estate, and in a place by the river that the Clairemonts had allowed all in the village to use as common greensward when they'd lived there. It was obvious that Mr Stratford had thought of nothing but his own convenience in choosing this site.

Though he showed no signs of recognising the impropriety of the location, he'd built a fence around a place that had once been the home of picnics and fêtes, trampling the freshness to hard-packed mud. Barbara was convinced it demonstrated on some deep and silent level that the master of it knew he was in the wrong and expected to receive trouble for it. The wrought-iron border surrounding the yard separated it from the people most likely to be angry: the ones whose jobs had been taken by the new mechanised looms.

She pushed her way through the crowd to the place where her father stood at the foot of the stone gatepost, rallying the men to action. Though recent misfortune had addled his wits, it had done nothing to dull the fire in his eye or the clarity in his voice. While his sentiments might be unwise, there was nothing incoherent in the nature of his words.

'The Orders in Council have already depressed your trade to the point where there is no living to be made by an honest man—no way to sell your cloth to America and other friends of France.'

'Aye!'

There were shouts and mutters, and the brandishing of torches and axe handles in the crowd. Barbara's heart gave an uneasy skip at the thought of what might happen should any man think to bring a firearm into the already volatile situation. She was sure that the mill owner towards whom the ire was directed sat in the closed black carriage just behind the gates. From there he could listen to every word. Perhaps he was even noting the name of the speaker and any others preparing to act against him.

But her father cared nothing for it, and went on with his speech. 'The new looms mean less work for those of you left and more jobs falling to inexperienced girls, while their fathers and brothers sit idle, dreaming of days past when a respectable trade could be plied in this country.'

The mutterings in answer were louder now, and punctuated with shouts and a forward surge of bodies, making the gates rattle in response to the weight of the crowd.

'Will you allow the change that will take the bread from your children's mouths? Or will you stand?'

She waved her arms furiously at her father, trying to stall what was likely to occur. The government had been willing to use troops to put down such small rebellions, treating their own people as they would Boney's army. If her father incited the men to frame-breaking and violence they would be answered with violence in return. Mr Stratford might be as bad as her father claimed, but he was not the timid man Mackay had been. He would meet strife with strife, and send for a battalion to shoot the organisers.

'Father!' she shouted, trying to catch his attention. But the workers towered around her, and her voice was swallowed up by the din. Before she could speak a calming word the first shot rang out—not from the crowd, but from the door of the carriage in front of them. Even though it was fired into the air, the mob drew back a pace like a great animal, startled and cringing. Barbara was carried along with it, relieved all were safe and yet further from her goal.

The carriage door opened and Stratford appeared, leaping to the ground before his worried footman could help him and springing to the same stone post where her father stood. He climbed easily up the back of it until he stood at the top and towered over her father and the other men. He held what looked like a duelling pistol in his right hand. With his left he drew back his coat, so the crowd could see its mate was tucked into his belt. He looked like a corsair—nimble, fearless and ready for battle. Barbara could easily imagine him with a blade between his teeth, rushing the crowd.

She was just as sure that he would be the sort to take no prisoners. Though he was a handsome man, in a dark and hungry sort of way, there was nothing in his sharp features that bespoke a merciful nature. His grey eyes were hard and observant. His mouth, which might be capable of a sensual smile, was twisted in a sneer.

Her father thought him the very devil, set upon the ruin of all around them.

But if devil he was then he was a handsome devil as well. Although she could think of a hundred reasons she should not notice it, she thought him a most attractive man. She schooled herself not to stare up with admiration, as she had caught herself doing on those few times she'd seen him in the village.

Perhaps she should have found him less impressive, for that sneer on his face quite spoiled the evenness of his features. While she had thought the position he took on the wall made him look taller than average, he hardly needed the advantage. He stood well over six feet. Today he was a fearsome thing, and nothing for a young lady to gawk at.

To match his physical presence he had the sort of forceful personality that seemed to incite strong emotion in friends as well as enemies. And, frightening though he might be, Barbara was sure that once she was focused on him she would not be able to look away.

'Who will be the first through the fence, then?' Stratford shouted down at the crowd. 'I swear to you, that man will lose his life along with his livelihood.'

The workers shrank back another pace, huddling against each other as though seeking warmth in the cold.

The man on the post laughed down at them. 'I thought as much. All bluff and bluster when there is no risk to you, and cowardice when there is.'

Her father turned, shouting up at him. 'It is you who are the coward, sir. Vain and proud as well. You hide behind your gates with your idle threats, unwilling to walk among the common man and feel his pain, his hunger, his desperation.'

Stratford glared back at him. 'I do not have to walk among you to know about you. I can go to the ruins of Mackay's place—a mill that you destroyed—to see the reason for your poverty. If you could, you would burn my factory as well—before I've even managed to open it. And then you'd complain that I'd treated you unjustly. I tell you now, since you have so conveniently gathered here, that I will not listen to your complaints until you begin making sense.'

It was unfair of him to compare this gathering to the burning of Mackay's place. Most of the men here had taken no part in that, rushing to save their workplace and not destroy it. The matter was much more complicated than Stratford made out. He was too new here to know and unwilling to listen, just as her father had said. Barbara pushed against the men around her, trying to work her way to the front again so that she might be heard.

Just as she thought she might reach her objective a man's boot caught in the hem of her gown and she started to fall forwards under the crush. She felt a rush of panic as she realised that no one around her was noticing as she fell. They had forgotten their fear of the second gun and were advancing to disprove Stratford's claims of cowardice.

She called out again, hoping that her father might hear and help her. But his back was to her as he shook a fist to threaten Stratford. He was too preoccupied to notice what was happening. In a moment she would be knocked to her knees. Then she would be dragged under, as though sinking beneath a human wave, and stamped into the mud in the trample of hobnailed boots.

'Ay-up!' She felt a sudden change, and the crowd parted around her. A hand caught her by the shoulder and yanked her to her feet with a rip of cloth. There was a shout as loud and ringing as her father's. But it came from close at her side, easily besting the noise of the crowd. 'Mind what you are doing, you great oafs. You may say what you like to me, but mind that there is a lady present. Have a care for her, at least. Perhaps I judge you unworthy of employment because you behave no better than animals.'

Then she was back on her feet, and the support was gone from her arm. She felt the crowd swirl around her again as her rescuer retreated. But for a moment there was a subdued quality to the actions of the mob, as though their frenzy had been defused by shame.

And the man who had saved her was back at the front of the group again, pushing past her father and climbing back onto the pillar that held the gate. She had thought Mr Stratford an intimidating figure even while behind the gates. But it was even more startling to have been so close to him, even for a moment. He had used his strength to force others out of the way, and his agility to be down to the ground and back up the fence before the mob had realised that he had been in their grasp. He was staring down at them again, his expression more disgusted than angry, as though they had proved to him that he was correct in his scorn.

'Go home to your families, if you care so much about them. A new year is coming, and a new age with it. You had best get used to it. When Stratford Mill is open in a month there will be work for those of you willing to put aside this nonsense and tend to your shuttles again. But if you rise against me I will see the lot of you transported and run it with your daughters. They will cost me less and have the sense to keep their tongues.' He reached towards his belt, and the group before him gasped. He withdrew not a pistol, but a purse, showering the coins into the crowd.

'A Merry Christmas to you all!' he shouted, his laugh both triumphant and bitter as he watched the threat dissolve as the crowd scrambled for the money. 'Do not bother to come here again. As long as I breathe, I will not be stopped. If you destroy the machinery I will get more, until you wear yourselves out with breaking it. Take my money and go back to your homes. I have summoned the constable. If you are here when he arrives you will spend Christmas Day in a cell, longing for your families. Now, be off.'

It shamed her to watch the men of the village too

busy on the ground to notice this new threat. They were a proud bunch. In better times they would have thrown the coins back in the face of this stranger rather than accept his charity and his scorn. But the recent economic troubles had left most of the village without work and in need of any money they might find to make any kind of a Christmas—merry or otherwise—for their families.

Her father's rallying cries were lost in the scuffle as men scrabbled in the dirt for pennies. Barbara pushed through them easily this time, until she could lay her hand upon her father's arm. 'Come away,' she whispered. 'Now. Before this goes any further. You can speak another day.'

It seemed the mood had left him, passing out of his body like a possessing spirit, leaving him quiet and somewhat puzzled, as though he did not quite know how he had come to be standing here in front of so many people. He would come away with little struggle, and she would have him home before the law arrived. All would be well. Until the next time.

Directly above her, and removed from the chaos, Joseph Stratford observed—distant and passionless, as though he did not know or care for the pain he was causing. When she looked at him all her father's anger and frustration seemed to rush into her. If the Lord had bothered to imbue her with reason, then why could he have not made her a man, so that other men might listen to her?

She turned and shouted up at the dark man who thought himself so superior to his fellows. 'You blame the men around me. But you should be ashamed of yourself as well. You stand over us, thinking yourself a god. You are mocking a level of hardship that you cannot possibly understand. You act as if you are made of the same rough wood and cold metal gears that fill your factory. If I could see the contents of your heart it would be nothing but clockwork, and fuelled by the coal running in your veins.'

Just for a moment she thought she saw a change in his face, a slight widening of the eyes as though her words had struck home. And then he gave a mirthless, soundless laugh, little more than a lifting and dropping of the shoulders. 'And a Merry Christmas to you as well, my dear.' Then he turned and stepped easily from his perch, dropping to the ground, though it must have been nearly eight feet, and strolling back to his carriage and his nervous grooms and coachman. They came cautiously forwards to open the gates so that the carriage could get through. They needn't have worried, for the men who had blocked the way had turned for home in embarrassed silence as soon as the money on the ground had been collected.

She pulled her father to the side of the road so that the horses could pass. But there was the signalling tap of a cane against the side of the box as the vehicle drew abreast of them, and the driver brought it to a stop so that Stratford could lean out of the window and look at them.

'This is not the end of it, Stratford,' her father said in a quieter voice. Now that the crowd was gone he sounded capable of lucid argument, and quite his old self.

'I did not think it was, Lampett,' Stratford replied, smiling coldly down at her father, staring into his eyes like a fighter measuring the reach of his opponent before striking.

'I will not let you treat these people—my people—like so many strings on your loom. They are men, not goods. They should be respected as such.'

'When they behave like men I will give them respect. And not before. Now, go. You have lost your audience, and your child is shivering in the cold.'

I am not a child. She was full four and twenty. Not that it mattered. But she *was* shivering—both from fear and the weather. The slight made her stand a little straighter, and fight the shudders until she could appear as collected and unmoved as her enemy was.

It did not seem to bother Joseph Stratford in the least that the weight of the entire town was against him. They had broken his frames once already and sabotaged the building of the mill at every turn. Still he persevered. Barbara wished she could respond in kind with that careless, untouchable indifference.

The envy bothered her. Perhaps—just a little—she appreciated the man's sense of purpose. However misguided it might be. When she looked at him she had no doubt that he would succeed. While her father was all fire, he flared and burned out quickly. But Stratford was like stone, unchanging and unmoved. It would take more than a flash of anger to move a man like him once he had set himself to a goal.

She looked again at him and reminded herself that he was proud as well. That sin would be his downfall if nothing else was. He could not succeed if he reduced all men to enemies and herself to a faceless, valueless child.

As she watched the two men, locked eye to eye in a silent battle, she was relieved that her father did not own a firearm. Though she thought she could trust Mr Stratford—just barely—not to shoot without provocation, there was no telling what her father might do when his blood was up and his thinking even less clear than usual. She reached out for her father's arm again, ready to guide him home. 'Come. Let us go back. There is nothing more that you can do today. If he has truly called for the constable, I do not wish to see you caught up in it.'

He shook off the embrace with a grunt and stepped back, giving an angry shrug as the carriage moved again, travelling up the road to the manor house. 'It would serve him right if I was arrested. Then the world would see him for the sort of man he is: one who would throw an old man into jail to prove himself in the right.'

There was no point in explaining that the only lesson

anyone was likely to see was that Stratford sat in a mansion at a fine dinner, while Lampett sat hungry in a cell. 'But it would make me most unhappy, Father,' she said as sweetly as possible. 'And Mother as well. If we can have nothing else for Christmas, can we not have a few days of peace?'

'I will be peaceful when there is reason to be,' her father acceded. 'I doubt, as long as that man breathes, we will see that state again.'

CHAPTER TWO

JOSEPH Stratford rode home alone in comfortable, if somewhat pensive, silence. The conclusion to today's outing had been satisfactory, at least for now. The crowd had dispersed without any real violence. But if Bernard Lampett continued stirring, the town was likely to rise against him. Before that happened sterner measures would need to be taken.

In his mind, he composed the letter he would send to the commander of the troops garrisoned in York. It was drastic, but necessary. If one or two of them were hauled off in chains it might convince the rest of the error of their ways.

His carriage pulled up the circular drive of Clairemont Manor and deposited him at the door—so close that the chill of the season barely touched him on his way into the house. He smiled. How different this was from his past. Until last year he'd frequently had to make do on foot. But in the twelve months his investments had turned. Even with the money he'd laid out for the new mill he was living in a luxury that he would not have dreamed possible in his wildest Christmas wishes.

Joseph handed hat, gloves and overcoat to the nearest footman and strode into the parlour to take the cup of tea waiting for him by the second-best chair near the fire. As he passed the closest seat he gave a gentle kick at the boot of the man occupying it, to get Robert Breton to shift his feet out of the way.

Breton opened a sleepy eye and sat up. 'Trouble at the mill?'

'When is there not?' He lifted his cup in a mock salute and Breton accepted it graciously, as though *he* owned the house and the right to the chair he usurped. While Joe might aspire to knock away at his own rough edges, affect the indolent slouch and copy the London accent and the facile gestures, he would never be more than false coin compared to this second son of an earl. Bob had been born to play lord of the manor, just as Joe had been born to work. He might own the house, but it was Bob's birthright to be at ease there.

And that was what made him so damned useful—both as a friend and an investor. The Honourable Robert Breton opened doors that the name Joseph Stratford never would, and his presence in negotiations removed some of the stink of trade when Joseph was trying to prise capital from the hands of his rich and idle friends.

Joseph took another sip of his tea. 'Lampett has been

giving mad speeches again—raising the population to violence. Lord knows why Mackay did not run him off before now, instead of allowing himself to be scared away. He might have nipped the insurrection in the bud, and his business would still be standing.'

Breton shrugged. 'Anne tells me that Lampett was not always thus. There was some accident when the men fought the mill fire. He has not been right in the head since.'

'More's the pity for him and his family,' Joe replied. 'If he does not leave off harassing me he will be the maddest man in Australia by spring.'

'Anne seems quite fond of him,' Breton said. 'Until they closed the school he was a teacher in the village and a respected member of the community.'

Joseph reminded himself to speak to Anne on the subject himself, if only so that he might say he had. It did not seem right that one's best friend got on better with one's prospective fiancée than one did oneself. But Bob and Anne enjoyed each other's company—perhaps because Bob was able to converse comfortably on subjects other than the price of yard goods and the man hours needed to produce them.

'If Anne respects him, then she has not seen him lately. From what I have observed he is not fit company for a lady. There was a girl at the riot today who must have been his daughter, trying to drag him home and out of trouble. She came near to being trampled by the crowd and Lampett did not notice the danger to her. I rescued her myself, and did not get so much as a thank-you from either of them.'

'Was this before or after you threatened to have the father arrested?' Breton asked dryly.

'In between threats, I think.' Stratford grinned.

Breton shook his head. 'And you wonder why you are not loved.'

'They will all love me well enough once the mill is open and they are back to work.'

'If there is work to be had,' Breton said. 'The Orders in Council limit the places you can sell your wares. As long as America is a friend of France, there is little you can do.'

'They will be repealed,' Joseph said firmly.

'And what if they are not?'

'They will be. They must be. The merchants are near at breaking point now. The law must change or we are all ruined.' Joseph smiled with reassurance, trying to imbue confidence in his faint-hearted friend. 'It will not do to hesitate. We cannot err on the side of caution in this darkest time. If we wish for great profit we must be more sure, more daring, more active than the others. A busy mill and a full warehouse are the way to greatest success. When the moment comes it will come on us suddenly. Like the handmaidens at the wedding, we must be ready for change.'

Breton shook his head in wonder. 'When you tell me this I have no trouble believing.'

'Then take the message to heart and share it with

your friends.' Joseph glanced out of the window at weather that was slate grey and yet lacking the snow he wished for. 'When we have them here for Christmas I will wrap them tight in a web of good wine and good cheer. Then you shall explain the situation, as I have to you. Once they are persuaded, I will stick my hand into their pockets and remove the money needed for expansion.'

Breton laughed. 'You make me feel like a spider, waiting for so many fat flies to ride up from London.'

'But that is not the case at all, my dear fellow. I am the spider. You are the bait—if spiders use such a thing. Without you, they will not come.'

'We will be lucky if they come at all. Here in Yorkshire you are quite far out of the common way, Stratford.'

'And you are the son of the Earl of Lepford. There must be a few in London, particularly those with eligible daughters, who would be eager to spend a holiday in your august presence.'

'Second son,' Breton corrected. 'No title to offer them. But I am rich, at least. In much part I can thank you for that.'

'Be sure to inform your guests of the fact, should the opportunity present itself.'

Breton made a face. 'Talking of money at a Christmas house party is just not done. They will not like it if they get wind of your scheme, Joe.'

'That is why you will do it subtly—as you always do,

Bob. They will hardly know what has happened. You may apologise to them for my lack of manners and let them plunder my cellars to the last bottle. Talk behind your hand about me, if you wish. Dance the pretty girls around the parlour while I am left to their fathers. They will think me common at the start. But by the time I leave I will have their cheques in my pocket. To one in business, Christmas must be a day like any other. If your friends wish to invest in this new venture they will see a substantial return to make their next Christmas a jolly one.'

The door opened, and the housekeeper, Mrs Davy, entered, with an apology for the interruption and a footman carrying a large armful of greenery. As he began swagging bows from the mantel, Joseph stood and quizzed the woman, ticking things off the list in his head as he was satisfied that they had been taken care of.

'Everything must be in perfect order,' he said firmly. 'While nearly every mill owner in the district has had some problems with frame-breakers and followers of Ludd, it would reflect poorly on me if my guests see a lack of control over my own household. I cannot fault the cleaning you have done, for I would swear you've scrubbed the house with diamonds it sparkles so.'

The housekeeper bobbed her head in thanks, and showed a bit of a blush. But his praise was no less than the truth. Everywhere he went he could smell the beeswax that had been worked into the oak panelling 'til it reflected the light from multitudes of candles and fires with a soft golden glow.

'And the larder has been stocked as well, I trust?'

'It was difficult,' Mrs Davy said modestly. 'There was little to be had in the shops.'

'You sent to London, as I requested?'

She nodded.

'There is no shortage of food in the city, nor shortage of people with money to buy it. My friends from the South will not understand the problems here, and nor do they wish to be enlightened of them. If they come all this way to visit me, I mean to see that their bellies are filled and their hearts light.' He grinned in anticipation. 'And their purses emptier at the end of the trip.'

The housekeeper's smile was firm, if somewhat disapproving. 'They shall eat like lords.' She passed him the menus she had prepared. 'If you will but select the meals, Mr Stratford.'

Given the bounty she presented, it was impossible to make a choice. He frowned. 'There must be goose, of course, for those who favour it. But I would prefer roast beef—and lots of it. With pudding to sop up the gravy. Swedes, peas, sprouts.' He pointed from one paper to the other. 'Roasted potatoes. Chestnuts to roast beside the Yule Log. And plum pudding, Christmas cake, cheese…'

'But which, sir?' the housekeeper asked.

'All of them, I should think. Enough so that no one

will want, no matter what their preference. It is better to have too much than too little, is it not?'

'If we have too much, sir, it will go to waste.' From the way she pursed her lips he could tell that he was offending her to the bottom of her frugal Northern heart.

'If it does, I can afford the loss. A show of economy in front of these investors will be seen as a lack of confidence. And that is something I will not be thought guilty of.' He paced past her, down the great hall, watching the servants tidying, examining ceilings and frames with a critical eye and nodding with approval when he found not a speck of dust. 'All is in order. And, as just demonstrated, you have seen to the greenery.'

'There are still several rooms to be decorated,' she admitted. 'But some must be saved for the kissing boughs.'

'Tear down some of the ivy on the south wall. There is still some green left in it, and the windows are choked to point that I can barely see without lighting candles at noon. With that, you should be able to deck the whole of the inside of the house. Clip the holly hedge as well. Trim it back and bring it in.' He gave a vague sweep of his hand. 'Have them search the woods for mistletoe. I want it all. Every last bit of the house smelling of fir and fresh air. Guests will begin to arrive tomorrow, and we must be all in readiness for them.'

'Yes, sir.'

From behind him, Breton laughed. 'You are quite the

taskmaster, Stratford. Lord help the workers in your mill if this is the way you behave towards them.'

'I mean to master you as well, Bob. I will expect you to get up from your chair to help lead the games.'

Breton looked stricken at the prospect. 'Me, Stratford?'

'Of course. They are your friends. You will know what it takes to entertain them.'

'I don't think it is my place.' The man was almost physically backing away from the task. 'You are the host, after all.'

'I am that in name only,' Joseph insisted. 'I can manage to pay the piper, of course. But in God's name, man, do not expect me to dance to the tune. There has been little time for that in my life, and I never got the knack of it. I fear I am much better with machines than with people.'

'But I…' Breton shook his head. 'I am not the best person to stand at the head of the set for you.'

'At best, all they want from me is a hearty meal and a full punchbowl. At worst, they are coming to gawk at what a common mess I am likely to make of a grand old house. They would do without me if they could. For I am—' he made a pious face '*—in trade*. Too humble by half for the people who have invested in me. But the money draws them like flies. Everyone wants their little bit of sugar, Bob. We will provide it for them. Though they sneer into their cups as they drink my wine, they will not be too proud to swallow it.'

'But must I be a part of it? If they do not want you, then surely…?'

'You are one of them,' Joe said firmly. 'I will never be. I am lucky to have won over Clairemont, and will have his daughter to dance with, of course. If she means to accept my suit then she had best get used to being seen with me. The rest of the ladies I leave to you.'

'And what am I to do with them?' For all his town bronze, Bob could be obtuse when he wished to be.

'Smile at them. Flatter them. Keep their glasses filled. You could do worse than following my example and taking a wife, you know. Oaksley has three daughters, from what I understand. Perhaps one of them will do for you.'

There was also the daughter of that firebrand in the village. She had not been invited to the festivities. It would show a considerable lack of wisdom to have that man and his family here, to undermine his success. But she would be a fine match for Bob. She was both pretty and intelligent, and a gentleman's daughter as well. She was more respectable than he himself would have aspired to be just a few short years ago. Miss Lampett would be perfect for his friend in every way. Although now that the opportunity presented itself to suggest a meeting, Joseph found himself strangely unwilling to voice his thoughts.

'I have no intention of marrying,' Bob said firmly. 'Not now. Not ever.'

'Then take advantage of some more earthly pleasures,'

Joseph said, oddly relieved. 'There will be enough of that as well, I am sure. I've heard that Lindhurst's wife rarely finds her own room after a night of revels. I hope I do not have to explain the rest for you. Avail yourself of my hospitality as well. Eat, drink and be merry.'

For tomorrow we die.

Joseph shuddered. He was sure he had not finished the quote. But he'd heard the words so clearly in his head that he'd have sworn they'd been intoned aloud, and in a voice that was not his.

'Stratford?' Bob was staring at him as though worried.

'Nothing. A funny turn, that's all.' He smiled in reassurance for, though he liked the idea of socialising with strangers no better than Bob, he could not let his nerve fail him. 'As I was saying. I expect you here and making merry for the whole of the week. I mean to keep my nose to the grindstone, of course. But we have made a success of this venture, and you should be allowed to take some pleasure in it. There is more to come in the New Year. Now is the time to play.'

CHAPTER THREE

THAT evening, as ever, Joseph's trip to his own bedroom was a little disquieting. Much as he knew that he owned the house, he did not really feel it suited him. It was beautiful, of course. But at night, when the servants had settled in their quarters and it was mostly him alone, he walked the wide corridors to reassure himself that it existed outside of his boyhood fantasies of success.

The place was too large, too strange and too old. It would not do to let anyone—not even Breton—know how ill at ease he was, or that this late-night walk was a continual reminder of how far from his birth and true station he had come.

It was not as if a pile of stones could come to life and cast him out. It was his, from cellar to attic. He had paid for it and had got a good price. But when it was dark and quiet, like this, Clairemont Manor felt—for want of a better word—haunted. Not that he believed in such things. In an age of machines there was hardly room for spirits. Clinging to childish notions and common superstition bespoke a lack of confidence that he would not allow himself.

With a wife and children in it, the house would fill with life and he would have no time for foolish fancies. But since the wife he was in the process of acquiring rightly belonged here, it sometimes felt as though he was trying to appease them rather than banish them. Setting Anne Clairemont at the foot of the table would restore the balance that had been lost. It had been her father's house, whether he'd been able to afford to keep it or not. Returning a member of the family to the estate, even if it *was* a female, might pacify some of the ill feelings he had created in the area. It fell in nicely with his plans for the business. There was nothing superstitious about it.

It was a pity the girl was so pale and lifeless. Had he the freedom to choose a woman to suit himself, it would certainly not be her. He'd have sought someone with a bit more spirit, not some brainless thing willing to auction herself to the highest bidder just to please her father.

He'd have wanted—

He stopped in his tracks, smiling to himself at the memory. He'd have wanted one more like the girl he'd seen in the crowd today. Fearless, that one was. Just like her father, that barmy Bernard Lampett who led the rebellion against him. What was the girl's name? Barbara, he thought, making a note to enquire and be sure. She did not seem totally in sympathy with her father, from the way she'd tried to drag him away. But neither did she support Joseph, having made it quite clear that she disapproved of him. Barbara Lampett knew her own mind, that was certain. And she had no fear of showing the world what she thought of it.

But it wasn't her sharp tongue that fascinated him. She was shorter than Anne, curved where Anne was straight, and pink where his prospective fiancée was pale. When he'd been close to her, he'd seen a few freckles on her turned-up nose, and handfuls of brown curls trying to escape from her plain bonnet.

But it was her eyes that had drawn him in. Her gaze had been cool and direct, like blue ice, cutting into him in a way that simple anger could not. She judged him. It made him doubt himself. For could any cause be wholly in the right if it might result in harm to such a lovely thing as a Barbara Lampett, tramping her casually into the dirt? While he was sure he bore a greater share of the right than the men who stood against him, the truth of what might have happened to her, had he not intervened, weighed heavy on his conscience.

And so tonight he walked the halls more slowly than usual, thinking dark thoughts and counting the many rooms as though they were rosary beads. If the servants had noticed this ritual, they were too polite or well trained to comment. But he found himself taking the same path each night before retiring, as though he were touring someone else's great house and marvelling at their wealth. Reception room the first, library, breakfast room, dining room, private salon, stairs, reception room the second, card room, music room, ballroom. And then a climb to the second floor: red bedroom, blue bedroom, master bedroom… There was a third floor as well, and servants' rooms, larders, kitchens and possibly some small and useful places he had not bothered to investigate.

It was a sharp contrast to his childhood. When it had been but one room they'd lived in there had been no reason to count. As his father's business had grown, so had the rooms. A three-room flat. A five-room cottage. A house. They had risen from poverty in the days long before the war, when trade was unobstructed and money easier. But the successes had been small, and the work hard and unpleasant. He had hated it.

He had broken from it, rebuilt the work in his own image. And now he lived in the grandest house in the county—and was not happy here either. Perhaps that was his curse: to hurry through life reaching for the next great thing, whether it be invention or business. Each time he succeeded he would be sure that this time he had gained enough to please himself. Then the success would pale and he would seek more.

The thought left him chilled, and he felt the unease that seemed to stalk him through these halls. He remembered again the eyes of Barbara Lampett, who could see through him to his clockwork heart. It made him want to grab her and prove that his blood flowed just as hot as other men's, and perhaps a little warmer for the sight of her. If the girl were the daughter of any other man in the village he'd have at least attempted a flirtation. But she was too young and too much of a lady to understand the discreet dalliance he had in mind. Even if she was of a more liberal nature it would not do to have her thinking that sharing her charms might lead him to show mercy on her father.

While he might consider offering a bijou, or some other bit of shiny to a pretty girl, something about Barbara Lampett's freckled nose and the sweet stubbornness of her jaw convinced him that she was likely to bargain for the one thing that he was not willing to share: clemency for the man who plotted his undoing.

He shook his head, rejecting the notion of her as the long-case clock in the hall struck twelve and he opened the door to his room. To be sure he would not weaken, it was best to leave all thoughts of her here in the corridor, far away from his cold and empty bed.

'Boy.'

Joseph started at the sound of a voice where there should have been nothing but the crackle of the fire and perhaps the sounds of his valet laying out a nightshirt. The opulence of the room, the richness of its hangings and upholstery, always seemed to mute even the most raucous sound.

But the current voice cut through the tranquillity and grated on the nerves. The familiar Yorkshire accent managed to both soothe and annoy. The volume of it was so loud that it echoed in the space and pressed against him—like a hand on his shoulder that could at any moment change from a caress to a shove.

He looked for the only possible if extremely unlikely source, and found it at the end of the bed. For there stood a man he'd thought of frequently but had not seen for seven years. Not since the man's death.

'Hello, Father.' It was foolish to speak to a figment of his imagination, but the figure in the corner of his bedroom seemed so real that it felt rude not to address it.

It must be his distracted mind playing this trick. Death had not changed his da in the least. Joseph had assumed that going on to his divine reward would have softened him in some way. But it appeared that the afterlife was as difficult as life had been. Jacob Stratford was just as grim and sullen as he'd been when he walked the earth.

'What brings you back? As if I have to ask myself… It was that second glass of brandy, on top of the hubbub at the mill.' When he'd rescued the Lampett girl he'd been literally rubbing shoulders with the same sort of man as the one who had raised him. The brutal commonality of them had attached itself to his person like dust, sticking in his mind and appearing now, as he neared sleep.

'That's what you think, is it?' The ghost gave a disapproving grunt. 'I see you have not changed a bit from the time you were a boy.' Then he ladled his speech thick with the burr that Joseph had heard when he was in the midst of the crowd around his mill. 'Th'art daft as a brush, though th' live like a lord.'

'And I will say worse of you,' Joseph replied, careful to let none of his old accent creep back into his speech. No matter what his father might say of him, he had changed for the better and he would not go back. 'You are a stubborn, ignorant dictator. Two drinks is hardly a sign of debauchery. And I live in a great house because I can afford to. It is not as if I am become some noble who has a line of unpaid credit with the vintner. I pay cash.' He'd been told by Bob that the habit was horribly unfashionable, and a sign of his base birth, but he could not seem to break himself of it. It felt good to lie down knowing that, though he might need investors for the business, he had no personal debts.

Although why his rest was now uneasy he could not tell. The bad dream staring him down from the end of the bed must be a sign that all was not right in his world.

His father snorted in disgust. 'No matter what I tried to teach, you've proved that buying and selling is all you learned. You know nothing of art, of craft or the men behind the work.'

'If the men behind the work are anything like you, then I think I've had enough of a lesson, thank you. You may go as well.' He made an effort to wake and cast off the dream. To be having this conversation at all was proof that he was sleeping. To rouse from slumber would divest the vision of the last of its power.

His father gave a tug on his spectral forelock. 'Well, then, Your Lordship, I am put in my place. I hope by now you know that you don't fit with the posh sort that you suck up to. You are as much of a dog to be kicked from their path as I am to you.'

'Probably true,' Joseph admitted. There was no point in lying about that, even to himself. Though the gentry might be forced to mix with those in trade, there was nothing to make them enjoy it. 'But if I am a dog, then I am a young pup with many years ahead of me. Their time is ending, just as yours did. In the day that is coming men of vision will be rewarded.'

'At the expense of others,' his father replied.

'Others can seize this opportunity and profit as well, if they wish to,' Joe snapped back. 'It is not my responsibility to see to the welfare of every man on the planet. They had best look out for themselves.'

'That is no better than I expected from you,' his father replied. 'And not good enough. Believe me, boy, I can see from this side of the veil that it is not nearly enough. It is no pleasant thing to die with regrets, to have unfinished business when your life is spent and to know that you have failed in the one thing you should have profited at: the care of another human life.'

The statement made the speaker uncomfortably real. It was most unlike anything in Joseph's own mind. It sounded almost like an apology. And never would he have put those words in his father's mouth—no matter how much he might have wished to hear them. If things went as planned Joseph would be a father soon enough. It would not take much effort on his part to do a better job of it than his father had done with him.

'You would know better than I on that, I am sure. As of this time, I have no one under my care. I answer only to myself, and I am happy with that.' Surreptitiously he made a fist and dug his nails into his palm, pinching the skin to let the pain start him awake.

'Boy, you are wrong.'

'So you always told me, Father. Although why I should dream of your voice now, I do not know. I have only to wake up and look around me to prove that I am doing quite well for myself.' Although, thinking on it, he could not seem to recall having fallen asleep in the first place. But it was the only explanation for this. He was not in the habit of conversing with ghosts.

He was sound asleep in this bed and having a dream. No. He was having a nightmare. If he could not manage to wake, he must try to go to a deep, untroubled rest where his father would not follow. To encourage the change he sat upon the edge of the bed and began to undress himself. While it seemed strange to do so during a dream, he could think of no other way to set things right.

As he leaned forwards to pull off his boots his father stepped closer and brought with him the smell of the grave—damp earth, a faint whiff of decomposition and the chill of a cold and lifeless thing made even colder by the season. 'Do not think to ignore me. You do so at your peril.'

'Do I, now?' Joseph could not help it and stole a glance up at the spirit—if that was what it was. And he wondered when he had ever had a dream this real. He could smell and feel, as well as hear and see. He had to struggle to keep himself from reaching out to touch the shroud that the man in front of him carried like a mantle draped over his bony arm. He stared at the ghost, willing it to disappear. 'I ignored you in life as best I could. Because of it I gave you enough money to die in comfort, instead of bent over a loom. But that was years ago. Go back to where you have been and leave me in peace.'

'You do not have peace, if you would be honest and see the truth. Just as it always was when you were a boy, you are careless. You have not attended to both the warp and the weft. The tension is uneven. You have done much, and done it quickly with your fancy machines. But your work is without shape.'

Joseph glared into the hollow eyes before him, too angry at the slight to stay silent. 'I bore enough of that needless criticism from you when you lived—trying to teach me to weave when it was clear I had no skill for it. The last piece of work you will ever see me make on an old-fashioned loom was the shroud I buried you in. I wove it on your old machine with my own hands. I made it out of wool in respect for custom and your trade. If you have come to me to complain of the quality, then go back to your grave without it. As for my current life—there is no basis for this criticism. I can measure my success by my surroundings. This Christmas I will have a house full to the brim with guests and a table creaking with bounty. I have a new mill. When it opens I will be able to afford to fill the warehouse with goods, ready to ship when the sanctions are lifted.'

The ghost shook his head, as though all the achievement was nothing, and waved the shroud before him. 'Shapeless. Tear it out. Tear it out before it is too late. Your grain is off, boy.'

Joseph finished with his undressing and pulled a nightshirt over his head. Then he lay down on the bed with his arms stiff at his sides, fighting to keep from stuffing his fingers in his ears. He could hear the old man's death rattle of a breath, along with the same repeated criticisms that had tortured him all through his failed apprenticeship.

Then he thought of the girl who had been clinging to Bernard Lampett's arm in front of the mill. Her difficulties with her father had raised these memories in him. He felt a sympathy with her. And, for all his convictions that there could be no mercy shown, he would not rest easy until he had found a peaceful solution.

He looked at the shade of his father again, half hoping that it had evaporated now that he'd found the probable cause. But it was still there, as stern and disapproving as ever he had been. 'If you are my own guilty conscience, the least you could have done,' Joseph said, 'was come to me in the form of Barbara Lampett. And I'd be much more likely to listen if you told me plainly what you wanted.'

The ghost looked at him as though he was both stupid and a disappointment. It was a familiar look. 'It will not go well for you if you persist in talking nonsense. I came here hoping to spare you what is soon to come. My time is wasted, for you are as stubborn as you were right up 'til the day I died.'

'You? Spare me?' Joseph laughed. 'When did you ever wish to spare me anything? It was I who saved myself, and none other. I used my own brain and my own hands to make sure that I did not live as you did. And I succeeded at it.'

The ghost looked troubled, but only briefly. 'My goal is not to make you into myself. I was a hard man in life. A good craftsman, but a poor father.'

'Thank you for admitting the fact now that it is years too late,' Joseph snapped, annoyed that his mind would choose his precious free hours to remind him of things he preferred to forget.

'I bear the punishment of my errors even now. But my goal was to make you something more.' The ghost pointed with a pale, long-fingered hand that in life had been nimble with a shuttle. 'Here you are—proof that my job was not done. You are less than you should be. You are certainly less than you must be. That is why you must tear out what you have done. Tear out the work and start again, while you are able. It is not too late to go back. Find the mistake and fix it. Start again, before tomorrow night, or face another visitor.'

'I have no intention of destroying the work of a lifetime to please some niggling voice in my own mind that will be gone in the morning.' He pulled up the coverlet and waved a hand. 'Now, go, sir. Come again as some more interesting dream. You do not frighten me, though I will be glad to see you gone. Bring the girl instead.'

He smiled at the thought. If he could choose a bedtime fantasy, she was better than most. Then he pulled the sheet over his head and rolled away from the figure, trying to ignore the strange green glow that seemed to seep through his closed eyelids. What sort of dream remained even after one ceased to look at it?

One that could still speak, apparently. His father's voice came from just above him, unbothered by his ignoring of it. It was louder now, and Joseph had his first moment's fright, thinking if he pulled the blankets away he might find himself inches away from a corpse—close enough to choke on the smell of rotting flesh and see the waxy vacancy of a dead man's eyes.

'Very well, then. It is as was feared. You will not listen to me. Be warned, boy. If you have a brain, you will heed before Christmas Eve. From here, I can see what is coming, and I would not wish that—even on you.'

'Thank you so much, Father, for such a cold comfort.' Joseph snuggled down into the pillow.

'There will be three before Christmas. Look for the

first when the clock chimes one tomorrow. If you have any sense you will heed them, before it is too late.'

Joseph laughed into the bedclothes. 'You mean to ruin my sleep between here and Christmas, I suppose? And destroy every last pleasure I take in this holiday. Only *you* would be trying to visit me with dire predictions on this of all weeks. Come back after Twelfth Night and perhaps I shall care.'

'Sir?'

Joseph opened his eyes.

The voice was not that of his father but of his valet, who sounded rather worried. 'Were you speaking to me, Mr Stratford? For I did not quite catch…'

When he pulled back the covers the candles were still lit and there was no sign of the eldritch glow he had been trying to shut out, nor the figure that had cast it. 'No, Hobson. It was only a dream. I was talking in my sleep, I think.' It must have been that. He had come back to his room and dozed, spinning a wild fancy without even bothering to blow out the light.

His valet was standing in a litter of clothes, looking around him with disapproval. 'If you were tired, you had but to ring and I would have come immediately to assist you.' Hobson picked the jacquard waistcoat from off the floor, smoothing the wrinkles from it and hanging it in the wardrobe.

'I was not tired,' Joseph insisted. Although he must have been. Why had he been dreaming? Though he could remember each piece of clothing as he'd dropped it on the floor, he could not seem to manage to remember falling asleep at any point—dressed or otherwise.

'Then might I bring you a warm drink before bed? A brandy? A posset? In keeping with the season, Cook has mulled some wine.'

'No, thank you. No spirits before bed, I think.' At least not like the one he'd had already.

There will be three.

He looked to the valet. 'Did you say something just now?'

'I offered wine…' The man was looking at him as though he was drunk.

'Because I thought I heard…' Of course he was sure that he had not heard Hobson speak. It had been his father's voice for certain, come back to repeat his warning. Although, looking around the room, he could see no sign of a spectre. 'Did you hear a voice?'

The valet was looking behind him, about the empty room. Then he looked back at his master, struggling to keep the worry from his face. 'No, sir. Just the two of us conversing.'

Joseph gave a laugh to mask the awkward moment. 'I must be more tired than I thought. Pay me no mind. And no wine tonight, please. A few hours' untroubled rest is all I need.'

But if there were to be another evening such as this one he doubted that serenity would be a quality it possessed.

CHAPTER FOUR

IN THE little corner of the Lampett kitchen set aside as a still room, Barbara inhaled deeply and sighed. After the ruckus of yesterday it was comforting to be home again, immersed in the sights and scents and sounds of Christmas preparation. There were mince pies cooling on a shelf beside the pudding bowl, and the makings for a good bowl of punch set aside against any guests they might have between now and Twelfth Night. Before her she'd arranged what fragrant ingredients she could find—dried rose petals and lavender, cloves, the saved rinds of the year's oranges and handfuls of pine needles to refill pomanders and refresh sachets in recently tidied closets and drawers.

She glanced down at her apron, pleased to see that there were few marks on it to reveal the labours of the day. Everything spoke of order, cleanliness and control. She smiled. All was as it should be, and as she liked it.

Suddenly the back door burst open and her mother rushed into the room, dropping the empty market basket and looking hurriedly around her.

Barbara stood, fearing the worst. 'What has happened?'

'Your father? Is he here with you?'

'No. He was in the parlour, reading his paper. I've heard nothing unusual.' Barbara rushed to the kitchen door, opening it and staring into the empty front room.

'On the way to the village I passed Mrs Betts. She had seen him heading towards the mill. He was carrying the axe.'

Barbara stripped off her apron, pushing past her mother to grab a shawl and bonnet from pegs by the door. 'I will go. You stay here. Do not worry. Whatever he is up to, I will put a stop to it before any real damage is done.'

There could be little question as to what he meant to do if he had taken a tool of destruction. The papers were full of reports from other villages of the frame-breakers—followers of Ned Ludd got out of hand—destroying machinery. And of mill owners dead in their beds or at their factories by violence. While there was much that annoyed her about Mr Stratford, he hardly deserved death.

It might go hard for her family if her father was left unchecked. He could well lose his freedom over this—or his life. She thought of the pistol in Stratford's hand the previous day. His first shot had been fired into the air. If he felt himself sufficiently threatened he might aim lower, and her father would be the one to suffer for it.

She ran down the path from the Lampett cottage, forgoing the road and heading cross-country over the patch of moor that separated the mill from the village. She splashed through the shallow stream, feeling the icy water seeping into her shoes and chilling her feet near to freezing, making her stumble as she came up the bank. The thorns in the thicket tore at her skirts and her hem was muddy, the dress practically ruined.

It was a risky journey. But if she wished to catch her father before he did harm she must trust that the ground was solid enough that she would not be sucked down into the peat before she reached her destination. Even the smallest delay might cost her dearly.

When she reached the front gate to Stratford's mill she found it chained and locked. She wondered if Mr Stratford had left it thus, or if her father had gone through and then locked it behind him, the better to do his mischief in privacy. For a moment she imagined Joseph Stratford, working unawares in the office as an assailant crept stealthily up behind him, axe raised…

She threw herself at the wrought-iron bars, crying out a warning, shaking them and feeling no movement under her hands. And then she was climbing, using the crossbars and the masonry of the wall to help her up. Mr Stratford had made it look simple when he had climbed to face the crowd. But he had not done so in a sodden dress and petticoats. She struggled under the weight of them, stumbling as she reached the top. What she'd hoped would be a leap to the ground on the inside was more of a stagger and a fall, and she felt something in her ankle twist and give as she landed.

It slowed her, but she did not stop, limping the last of the way to the wide back entrance. She passed through the open dock, where the vans and carts would bring materials and take away the finished goods, through the high-ceilinged storeroom waiting to hold the finished bolts of cloth. She passed the boiler room and the office and counting house, which were quiet and empty, and continued on to the floor of the factory proper, with its row upon row of orderly machinery, still new and smelling of green wood and machine oil.

From the far side of the big room she heard voices. Her father's was raised in threat. Mr Stratford's firm baritone answered him. The two men stood facing each other by the wreckage of a loom. Her father's axe was raised, and the look in his eyes was wild.

Stratford must have been disturbed in working with the machinery. He was coatless, the collar of his shirt open and its sleeves rolled up and out of the way, with a leather apron tied around his waist and smudged with grease. In one hand he held a hammer. Though his arm was lowered, Barbara could see the tensed muscles that told her he would use it in defence when her father rushed him.

'Hello?' she called out. 'What are you doing, Father? I have come to take you home for dinner.'

'Go home yourself, gel, for you do not need to see what is like to occur.' Father's voice was coarse, half-mad and dismissive. There was nothing left of the soft, rather pedantic tone she knew and loved.

'Your father is right, Miss Lampett. It is unnecessary for you to remain. Let we gentlemen work this out between us.' Stratford sounded calm and reassuring, though the smile he shot in her direction was tight with worry. His eyes never left the man in front of him. 'You will see your father directly.'

'Perhaps I will,' she answered. 'In jail or at his funeral. That is how this is likely to end if I allow it to continue.' She hobbled forwards and stepped between them. And between axe and hammer as well, trusting that neither was so angry as to try and strike around her.

'Miss Lampett,' Stratford said sharply. 'What have you done to yourself? Observe, sir, she is limping. Assist me and we will help her to a chair.' He sounded sincerely worried. But she detected another note in his voice as well, as though he was seizing on a welcome distraction.

'My Lord, Barbara, he is right. What have you done to yourself now?'

Her father dropped his axe immediately, forgetting his plans, and came to take her arm. Sometimes these violent spells passed as quickly as they came. This one had faded the moment he had recognised her injury.

Stratford had her other elbow, but she noticed the handle of his hammer protruding from an apron pocket, still close by should he need a weapon.

'I fell when climbing down from the gate. I am sure it is nothing serious.' Though the pain was not bad, and she could easily have managed for herself, she exaggerated the limp and let the two men work together to bear her forwards towards a chair.

'The front gate?' Stratford said in surprise. 'That is nearly eight feet tall.'

Her father laughed, as though lost in a happier time. 'My Barb always was a spirited one as a youngster. Constantly climbing into trees and taking the short way back to the ground. It is a good thing that the Lampett heads are hard, or we'd have lost her by now. Sit down, Barbara, and let me have a look at your foot.'

She took the seat they had pressed her to, and her father knelt at her feet and pulled off her muddy boot, probing gently at the foot to search for breaks.

She sat patiently and watched as Stratford's expression changed from concern to interest at the sight of her stocking-clad leg. Then he hurriedly looked away, embarrassed that he'd been caught staring. He gave her a rueful smile and a half-shrug, as if to say he could hardly be blamed for looking at something so attractive, and then offered a benign, 'I hope it is nothing serious.'

'A mild sprain, nothing more,' her father assured him.

For a change, his tone was as placid as it had ever been. He was the simple schoolmaster, the kind father she remembered and still knew, but a man the world rarely saw. She wanted to shout into the face of the mill owner to make him notice the change.

This is who he is. This is who we all are. We are not your enemies. We need you, just as you need us. If only you were to listen you might know us. You might like us.

'Would it help for her to sit with her foot on a cushion for a bit?' Mr Stratford responded as he was addressed, behaving as though she had twisted an ankle during a picnic, and not while haring to her father's rescue. 'My carriage is waiting at the back gate, just around the corner of the building.'

'That will not be necessary,' she said. This had hardly begun as a social call, though both men now seemed ready to treat it as such. While she doubted her father capable of guile, she did not know if this new and gentler Stratford was the truth. What proof did she have that they were not being led into a trap so that he could call the authorities? Even if he did not, at any time her father might recollect who had made the offer and turn again to the wild man she had found a few moments ago.

'A ride would be most welcome,' her father said, loud enough to drown out her objections. His axe still lay, forgotten, on the floor behind them. For now he was willing to accept the hospitality of a man he'd been angry enough to threaten only a moment ago.

'Then, with your permission, Mr Lampett, and with apologies to you, miss, for the liberty…' Joseph Stratford pulled off his apron, tossed it aside, then reached around her and lifted her easily off the stool and into his arms.

While it was a relief to see how easily he'd managed her father, it was rather annoying to see how easily he could manage her as well. He was carrying her through the factory as though she weighed nothing. And she was allowing him to do it—without protest. The worst of it was, she rather liked the sensation. She could feel far too much of his body through the fabric of his shirt, and her face was close enough to his bare skin to smell the blending of soap and sweat and cologne that was unique to him. Such overt masculinity should have repelled her. Instead she found herself wishing she could press her face into the hollow of his throat. At least she might lay her head against his shoulder, feigning a swoon.

That would be utter nonsense. She was not the sort to swoon under any circumstances, and she would not play at it now. Though she *did* allow herself to slip an arm around his neck under the guise of steadying herself. His arms were wrapped tightly, protectively, around her already, and such extra support was not really necessary. But it gave her the opportunity to feel more of him, and to bring her body even closer to his as he moved.

'It seems I am always to be rescuing you, Miss

Lampett,' he said into her ear, so quietly that her father could not overhear.

'You needn't have bothered,' she whispered back. 'I am shamming.'

'As you were when the crowd knocked you down yesterday?'

Then he spoke louder, and directly to her father. 'If you would precede us, sir? I do not wish to risk upsetting the lady with too rough a gait. Tell the coachman of our difficulties. Perhaps he can find an extra cushion and a lap robe so that Miss Lampett will be comfortable on the journey.'

'Very good.'

As her father hurried ahead, Stratford stopped to kick the axe he had been wielding into a darkened corner. 'Though you may not want my help, I think it is quite necessary today, for the safety of all concerned, that we play this to the very hilt.' He started again towards the carriage at a stately pace, stopping only long enough at the door to lean against it and push it shut behind him. 'Do you really wish to protest good health and risk your father remembering and using his weapon?'

She shifted a little in his grasp, feeling quite ridiculous to be treated as some sort of porcelain doll. 'Of course not. But I do not wish you to make a habit of swooping in to care for me when I am quite capable of seeing to my own needs.'

'Your independence is duly noted and admired,' he said. Then he dipped his head a little, so he could catch her scent. 'Though I find your infirmity has advantages as well.'

She slapped hard at his arm. 'You are incorrigible.'

'You are not the first to have told me so. And here we are.' He said the last louder, for the benefit of her father, to signal that their intimate conversation was at an end.

She frowned. Stratford could easily have ridden the distance between the manor and here, or perhaps even walked. To bring a full equipage and servants to wait after him while he worked was just the sort of excess she had come to expect from him—and just the sort of thing that was angering the locals. Or it could mean that he had a sensible fear of being set upon, should he travel alone and vulnerable along a road that might be lined with enemies.

He set her down briefly, only to lift her again, up into the body of the carriage, settling her beside her father on a totally unnecessary mound of cushions, her injured ankle stretched out before her to rest on the seat at Stratford's side.

The carriage was new, as was everything he owned, and practically shining with it. The upholstery was a deep burgundy leather, soft and well padded. There were heavy robes for her legs to keep out the cold, and a pan of coals to warm the foot that still rested on the floor. The other was tucked up securely, the stocking-clad toes dangerously close to the gentleman there. The foot was chilled, and she resisted the urge to press it against his leg to steal some warmth.

Stratford had noticed it. He stared down for a moment, and then, as unobtrusively as possible, he tossed the tail of his coat over it and shifted his weight to be nearer.

Barbara warmed instantly—from the contact with his body and the embarrassment accompanying it. It was a practical solution, of course. But she would be the talk of the town if anyone heard of it. And by the smug smile on his face Joseph Stratford knew it, and was enjoying her discomfiture.

Then he signalled the driver and they set off, with barely a sway to tell her of the moment. It was by far the richest and most comfortable trip she'd taken, and she had to struggle not to enjoy it. Her subdued pleasure turned to suspicion, for at another signal to the driver they proceeded through the unlocked gates down the road towards Clairemont Manor.

'This is not the way to our home,' she said, stating the obvious.

'My house is nearer. You can both come for tea. I will send you home once I am assured that you are warmed and refreshed, and that no harm has come to you while on my property.'

'That is most kind of you,' her father said.

It was not at all kind. It was annoying. And she was sure that there must be some sort of ulterior motive to his sudden solicitousness.

But when she opened her mouth to say so, her father went on. 'There are not many who are such good neighbours. And are you new here, Mr…?' He struggled for a name. 'I am sorry. My memory is not what it once was.'

Barbara coloured, part relieved and part ashamed. She needn't worry that her father was likely to turn violent again, for it was clear that he had lost the thread of things and forgotten all about Mr Stratford while concerned for her ankle. But what was she to do now? Should she remind him that his host was the same man who, according to her father's own words, treated his workers 'like chattel to be cast off in pursuit of Mammon'? Or should she continue to let him display his mental confusion in front of his enemy and become an object of scorn and pity?

Stratford seemed unbothered, and responded with the barest of pauses. 'We have met only briefly, and I do not fault you for not recalling. I am Joseph Stratford, and I have taken residence of Clairemont Manor now that the family has relocated closer to the village.'

Her father gave a nod in response, still not associating the man across from them with the evil mill owner he despised.

'Would you do me the honour of an introduction to your daughter, sir?'

As her father presented her to this supposed stranger with all necessary formality, she thought she detected a slight twitch at the corners of Stratford's mouth. If he meant to make sport at the expense of her father's failed memory she would find a way to pay him out. But, after the briefest lapse, he was straight-faced and respectful again, enquiring after her father's work and commiserating with him on the closing of the little school where he had taught, and his recent difficulties in finding another occupation.

Mr Stratford had changed much since the last time she'd seen him brandishing a pistol and taunting the crowd. Though she could not say she liked him, she'd felt an illogical thrill at the power of him then, and the masterful way he had come to her aid. Now she was left with time to admire him as he conversed with her father, displaying intelligence and a thoughtful nature that had not been in evidence before. She found herself wishing that things could be different from the way they were and that this might be their first meeting. If she could look on him with fresh eyes, knowing none of his behaviour in the recent past, it might be possible to trust him. But she could not help thinking that this display of good manners was as false as her sprained ankle.

He had let the groom help him on with his coat again before they had taken off, and she could see that it was the height of London fashion, tailored to perfection and designed to give a gentlemanly outline to the work-broadened shoulders she had felt as he carried her. He was clean-shaven. But his hair was a trifle too long, as though he could not be bothered to spare the few extra minutes that the cutting of it would take. A lock of it fell into his eyes as he nodded at something her father had said, and he brushed it out of his face with an impatient flick of his hand. Though she could not call them graceful, his movements were precise. She could imagine that these were hands better at tending machinery than creating art, more efficient than gentle.

He made conversation with her father in an accent carefully smoothed to remind the listener of London, though she doubted that his tongue had been born to it. He spoke nothing of himself or his own past. But in the questions that drew her father to conversation Barbara heard the occasional lilt or drawl that was the true Joseph Stratford. He was a Northerner. But for some reason he did not like to show it.

She looked away before he could catch her staring. Even if he was nothing more than a tradesman masquerading as gentry, he deserved more courtesy than she was giving him. They were drawing up the long drive towards the great house where she had played as a child. That was before Mary had died, of course, and before her sister Anne had grown into such a great and unapproachable lady. Had the manor changed as well? she wondered. Were the places she'd hidden under chairs and behind statues the same or different? Although she wished the circumstances had been different, she very much wanted to see the place—just once more.

She could feel the eyes of the other man on her, watching her reaction to the house. So she worked to relax her posture and not stare so, or appear eager for a visit to it. It was little better than staring directly at him to admire his property as though she coveted or desired the luxury he took for granted.

'I had a friend who lived here once,' she blurted, to explain her interest.

'And perhaps you will again,' he replied easily.

She looked up sharply into a face that was all bland innocence. The carriage pulled up before the great front entry, and as it stopped he signalled for the door to be opened, allowing her father to exit first so that he might help her on the steps.

For a moment they were alone again, and he touched her hand and smiled. 'There is no reason for us to be enemies,' he said.

'Nor any particular reason for friendship,' she reminded him, drawing her hand away.

'I think it is too soon for either of us to tell,' he announced, ignoring her animosity.

The process of entering the house was much the same as their setting off from the mill had been, with him carrying her while she protested, her shoeless foot waving in the air. There was a flurry of alarm amongst the servants, many of whom recognised her and her father.

'Put me down now,' she insisted. 'Talk of this will reach the village. It will be the ruin of me.'

'If it is, your father is right here to set them straight.' He was smiling again, as though he knew how likely it was that her father would have no real memory of the event, for good or ill.

'I would prefer that no explanation be needed,' she said.

'And I would prefer that people think me less of an ogre,' Stratford replied. 'I will not have you limping about my house while I offer no assistance. Then it will get round that I let you suffer as a punishment to your father.'

For her own sake, and to preserve her reputation, he explained in a loud voice for the benefit of the staff that Miss Lampett had fallen, and he did not wish to risk further injury until she had rested her foot. But as he did so his hands tightened on her body, to prove to Barbara that he was enjoying the experience at her expense.

'You may put me down, and I will take my chances,' she said, glancing at a parlour maid who stood, wide-eyed, taking in the sight. 'I feel quite all right now.'

He pretended that he had not heard, and called for tea to be brought to the library, carrying her down the wide hall and depositing her on a couch by the fire.

How had Mr Stratford known, she wondered, the calming effect that the presence of books had on her father? Though he seemed to have more difficulty with people since the accident, the printed word still gave him great comfort. The Clairemont Manor library was the largest in the area and the best possible place to cement her father's recovery.

As the servants prepared tea, her father stood and ran a hand along the rows of leather-bound volumes. Stratford studied the behaviour and then invited him to help himself to whatever he liked, lamenting that business gave him little time to enjoy the books there.

Her father gave a grateful nod and fell quickly to silence, ignoring the cup that had been poured for him, and the plate of sandwiches, in favour of the Roman history in his hand.

Stratford gave her a wry smile. 'While your father is preoccupied, would you enjoy a brief walk down the corridor? If your ankle is better, as you claim, a spot of exercise will assure me that it is safe to send you home.'

She wanted to snap that she did not need him seeing to her safety. She had not wanted to come here at all. And now that she was here she would go home when she was ready, and not at his bidding. But it would be shaming to discuss her father's rude behaviour while she shared a room with him, so it was best that she allow herself to be drawn away.

'That would be lovely,' she lied.

He went to fetch her boot and helped her with the lacing of it, commenting that the lack of swelling was an encouraging sign. Behind a placid smile, she gritted her teeth against the contact of his fingers against her foot and ankle. He was very gentle, as though he cared enough not to cause injury to a weakened joint. But she suspected the occasional fleeting touches she felt against her stocking were not the least bit accidental. He was touching her for his own pleasure. Much as she did not wish to, she found it wickedly exciting.

Then he rose and went ahead to open the door for her,

standing respectfully to the side so that she might pass. She forced herself to stifle the unquiet feeling that it gave her to have him at her back—even for a moment.

It was possible that this latest offer masked something much darker. Perhaps he had designs upon her virtue. For, this close, she could not deny the virile air that he seemed to carry about with him, and the sense that he had a man's needs and would not scruple to act upon them. She gave a small shudder, barely enough to be noticeable.

'Is the house too cold for you?' he prompted. 'If so, I could have a servant build up the fire, or perhaps bring you a wrap…'

'No, I am fine. I suspect that I took a slight chill on the moors.'

'Your clothing is still damp from the fall. And I took you away from the tea I had promised.' He frowned. 'But I wished to speak alone with you for a moment, so that you might know I bear you no ill will because of recent events.' He rubbed his brow, as though tired. 'One can hardly be held responsible for the actions of one's parent. I myself have a troublesome father.'

He stopped.

'Had,' he corrected. 'I *had* a difficult father. He is dead now. For a moment I had quite forgotten.'

'I am sorry for your loss,' she said politely. 'I assume the passing is a recent one, if you still forget it?'

He looked away, as though embarrassed. 'Almost

seven years, actually. It is just that he has been on my mind of late. He was a weaver, you see.'

'You are the son of a weaver?' she said.

'Is that so surprising?' There was a cant to his head, a jutting of the chin as though he were ready to respond to a challenge. 'With all your father's fine talk of supporting the workers, I did not think to find you snobbish, Miss Lampett.'

'I am not snobbish,' she retorted. 'It merely surprises me that my father would need to tell a weaver's son the damage automation does to the livelihoods of the men here.'

'What you call damage, Miss Lampett, I call freedom. The ability to do more work in less time means the workers do not need to toil from first light to last. Perhaps they will have time for education, and those books your father finds so precious.'

'The workers who are put from their places by these machines will have more time as well. And no money. Time is no blessing when there is no food on the table.'

He snorted. 'The reason they are without work this Christmas has nothing to do with me. Was it not they and their like who burned the last mill to the ground and ran off the mill owner and his family? Now they complain that they have no source of income.'

'When men are desperate enough, they resort to desperate actions,' she said. 'The owner, Mr Mackay, was a harsh man who cared little for those he employed, taking them on and casting them off like chattel. It is little wonder that their spirits broke.'

'And I am sure that it did not help to have your father raising the rabble and inciting them to mischief.' He looked at her with narrowed eyes.

'That is a lie,' she snapped. 'He had nothing to do with that argument. He did not support either side, and worked to moderate the cruelty of the one with the need of the other.'

Stratford scoffed. 'He saves his rage for me, then, who has not been here long enough to prove myself cruel or kind?'

'He was not always as you see him,' she argued. 'A recent accident has addled his wits. Until that night he was the mildest of gentlemen, much as you see him now. But of late, when he takes an idea into his head, he can become quite agitated.' When he recalled the scene she had come upon at the mill, just a short time ago, he must know that 'agitated' was an understatement. 'Mother and I do not know what to do about it.'

'You had best do something,' Stratford said. 'He appears to be getting worse and not better. If you had not come along today…' He paused. 'Your arrival prevented anyone from coming to harm, at least for now.'

From his tone, it did not seem that he feared for his own life. 'Are you threatening my father, Mr Stratford?'

'Not without cause, I assure you. He is a violent man. If necessary I will call in the law to stop him. That would be a shame if it is as you say—that the rage in him is a thing which he cannot control. But you must see that the results are likely to be all the same whether they proceed from malice, madness or politics.'

'Just what do you propose we do? Lock him up?'

'If necessary,' Stratford said, with no real feeling. 'At least that will prevent me from having him transported.'

'You would do that, wouldn't you?' With his understanding behaviour, and his offers of tea and books, she had allowed herself to believe—just for a moment—that he was capable of understanding. And that if she confided in him he might use his ingenuity to come up with a solution to her family's problems. But he was proving to be just as hard as she'd thought him when she'd seen him taunting the mob of weavers. 'You have no heart at all to make such threats at Christmas.'

Joseph Stratford shrugged. 'I fail to see what the date on the calendar has to do with it. The mill will open in January, whether your father likes it or not. But there is much work I must do, and plans that must be secured between then and now. I will not allow him to ruin the schemes already in progress with his wild accusations and threats of violence. Is that understood, Miss Lampett?'

'You do not wish our coarseness and our poverty to offend the fancy guests you are inviting from London,' she said with scorn. Everyone in the village had heard the rumours of strangers coming to the manor for the holiday, and would be speculating about their feasting and dancing while eating their meagre dinners in

Fiddleton. 'And you have the nerve to request that I chain my father in our cottage like a mad dog, so that he will not trouble you and your friends with the discomfort of your workers?' She was sounding like her father at the beginning of some rabble-rousing rant. And she was foolish enough to be doing it while alone with a man who solved his problems with a loaded pistol.

'There was a time when I was little better than they are now,' he snapped.

'Then you must have forgotten it, to let the people suffer so.'

'Forgotten?' He stepped closer, his eyes hard and angry. 'There is nothing romantic about the life of a labourer. Only a woman who has known no real work would struggle so hard to preserve the rights of others to die young from overwork.' He reached out suddenly and seized her hands, turning them over to rub his fingers over the palms. 'As I thought. Soft and smooth. A lady's hands.'

'There is no shame in being a lady,' she said, with as much dignity as she could manage. She did not try to pull away. He could easily manage to hold her if he wanted to. And if he did not respond to her struggle the slight fear she felt at the nearness of him would turn into panic.

His fingers closed on hers, and his eyes seemed to go dark. 'But neither is there any pride in being poor. It is nice, is it not, to go to a soft bed with a full belly? To have hands as smooth as silk?' His thumbs were stroking her, and the little roughness of them seemed to remind her just how soft she was. There was something both soothing and exciting about the feel of his fingers moving against hers, the way they twined, untwined and twined again.

'That does not mean that we should not feel sympathy for those less fortunate than ourselves.' He was standing a little too close to be proper, and her protest sounded breathless and excited.

'Less fortunate, eh? Less in some ways, more in others. Without the machines they are fighting I would be no different than they are now—scrabbling to make a living instead of holding the hands of a beautiful lady in my own great house.'

It was not his house at all. He had taken it—just as he had taken her hands. 'I did not give you leave to do so,' she reminded him.

'You gave me no leave to carry you before either,' he said. 'But I wanted to, and so I did. You felt very good in my arms.' He pulled her even closer, until her skirts were brushing against the legs of his trousers. She did not move, even though he had freed her hands. 'It is fortunate for me that you are prone to pity a poor working man. Perhaps you will share some of that sweet sympathy with me.' He ran a finger down her cheek, as though to measure its softness.

She stood very still indeed, not wishing him to see how near she was to trembling. If she cried out it would draw the house down upon them and bring this meeting to a sudden end. But her words had failed her, and she could manage no clever quip that would make him think her sophisticated. Nor could she raise a maidenly insistence that he revolted her. He did not. His touch was gentle, and it made her forget all that had come before.

He seemed to forget as well, for his voice was softer, deeper and slower. 'Your father broke one of my looms today. But it will be replaced, and I will say nothing of how the destruction happened.'

'Thank you,' she whispered, wetting her lips.

'If you wish to make a proper apology, I would like something more.' His head dipped forwards, slowly, and his lips were nearing hers.

Although she knew what was about to happen she stayed still and closed her eyes. His lips were touching hers, moving lightly over them. It was as it had been when he had touched her ankle and held her hands. She could feel everything in the world in that single light touch. Her whole body felt warm and alive. Hairs rose on her arms and neck—not from the chill but as though they were eager to be soothed back to smoothness by roving hands.

She kissed him back, moving her lips on his as he had on hers. His mouth was rough, and imperfect. One corner of his smile was slightly higher than the other, and she touched it with the tip of her tongue, felt the dimple beside it deepen in surprise.

In response, he gave a playful lick against her upper

lip, daring her. Her body's response was an immediate tightening, and she pressed herself against him, opening her mouth. And what had been wonderful became amazing.

He encircled her, and his arms made a warm, safe place for their exploration—just as they had when he'd carried her. The slow stroking of hands and tongue seemed to open her to more sensations, and the tingling of her body assured her of the rightness of it, the perfection and the bliss. Although she knew all the places on her body that he must not touch, she was eager to feel his fingers there, and perhaps his tongue.

Just the idea made her tremble with eagerness, with embarrassment, and the knowledge that had seemed quite innocent was near to blazing out of control. And it was not only his doing. Even now she had taken his tongue into her mouth, and it was she who held it captive there, closing her lips upon it.

She could tell by his sigh of pleasure that he enjoyed what she'd done. But his only other response was to go still against her. His passivity coaxed her to experiment, raking his tongue with her teeth and circling it with her own, urging him to react.

He had trapped her into being the aggressor. At the realisation, she pulled away suddenly. He let her go, staring down at her in mock surprise, touching his own lips gingerly, as though they might be hot enough to burn his fingers.

'Stop that immediately,' she said.

He smiled. 'You have stopped it quickly enough for both of us. And now I suppose you wish me to apologise for the way *you* kissed *me*?'

'Only if you wish me to think you any sort of gentleman,' she said, feeling ridiculous.

'But I am not a gentleman,' he said with a shrug. 'Isn't that half the problem between us? I sit here, a trumped-up worker, in a house that should belong to my betters, had they not lost it through monetary foolishness. My presence in this house upsets the natural order of things. My touching you…'

'That is not the problem at all,' she snapped. 'I do not care who you are.'

'If you do not care who I am, it was highly indiscriminate of you to allow me the kiss. And even worse that you returned it.'

'You are twisting my words,' she said. 'I meant that it should not have happened at all. Not with any man. But especially not with you.'

'I don't know,' he said with an ironic laugh. 'I might be the best choice for such dalliance. If you complain to your father, I would be obligated to do right by you. Then my house and my fortune would be yours. You might trap me with your considerable charms and force me to marry you.'

'But to do that I would have to admit to Father that you had touched me, Mr Stratford. I think we can safely say that such a circumstance will never happen. Not for all the money in the world, and Clairemont Manor thrown into the mix. Now, please return me to the library.'

He smiled in triumph, as though that had been his end all along. 'Very well, then. Let us go back to your father, and both of you can be gone. I trust that now we have spoken on the subject I will see no more of you, or be forced to endure any more of your father's tirades? For, while I can see that there is more than a little madness to them, they cannot be allowed to continue. If arms are raised against me and the opening of the mill disrupted, or my equipment damaged further, I will be forced to take action. While I am sure that neither of us wants it, you must see that I do not intend to be displaced now that I am so near to success.'

He turned and led her back towards the library. As he opened the door he made idle comments about the furnishings and art, as though they had just returned from a tour of his home. It was all the more galling to know that some of the things he said were inaccurate, proving that he knew little more about the things he owned than how to pay for them. He really was no better than he had said: a man ignorant in all but one thing. He had made a fine profit by it. But what did that matter if it had left him coarse and cruel?

As they entered, her father looked up as though he had forgotten how he had come to be there. 'I think it is time that we were going, Father,' she said firmly. 'We have abused Mr Stratford's hospitality for quite long enough.'

Her father looked with longing at the book in his hands.

Joseph Stratford responded without missing a beat. 'I hate to take you from your reading, sir. Please accept the volume as my gift to you. You are welcome to come here whenever you like and avail yourself of these works. It pleases me greatly to see them in the hands of one who enjoys them.'

Because you have no use for them, you illiterate lout, she thought. She responded with a smile that was almost too bright, 'How thoughtful of you, Mr Stratford.'

Her father agreed. 'Books are a precious commodity in the area, and it is rare that we get anything new from London that is not a newspaper or a fashion plate.' He wrinkled his nose at the inadequacy of such fare to a man of letters.

Stratford nodded in sympathy. 'Then we will see what can be done to correct the deficiency. If there is anything you desire from my library, send word. I will have it delivered to you. And now it appears that your daughter is properly recovered. If I may offer you a ride back to the village?'

Her father stood, and the men chatted as they walked to the door as though they were old friends. In a scant hour Bernard Lampett had quite recovered from his fit of rage, and Mr Stratford was behaving as though the incidents in the mill and in the hall had not occurred. If he remembered them at all, he appeared untouched by them.

But in the space of that same hour Barbara felt irrevocably changed, and less sure of herself than she had ever been.

CHAPTER FIVE

LATER that evening the guests began to arrive, and Joseph was relieved to have no time to think of Barbara Lampett. Even when he should have focused his energy elsewhere, he could feel the memory of her and her sweet lips always in the background. It had been madness to take her out into the hall. He had known that he could not fully trust himself around her. When they were alone he should have limited himself to urging her to moderate her father's actions. But he'd had the foolish urge to show her his house, so that she might see the extent of his success. There might even have been some notion of catching her under a kissing bough and stealing one small and quite harmless kiss. He had been eager to impress her, and had behaved in a way that was both foolish and immature.

All of it had got tangled together in an argument, ending with a brief and heated display of shared emotion. It had been as pleasant as it had inappropriate. While such little indiscretions happened all the time, ladies like Barbara Lampett did not like to think themselves capable of them. She would not wish to be reminded, nor to risk a repeat display. He would not see her again.

And that was that.

He turned his attention to more important matters. After the rejections in today's post, it appeared that his house would be barely half-full for Christmas. There had been several frosty refusals to the offer of a trumped-up tradesman's hospitality. But it would not matter. Even one or two would be plenty—if they were rich enough and could be interested in his plans.

As promised, he let Bob take the lead in introductions and in the planning of activities, doing his best to respond in a way that was not rough or gauche. His casual offer that tomorrow's skating on the millpond might end with cakes and punch served in the empty warehouse was accepted graciously—once the ladies were assured that it was quite clean and that no actual work was being done. While they were there he would arrange a tour of the tidy rows of machinery. Breton would make mention of the successes they'd shared with the production and sale of such looms to others. The seed would be planted.

Before they returned to London one or two of the men would come to Bob, as they always did after such gatherings, making offhand remarks about risk and reward. A discreet parlay would be arranged in which no money would change hands. There would be merely a vague promise of it, for such people did not carry chequebooks with them. They carried cards and wrote letters of introduction to bankers, who stayed in the background where they belonged. But if they offered, they would deliver. Honour was involved. A true gentleman's word was as good as a banknote.

He frowned as the last of his guests took themselves off to bed, leaving him free for a few hours of rest. He was tired tonight, after last night's uneasy rest. Dinner had tired him as well. It was like speaking another language, dealing with the gentry and their need to seem idle even while doing business. So much easier to deal with the likes of mad Lampett. Though he was of a changeable nature, he would at least speak what was left of his mind.

For plain speaking, Lampett's lovely daughter was better than ten of the milk-and-water misses he was likely to see this week. Even Anne Clairemont, whose family had put in a brief appearance this evening, had looked puzzled by the conversation, and nervous at the prospect of a little skating on a properly frozen pond. He would not have faulted her if she had politely excused herself from it. But she had looked from her father to him, blinked twice and then forced a smile and declared it a wonderful notion.

Miss Lampett, in a similar situation, would have likely announced to the assembly that the whole trip was a thinly disguised attempt at business and refused to take any part in it. For some reason the imagined scene did not bother him. He could just as easily imagine drawing her out in the hall to remonstrate with her, only to have the conversation degenerate into another heated kiss.

When his valet had left him for the night he settled back into the pillows and pulled the blankets up to his chin, closing his eyes and thinking of that kiss. He really shouldn't have taken it. It had been improper and unfair of him to take advantage of her innocence. But he would do it again if he had the chance. That and more…

He awoke hungry. It made no sense. The clock was only striking one, and dinner had been a feast, stretching late into the evening. He had partaken of it with enthusiasm. But it was gone from him now, leaving his guts empty and gnawing on themselves in the darkness.

He had not known want like this since he'd become master of his own life. This was the kind of nagging hunger he'd felt as a child, going to bed with an empty belly and knowing that there would be nothing to fill it again tomorrow. It was a kind of bleak want that existed in the body like an arm or a leg: something that one carried with one from moment to moment, place to place, always there and impossible to cast off.

But it was easily rectified now. He had but to sit up in bed and ring for a footman. He would explain the need and have it filled. It would mean getting some poor maid out of her bed to do for him. But what was the point of having servants if one could not make unreasonable demands upon them?

When he opened his eyes, the room was strange. Not his own bedroom at all, but a different, emptier room, filled with a strange, directionless golden haze.

From the corner of the room there was a sigh.

Joseph sat bolt upright now, searching for the source of the sound. And with it he found the origin of the glow. A man sat in the corner—a Cavalier, in a long well-curled wig and heavy-skirted coat. The light seemed to rise from the gold braid upon it, diffusing into a corona around him.

This man was a stranger, and yet strangely familiar. He looked around the room and sighed again. He glanced across at Joseph and gave a pitying shake of his head. 'When I was summoned here, I must admit I expected better. These are not the surroundings to which I am accustomed. But I suppose if there is no problem, then there is no need…' The Cavalier gave another heavy sigh.

'Just what do you mean by that?' snapped Joseph, rubbing his eyes. 'I grew up in a room not unlike this one, and…'

As a matter of fact he'd grown up in a room exactly like this one. Its appearance was softened somewhat, by the glow of the phantom and by his own fading memories, but it was the same room. It was where he'd felt the hunger that plagued him now, which was still as sharp and real as ever it had been.

'I belong at the manor and have been sent to fetch you back to it,' the man said bluntly. 'Although even that is no treat. For I must tell you the place under your governance is not as nice as it once was.'

'Now, see here,' Joseph said, sitting up in his bed only to realise that it was not the thing he'd lain down on but a narrow bunk, with a rush mattress and thin blankets that could not keep the cold from his feet. 'You need not take me back, for I did not go anywhere. I am still there, fast asleep and dreaming.' This time he gave himself a hard pinch on the back of the hand, not caring if the spirit before him saw it.

'I was told that this had been explained to you. Three visitors would come. We would show you your errors. You would learn or not learn, as was your nature…' He droned in an uninterested way that said he did not care what Joseph learned, so long as he did it quickly and with as little bother as possible.

Joseph glared at the spirit, annoyed that it was still before him. 'I was told by my father. Who is dead and therefore should not be telling me anything. While he said there would be three, he did not say three of what. If there was any truth in it he might as well have said four, thus counting himself.'

'Do not think you can reason like a Jesuit to get yourself out of a situation that you yourself have created.' The Cavalier sighed again, and flicked a lace handkerchief in front of his nose as though offended by the stench of such humble surroundings. 'Be silent and I will explain. And then we might be done with this vision and go back to the house.'

'But you are not real,' Joseph argued. It was most annoying to be lectured at by one's own imagination. And then he placed the identity of the thing sitting before him. 'You are Sir Cedric Clairemont, and nothing more than a portrait hanging in the gallery on the second floor. This room is the place where I was born. I am blending memories in a dream.'

Sir Cedric gave a resigned glare in his direction, and sighed again as though facing a difficult child. 'Let me put this plainly, so that you might understand it. I would say I am as real as you, but that would lack truth. I was real. Now I am a spirit, as is your father. As are the two that will come after. By the end of it you will know where you were, where you are and what you will become.'

'I know all these things for myself, without your help. I will not be frightened into a change of plans by some notion created out of a second helping of trifle after a roast pork dinner.'

'Touch me,' commanded the spirit.

He did look almost real enough to touch, and just the same as he did in his portrait. But from what memory had Joseph created the man's voice, which was a slightly nasal tenor? Or his mannerisms as he swaggered forwards with his stick and looked down at Joseph with amused superiority? This man was not some ghost from a painting, but so real that he felt he could reach out and…

Joseph drew his hand back quickly, suddenly aware of the gesture he'd been making—which had looked almost like supplication.

The ghost stared at him with impatience. Then he brought the swagger stick down upon Joseph's head with a thud.

'Ow!'

'Is that real enough for you, Stratford? Or must I hit you again? Now, get out of the bed and take my hand—or I will give you a thumping you will remember in the morning.'

The idea was ludicrous. It was one thing to have a vivid dream. Quite another for that nightmare to fetch you a knock to the nob then demand that you get out of bed and walk into it.

'Certainly not.' Joseph rubbed at the spot where he'd been struck. 'Raise that stick to me again and, dream or not, I will answer you blow for blow.'

Sir Cedric smiled ironically. 'Very well, then. If you wish to remain here I can show you images of your childhood. Although why you would wish to see them, I am unsure. They are most unpleasant.'

As though a candle had been lit, a corner of the room brightened and Joseph felt increasing dread. It was the corner that had held the loom.

'Tighten the warp.' He heard the slap and felt the

impact of it on the side of his head, even though it had landed some many years before on the ear of the young boy who sat there.

'S…sorry, Father.' The young Joseph fumbled with the shuttle.

The man who stood over him could barely contain his impatience. 'Sorry will not do when there is an order as big as this one. I cannot work the night through to finish it. You must do your share. Sloppy work that must be unravelled again the next day is no help at all. It is worse than useless. Not only must I do my own part, I must stand over you and see to it that you do yours. You are worse than useless.'

'I was too small,' Joseph retorted, springing from the bed and flexing his muscles with a longing to strike back. 'My arms were too short to do the job. All the bullying in the world would have made no difference.'

'He cannot hear you,' the ghost said calmly. 'For the moment you live in my world, as much a spectre to him as he is to you.'

'It was Christmas. And it was not fair,' Joseph said, trying to keep the childish petulance from his voice.

'Life seldom is.'

'I made it fair,' Joseph argued. 'My new loom is wider, but so simple that a child can manage it.' The weavers of Fiddleton and all the other places that employed a Stratford loom would not be beating their children at Christmas over unfinished work.

But the ghost at his side said nothing, as though

Joseph had done no kindness with the improvement. He held out his hand again. 'Do you need further reminders of your past?'

Without thinking, Joseph shook his head. The past was clear enough in his own mind without them. It had been hard and hungry and he was glad to be rid of it. 'I made my father eat his words before the end,' Joseph said coldly. 'He died in warmth and comfort, in a bed I bought for him, and *not* slaving in someone else's mill.'

'Take my hand and come away.' Sir Cedric sounded almost sympathetic, his voice softer, gently prodding Joseph to action.

Joseph turned his back on the vision and reached for the arm of the spectre, laying his hand beside the ghostly white one on the stick he held. The fingers were unearthly cold, and smooth as marble, but very definitely real to him in a way that the man and boy in the corner were not. 'Very well, then. Whatever you are, take me back to the manor and my own bed.'

There was a feeling of rushing, and of fog upon his face, the sound of the howling winds upon the moors. Then he was back in his own home, walking down the main corridor towards the receiving rooms in bare feet and a nightshirt.

'What the devil?' He yanked upon Sir Cedric's arm, trying to turn him towards the stairs. 'I said my bedroom, you lunatic. If my guests see me wandering the house in my nightclothes, they will think I've gone mad. All my plans will be undone.'

If this was a ghost that escorted him, the least it could do was to be insubstantial. But Sir Cedric was as cold and immovable as stone. Now that they were joined Joseph could not seem to pull his hand away. He was being forced to follow into the busiest part of the house, which was brightly lit and brimming with activity, though it had been empty when he'd retired.

'Don't be an idiot, Stratford. Did I not tell you that I am a spirit of the past, and that you might pass unseen through it?' The ghost sniffed the air. 'This is the Christmas of 1800, if I have led us right. It is the same night when we saw you clouted on the ear. Well past my time, but the holiday is much as I remember it from my own days as lord here, and celebrated as it has always been. The doors are open to the people of Fiddleton. Tenants and villagers, noble friends and neighbours mix here to the joy of all.'

The ghost gave a single tap of his stick and the ballroom doors before them opened wide. The same golden glow Joseph had seen before spilled through them and out into the hall, as if to welcome them in.

This is how it should be.

The thought caught him almost off guard, as though the sight of this long-past Christmas was the missing piece in a puzzle. The rooms were the same, the smells of Christmas food very nearly so. But it was the people that made the difference.

Even in mirth, his current guests were polite and guarded. The men considering business looked at him as though calculating gain and loss. Anne's family treated him with an awkward combination of deference and contempt. A few others avoided him, acting as though the wrong kind of mirth on their part would admit that they did not mind his company and would result in some life-changing social disaster.

But the very air was different in this place. It was not simply the quaint fashion of the clothes or the courtliness of the dancing. There was a look in their eyes: a confidence in the future, a joyful twinkle. As though there was no question that the future would be as happy as the past had been. But they were not bending, more than ten years on, under the weight of a never-ending war, or the feeling that their very livelihood might slip from their fingers because of the decisions made by men of power and wealth. They were dancing, singing and drinking together, unabashed. The spirit was infectious, and Joseph could not help but smile in response to the sight.

There was a pause in the music and he heard the laughter of young girls—saw a pair, still in the schoolroom, winding about the furniture in a game of tag.

'Do you not wish they would stop?' the ghost prodded gently. 'It is most tiresome, is it not? All the noise and the bustle?'

'No. It is wonderful.' For all the quiet dignity of the party he was throwing, there was something lost. It lacked the life of this odd gathering so bent on merriment. He could see village folk amongst them—the grocer, the miller and younger versions of the same weavers who had threatened only yesterday to break the frames in his factory. But now they danced with the rest, as though they were a part of the household.

He cast a questioning glance at the ghost.

'It is the annual Tenants' Ball,' Sir Cedric supplied. 'Held each Christmas night—until the last owner could no longer keep the spirit of the season or afford the house.'

'Perhaps if he had been a wiser steward of his money and not spent it on frivolities such as this he would still reside here.' But his own conscience told him that was an unfair charge. The celebration *he* was throwing was far more elaborate than this, and not a tenth as happy.

'He seems successful enough there, doesn't he?' Sir Cedric raised his stick and pointed towards the corner, where stood Anne's father, Mr Clairemont, looking happier and less careworn than he had done since Joseph had known him. And there was Mrs Clairemont, who showed a change even more drastic. Eleven years ago she had been a gracefully aging beauty. Now she was grey, pinched and nervous.

'Whatever the reason, the Clairemonts are gone from here and none of your concern. I hear the house is held by a harsher master now.' The ghost gave him a look one part disappointment and one part disapproval, followed by another heavy sigh.

'I am harsh because I did not invite the whole village for Christmas dinner?' Joseph waved a hand at the assembly. 'How was I expected to know of this? It is not as if I was born of this area. The cottage we began the night in was miles from here. Clairemont said nothing of this responsibility when he sold me the house.'

'And you are so tragically robbed of speech that you could not enquire.' The ghost nodded in mock sympathy.

Now the lord of the manor was offering baskets to the families that had come, shaking hands and slapping backs as though every last man was an old friend. If the Clairemonts were still in the house, it must mean that the woman he now meant to marry was somewhere in the throng—and no older than the girls at play. He searched for the pair he had seen and dismissed earlier, but there were so many children, and they seemed to swarm out of doorways and hiding places, tearing down the halls, heedless of the other guests.

Then he spied Anne. Even now he could not quite manage to think of her as 'his' Anne. The unfamiliarity of her youth made it no easier. This little girl was as unlike her in manner as she was like in face. In childhood there had been none of the sombre grace that the woman carried now. She was a mischievous imp who did not care that her hair ribbons had come untied so long as she was not caught by the one who followed.

And the other, following close on her heels, was just alike. A twin? Or very nearly so? For the girls were very similar in looks. If they were not birthed together, then no more than a year could have separated them.

'Mary! Anne! Wait for me.' A third girl appeared, as though out of nowhere, seemingly forgotten as the game of hide-and-seek went on without her. When he turned to the sound of her voice he saw a hanging on the wall that had concealed her still rustling back into place.

Focused as she was on the two who had passed, she did not see him until it was too late, striking his legs with a surprisingly solid thump. 'Excuse me, sir.'

As he reached out a hand to steady her, her little face turned up to his. Barbara Lampett. It must be her. For there was the same turned-up nose. And those were her blue eyes, as bright and searching as a beacon, with the curiosity of unvarnished youth. No one had told her not to stare, or taught her to cloak the energy of her spirit in courtesies and false manners.

He felt the same connection he had at the riot, and again in this very hall. But this was different. Tonight she knew nothing about him. She'd had no chance to form an opinion, no reason to think him anything less than a gentleman. She had no cause to dislike him. She was smiling at him with those same pursed lips that had shown such disapproval this afternoon.

The thought staggered him. Seeing her here, as she had been, he very much wished that he might have met the girl full-grown tonight, and had even the smallest opportunity to let the woman she had become see him as anything else than an enemy.

He steadied her, and stepped out of her way. 'No harm done, Miss Lampett. Go and find your friends.'

But the other girls had come back for her, grabbing her hands and pulling her away, paying no heed to him.

'Barbara, what are you waiting for? Come.'

Then she was gone from him, with one passing look and a tip of her head, as though she could not quite make out his purpose in standing in the hall, staring.

'Who is the man in the nightshirt?' she said to the nearest girl, looking back at him again.

'What man?' Her friends looked back, through him.

'I… Never mind.' Barbara smiled and looked away again, as though the memory of him was already fading.

'She saw me?' he said in wonder, looking down at his own hand as though he could still feel the muslin of her gown under his fingers.

'It seems so,' said the ghost, barely interested. 'There are those who see the world around them plainly, and those who don't. Miss Lampett is more perceptive than most.'

Joseph thought again of her ill opinion of him. That was hardly a sign of keen perception. Her animosity seemed to be shared by most of the community.

'And some others can learn to see properly if they are shown,' the ghost added.

'You are speaking of me, I suppose?' Joseph answered.

'You do seem to be most singularly blind to your surroundings.'

'I see it more as an ability to avoid distractions and to focus on the future.'

'Really?' It was more a question than a statement. 'The future is not my purview. There is another...' The ghost stopped for a moment and gave a slight shudder. 'You will see soon enough how clear a view of the future you hold. But for now I bring you to the past so that you might learn from it. Do not forget it, my boy.'

'Stratford! What the devil? Joseph, get up immediately. What are you about, sleeping in a common hallway?'

Joseph started awake, focusing in confusion for a moment on a man's legs, before looking up into the worried face of Breton. 'Hallway?' he echoed in puzzlement, struggling to remember the details of the previous evening. It had begun normally enough. But now...

He looked around him. He was slumped on the floor in the hall, in front of the ballroom, still clad in his nightclothes. He stood up quickly, glancing around to make sure they were alone. 'Did anyone...?'

'See you? Dear God, I hope not. I am sure we will hear of it if they have. But you must consider yourself fortunate that I am an early riser and can help you out of this fix. What happened?'

'I am not sure. I must have roamed in my sleep. I had a very vivid dream.' And vivid it must have been. He could see the bruise on his hand where he had pinched himself. And feel a small knot on his skull where he had been rapped by the Cavalier's beribboned walking stick.

'Well, you look like the very devil. Grey as a paving stone and just as cold.'

Joseph turned behind him to the curtain that hung on the wall and swept it aside, to reveal a small alcove with a stone bench just large enough to hide a pair of lovers. Or a girl playing at hide-and-seek.

'I did not know of this before now,' he said numbly to his friend. 'But I dreamed it was here.'

Breton was staring at him as though he were as barmy as Bernard Lampett. 'If you wish to search the house for priests' holes, it might be best to continue when fully dressed.'

'Perhaps so.' He frowned. 'But I am surprised I had not noticed this before.'

His friend took him by the arm, tugging him towards the back stairs. 'That is little shock to me. It has nothing to do with the running of the mill. That is all you seem to care about lately.'

'Unfair,' Joseph charged. 'I care about many things. It is not as if I am made of clockwork, you know.' Who had told him he was?

They mounted the steps and Breton hurried him towards his room, his valet and his clothing. 'Sometimes I wonder. But, if you have them, tell me of these other interests. I defy you to name one.'

Now that he was pressed, Joseph could not seem to think of any. Unless he could count Lampett's fractious daughter as an interest. If the spirit of Sir Cedric had taught him anything, it was of his desire to see another of the smiles she had worn as a child.

In response to his silence Bob gave a snort of disgust. When he spoke, the amusement in his voice had been replaced with sincere annoyance. 'That was where you should have announced your excitement at your impending engagement. Have you forgotten that as well?'

'Of course I have not forgotten.' But he had responded too late to be believable.

'I might just as well have included it as part of your business. It is little more than that to you, isn't it?'

'Little more to her as well,' Joseph said, a little defensively. 'Her father wishes her back living in this house. This is the most efficient way to accomplish it.'

Breton pushed him towards his room. 'Once she is here, you will notice her as little as you do your own furnishings—or that hole in the wall you found so fascinating. And that is a pity. Anne is a lovely girl, and deserving of better.'

There was that prickling of his conscience again, and the echoing warning of his father to unravel his plans and start fresh. Perhaps that was what he'd meant. His other business plans were sensible enough. He hardly needed a wife to cement his place. But he could think of no honourable way to back out of the arrangement he had made with Clairemont.

'There is nothing to be done about it now,' Joseph said with exasperation. 'We are as good as promised to each other. Everyone knows I mean to make the announcement on Christmas Eve. I cannot cry off, even if I might like to. The scandal to the girl would be greater than any that might befall me.'

'Then the least you can do,' Breton said more softly, 'is to recognise that you have won a prize, and treat the girl as such. For if I find that you are neglecting her, or making her unhappy, I will be forced to act.'

Joseph looked at his friend as if for the first time. Bob, who had been ever loyal, friendly and trusting, was acting as strangely as though he had been receiving nightly revelations as well. He looked angry. It was disquieting.

'Very well, then,' Joseph answered, searching his friend's expression for some understandable reason for this change. 'I will take your words to heart. Although it will not be a love match, I will make sure that she does not suffer for my neglect.'

His friend sighed. 'I suppose it is as much as I can expect from you. But see that you remember your words.'

And mine as well.

The echo of a voice from the portrait gallery caused him to start nervously.

His friend gave him another suspicious look. 'Is there something wrong, Joe?'

'Nothing,' he said hurriedly. 'You are right. I have been working too hard. I have not slept well for two nights. And I am neglecting Anne. Today I will change. I promise. But for now I must dress. I will see you in the breakfast room shortly.' He backed hurriedly into his bedroom and shut the door before the conversation could grow any more awkward.

He would make a change—if only to avoid another night like the one he'd just had. Although, with the minimal direction his nightly ghosts had given him, God only knew what that change was supposed to be.

CHAPTER SIX

'WILL that be all, Miss Lampett?'

Barbara checked carefully through the list she'd set for herself to finish the Christmas shopping. A matching skein of wool to complete the warm socks she was knitting for Father, and the new fashion plates that her mother would enjoy, along with enough lace to make her a collar. 'I can think of nothing more.'

'Do you want this sent round to the house, Miss Lampett?' The girl behind the counter looked at her expectantly.

There was plenty of space left in her market basket on top of the groceries: three oranges, one for each of them, and a pound of wheat for her father's favourite frumenty. The roast she'd got from the butcher sat in the bottom of the basket, wrapped tightly in brown paper so that it would not spoil the rest. The poor bit of meat was leaner than she'd wished for. But then so was the butcher. What with the war, and the general poverty of the area, Christmas itself would be sparse for many people, and she had best be grateful that her family had the money to purchase a feast.

Barbara counted the remaining coins in her purse, calculating the pennies needed to reward the boy at the end of his journey. 'No, thank you. It is a fine day, and not far. I will carry this myself.'

The shop girl gave her a doubtful look and wrapped the package carefully, placing it on top of the others.

Barbara hefted the basket off the counter, feeling the weight shift. It was heavy now. In a mile it would be like lead on the end of her arm. Her muscles would ache with carrying it. But she smiled in gratitude, to show the girl that it was all right, and pulled it to her side, turning to go.

'Allow me, Miss Lampett.' Without warning, Joseph Stratford was there at her side, as suddenly as he had been two days past in front of the mill. He had a grip on the basket handle, and had pulled it from her without waiting for her to give him leave.

'That will not be necessary,' she said, trying not to sound breathless from the shock of the sudden contact. It was strange enough to see him in the village, shopping amongst the peasants in the middle of a work day. But it was doubly disconcerting to have him here, close to her again, after the intimacy of yesterday.

'Perhaps you do not think it necessary,' he agreed. 'But I would not be able to stand aside and watch you struggle with it. You had best take my assistance, for both our sakes.'

'I would prefer not.'

'But I would not be able to sleep, knowing I had left a lady to carry such a burden.' He smiled at her in a way that might have been charming had she not known so much of the source. 'I can hardly sleep as it is.'

The charm faded for a moment, and she saw shadows under his eyes that had not been there two days ago. Maybe her father was weakening him, after all. She reminded herself that he deserved any suffering he felt, and gave him a false smile in return. 'Heaven forefend that you are uneasy in your rest, sir.' She reached again for the basket, but he pulled it just out of reach.

'Come. You and your packages will have a ride home in my carriage.'

'It is a short distance,' she argued.

'The weather is turning. Come with me, and you will stay warm and dry.'

'My reputation…'

'Will be unharmed,' he finished, glancing at the people around him for confirmation. 'I mean you no mischief. I will take you directly home. It is on my way.' He looked around with a glare, cowing the shop girl and the other customers. 'No one will cast aspersions if I attempt to do you good. They can see plain enough that you are resisting, but I am giving no quarter. Come along, Miss Lampett.'

Then he and her basket were ahead of her, out of the

door and walking towards the large and entirely unnecessary carriage. She had no choice but to trail after.

As she passed, his groom jumped to attention, rushing to take the basket, get the stair down and hold the door as he helped her up. Across from her, Joseph Stratford leaned back into the seats as though he was ascending to a throne.

Then he smiled at her, satisfied. 'There. As you can see, you are perfectly safe, and still in clear view of those in the street. I am all the way over here—properly out of reach of you. There will be no such incident as there was the last time we were alone together.'

'I had no doubt of that, Mr Stratford. I would die first.'

He laughed at her for her primness. 'You are a most ungrateful chit, Miss Lampett. One kiss did you no permanent harm. And, if you will remember the altercation outside the mill two days past, you must admit I have shown concern for your welfare. If I was as awful as you pretend, I would have let the mob trample you.'

'You would not have.' He'd moved with such speed to get to her side that she was sure it had been all but involuntary.

He looked surprised. 'You give me credit for that much compassion, at least. Thank you for it.'

The silence that came after served to remind her just how unequal things had become, and just how unfair she was being to him—even if she did not particularly like the man. 'I deserve no thanks, Mr Stratford. I owe them to you. At least for that day. I am perfectly aware that if you did not save my life, you at least spared me serious injury.'

'You're welcome.' He seemed almost embarrassed that she had noticed the debt she owed.

'But now you are giving me a ride, when I told you I did not wish one. After yesterday…'

'Can you not accept this in the spirit with which it was given?' he asked with a smile. 'It is foul outside, but it appeared that you wished to forgo even the help of a delivery boy and struggle home by yourself. There was no reason for it.'

He looked at her sideways for a moment, and then out of the window, as though his next comment was of no consequence.

'Perhaps I remember what it was like to count pennies as though they were pounds, and do without the smallest luxuries.'

He had guessed her reason for walking? 'Then I also apologise for the comment I made in our last conversation, accusing you of being unsympathetic to those in need.'

He was frowning now, and hardly seemed to speak to her. 'You were right in part, at least. I had meant, when that time passed, to remember it better. I pledged to myself that I would be of aid to those who were impoverished, as I had been while growing up. It seems I have forgotten.'

'Do not think to make my family an object of pity to

salve your stinging conscience,' she snapped. 'If you wish to offer charity, there are others that need more of it.' Then she looked out of the window as well. She felt bad to have spoken thus, for it was very ungrateful of her. He seemed able to put her in the worst temper with the slightest comment. But then, he could arouse other emotions as well.

Her cheeks coloured as she thought again of the kiss. When she'd accepted this ride, had there been some small part of her that had hoped he would attempt to do it again? Was that what made her angry now? She was a fool if she thought that his offer had been anything other than common courtesy. She meant nothing to him. Nor did the kiss.

'It is hardly charity to offer another person a ride on a cold and rainy day,' he said gently. 'I'll wager you'd have accepted if the offer had come from Anne Clairemont or her mother.'

'That would not have been likely,' she said.

'Why not? You were friends with the Clairemont girls as a child, were you not?'

She turned and looked at him sharply. 'What gave you that idea?'

His gaze flicked away for a moment. 'You mentioned it as we were driving towards the house yesterday.'

'I said I'd had a friend there. But you said "girls" just now. I did not mention Mary.'

'Perhaps Anne did,' he said, still not looking at her. 'Mary was her sister, then?'

The idea that Anne might have mentioned her seemed highly unlikely. Something about the calculated way he spoke made her suspect he fished for information and was piecing the truth together with each slip Barbara made. 'Mary has been dead for quite some time,' she said, praying that would be the end of the conversation.

'What happened to her?'

'There was nothing mysterious about her death. She took ill, faded and died. If you wish to know more you had best ask your fiancée, Miss Clairemont.'

'I have not offered as of yet.'

'But you will. The whole village knows that the festivities you have organised are meant to celebrate your engagement to her.'

'Do they, now?' His voice had dropped briefly, as though he was talking to himself. 'I did not know that the world was sure of plans that I myself have not spoken.'

Were they not true? Anne seemed sure enough of them, as was her father. But Stratford's response gave Barbara reason to fear for them. It would be most embarrassing should they have misunderstood this man's intent so completely and allowed themselves to be used to further his business. 'I am sorry. Perhaps I was mistaken.'

'Perhaps you were.' He was looking at her rather intently now, as though trying to divine her opinion on the subject.

She reminded herself that she had none. Perhaps she

was a little relieved that he was not riding with her or kissing her while planning to marry Anne. She had no wish to hurt that family again by seeming too interested in Mr Stratford. Nor did she want to do anything that might encourage him to become interested in her if he was otherwise engaged.

But his eyes, when seen this close, were the stormy shade of grey that presaged a violent change in the weather. The slight stubble on his chin only emphasised the squareness of his jaw. Now that she had noticed it she found it hard to look away.

He broke the gaze. 'Then again, perhaps you were not mistaken about my engagement. I have not yet made a decision regarding my future, or that of Miss Anne Clairemont.'

She looked down at her feet, embarrassed for having thought anything at all other than cursory gratitude that she was not walking in the rain. 'Either way, it is rude of you to discuss it with me. And, I might add, it does not concern me whatever you do. You might marry whoever you like and it will not matter to me in the slightest.'

'It is good to know that. Not that I planned to seek your approval.' This was more playful than censorious, and delivered with a strangely seductive smile, as if to say it was in his power to make it matter, should he so choose. 'But why do you say that the Clairemonts would not offer you a ride if you needed one? They seem like nice enough people, from what I know of them.'

Perhaps enough time had passed that they were better. Barbara was not sure of the mood in the Clairemont household. But she would rather cut her tongue out than ask Anne, for fear the answer she might receive would open old hurts afresh. She gave a firm smile. 'It is an old family quarrel, and nothing of importance. I would not seek to bother them if I did not have to.'

'But I would like to hear of it, all the same.'

'You will not hear it from me,' she said, shifting uncomfortably in her seat. 'You are new to Fiddleton, Mr Stratford, and might not know the ways of small villages. When one lives one's life with the same people from birth, it sometimes happens that one makes a mistake that cannot be corrected and that will follow one almost to the grave.'

'Are you speaking of the Clairemonts, then? What mistakes could you have made to render you less than perfect in the eyes of this village? From where I sit, I see a most charming young woman—and well mannered.' He smiled. 'Although not always so to me.'

'You do not always deserve it, sir.'

'True enough,' he agreed. 'But you are kind to others, modest, clearly devoted to your family. And beautiful as well.'

'Though too old to be still unmarried,' she finished for him, sure he must be thinking it. 'The verdict has already been rendered as to my worth in that regard. I have learned to accept it.'

'Then we are of a kind,' he said. 'Although I am the

worse of the two of us. I have just got here, and I have made myself universally hated. But I do not let it bother me. I do not care a whit for the opinions of the locals. I am who I am, and they had best get used to it.' He looked her up and down again. 'If they think less of you, for some foolish reason or other, I cannot give their views much credence.'

Between the kiss they had shared and the look he gave her now, she suspected he had got quite the wrong idea about it all. He was hoping that there had been a man involved in her downfall. But their trip was almost over, and he had offered no further insult, so it was hardly worth correcting him. As long as they were not alone again he would give her no trouble.

But his disregard for his own reputation bothered her. 'Perhaps you *should* care what people think. There are worse things than social ostracism, you know. Mill owners have been accosted in their own homes and on their ways to and from the factories they own.'

'That is why I carry this,' he said, patting the bulge in his pocket and reaching in to draw out the handle of a pistol.

'Are you really going to use it?'

'Do you doubt my bravery?'

'I do not doubt your foolhardiness,' she said. 'It has but one bullet in it. If there is trouble, there will likely be a gang behind it.'

'Then I will be forced to appeal to the garrison for aid, and it will not go well with them,' he said, as though that settled the matter. 'I do not seek violence, Miss Lampett. But if I feel myself threatened I will resort to it. You need have no doubt of that.'

She imagined the possible consequences with a sinking heart. 'Since the violence you describe is likely to be turned against my father, I believe we have nothing more to say to each other. It is fortunate that we have arrived at my home.'

Stratford glanced out of the window. 'So we have.' He turned and tapped on the door to signal the driver. 'Another turn around the high street, Benjamin. The lady and I are not finished with our discussion.'

'And I have just said we are.' She reached for the door handle, only to fall back into her seat as she felt the carriage turning. 'This is most high-handed of you, Mr Stratford.'

'But, knowing me as you do, you must expect nothing less of me, Miss Lampett.' He smiled again, as though they were doing nothing more serious than dancing around a ballroom. 'The subject we discuss is a serious one. I think I may have found an agreeable solution to several dilemmas at once. But it requires your cooperation, and the chance for us to speak privately for a little while longer—as we are doing now.'

Which explained the ride, she supposed. She should be relieved that he had not sought her out of any deeper desire for her company. But, strangely, she was not. 'Very well, then. Speak.'

'As you say, in a small village news travels fast. You

say that you know of my plans for the Christmas holidays?'

'You are entertaining guests from London. The only people of the village who will be in attendance are the Clairemonts. If it is not an engagement, then I suspect the gathering has something to do with the opening of the mill.'

'Why would you think that?' he asked, surprised.

'Because you are the host of it. Having met you, Mr Stratford, it seems unlikely that the people coming are old friends.'

'Ha!' Rather than being angered by her insult, he seemed amused by it.

She continued. 'Everything you do has to do with your business in some way or other. This Christmas party is like to be the same.' Then she allowed her true feeling of distaste to show. 'It is vulgar in the extreme to use the Lord's birth as a time for doing business, if that is what you mean to do.'

'Whether you have reached your conclusion from local gossip or shrewd deduction, you are correct, Miss Lampett. I am entertaining investors from London.' He gave a slight frown. 'Because, apparently, I think of nothing but business.' He paused for a moment, as though he had forgotten what it was he meant to say. 'I do not have quite so many guests as I had hoped. There were more negative replies in today's post.'

'Probably from gentlemen who understand the impropriety of it,' she said.

He shrugged. 'Or perhaps they do not wish to associate with one who is in trade, even though he offers them the opportunity to do it far from the prying eyes of the *ton*. It does not matter, really. As you have pointed out, they are not my friends. But I need only one—perhaps two—to come, agree and invest. Then, for me, this Christmas will be a happy one.'

It appeared that her father was right about the man, if that was how he measured his happiness. 'There would be far more joy for all should you choose to spend that time in meeting your neighbours, sir. If you could not manage that, then perhaps you could release the Clairemonts from their obligation to attend? For I suspect it will pain them greatly to see their home treated as the London Exchange.'

'It is no longer their home, Miss Lampett. It is mine to do with as I please.'

'But I do not see why you wish to tell me of it. It is no business of mine,' she said, almost leaning out of the window in an effort to put space between them.

'On the contrary. I mean to make it your business. I understand that there has traditionally been a gathering of villagers at the house for Christmas. You have been in attendance at it, with Miss Anne Clairemont and her sister.'

'But that was years ago,' she admitted. 'Not since…' Not since Mary died and the Clairemonts shut up the house at Christmas. But the circumstances were no business of Stratford's.

'You and your family will honour me with your attendance this year as well,' he said. 'I am short of ladies, and there are likely to be several young bucks who would prefer an eligible young partner to dancing with their sisters.'

'On our limited acquaintance, you expect me to sit in attendance on your guests? That is rude beyond measure, sir.'

'Nothing of the kind. I invite you to be one of my guests. There would be no obligation to dance if you did not wish to do so. Though should you meet someone and form an attachment to him it would solve the question of your unmarried state quite nicely. Between your father's trouble, and the problem you have hinted at with local society, it must be difficult for you to be so removed from the company of equals.'

It was. Though she tried to control it, a wistful longing arose in her at the prospect of a chance to put on her nicest gown and dance. 'I do not need your help in that situation,' she said primly. 'I am quite fine on my own.'

'So you keep telling me. But I need *your* help, Miss Lampett,' he said, his hands open before him. 'My business negotiations, whether they are improper or no, are at a delicate juncture. I dare not risk your father giving another angry speech while the investors are here to see it. Nor do I wish to call the law down on him with Christmas dinner.'

'Then I think you would want us quiet at home for the holiday, and not dancing at the manor.'

'On the contrary. I have seen your father's interactions with you. When he is concerned about your welfare, all thoughts of violence go quite out of his head. If you told him that you wished to come to my party he would not disrupt it for fear of spoiling your enjoyment.'

'Even so, I would not trust him for any length of time in the company of strangers.'

'Then I shall send him a selection of books from the library. Old favourites of mine that are sure to occupy his mind for the duration of the week.'

'Old favourites of yours?' she said in surprise. 'You gave me to understand that you had no time for books.'

'Not now, perhaps. But I'd read most of the volumes in the Clairemont library long before my arrival here. In the coming year, when the mill is employed, I hope to have some evenings to myself and might read them again.'

'You said you were a weaver's son,' she said, thinking of her father's recalcitrant students and wondering if she had misunderstood him.

'I did not say I was clever at the trade. I was a horrible weaver, and no amount of teaching could make me better. I was more interested in books than the loom. When Father did allow me to go to school I taught myself, in whatever way I could manage.' He smiled bitterly. 'I fear I was a grave disappointment to him.'

'But why did you remain involved in the trade? Surely there might have been another occupation more suited to your tastes?'

'The life I wanted was forever closed to me, for I was not born a gentleman, Miss Lampett. It appeared that, no matter my lack of skill, I was destined to weave. So I redesigned the loom to make it easier for my clumsy fingers to manage. The machines to be used at the factory are of my own invention.'

Somehow she had imagined him purchasing the frames he used with little knowledge of their workings. But there was real passion in him as he talked of cold and unfeeling machines, and an energy that drew her in like a lodestone. It was only with effort that she noticed the fact that there was no mention of anyone other than himself.

'Is that why the talk of frame-breaking bothers you so? It must be difficult to see your work destroyed.'

He shrugged. 'Not really. Before coming here, my business was mostly in the supplying of other mills. When their looms were damaged by vandals, I made additional money in the repair and replacing of their machinery. While the production of cloth is a risky business, there can be no surer trade right now than the making of a thing that is useful, and very much in demand, but needs to be purchased multiple times when it is ruined. That business was the source of my wealth. Though your father and his friends might seek to see the end of me, like men have been my making.'

'You view the misfortune of others as the source of your success?' she said, amazed at how far removed he was from the people around him.

'So it has been. But enough of me and my business. Tell me what your response to my offer is likely to be.'

'It would be most improper for a single lady to accept an invitation from a gentleman if there is no understanding between them,' she said, wondering what he could be thinking to ask her in this way.

'Of *course.*' He pounded his fist against his leg once, in irritation. Then he gathered himself a little straighter. 'Please accept my apologies. It was forward of me. I will extend a formal invitation, in writing, for your whole family to join in whatever activities take place. There will be nothing to upset your father, I assure you. There will be dinners, dancing, games. I expect that it will be a very jolly time. If your parents do not wish to come, you must come alone—in the company of Miss Anne Clairemont and her family.' He gave her a firm look. 'There will be no trouble on that front. The doors of my house are open to you.'

There was a faint emphasis on the word 'my' to remind her that things had changed. She wondered if he would put the situation to the Clairemonts in the same blunt tone. It almost made her pity them.

But, no matter what he did, it would not be as it had once been. The merriment would not touch the community that it bordered. 'No, thank you,' she said. 'It hardly seems appropriate to celebrate when so many people are unhappy.' They had reached the gate of the cottage again, and she looked longingly in the direction of her home.

'How very pious of you.' He had noticed their destination as well, and tapped to signal the driver. 'It is a lovely day. Let us make another pass of the high street, shall we?'

'Do you mean to hold me prisoner in this carriage until I agree to your scheme?'

He held his hands up in a symbolic gesture of release. 'The thought had occurred to me. But I will let you go home to consider this and see if you do not think it a temporary respite from our troubles. Either way, the mill will open in January. Change is coming and there will be no avoiding it. Once it is open, and at least some of the locals are employed in it, we will find them less likely to raise a hand against me. Until then we must find together a way to stall your father from upsetting my plans—or I will take steps that are pleasant to neither of us.'

The carriage drew smoothly to a stop, and when the door opened he went before her, offering his hand to help her to the ground. Then he signalled for a footman to carry her basket to the house and returned to his seat, closing the shiny black door behind him.

CHAPTER SEVEN

WHEN she was through the door of the cottage she saw her father waiting in the front room, arms folded across his chest. Today she did not fear him so much as dread the weight of his displeasure.

'Well?' There was so much disappointment in the one word that Barbara glanced behind her, out of the open door and down the road, thinking that the burden of carrying the weight of her loaded basket could not possibly have equalled this.

She turned back, squared her shoulders and explained. 'Mr Stratford offered me a ride from the shops because the weather was changing.' She gave a little shake of her cloak to show the patter of icy drops that had hit her in the short walk from the carriage to the house. 'He was quite insistent. It seemed that I was likely to create more of a scene by refusing than accepting. So I relented.'

'There was time enough for someone to come from the village and inform me of the fact and be gone again,' her father said suspiciously. 'One would think that a man on foot could not best a team of horses in traversing the distance.'

She cleared her throat. 'Mr Stratford was deep in conversation with me as we neared the house. To continue it, he turned the carriage and we travelled once more around the village.'

'Thus it became a social drive.' Her father shook his head. 'That is a demonstration of the perfidy of the man. It is much like the mill—offered as an olive branch to the people of this community, only so he can snatch it away as they draw near. He took you, just as he took their jobs, and he dangles you like a bauble, just out of reach, and plays with you at his leisure.'

'Hardly, Father. We talked for but a few moments. The carriage remained on the high street and I sat in the window of it. I am sure that many in the community could see me and know that nothing untoward was happening.'

The argument seemed to have no effect on him, for he went on with increasing anger. 'The man is the very devil, Barb. I swear. The *devil.* He is here to ruin the village and all the people in it with his new ideas and his cheap goods. Nothing can come of cheapening the quality of the work, I am sure. It is the veritable road to hell.'

'And nothing to do with the matter at hand,' her

mother added firmly from behind him. She looked past him at her daughter. 'You say that you were seen the whole time? The carriage took no side trips, nor left the sight of the high street?'

'Not at all, Mama.'

'You could not have waited until the rain had passed? Or hurried home before it?'

'I did not want to spare the penny for the boy if I did not have to. The basket was heavy. And Mr Stratford would not take no for an answer.'

Her mother nodded. 'The offer of transport was fortuitous, even if there was an ulterior motive. What did you speak of?'

'His business.' And Mary, of course. They had spoken of her. But it was hardly worth mentioning.

'Then it had nothing to do with you?'

'Just as I suspected. It was an effort to turn you against me, and the village against us. The man is the devil,' her father insisted.

'Enough!' her mother snapped, ignoring her husband again and turning back to Barbara. 'We must deal with the more important matter first. And that should be the honour of our only child, which has not been harmed in the least by the trip, whether it was social or practical.'

'He invited us to the manor for Christmas,' Barbara added. 'He suggested that there might be gentlemen there, and dancing.' She tried to sound matter-of-fact about it, as though it did not matter one way or the other. She did not particularly wish to meet gentlemen.

There was one in particular that she might like to know better, but her father was probably right to call him a persuasive devil who was best avoided.

Still, it had been a long time since she'd danced—with or without demons. Would it really do any harm?

'Dancing at the manor? Of course you should go, then.' Her father's sudden change caught them unawares, as it often did. Though he had been angry only a few moments before, now he was smiling at her. 'You have not been since last Christmas, and you always enjoy it so. Visiting Anne and Mary will do you a world of good.'

She shot a worried glance over his shoulder to her mother, and then said, 'Father, Mary is dead. The Clairemonts no longer live at the manor. There has not been a Christmas celebration there in six years.'

'I know that,' he said quickly, embarrassed at his lapse. 'I only meant that you would be better off dancing at the manor than driving on the high street with Lucifer in a silk waistcoat.' He darkened again, as suddenly as he had brightened. 'A silk waistcoat made by hands that slaved for pennies so that he might ride high and mighty like a prince.' His eyes lit at the sound of his own words. 'I must write this down. It will be the basis of my next speech.'

'You do that, Father.' Barbara hurried to the little desk in the corner, setting out paper, uncapping the ink and trimming the nib of the pen. Then she pulled out his chair and took time to settle him there. It seemed to give him comfort, for he sat down and began writing industriously, staring out of the window before him into the sleet-streaked sky as though the next words were written on it and he could pluck them from the air.

'Come into the kitchen, Barbara. Let us see what you have brought back from the market.' Her mother turned quickly, but not before Barbara could see the trembling of her lip that was the beginning of tears.

'A moment, Mama.' She hurried to the sewing basket, to conceal her mother's Christmas gift. Then she followed her out of the room.

By the time she had reached her in the kitchen her mother was more composed, though clearly worried.

'What are we to do, Mama?' she whispered. 'He is like this more and more.'

'There is little for us *to* do. There is no changing him.' Her mother gave a brief, bitter laugh. 'He changes often enough on his own. Like the tides, he goes to extremes at both ends.'

If he continued thus there would be no chance of him returning to employment, and they would end their days living off the dwindling inheritance her mother had received from her own family. Barbara thought of the pennies in her purse again, and gave quiet thanks to Mr Stratford. Even if he was the devil, he had saved her the bother of a wet walk.

Her mother seemed to be thinking of him as well. 'Tell me about this Christmas invitation you have received. It does seem to be a lone bright spot in the day.'

'I told him it was improper,' Barbara said, frowning. 'For I did not think Father would approve.'

'Your father is lucky to remember from one minute to the next why he hates the man. We will tell him that you are gone to see Mary. For if there are gentlemen there, as he said…' Her mother was thinking forward, hoping for a bright future in which a wealthy stranger would appear with an offer and solve all their problems.

'But I refused,' Barbara said, dashing her hopes.

'Oh,' said her mother, properly disappointed.

'He offered again—including the family. When I told him that there was no way Father could manage such a gathering, he offered a selection of books as Christmas gifts—to keep him home and quiet over the holiday. He said he would send something written, so that I would know he spoke with sincerity.'

'A written invitation to the manor?' Her mother positively glowed with the prospect.

'I doubt he will remember,' Barbara said hurriedly. 'I am sure it was said only in passing, to make conversation. It was just an effort to be social.'

'A most curious effort, then.' Her mother was looking closely at her, trying to determine what she might be concealing. 'He has made no attempts at civility to the rest of the village. And yet he singles you out. A gentleman would know better than to make promises he cannot keep—especially when he is courting another.'

'One can hardly call him a gentleman, Mother. He is in trade. He admitted to me that he was a weaver's son.'

'Really?' Her mother's eyebrows arched. 'You speak like your father, my dear. It is idealistic to set men of business firmly below us and to act as though birth is all. Perhaps realism would be a better path, considering our circumstances. It is possible to be a gentleman and poor as a church mouse, while the weaver's son dines and dances in a manor. The world is changing. While we might not approve of all the changes, we must make the best of them. Let us hope that Mr Stratford is as good as his word.'

And his offer proved true. A short time later, while her father still pondered his latest diatribe, there was a knock on the door. Outside, the same coach that had deposited her waited for the liveried servant who held a properly sealed and decorated invitation and a package of books.

Before her father could say otherwise, her mother had snatched it from the poor man's hand and instructed him to wait upon the response. Then she pushed her husband's work aside and reached for paper and pen.

'As usual, Satan sends his handmaidens in fine garments to tempt the unwary,' her father barked.

The footman looked rather alarmed and peered behind him, unaware that he was the handmaiden in question.

'Nonsense, dear. It is an invitation to the manor. Nothing more. It can do us no harm to accept, surely?'

'Well, then.' Her father beamed. Then he waved a hand at the man who waited. 'My regards to Lord

Clairemont, his wife and his daughters. Tell them to be wary, just as they are merry.' Then he opened the first of the books and immediately forgot the source of his discomfiture.

The man gave a hesitant nod, and waited upon the hurriedly scribbled response from her mother before returning to the carriage.

Mother and daughter returned to the kitchen.

'You cannot mean for us to go, Mama,' Barbara whispered. 'Look at Father. There is no way for us to keep the pretence that it will be as it was. And no way to predict, once he is there, what he will say in front of Mr Stratford and his guests. It would be better if we refused politely and stayed home.'

'It would be better if your father and I stayed away. But there is no reason why you cannot go,' her mother said firmly. 'While I like dinner and a ball as well as the next person, I am content to sit here with your father and allow you to get the benefit of an invitation. He said there might be gentlemen?'

'Friends from London.'

'Stratford means to marry Anne. She and her parents will be there to recommend and chaperone you. I am sure, if you wrote to her, she would offer you a space in their carriage so that you needn't walk to the manor.'

'That was what Mr Stratford suggested as well. He said he would speak to them. But I do not think they would like it very much. Perhaps there is another way.' Although Barbara could think of none.

'I will not let you walk to the manor in dancing slippers. Nor will I allow you to refuse this invitation,' her mother said, giving her a stern look. 'I will write to the Clairemonts about it. I will choose my words with care. Perhaps, after six years, you should not blame yourself for something that was no fault of your own, and they should find it in their hearts to forgive you.'

It was not nearly enough time, Barbara was sure. It had been just this morning that she'd met Lady Clairemont walking down the street and seen the way the lady looked sharply in her direction, and then through her. 'Please, Mother, do not.'

'There is no other way. This is an opportunity that you dare not turn down. If there were other suitable men anywhere in the area I might think twice. But if there is a chance of a match amongst Mr Stratford's guests we must seek it out for you. One of your old gowns will have to do. But we can trim it up with the lace you bought this morning and I am sure it will look quite nice.'

'Mother!' Despite her best efforts, her mother had seen into the shopping basket. 'That was intended as a gift.'

'For someone who has less need of it than you,' her mother said, laying a hand on hers, 'it would do my heart good to know that you are out in society again—even if it is only for a day or two. I will write the letters, and then we will see what can be done with the gown. You must go where you are invited, Barbara, and dance as though your future depended on it. For it very well might.'

CHAPTER EIGHT

JOSEPH went to his bed that night in the knowledge that his rest would be well and truly settled. He had managed his guests—impressing the men with his plans for the mill, and charming the ladies without appearing ill-mannered or common. He had skated Miss Anne Clairemont twice around the millpond without falling or precipitating a fall in her. Then he had gone into the village, located Miss Lampett and presented his proposition.

If the ghost, or whatever it had been, had meant to upbraid him on the fate of that poor girl, he had done his best to return her to the society to which she was accustomed. Although why her fate should fall to him, he had no idea.

Perhaps it was because he was the one with the most power to change it. When his future mother-in-law had protested that she would not be seen in the company of 'that girl', he had explained tersely that it would be so because he wished it so, and that was that.

He wondered for a moment what Barbara had done to deserve such frigid and permanent rejection, but concluded it was nothing more than the usual fall from grace involving some young man—possibly a suitor of Anne or the departed Mary. If that was the case Miss Lampett had well and truly atoned for it, after years of modest dress and behaviour.

And more was the pity for it. If the kiss they'd shared had been any indication of her capability for passion, he'd have liked her better had she *not* found her way back to the straight and narrow. He smiled, imagining a more wanton Barbara, and the sort of fun he might have had with her.

The clock in the hall struck two.

'Leave off having impure thoughts about the poor girl, for your work is far from finished.'

Joseph sat bolt upright in bed at the sound of another unfamiliar voice, booming in the confines of the chamber. He had not even risked wine with supper, and had shocked his valet with a request for warm milk before bed. But now he wondered if perhaps it might have been better to forgo the milk and return to a double brandy in an effort to gain a sound and dreamless sleep. 'Who might you be, and what makes you think you can read the contents of my mind?'

'You are young enough, and healthy enough, and smiling at bedtime. If you are not thinking of a young lady then I do not wish to know what it is you *do* think on.'

This night's ghost wore a scarlet coat of a modern cut trimmed in gold braid. His buff trousers pulled tight across his ample belly as he laughed at his own joke. The brass of his buttons was gleaming as bright as the gold leaf upon the coach he must drive. But tonight it seemed to be even brighter than was natural, as was the coachguard's horn he carried in his right hand as further indication of his job.

'As to who I am, you may call me Old Tom, and know that I departed this life just a year ago, along the Great North Road. You would not have had to ask my name had you lived any great time in this country. All know me here. At least those who are not so high and mighty as to have no need of public conveyance.'

Joseph snorted. 'Although I have no real memory of you, I've heard of you—driving drunk and taking your passengers with you to the next life when you upset the coach. I must be running out of ideas. I am reduced to populating my own dreams with little scraps of facts that do not even concern me.'

The driver laughed again. 'You give yourself far too much credit, Joseph Stratford. Even if you think yourself clever with machines, you are rather a dull sort for all that, and not given to colourful imaginings.'

'Dull, indeed.' Joseph rather hoped the ghost was real. If it was not, it was proof that his own imagination was prone to self-loathing and insult. 'If I refuse to believe in spirits it is a sign of a rational mind, not a slow one. For ghosts do not exist.'

'If you do not believe in ghosts, then why are you sleeping in your clothing?' asked the shade, drawing back the bedclothes to reveal Joseph still in shirt, trousers and boots.

'Because I woke this morning near naked in a downstairs hallway. Ghost or not, the situation will not be repeated.'

'Very well, then. You are not dull. More like you are so sharp you'll cut yourself. You are willing to believe anything, no matter how unlikely, so that you don't have to accept what is right before your eyes.' Old Tom glared. 'For your information, I was not drunk on the night I crashed. I did sometimes partake, when a glass was offered. Who would not, with the night air being chill and damp? But that night I was sober as a judge and hurrying to make up time. A biddy at the Cock and Bull had dawdled over her supper and left us to run late.' He leaned closer and added in a conspiratorial tone, 'And she will not leave off nagging and lamenting about the time, even now on the other side. Some people never learn, as you well know.'

The ghost looked him up and down and laid a finger to the side of his nose, as though Joseph should learn something from the comment. Then he went on. 'I was late, and pushing the horses to their limit, when a rabbit darted out from the hedge and right under 'em. It spooked the leader and he got away from me. Just for a moment. And that was that.'

Joseph swung his feet out of bed and sat up to face the ghost. 'An interesting tale, certainly. But there is no way to prove it, and nor am I likely to try.'

'You would not believe it even if you found the truth,' Old Tom replied in disgust. 'You are cold as ice, Joseph Stratford, and just as solidly set. I gave you too much credit when I arrived. It is just as likely I found you warming your thoughts not with some beautiful lady but with fantasies of machinery and ledger books.'

'So I have been told,' Joseph said with bitterness. 'Yet I have spent a portion of this day seeing to the wants of others, with no chance of personal gain likely to come of it.'

'No gain at all?'

He remembered the way he had phrased his offer to Barbara, as an effort to keep her father safely at home. 'Very little gain. The majority of the good done will benefit others. After last night's visitor, I made a change in my plans and invited Miss Barbara Lampett back to the manor house. There is my proof that I have learned something and rendered tonight's lesson unnecessary. I am making an effort to help the daughter of my enemy.' He gave a wave of his hand. 'And so you may depart.'

'Well, thank you, Yer Lordship,' the ghost said with a sarcastic bob of his head. 'But for your information it is I who will set the time of my departure, and not you. Before I can complete my final journey I have been called back for one task alone to make up for the carelessness of my end. I mean to do the job properly. When I leave here you will be well and rightly schooled.'

The ghost shuddered for a moment, as though uncomfortable in his surroundings. 'I'd have thought that if called to haunt I could have taken to the road, just as I did in life. Instead they sent me to *this* dreary place, colder than a moor in December.'

Again Joseph was annoyed that his spiritual visitor seemed less than satisfied with surroundings it had taken him half a lifetime to afford. 'This is the finest house in twenty miles, as you should know. The fire is lit, as are the candles. There is tea on the hob and brandy in the flask. Or perhaps you would like a shawl, like an old woman?'

Tom snorted. 'As if I could take pleasure in such, here on the other side. I am quite beyond feelings such as that.' He shuddered again. 'But I can see things you cannot. There is a cold coming off you like mist from a bog.'

He raised a finger to point at Joseph. In an instant the friendly driver was gone, and before him Joseph saw only a tormented spirit with a dire warning.

Then Tom smiled. 'But I have been set to warm you up a bit. A hopeless task that is like to be. Now, come on. We haven't got all night.' The ghost reached out a hand. 'Tonight you will walk with me, and if you are lucky you will learn to see the world as others do. At the least you will see what you are missing when you cannot take your nose from the account books and your feet from the factory floor. You will learn what people think of you. It should do you a world of good. Now, take my hand.'

Joseph's mind warred with itself, but the battle was shorter than it had been on the previous two nights. Whether real or imagined, Tom would not leave until he was ready to. And Joseph did not like being afraid of men—in this world or the next. So he reached out and grabbed the hand that was offered to him.

To touch it was even worse than touching Sir Cedric the previous night. Old Tom's hand was large and doughy, and thick with calluses from handling the reins. But it was freezing cold—like iron lying on the ground in December. The instant Joseph touched it his own fingers went as numb as if they'd died on his hand. And this, more than anything else, made him believe. His father might have been a memory, and Sir Cedric a walking dream. But in his wildest imaginings, he'd have conjured nothing like the feel of this.

He withdrew quickly, and after a stern look from the ghost adjusted his grip to take the spectre by the coat-sleeve instead. That was cold as well, but not unbearably so.

'The first stop is not far,' the ghost assured him, as though aware of his discomfort. 'Just beneath you, as a matter of fact.' Then they seemed to sink through the floorboards until they stood in the first parlour.

Though he'd thought that she had gone home with her

parents, he found Anne sitting in a chair by the fire and weeping as though her heart would break.

'There, there,' he said awkwardly, reaching out a hand to comfort her.

'Have you not yet learned what a pointless gesture that would be?' Old Tom asked. 'While you are with me she will not notice you.'

'Perhaps she will.' Joseph reached out to pat her shoulder, only to feel his hand pass through her as though she was smoke. He looked helplessly at the ghost. 'Last night, it was not always so,' Joseph argued, remembering the young Barbara.

'And tonight it is,' Old Tom said.

Behind them, the door opened. Though he needn't have bothered, Joseph stepped to the side to allow a man to enter the room.

Robert Breton glanced into the hall, as though eager to know that he was not observed, and then shut the door behind him and went quickly to the seated woman and took her hand.

'Bob?' Joseph knew then that he must indeed be invisible, for never had he seen such a look on his friend's face—nor was he likely to. The gaze he favoured Anne with was more than one of sympathy to her plight. It had tenderness, frustration and—dared he think it?—love.

On seeing him there, Anne let her tears burst fresh, like a sudden shower, and her shoulders shook with the effort of silence.

'Tell him,' Breton said. 'I have confronted him on the subject. He will not break off at this late date for your sake. He fears for your reputation even more than you do. If you do not end it for yourself, it is quite hopeless. I will not speak if you say nothing, no matter how much I might wish to. I have said more than enough already. You must be the strong one, Anne.'

'And I never was,' she answered, not looking up. 'Perhaps if Mary was here...'

'Then the lot would have fallen to her. Or it might never have occurred at all. But it does not matter,' Breton said firmly. 'She is dead and gone, much as no one wishes to acknowledge the fact. You cannot rely on her for help. You must be the one to speak, Anne.'

'Speak what? And to whom? To your father? To me?' Joseph took his place on her other side, as though he could make himself heard to the woman through proximity. But she said no more and, realising the futility of it, he looked up at the ghost. 'What do you want? I will give it to you, if I can. I am not totally without a heart, you know.'

'I think you can guess what she wants,' the ghost said. 'And why she does nothing about it.'

'It is not as if I am forcing the union on her. She agreed to it. And what does Bob have to do with any of it?'

'Not a thing, I expect, if it all goes according to your plan. He is a gentleman, is he not?'

'But he is a man first,' Joseph said. 'If he wants the girl for himself, then why does he not say something?'

The coachman laughed in response. 'You make it all sound quite simple. I envy you, living in a world as you do—where there are no doubts and everyone speaks their mind. The woman he loves has chosen another. He has been bested by a richer man. He will step out of the way like a gentleman.'

'But not before warning me to care for her,' Joseph said glumly. Their conversation in the hall that morning made more sense to him now. 'I cannot cry off now that there is an understanding. Unless she finds the courage to speak, we must all make the best of it.' But now that he knew the mind of his would-be fiancée it would be dashed hard to pretend a respect where none existed.

'Is this all, then?' he asked of the ghost.

The ghost smiled in a way that was hard and quite out of character with his jolly demeanour. 'Did you think it was likely to be? Your sins, when added together, total more than just heartlessness to this poor, foolish girl.'

'If you mean to brand me sinner, show me the proof of it so that I may go back to my bed. Take me away from here, for I have seen all you intended me to in this place.' He did not wish to follow the ghostly coachman, and this might still be little more than an unsettling dream, but the sight of his friend and Anne together felt like a violation. If he could not find a way to change things, then the least he could do was allow the two who were suffering a moment's privacy.

'Very well.'

Old Tom stepped forwards, and Joseph along with him. There was a rushing of wind, and in the time it took for his foot to fall he was stepping into another room, in another house. This place reminded him of his visit to his childhood home the previous night, though it was not so grim. It was sparsely furnished, and bare of ornament, but the kitchen where they stood was kept with the sort of earnest tidiness he expected of a home with a living wife and mother. A woman was busy at the hob. Her husband sat at the table, shoulders slumped and head bowed as though in prayer.

'Who might this be?' Joseph asked, for though the man's face was familiar he could not attach a name to it.

'If you had bothered to speak to him, or any other in this community, you would know him already.'

'I know that he was waving a sledgehammer at me when last I saw him, just two days ago,' Joseph said testily. 'It did not put me in the mood for gaining a proper introduction.'

'His name is Jonas Jordan,' replied Old Tom, ignoring his retort. 'He is the most skilled worker in the area, and might be your foreman should you and your mill survive long enough to hire him. And this is his family, preparing for the Christmas you and your kind have made for him.'

The man had not moved from his place, though his wife now gathered the children for their meal, overseeing the washing of hands and the setting of places. There were five of them. The youngest was a babe that was likely still at breast, and the oldest was too young to work.

In this little house, on a narrow side road just off the high street, there were none of the smells he had come to associate with the season—neither burning Yule Log nor sizzling fat and fresh bread. The fire in the grate burned low with the meagre handful of coal that made it, so that the cold crept out into the corners of the room, and the children, who should have been boisterous, huddled together as though they had little energy to do else.

'Mama,' said the second youngest, 'I am hungry.'

Without a word, the woman brought out bowls and set them around the table. The children gathered to take their places. Then she ladled some thin porridge from the pot that sat by the fire, and reached for the jug that sat upon the table. She poured out water rather than milk. The children took it in silence and she looked on, worried. When she reached to set a bowl before her husband he pushed it away, without a sound, until it sat before her.

She watched, her own supper untouched, as the children finished what they had. Then she shared the contents of the last bowl between them. She sat hungry, as did her man.

'It would be more nourishing for the children to have a bowl with a good dollop of cream in it,' Joseph said stupidly, knowing that there would be none of that in this house.

'Perhaps if the lord of the manor had not sold off the herd that once grazed where the new mill stands they might have. It has been the nature, these many years, of the Clairemonts to keep the dairy and to graze the herd. All those who wished might come with jugs and buckets to take their share. But now they must send for milk from the next village. It is one more thing, along with all the rest, that this family cannot afford.'

'So they are starving?' Joseph said, doing his best to harden his heart. 'They were just so before I arrived. It might well be because this very man stood up against the last master and burned his place to the ground.'

'When men are pushed to the edge of reason by circumstances they act without thinking!' The ghost shouted the words at him, as though even a spirit could be pushed beyond endurance. 'Jordan and his family were hungry before. But they ate. He stayed at home with his babes the night the old mill burned. What has happened was no fault of his.'

'Then when the new mill opens he shall have work,' Joseph promised. 'If that is the only reason you visit me, you have no reason to fear. I am bringing employment to the area.'

'For some,' the coachman said.

'For as many as I need,' Joseph answered him. 'If it means so much to them, I will enquire with Clairemont about the dispersal of the herd and decide what can be done to reopen the dairy on different ground. It was never my intention to cut people out of their places or make their children suffer.'

'But neither did you make enquiries into their needs when you came here. I am sure if I asked you to quote figures about your building and your products you would know them, chapter and verse, without even opening a ledger. Yet this man, who will be your good right hand if you let him, might starve and die as a stranger to you.' The ghost's brow furrowed as though he were working a puzzle. 'It is a wonder that the only way you can be made to look clearly at the suffering right before your eyes is to be dragged from your bed by a supernatural emissary.'

The ghost was hauling him forwards, through a closed door towards God only knew what fresh nightmare, and Joseph pulled back, struggling in futility against his grip.

'Very well, then. I see my present clearly,' Joseph shouted back. 'The people I need to work in my mill are starved to the point of hatred. My best friend betrays me. The woman who I would take to wife cannot be bothered to speak a word of truth to my face and set me free of the promise I made to her family. I have seen enough. I will do what I can. Take me back to my room.'

'Not just yet. There is one more you must see.'

Now they were in the home of his nemesis: Lampett.

'Not here,' he said to the ghost. 'I get quite enough of

what I am likely to find here without a ghostly visitation.'

'And what is that?'

'Abuse heaped upon abuse. Violence from the father, and scorn from the daughter.' He thought of the previous evening. 'It is likely she will see me, as she did last night. How will I explain myself to her?'

The ghost crooked a smile. 'She is grown into the sort of woman who is much too sensible to see ghosts. And she has given you more than abuse, if I have heard correctly.'

'You mean the kiss?' Joseph scoffed. 'It was hardly a gift freely given. I took it from her, and then I tricked her into responding.'

'Did she enjoy it?'

'I expect that Eve enjoyed her taste of the apple. But that hardly made hers a wise decision.'

The coachman laughed all the harder. 'You think yourself the devil?'

'They do.'

'Let us see, shall we?'

Just in case, Joseph huddled inside the brassy glow of Old Tom's shadow, thinking that the light would render him invisible if nothing else could. Perhaps this Barbara *was* too sensible for ghosts. But she could see through him easily enough if she chose to do so—just as he could see more of her heart than he wished to.

More of her life as well. He should not want to spy upon her. Her life, her family, her thoughts and words when she was not with him should be no concern of his. But there was a dark undercurrent growing in the curiosity he felt tonight—a possessiveness that was stronger than anything he felt for Anne, or even for his business. Suddenly he was hungry for any detail he might learn of her. Secretly he was glad that the spirit had brought him to her again. Once he had married there would be little chance for any conversation with her. For now, he would rather hear a bitter truth from her lips than the silence he deserved.

To hide his confusion, he examined his surroundings. The Lampett house was nicely though simply kept, and too small to need a servant. There was no sign of strife or need except for the worried look in the eyes of the pretty girl as she stood at the shoulder of the man sitting at a desk by the window.

'Please, Father, take some stew. It is supper, and you must not go without eating.' She set the dinner on his desk, nudging it in the direction of the paper he had been writing upon. Unlike in the last house, there was meat in the bowl she offered, and Joseph could smell fresh bread and mince pies cooling in the kitchen. His mouth watered.

But her father seemed unaffected by the sight and smell of the food. 'Don't want it. There is work to be done. I must stop Stratford before this goes any further.' The man pushed the bowl to the side, and his daughter shot a worried glance in the direction of her mother, who sat by the fire, stitching a piece of blond lace on to a blue muslin gown.

Joseph wished he could offer some reassurance—prove that they had nothing to fear from him, or his mill. When it had opened, and the men were back to work, he might be able to sit at their table as a guest, talking about books with her father and offering polite compliments about the housekeeping of the mother and the prettiness of the daughter. Despite the tension in the air there was a feeling of love and family that was lacking in the manor, just as it had been missing from his childhood.

Then he remembered that he was in the last house in Fiddleton where he might be welcomed as a friend. The disappointment he felt was sharpest when he looked at Barbara. While he was used to hearing her father rail against him, she had much more personal reasons to despise him and he deserved every scornful word.

'Go on, then,' Joseph said, bracing himself. 'Give your opinion of me. When I am with you, you do not have a word of kindness for me other than the few thank-yous I have forced out of you. What do you say when we are apart?' It would hardly be a surprise. She was quite plain about it when they were together. She did not like him in the least. But all the same he tensed, waiting for her words.

'While many of the things he has been doing are wrong, they are not so much evil as they are misguided,' she said, as slowly and carefully as possible. 'I am sure, with time, he will come closer to your way of thinking.'

'Defending him, are you now?' Her father was staring at her, hurt, betrayed and sullen. She was clearly torn by the sight of his agitation.

'Go ahead,' Joseph said softly to her, putting aside his bitterness at the sight of her distress. 'Say what makes this the easiest. It is not as if one more harsh word will hurt me. His mood upsets you. Agreeing with him will calm him down.'

'Yes,' she said suddenly. 'I *will* defend him against your more unreasonable charges. The men in the district need work, Father. You must see that. There must be a mill of some sort, and Mr Stratford has built one where there was nothing. He has done it at great expense and risk to himself. Do the papers not say that it is a bad time to be doing business? He could just as easily have tried his hand at something more profitable. He could have stayed in London. Or built elsewhere.'

'So he brings a few jobs to the Riding?' her father said dismissively. 'He will find another way to make the men starve once it is opened.'

'Perhaps,' Barbara admitted. 'But perhaps not. If we show him reason and kindness and make him feel welcome here he might respond in kind. He does not have to be like Mr Mackay. He might provide a safe and clean work place, and be a benefit to the community. He is an extremely clever man. In talking to him, I find that he is well read and ingenious. If there is anyone who can help the people here, I believe it might be him. You will like him when you know him better. Do you remember the books he sent to you?'

'Yes,' her father said grudgingly, like a child forced to be mannerly.

'They are his favourites, and you like them as well. Might that not be a sign of a kindred spirit? But he must be given a chance to prove it to you.'

Joseph sank to the bench in the corner, quite taken aback by the flood of warmth he heard from her. 'You listened to me, didn't you?' He grinned at the ghost, his own spirit much lighter than it had been. 'It was not all anger on her part. Her chiding had some bluster in it. Perhaps there is some hope for me, after all.'

Old Tom laughed. 'I wonder how your wife will feel about your success with this girl. Since she does not care for you, she will likely be relieved that you seek the affections of another. And you will have this one talked around in no time. If you wished to get her into bed—'

Joseph jumped to his feet, fists balled. 'Do not say another word, sir, about the honour of that lady, or you will answer to me at dawn.'

The ghost observed him with a deathly expression. And, coming from one with such an intimate experience with that state, it was a truly fearsome thing. 'You are a year too late to threaten me, Mr Stratford. Being from beyond the grave gives one the ability to say what one likes without fear of repercussion. So I will tell you that you're only pretending to be a gentleman towards her. You care little enough for people unless they can be of benefit to you. You would bed this girl in a heartbeat if you saw the chance to do it. You would do it even faster if you thought it would give you an advantage over her father.'

Joseph opened his mouth to defend himself, and then closed it again as he realised he had considered doing just that. The fact that he had not acted on the impulse was hardly a point in his favour. As the ghost pointed out, he'd had no opportunity.

Old Tom held up a hand to silence him, for the Lampetts were speaking again.

'Let us talk of something more pleasant.' Her mother interrupted the argument between father and daughter. 'It is almost Christmas, after all.'

'And a time for gifts,' said Barbara, seizing upon the subject. 'Although I do not know how I shall surprise you, Mama, if you keep rummaging through my sewing basket and stealing the contents for other purposes.'

'Never mind what we want. What are we to get for you, my dear?' her father asked, turning back into the doting parent that Joseph had seen the other day. 'You still have not said. And it is too late to send to London for anything special.'

'You know that is not necessary,' the girl said, dropping her head.

'We wish to get you something,' her mother insisted. 'It gives us pleasure to know that you are happy.'

'You should know by now that I am happy just to

have the days pass,' Barbara said, staring into the fire. 'It is never an easy time for me.'

'But by now it should be. It has been years, Barbara,' her mother said firmly.

'Almost six,' Barbara said absently.

'It is not as if we expect you to forget.'

'Very good. Because I shall not.'

'Only that it is time to cease punishing yourself for a thing which was none of your fault.'

'There are still those that blame me,' she said, without looking up.

'Fools,' her father grumbled.

'Let us not talk of them, or of the past,' Barbara said quickly, as though eager to avert another dark mood. 'Let us simply say that I am not overly fond of Christmas. I would prefer to celebrate it by knowing that those I love are safe and happy, and not by focusing on my own wants and needs.'

The scene seemed to fade from view again. Joseph could see the players in it, but could no longer hear their words, though he strained to catch some whisper of them. He turned back to Old Tom, frustrated. 'Very well, then. You are right. I have been base and callous in regard to the people of Fiddleton, and this family in particular. But it would help me to understand them better if they were more open about the truth. Six years,' Joseph said, counting on his fingers. 'She would have been eighteen then.' He stared at the ghost of the coachman. 'You were still alive. What happened?'

'I am here to show you the present, not explain the past to you,' the ghost said, a little impatiently. 'If the information is important to you, then you should talk to the girl before you.'

'Did you not just hear her?' Joseph retorted. 'Whatever it is, she will not speak of in front of her own family. How likely is it that she will reveal all when I question her?'

The ghost gave him another sidelong glance. 'I expect it will depend on how you ask her.'

'Stop tormenting me with the idea that I will seduce her,' Joseph said, setting his jaw against the idea. 'It is clear that she has unhappy memories associated with Christmas time. I do not mean to be another of them. If that is what you wished me to learn this night, then let me go.'

In the blink of an eye he was in his bedroom again, standing alone and fully dressed before the fire, and lecturing the mantel clock as it struck three.

'I will not forget,' he said, just in case some wisp of the spirit remained. 'I will be better. You will see. Let this be the last of these nightly visits. For I have had quite enough of them.'

He changed for bed, then—cautiously, as though at any moment he might be interrupted and dragged away again. It was nearly dawn before he closed his eyes.

CHAPTER NINE

THE next evening found Barbara packed as an unwelcome fourth into the Clairemont carriage, trundling through the sodden streets towards the road that led to the manor. The drizzle had continued for most of the day, as though trying to decide minute to minute whether it would be rain or snow. Barbara felt in sympathy with it. Her own heart was as changeable as the weather, still unsure whether it wished to run towards this evening and its host, or away from it.

But Anne seemed unbothered. 'I am sure it will be a delightful time,' she said, with a wan smile. 'There is to be dancing. And cases of champagne. Cook is preparing a fine buffet, and a cold supper at midnight. Joseph has promised a celebration to rival anything in London.'

'Hmmmf,' said her father, and scowled out of the window.

Her mother said nothing at all, unwilling to acknowledge either their destination or the extra passenger they had accrued for the short journey. The Clairemont family had moved to the largest house in Fiddleton proper, with five servants and room enough to keep both a carriage and horses, but it was nothing compared to the manor. Returning to it as guests was obviously a source of irritation that they would conceal only when absolutely necessary.

But Anne seemed to feel less of it, looking from one to the other of them with a kind of desperate enthusiasm, as though she could imagine nothing better than visiting her old home only to leave it again at the end of the evening. 'Joseph says the chestnuts are particularly good this year. He has sampled them already.'

'I imagine he would have,' her father retorted. 'He goes to excess in all other things. If he is not careful he will be prone to gluttony.'

'I doubt it will come to that,' Anne assured him. 'He will not sit still long enough to grow soft. It is more likely that when he is in the throes of work he will need to be reminded to eat.'

Her father muttered something barely audible beyond the word 'trade'.

Anne fell to silence again, and Barbara could almost hear her thoughts. She was wishing that she had not brought up the subject of her prospective fiancé having an occupation at all. It was clearly another sore spot in the conversation.

She looked desperately to Barbara, who said gamely,

'He seems a most solicitous gentleman. When I was struggling in the shop yesterday he offered to transport myself and my basket in his carriage.'

Anne gave an approving nod, as if to say she would not have thought any less of him.

Her mother responded, 'That might just as easily show a fickle nature. What is he doing, offering courtesies to others when he is promised elsewhere?' She narrowed her eyes at Barbara. 'Unless you were angling after a ride?'

Anne sucked in her breath, but Barbara managed to keep her reaction invisible to the other passengers. She knew Lady Clairemont's opinion of her. But she'd hoped to see no obvious demonstration of it tonight.

'Mother,' Anne said quickly, 'I am sure it was nothing of the kind. Though you might not think it so, Joseph has a kind and generous heart. I am not the least bit surprised that he should offer to aid Miss Lampett.'

'Until his ring is on your finger you had best be less generous and more sensible,' her mother informed her. 'This party would be an excellent time to finalise the arrangement between you.'

'I cannot very well demand that he make the announcement,' Anne said, obviously embarrassed by her mother's bluntness.

'But his inviting other young ladies to this ball does not bode well.'

'I think there is someone he wishes me to meet,'

Barbara said hurriedly. 'He was quite clear about there being eligible gentlemen in attendance.'

'Probably that Breton fellow,' Anne's father grunted. 'He's a bit high in the instep for you, my dear. But a bit low… Second son…' His comment trailed off into inaudibility again.

'You have not even met him, Father.' Anne gave Barbara another silent apology. 'He is really very nice. A true gentleman—neither too high nor too low.'

'And no concern of yours, no matter what his birth. He will do for Barbara, here, if that is what Stratford intends for them. But he cannot be much of a man if he lets a business associate make such decisions for him.'

Anne stared out of the window, as though searching for another topic of conversation. 'I hope the weather favours us this evening. It seems likely that the rain will turn to snow.'

'Then we shall be forced to remain at the manor,' her mother said, showing the first signs of cheerfulness. 'I assume that Stratford has taken the master bedroom. But we shall make do in the next best suite, and you shall have your old room back, Anne.'

'Then I hope that travel is not made difficult,' Barbara said, considering the awkwardness of the situation. 'I am quite unprepared to stay the night.'

'Oh.' Lady Clairemont gave a sad little moue that ended in a smile. 'Do not worry upon it, my dear. I am sure there is a maid that can lend you a nightdress, should we be stranded.'

When they had arrived at the manor, the Clairemonts' behaviour grew no warmer. Lord and Lady Clairemont swept into the ballroom as if they still owned it, greeting other guests as though they were old friends. Anne trailed along in their wake, polite and silent.

When Barbara made to follow, Lady Clairemont turned, giving her a cold and very deliberate look. The direct stare seemed to change as she held it, to look past Barbara and then through her, as though she did not exist at all. The cut was so beautifully made that for a moment Barbara longed for a mirror, convinced that it was she who had faded to transparency. With a single look, Lady Clairemont had made it clear to her that, whatever Joseph Stratford might think, Barbara Lampett was an unwelcome guest here. If there were introductions to be made, he had best appear and make them himself, for the Clairemonts planned to pretend she did not exist.

She had to admire the perfection of the revenge Lady Clairemont had devised. The room was full of strangers. And, if she wished to be thought a well-mannered young lady, Barbara could hardly introduce herself to any of them. She would spend her first night in ages as a sort of social ghost, separated by a glass wall of propriety from the merrymaking.

Nor would Anne come to her aid. Though she did not hold the deep animosity for Barbara that her parents did, she lacked the spine to stand against them.

She was sure that Joseph Stratford would help her, if

she could find him. But there was no sign of him, and she assumed that he must be in a card room somewhere, talking business. She could expect little else. To him, that was the only purpose for the gathering. Even if he had meant to be a proper host, it should be Anne standing at his side and not her.

But it was just as well Mr Stratford did not see her. Having taken a moment to admire the other women, she could see that she did not belong amongst them. While her dress had seemed quite nice in the cheval glass at home, it looked dowdy compared to the pale silks and fine embroidered shawls she saw tonight. And the loveliest amongst them was Anne Clairemont. Her net gown was trimmed with tiny pearls, her hair held in place with diamond pins. She glided through the room like a swan: pure white, slender and graceful.

In comparison, Barbara's retrimmed blue gown managed to be both too bright and too plain. Her neck was bare. Her hair was dressed simply, with no jewels to ornament it. Even if Joseph were to see her he would look on her with pity rather than desire. She was little better than a charity case here—just as she had been the last time she saw him. She must learn to face the reality of it and not let the disappointment show. Invited or not, she did not belong here.

She must remember not to call him Joseph—to his face or to others. Anne Clairemont had that right of intimacy. She did not. But she quite liked the sound of the name in her head. After receiving a secret kiss from him, and being alone with him on two occasions, in the privacy of her thoughts she did not need to think of him as Mr Stratford.

To save herself the embarrassment of another cut, Barbara withdrew, pretending to admire the hangings in the ballroom nearest the door and then easing through it to stroll towards the portrait gallery, as though engrossed in the quality of the art. She considered herself fortunate that the manor was so large, and she so familiar with it. She would steal her share of the refreshments and then wander away by herself to relive happier times in her mind.

When she went home she would concoct a story for her mother about the fine food and the dancing, and the courtly gentlemen who had paid her attention. None so specific as to make her expect a call, but she would claim that it had been a delightful night, and that she had enjoyed herself most thoroughly.

A group of gentlemen passed her in the hall, carrying heaped plates of cakes and sandwiches, clearly on the lookout for a quiet place to sit. Lord Clairemont was amongst them. To avoid further awkwardness she withdrew to one of the many hiding places she'd known as a girl—a chair behind a statue of Mars, which had been decorated in a most undignified manner with garlands of holly.

'Has anyone seen our esteemed host this evening?' asked the first, a rather large man with a lurid pink waistcoat.

'Still trying to do business,' the next remarked. 'He would not let me alone before. Stratford is a most persistent fellow.'

'Little else can be expected of his sort,' the other responded pityingly. 'In trade, you know. It seems they can think of nothing else.'

Unlike some, who thought of nothing but filling their bellies. Barbara looked hurriedly down at her empty glass and the plate of crumbs beside it. Of all the sins of which Joseph was guilty, she could not fault his hospitality to his guests. The portions were generous, and any whim would be indulged for one so fortunate to have been invited into his home.

It made the absence of the villagers more keenly felt. She was sure, had he bothered to include them, that he would have rewarded any stranger from the village with the same casual generosity.

It seemed Lord Clairemont viewed the abundance with less charity. 'There is too much of everything here.' He picked a leaf from Mars and flicked it to the floor. 'When Anne is mistress, I trust she will teach him manners. He is rich, of course, but quite common. Did you see what he has done to the ivy on the south side of the house? He has stripped away great patches of it and brought it here.'

'Decorations, man!' Pink Waistcoat laughed. 'It is hardly Christmas without the stuff.'

'But there is a time and a place,' Lord Clairemont said primly. 'One does not go about denuding houses.'

Barbara was in two minds about that. The rooms looked very nice with the fresh greens. And now that some of the troublesome vines had been removed from around the windows she suspected there would be daylight in the library and the ballroom. Both had been gloomy places even by day, and she recalled being quite frightened of them.

'Stratford and your daughter do make a lovely couple,' one of the men remarked grudgingly. 'It seems that birth does not show on one's face.'

'But it is plain enough in his conversation,' Lord Clairemont remarked. 'He goes to the best tailor in London, but he tells people that the fabric for his coat was woven by himself—on his own modern loom.'

'Perhaps we will find him in the parlour, knitting a muffler?' said Pink Waistcoat. The men around him laughed, moving on.

Barbara leaned back against the wall, eyes closed, wishing she had stopped her ears, before hearing a word of that conversation. She was ashamed of herself for eavesdropping, and embarrassed for Joseph as well. How awful must it be for him to be an object of ridicule amongst his guests and a source of amusement in his own home. She felt a rush of kinship with him. Of all the people in the manor tonight, maybe neither of them belonged.

'Playing at hide-and-seek, Miss Lampett? I understand it is a common game here at Christmas.'

Her eyes flew open to find her host, leaning against

the wall at her side, scant inches away, smiling down at her.

'I was doing nothing of the kind. I was simply—' she searched for a plausible explanation '—resting for a moment. The dancing is most strenuous.'

'It must be, for you to grow tired just by watching it. But you have not even done that, have you? I have been in and out of the ballroom all evening, and have not seen you there at all. Explain yourself.'

'Before I stand up to dance I must be asked,' she said. 'And before that there must be introductions.' She smiled politely. 'But I am having a lovely time, reacquainting myself with the house. It is beautiful—especially done up for Christmas. I thank you for your invitation.'

'Rubbish,' he said sharply. 'You came with the Clairemonts, did you not?'

'They were kind enough to give me a ride in their carriage.'

'But they did not make you known to the other guests?'

She could think of no proper answer for this, so she remained silent.

'And I was negligent in my duties as host and let you wander, alone and abandoned.' He swore then, a short colourful vulgarity that she had never heard before. She supposed she should be shocked by it, make some comment about his low birth and stalk off. But he had had enough of that reaction, she was sure, and she did not have the heart to add her censure to the rest.

He collected himself quickly, and gave a curt bow of apology. 'Come, Miss Lampett. We are going back to the ballroom so that you might dance with me.'

'Really, that is not necessary,' she whispered.

'There you are again, trying to tell me what is needed and what is not.' He grabbed her by the arm and pulled her out from behind the statue. 'You must know by now that it is quite hopeless to stop me once I have an idea in my head.'

'But I must try,' she said, pulling her arm from his grasp, and permitting him to escort her properly. 'I know that your invitation here was little more than a sop to gain my father's silence. But if we dance the Clairemonts are likely to think it was something more.'

'Do not ascribe such dark motives to me,' he said. 'Perhaps I merely thought that you would enjoy the opportunity of socialising and devised an excuse so that you would not refuse my invitation. Instead I see you are wedded to the wall because my future in-laws are unable to behave like the lady and gentleman they purport to be. I do not know what the gripe is between you. But it ends now.'

'This is a waltz,' she said, tripping along at his side as he stalked into the ballroom. 'And I do not know how. Perhaps if we waited…' But it was hopeless. He was tugging her very gently towards the dance floor.

'It is the simplest of all dances, and you will learn

it as we go,' he said, swinging her about to face him. 'People will call me rude and brash and inappropriate. But I am quite used to that already and will not be bothered.'

'And if people think ill of *me* because of it? Dancing so intimately with a man I barely know?' Although she quite liked the sound of the music and the feel of his hand on her waist. She liked even better the look of shock she saw on Lady Clairemont's face as she spun past her.

'I am your host,' he said, giving a gentle push on her hand to guide her. 'You can hardly refuse me. It is Christmas, which is traditionally a time for small latitudes. No one will say a word.'

'Even if they do, they are all from London and I will never see them again.' She sighed in satisfaction.

With his hand upon her ribs, he noticed. 'That was a happy sigh, I trust?'

She gave a hesitant nod. 'I have not had many opportunities to dance. Sometimes it seems as though I went directly from the schoolroom to the shelf, with no stopping between.'

He snorted. 'You? On the shelf? I should say not.'

'I am twenty-four years old,' she said, with a purse of the lips. 'There are few gentlemen in the area. And girls who are younger, prettier, more biddable…'

He laughed again. 'You make those sound like virtues.'

'Are they not?'

'Young and biddable is often synonymous with naive and without a fully moulded character. Easier at first, perhaps. But it would make for a most dull union to marry such a girl.'

Which was strange. Because it was exactly how she would have described the object of his own matrimonial plans, had she been called to compare with her. 'And beauty?' she asked. 'Surely you have no problems with that?'

'At your worst, you are quite pretty enough to suit even the most discriminating men,' he said, looking down at her with an appraising eye. 'Tonight you are looking most charming indeed. If you hear any complaints on the subject you must send the offenders to me.' His fingers flexed on her waist and his hand squeezed hers. Just for a moment his face dipped closer to hers, sharing a conspiratorial smile.

And she thought, with a sudden flash of insight, *If I allow it, he is likely to kiss me again. Right here on the dance floor. Or in a dark corner, when we can be alone.*

She knew, if the opportunity presented itself, that she would let him. She stumbled and broke the moment of intimacy.

He concentrated on the steps, easing her gently back onto the beat until they were steady again, pretending that the mistake was his to put her at her ease.

It made her feel quite awful. She had accused him of all manner of horrible things, directly to his face. She had thought even worse about him. But it was becoming plain that, though his nature seemed brusque, he was quite capable of behaving like a gentleman when he wished to. It was a shame that he was not being treated as such.

Though it was the height of bad manners to repeat what she had heard, neither did she feel right about keeping the truth from him. 'They are all laughing at you, you know. The other guests. Even Anne's family.' Then she realised that it might sound as if she was sabotaging a rival. 'Not Anne, of course. She is much too good for that.'

'Oh, of course not,' he answered back with sarcasm. 'But she and the rest are not too good to accept bread and board from likes of Mr Joseph Stratford. They lack the strength of their convictions. Some of the people I'd hoped to see tonight refused me outright. I have more respect for them. They are incapable of pretence.' There was no tension as he said the words, sweeping her further out on the dance floor, twirling her effortlessly with the other dancers.

'You realise what they are saying about you?'

'Of course,' he said, with a wry smile. 'You did not honestly worry I'd be hurt, did you? What a sensitive creature you must think me, Miss Lampett. I do not shrink from their displeasure, nor do I acknowledge their gossiping. I am willing to stand against your father and his armed mob, my dear. But to my knowledge no one has ever bled to death from the cut direct.'

'Maybe people would not act that way to you if only

you were not so…' She could not seem to find a word to describe it.

He sighed and smiled at her. 'I am too much of everything, I fear. But it is hard to explain the novelty of a full larder to one that has always had their fill.' He looked out of the window at the snow falling in the gardens, as though he could see past it into his own future. 'This is nothing compared to what it will some day be. Two years ago it was a few machines. Now it will be a factory. And before I am through? An empire.' He waved a hand towards the hall they had left. 'They may laugh behind their hands, if they like. But the gentleman in the horrid pink waistcoat has promised me ten thousand pounds. And the gentleman beside him another five. Both will see a good rate of return on their investments. Neither of them need fear that I will reveal our association or bother them with my presence in London. It will work well for all of us.'

'That is all that concerns you?'

He nodded. 'If I had chosen to behave properly and stay where I was born I would be on the other side of the gates right now, looking in at the people dancing. Tomorrow I would be standing outside another man's mill, threatening the master with violence, living in fear that the last crust of bread would be ripped from my hand.'

'You have a very grim view of the world, Mr Stratford.'

'And a very accurate one. I was once poor, Miss

Lampett. Now I am rich. But I will never clear the stink of poverty from my skin. I accept that.' He grinned. 'But, all the same, I cannot help but revel in the change.'

The dance ended and he walked her to the edge of the floor. As they approached the people standing there she hesitated, laying a hand on his arm to halt him. 'If they think so little of you, then what will they say to me, in last season's gown retrimmed in borrowed lace?'

'They will treat you with the utmost courtesy, I am sure. I will introduce you to Robert Breton, who is a true gentleman with impeccable manners. He will shepherd you about the room to the others. I recommend that once I am gone you comment at my boorish behaviour in forcing you to dance. Your future will be secure.'

She could not help it, and gave a short laugh. 'I would never…'

'I know you would not.' He was looking into her eyes again, and she felt the warmth, the pull. 'Although I am sure you have thought it.'

'No.'

'Do not lie,' he said, giving her hand a squeeze. 'But do not feel that I fault you. You cannot be blamed. My manners are rough. Considering our circumstances, I appreciate that yours are not, and thank you for it.'

Then he led her across the room to his friend, making another formal bow and as proper a presentation as she could have hoped for. In truth, it was a bit too formal, but that was better than the alternative of being forgotten.

In turn, Mr Breton made polite and much more polished conversation, then took her around the room to his friends and acquaintances, making sure that she was properly introduced to each of them. Her dance card for the evening was quickly filled with gentlemen of the *ton*—younger brothers and married men, who had been rousted from the card room to make up for the lack of dancers.

It was pleasant. She relaxed and remembered what it had been like to attend similar parties, before the house had been shut up in mourning and she'd felt the sting of rejection. But this night was different in that she longed to turn and find the eyes of a particular gentleman following her about the room, even though they had danced only once.

Joseph had taken a personal interest in her. It was to be expected, she supposed. He wished her to be at ease, just as he did the other guests. That was all it was. If there had been any proprietorial interest it was a fabrication on her part. His effusive compliments were another sign of his lack of social grace, not a partiality unique to her.

When she looked for him, as she found herself frequently doing, he was giving his attention to Anne, just as he should. The man was engaged to her, or near to it. He wanted nothing more than to see Barbara similarly happy.

As another dance ended, her partner returned her to Mr Breton, who offered her escort on a trip to the refreshment room. As they passed Joseph Stratford, Breton caught her gaze and looked back at his friend with a mixture of frustration and admiration. 'If you foster hopes in that direction you must know that there is an understanding with another young lady.'

'I know that,' she said, trying not to blush at how obvious he must think her. 'I am merely surprised at how kind he has been to me—though he barely knows me, except through Father. And that is…difficult.'

'So I understand,' said Breton. 'You must go home and explain to your father, if you can, that all is not as simple as it seems.' He looked across the room at his friend. 'For all his faults, Stratford is a visionary. We must trust him to know what is right.'

'I cannot say that I approve of his vision,' Barbara said, shaking her head. 'To the villagers, it seems to be nothing more than wanton destruction and change that benefits one man more than any other.'

'Not at all,' Breton insisted. 'I was there when he made the decision to come here. He was poring over a pile of maps, gazettes and indexes. He chose and then rejected several sites. Then he showed me this place. "Here," he said, "is the land, and here are the workers. Here is the river that will bring the finished goods to London and to the ports. Here are the fields, already full of the sheep to give us supplies, and the roads that will bring the coal."' Breton grinned with pride. 'He sees it all as though it were a pile of loose links, waiting to become a chain. Some men can come up with an idea for improvement, but he is one of the few that understands enough to put that change to work.'

'You are a gentleman,' she argued. 'I would think you knew better than to get so closely involved in trade.'

He shrugged. 'At one time, perhaps. I am a second son, and must make the best of my inheritance. I was dubious when he came to me with the idea for an improved loom. But he is very persistent. He would not leave. So I made one quiet investment. He turned my modest income into a fortune. When he suggested an expansion, I decided I would be a fool to refuse him.'

He glanced around at the largely empty dining hall. 'He expected there to be more speculators, since the chance to do business far outside the eyes of the *ton* would be a pleasant one. Joe's cellar is good, and his table groans. The house is as nice as any one might see in London. The beds are soft enough for a lord, certainly. I have no complaints.'

Barbara pursed her lips. 'He spoke to me of this, and he does not seem disappointed. But I wonder what the Clairemonts think of it all.'

'It hardly matters,' Breton supplied with finality. 'It has been demonstrated to me on several occasions that the God-given right to property does not automatically assume the wisdom or skill to keep it. While your friends the Clairemonts could not maintain their position, I am sure you will find Mr Stratford to be more than able. This is the first such fortune he will make in his lifetime, and the first house he shall purchase. While he continues to advance, the Clairemonts of the world shall be left with nothing more than the honour of their names. Genteel poverty is poverty nonetheless, Miss Lampett. Surely you must know that by now?'

The man they had been discussing rounded the corner, coming upon them without warning. He stopped suddenly and stared at the two of them in surprise, and then offered a hurried apology before turning back the way he had come.

'Whatever does he mean by that?' Barbara said in confusion.

Breton glanced up. 'He thinks he has caught us under a kissing bough. Although how we could manage to avoid them I am not sure. Stratford has them hung in nearly every room and doorway, despite the decidedly unromantic nature of this gathering.'

'Surely if there is an engagement to be announced, there must be a trace of romance in the air.' The thought did nothing to lift her spirits, and Mr Breton seemed equally pensive. He was looking up at the garland of mistletoe and ribbons and around at the empty room. 'I suppose we had best make use of it while we are here.' He hardly sounded enthused about the prospect.

Barbara did not wish to show her own lack of desire. 'If you wish, sir. It is Christmas, after all.' She closed her eyes and raised her face to his.

She had hoped it would be the briefest buss—over

quickly and forgotten. But it appeared that he wished for something more memorable, and did not immediately withdraw. Neither did he advance, or show any real enthusiasm for it. It was not exactly unpleasant, but it was most definitely awkward.

There was a gasp of surprise from the doorway, a stifled sob and then the pattering of lady's slippers down the hall. Breton jerked away from her and muttered a curse. 'If you will excuse me, Miss Lampett?' He gave a hurried bow and raced from the room, leaving her alone again.

CHAPTER TEN

JOSEPH Stratford practised the words of his proposal quietly to himself in the silence of the library. If he meant to do the deed he had best do it tonight, while there were guests to celebrate it. It was a culmination of sorts—a final proof to his investors of the confidence that the Clairemonts placed in him. It was another step in his entry into society.

In all ways it was an excellent choice. He had selected Anne with clinical precision, just as he had the household decorations. There was no question that she was a beauty, and her manners and breeding were impeccable. Though her father might be cold and abrupt to him, Anne paid just the correct amount of interest, making it clear without seeming inappropriately eager that when he chose to offer the answer would be yes.

His heart was not engaged, of course. Neither was hers. That was for the best. If he sought affection elsewhere she would likely be more relieved than upset. Though he would make every effort to see her happy, as he had promised Bob, he would expend nothing more to try to win a love that was not likely to appear. And if she sought comfort with another? As long as the first son looked like him, what right did he have to care?

He thought of the brief and unpleasant scene he had witnessed a few moments ago: Breton and Barbara standing awkwardly under the kissing bough. That had been his plan when he'd invited her. She should find someone who valued her, and he could think of no better choice than Bob.

But Joseph did not find his success nearly as enjoyable as the one dance he'd shared with her, or the heroic feeling of rescuing her from her hiding place in the portrait gallery. If he was not careful he'd destroy plans that had been months in the making in trying to interpret a few mysterious dreams and appease spirits that were entirely the makings of his own overtired brain. If he was lucky, the girl was even now getting on well with Breton, and he would never have to think of her again.

Anne was her superior in every way, he reminded himself firmly. Barbara's face was as far from patrician as one could imagine. To call her complexion ruddy was unfair, but it had a healthy glow about it—as though she partook freely of the northern air. She was not short, nor stout, though she appeared stunted next to the tall and slender Anne. In all ways she seemed less refined, less delicate, less of a lady.

And his body did not seem to mind that a bit. While Anne might be as lovely as a china doll, china dolls were made to be admired more than touched. They were expensive things, to be cherished, set upon a shelf and forgotten.

Other toys were meant to be played with. When he looked at Barbara Lampett, oh, how he wished for playtime. She made him think of Christmas morning, with gifts waiting to be unwrapped, games to be won, and nights full of pleasant surprises. The likelihood that she would spend her adult life as a spinster caring for her mad father seemed vastly unfair. He wondered yet again what the truth was in her disgrace and banishment from local society. If there was a stain already on her character, perhaps in time…

The door opened suddenly, and he was face to face with his intended. 'Anne,' he said dumbly, taking a moment to wipe his mind clear of its recent speculation.

'Joseph.' She seemed to need a moment's composure as well. He pretended not to notice the deep breath she took, and the fading flush on her cheeks. 'I am sorry. I did not mean to disturb you.'

'It is quite all right. I meant to seek you out just now. If you have a moment…?'

'Of course.'

Now that the time was upon him, he was unsure what the correct emotion was to suit it. Whatever was expected, he was sure that he was not feeling it. There was no tingle of nerves, no pleasant sense of anticipation, no triumph and no relief. He was certainly not feeling the desire he might wish for as she stepped into the room, closing the door behind her and leaving them alone together for the first time in their acquaintance.

She was totally composed again, staring at him with a pleasant, neutral smile, waiting for him to speak. He wondered if he should begin with some inane comment like, *I suppose you wonder why I've asked you here.*

But they both knew damn well the reason. To pretend there was doubt as to the question and its inevitable answer was an annoying ceremony that he could not quite manage.

So he waited until the click of the door latch no longer echoed in the still air of the room, took the few steps to her side, went down on one knee and said, 'Miss Anne Clairemont, would you do me the honour of becoming my wife?'

The words, though they were only a formality, were surprisingly hard to say.

'Thank you. I would be honoured in return.' It was good that he had not expected her to go into raptures. Her expression had not changed one iota from the one she had worn in the ballroom.

He rose. 'I have no ring to offer at this time. After Christmas I will take you to London, where you may choose something suitable that is to your taste.' It would save her being embarrassed at his lack of style, should he choose incorrectly.

'That will not be necessary,' she said, with the same

unfailing smile. 'I am sure Mother will have something appropriate in her jewel case.'

Apparently when he had purchased the house and its contents he had purchased the bride and her ring as well. He stifled a sudden and totally inappropriate desire to laugh.

'Very well, then. Let us meet in the ballroom at—' he checked his watch '—midnight exactly, to make the announcement. Until then…' They had almost three quarters of an hour. If he was wise, he would use the time to get to know his bride in a way that was more physical than social.

He leaned forwards and she closed her eyes, preparing herself to be kissed. He reminded himself to be gentle, though there was hardly a need. She did not seem frightened of him. Their lips met.

She was warm and pliable, and with a small amount of pressure her lips opened and she responded. It was clear that she knew what was expected of her, but she did not behave like a strumpet so much as a woman reconciled to the prospect of intimacy with a stranger. He had the sudden horrible feeling that now the words had been spoken she would permit whatever he might dare, greeting it with the same polite and placid smile.

To say that it was like kissing a statue was unfair. It was more like *being* a statue. Though he could feel the pressure and taste her tongue against his, it was little different from the walks with his ghosts had been, when he had been near the action but not really a part of it.

He broke the kiss. 'Until then I will allow you to refresh yourself. Now, if you will excuse me…?' He gave a brief bow and left her.

He was not fleeing the room, he told himself firmly. Merely returning with alacrity to the ballroom—to see to his other guests, prepare the musicians for the announcement and await his fiancée so that he could take her hand and make the biggest mistake of his life.

She would smile demurely, like the wooden poppet she was. She would colour with the faint blush of excitement that he assumed she was even now painting on her face in the ladies' retiring room. And he would smile, to prove himself aware of his good fortune, and accept the hearty congratulations that he would receive and the endless toasts drunk in their honour.

The very idea made him want to choke.

From the moment that he had kissed her—really kissed her, hoping to feel something of their impending life together—he had known it was a mistake. But by then the words were already spoken and it was too late to call them back.

In an act of supreme cowardice he swerved as he passed the little alcove in the hall, and ducked behind the curtain. He could not hide for ever. But even five minutes of privacy would be a welcome thing.

'Joseph!' Her voice was a hissing whisper that stirred his blood.

He turned in the tight, confining space and found Barbara Lampett hiding there as well. He put his hands to her waist, drawing her close, and though his mind roiled his body forgot that there was anything or anyone outside of this small niche and responded.

'Miss Barbara Lampett. Hiding again? And now, I assume, we are playing sardines?'

'Nothing of the sort,' she snapped.

'Then apparently you do not know what you are playing at,' he said suddenly, jerking her body until it rested against his, and relishing the feeling of being once again in control. Then he took her mouth, because he could not stand to be without her for another moment. She responded as he'd known she would, massaging his tongue with her own, urging him on. The taste of her sent the life rushing back into his body, and a joy so reckless that he knew it must be dangerous. He pulled away.

'Release me and exit from here immediately, or I swear I shall scream.'

Her words were the correct ones for any offended maiden. They had to be said, if only to be ignored. But as she spoke she made no struggle to escape him. Nor was there any fear in her voice. Instead she gripped his arms and leaned into him.

'Scream, then,' he said, half wishing she would. It would solve many of his problems. Anne would surely hear of it, and his engagement would be over before it had begun. But it seemed whatever indiscretion she had taken part in six years ago had left her devoid of outrage, and he was damned glad of the fact.

She took a deep breath, and for a moment he almost thought she might make good on her threat. Then she sighed, as though defeated. 'Just once, will you not do the proper thing? Why must you make this so difficult?'

'Perhaps it is because I do not wish to let you go,' he replied.

'And I lack the strength to resist you.'

'I doubt that very much,' he whispered, touching her lips with his. 'You are stronger than you know. Strong enough to break my will.' Then he brought his mouth back down to hers to give her the kisses he should have given another. And he felt her burst into flame again.

She took a breath, and he took it away again, letting the smell and the taste of her soak in, until it became a part of him to his very bones. His future might be as cold as a northern winter, but if he could have nothing else he would have a woman like this to remember. He thrust his tongue deep into her mouth and she raked it with her teeth, biting almost hard enough to draw blood, pushing her breasts eagerly against his waistcoat and swaying to excite herself.

He broke the kiss and pushed her away, stroking his fingers once down the front of her gown, making her tremble. 'I suppose you will now offer me some needless objections about how things must be between us,' he told her, making a half-hearted offer to let her leave.

And leave she should—rushing from the little alcove

after giving him a sharp word and a slap for his insolence. He deserved nothing less for behaving in a way that was everything despicable, everything he despised about himself and other men who would abuse their power over those in their debt.

But as he said it he reached around her and his fingers tightened on her bottom, flexed and then tightened again. She was round and lush, and he could imagine the feel of her naked flesh, cradling her in his lap as he pushed into her. His body gave a jump of desire in response.

With that little encouragement, she pulled him close again, and he felt another tremble as her body gave an answering surge.

He buried his face in her hair. 'No objections, then. Very good.' He forced her back with him, further into the darkness of the alcove and of his own soul.

He could hear the faint murmuring of couples in the refreshment room and a low moan from his partner, her quickening of breath and the shift of her gown against his coat. 'Someone might hear us,' she whispered.

He touched a finger to her lips. 'Then we will be careful.' He bent to kiss the slope of her breast, then tugged gently at the neckline of her gown, pushing the lace out of the way and probing beneath it to where her chemise had been tucked low and her breasts forced high to the top of her stays. At last his fingers found a nipple and coaxed it upwards to rest just outside her dress, so that he could latch upon it with a sigh.

She should be fighting for her virtue, or at least pretending to resist. He should be racked with guilt at his easy betrayal of Anne. But it felt so good to touch, and to feel a response. This was no mannequin but a living, breathing woman. The sort that a man could make a future with, have a house full of life and love and children.

She gave another gasp at the sudden shock of delight when his teeth closed upon the tip of her breast, and he swirled his tongue as he nipped and sucked. It was tender and sweet, and along with lust he felt the power of bringing her to life. And the bitterness of knowing that he had no right to this—that he was stealing it for his own pleasure, just as the villagers accused him of stealing their livelihoods.

'Tell me to stop,' he said, into her skin. For a moment he did, and looked up at her, admiring the fine line of her chin and cheekbones, for her head was thrown back as she panted in excitement.

'No.' She gasped, her face twisted as though it was agony to feel what he was making her feel. 'I want more.'

'I thought you did. When I saw you at the factory that first day I knew.' Even then her energy, her passion and her anger had shown, in that dull crowd, like a jewel in dross. She deserved more than this little village could offer her. She needed someone who could match her heat for heat. 'I want more as well. I want everything. I want to give you that as well. Everything you ever dreamt of. Let me set you free.' He dropped his head to her breast again.

He could feel that the intensity of his words frightened her. For a moment she seemed almost frozen by them, her frame stiff and rigid, neither welcoming nor resisting. But as he sucked rhythmically upon her he drew a greater response with each pull. Her hands rose to his shoulders, clutching, and then digging in with the sort of hard, painful, rhythmic massage that he might have expected from a cat that didn't know the power of its own claws. He cupped his hands beneath her breasts, holding them to his face before smoothing his fingers down over her skirts, outlining hips and thighs, and reaching behind one of her knees to urge her foot up on the bench beside him.

And she allowed him to do it. Her legs fell open to his touch. Her raised knee pressed encouragingly into his side as he stepped between them. His hand hovered at the fastenings of his trousers for only a moment before rejecting his own pleasure. There was not time, and this was not the place. She deserved more than a selfish coupling against a wall in a common passageway.

He pressed his lips to her ear and whispered, 'Relax for me. Trust me. Let me touch you.'

His hand went to her ankle, then slid up the silk of her stocking and higher, to the silk of her skin. He was teasing her gently, with playful strokes, between her legs, and he felt her surprised intake of breath cut short in an effort to keep quiet. Then he kissed her, and delved his fingers into the wonderfully warm, wet softness at their apex, circling and then pressing, pushing against the opening and then into it, gently, and then with more force. He deepened into a slow slide and thrust that matched the rhythm of his mouth.

She stifled her cry of surprise inside their kiss. There were people passing in the hall, barely feet from where they were. Discovery was inevitable if she could not keep silent, and she knew it.

He did not care. It would mean ruin for both of them. Anne and her family would leave in shame. The schemes he had built, largely from air, would collapse around him, leaving him with nothing but the woman in his arms.

But that would be more than enough. More than he deserved. He withdrew his hand and dropped to his knees before her, pleasuring her body with his mouth, first coaxing and then demanding a response from her. The harder she fought to keep silent, the more he teased, sucking the petals of her into his mouth and nursing upon them as he had at her breast. She bucked her hips against his tongue until he trapped them with his hands, held them still and had his way with her as her fingers twined in his hair, holding him close. Her trembling increased and he reached up again and gave a single hard thrust of his fingers. Her world unravelled, leaving her body throbbing and shaking, totally in his control.

He relaxed, letting his head loll against her thigh,

planting gentle kisses on the skin above her garter as he fought for mastery of his own body.

Above him, his lover turned her head and laid her cheek against the stone wall, as though trying to cool the heat in her blood. But her hands still played in his hair and stroked his temples, and her legs were still spread wide in welcome. She breathed slowly, deeply, in and out, waiting for him to accept the final gift she could offer.

In the silence he felt reality pressing against him, as it had when he'd come here to hide. He had thought only yesterday that he knew what he wanted. Wealth, power, respect, success. A moment ago he had been willing to risk it all—playing games with a woman who had been a stranger to him a week ago.

He reached with one hand to disentangle himself from her arms, and rose to his feet. But for a moment his other hand remained just where it was, fingers buried deep within her clenching body, to remind her who was controlling and who controlled, who was possessed and who possessed.

As though to confirm the truth, her body tightened on his fingers.

His gave an answering lurch of pleasure, even while he tried to regret what had happened. Then he withdrew his hand and stared silently into her eyes, which glittered in the darkness. He could not trust himself to speak. He dared not offer words of comfort or love. But neither could he dismiss her.

She read what she wished to into that silence and pulled away from him, as far into the corner of the little space as she could. She gave a snap of her skirt, to let it drop back into place, and straightened her bodice—which was in sore disarray and barely covering her luscious body.

'You are despicable. You know that, don't you?' she whispered, making sure that her voice was cold and controlled, even if it was the only part of her that was. 'You were trying to make me cry out just when the risk would have been greatest. You wanted discovery.'

'And you love me for it,' he said. 'The risk excited you. You climaxed. No harm was done. If I was as bad as you claim, I'd have taken the same pleasure. I could, even now, take the step that you could not retreat from, and you would go to whatever cold marriage bed fate has planned for you thinking not of your husband but of me.' It was an idle threat. For he would be damned before he'd let another man touch her from this night on.

'You flatter yourself, Mr Stratford.' She raised her chin, arrogant even in confusion.

'Frequently,' he admitted. 'But I am honest about it. I was born low, and not graced with connections or education. I would never call myself a handsome man. But I am the cleverest man in the room, and rich as Croesus. And I know that you want me.'

'That is quite different from loving you,' she said.

'Perhaps. But not for you. It is all of a thing to you.

For you could not love a man without wanting him, and you would never want a man that you did not love. At least a little,' he qualified, allowing her some pride.

'We have barely met, and yet you think you know me well.'

'I think I do,' he said. 'And I like what I know. I wish to know more of you. Come to my room tonight.' There would be no more ghosts with her at his side, and no fears of a cold and passionless future.

She shook her head and turned her face from his. 'After this shameful incident there is little left for you to learn of me. You must allow me to keep some secrets for myself, Mr Stratford. Now, if you will ascertain that we are alone so that I may exit, I will go to the retiring room. And you, sir, should return to your fiancée. While she will be too polite to notice your absence, I suspect that you will find others in the community less forgiving of it.' She pushed past him, not bothering to check the emptiness of the hall, and ran.

He sank to the bench behind him, frustrated and confused. What the devil was he doing? Her set-down stung, but he had no right to complain of it. Even if there was a secret in her past that tainted her virtue, it gave him no right to treat her like an experienced London widow. He had been planning, just now, to set her up and keep her for his pleasure, forgetting who she was and who her father was. To take a mistress while taking a wife was not unheard of. But he could not have picked a worse one than Barbara Lampett.

He was lucky that she had not raised a cry that would end his hopes with Anne. Or burst into tears and aroused some guilt in him for the way he had treated her, forcing him to cry off and offer properly. Even if he had sought, in a careless moment, to ruin himself, he had no right to do it at her expense. To finish by demanding entrance to her bed proved he was as uncouth and deserving of scorn as she seemed to think him. He was a base, simple creature, who answered with an enthusiastic affirmative to any temptation that called to him, and he had demanded that she be the same.

But even then she had not rejected him. She had merely refused to confirm the truth. While he suspected that Anne would be just as content to be a widow as a bride, Barbara could not keep her body from responding to his—though she clearly wished to.

She deserved better. And he deserved exactly what he was getting: a big house, a successful business and a wife who neither loved nor wanted him. It should have been enough. More than enough. It was certainly more than he had expected out of life. He had no right to complain.

He felt the desire in him dying, and realised that Barbara had been wrong on that first day. It could not be coal in his veins, for coal was never this cold. He stood, straightened his coat and brushed the dust from the knees of his breeches. Then he drew back the curtain enough to let in a ray of light by which he could check his watch. There was still a quarter of an hour left before midnight. If he applied himself in that time, he suspected he could get quite drunk and still be in the ballroom before the clock chimed twelve.

CHAPTER ELEVEN

FOR the third time tonight Barbara was hiding. At least this time she had chosen the ladies' retiring room, which seemed a bit more dignified than returning to her childhood haunts in a stranger's home.

The alcove had seemed like a clever idea when she'd wanted to think undisturbed about what she was sure she'd discovered. That had been Anne in the doorway, gasping and crying over an innocent Christmas kiss. The reaction might have been appropriate had she come upon Barbara a few days earlier, in the arms of Joseph Stratford. But she had seemed unusually distraught that Robert Breton might kiss another.

It was interesting. And it had given her a flutter of hope. Despite what everyone might say was the future, there were other forces at work tonight. If Joseph asked, and Anne refused… Or if Breton asked first, as his reaction to Anne's tears said he might…

She had sat alone behind the curtain, thinking the most delicious thoughts, smiling to herself and imagining Joseph, either stunned or relieved, turning to her for comfort. Despite her father's feelings on the subject, she would give that comfort gladly. Not tonight, of course. They were still almost strangers. But in the coming months they might grow closer, while her father grew used to the idea.

Then the man she'd been imagining had burst in upon her and everything had changed.

She looked at herself in the mirror, watching the blood rushing to her cheeks and wondering what to think of what had occurred. Maybe it was not as significant as she made it out to be. She'd kept her maidenhead, after all. But it would be a lie to think of herself as innocent. Another shudder went through her body at the memory, and she gripped the edge of the little table before her until her knuckles went white, trying to regain control.

His words after had been harsh and hurtful—but exciting as well. She had tried to respond in kind, aloof and yet passionate, not wanting to reveal her heart lest this all be a game to him. But she hoped it was not. She could not help but love Joseph. His passion and enthusiasm for his work drew her, and they were tempered with a kindness and generosity that few had seen but her. Given time, he could be made to see the errors he was making. Or perhaps it was he who was right, and her father in the wrong. There had to be a compromise of some kind to avert disaster. And she might be the only one who could bring it about.

The door opened behind her. When she glanced into the mirror she saw Anne Clairemont enter. Just for a moment the other girl shot a look of unvarnished loathing at the back of her head. Then she seemed to realise that it had been observed. Her features softened and her expression reformed into the placid mask that she so often wore. She went to a little bench on the opposite side of the room and began straightening hairpins, dabbing lightly at her eyes in an effort to disguise the tears she'd shed earlier, powdering her cheeks until the face in her own mirror was a deathly white.

'Here, let me help you.' Barbara turned and went to her, smoothing the loose curls at the back of her head and rubbing gently at the other girl's cheeks to get some colour back into them.

'Thank you,' Anne said, a little coldly. 'I fear this evening you are not seeing me at my best.'

'What you saw in the refreshment room was nothing,' Barbara said, wondering even now if she was apologising for the correct offence. 'Mr Breton was attempting to be kind to me, I think. I am grateful, of course. But that is all.'

'It does not matter,' Anne said quickly, but there was a flash of spirit in her eyes that quickly died again.

'I think it might,' Barbara said. 'Perhaps we could call the carriage and return home rather than going back to the party. If it would help, I could pretend an indisposition and you could pretend to help me.'

'No,' Anne said hurriedly. 'The snow has come, and I will be staying the night. You as well. Do not worry. Arrangements are being made. I will be quite all right—really. I must return to the ballroom. Father will be expecting me. And Joseph.'

'But what do *you* wish, Anne?' It was maddening to watch the girl, so obviously miserable, headed in lockstep towards the altar, unwilling to consider another option.

'I wish for everyone to be happy this Christmas,' the other girl said firmly. 'It does not matter what I want. That will not be possible. I think we can only hope to do as little harm as possible.' She lifted her chin, inspecting herself in the mirror. 'That is much better. Thank you, Barbara. Now, if you would be so kind, I would like to return to the ballroom, and I do not wish to walk alone.'

They linked arms and proceeded down the corridor towards the ballroom, chatting amiably of nothing in particular. And if Barbara felt Anne's arm tensing as they passed the kissing bough in the doorway of the refreshment room, then she ignored it—just as Anne needed to ignore Barbara's flinch as they passed the alcove.

Then they were back in the ballroom, and little knots of people glanced in their direction, Anne's father giving an approving look. There was Joseph, standing near the musicians, holding out a welcoming hand.

For a single, foolish instant Barbara thought that he was looking to *her*, offering that friendly gesture to coax her near. Then the moment passed and she realised that it was intended for the woman at her side.

Anne stiffened in a way that was imperceptible to any but Barbara. Then she fixed the serene smile more firmly in her lips and stepped forwards to take the offered hand and her proper place at Joseph Stratford's side.

He gave a nod of approval and cleared his throat. Although the noise was not particularly loud, it caught the attention of everyone in the room. They turned to look at him expectantly, and Barbara watched in admiration at his easy mastery of the crowd.

But in horror as well. For, despite all his vague words, and his actions towards her, and Anne's obvious penchant for another, Barbara could see what was about to happen—just as everyone else could.

'My pleasure to announce…done me…honour…hand in marriage.'

The words seemed to fade in and out of her hearing. It was clear that the others had no problem, for they smiled and clapped politely. Champagne was pressed into her hand by a ready servant. Barbara accepted it with a numb nod. All around her glasses were raised and toasts made to the happy couple—for that was what they appeared to be.

Just before her knees gave way she took a half-step back to the little chair against the wall, so that it would seem she sat rather than collapsed. As the music began again she shrank back, pulling it behind a pot of ivy, and sipped wine that seemed like vinegar on her tongue.

CHAPTER TWELVE

Too late, too late, too late.

It should have been a triumph. Joseph had acquitted himself as well as could be expected amongst the gentry who had accepted his invitation. He'd secured financing for his business plans, he had found himself a wife to secure his position in the area, and his truce with Lampett had lasted long enough to avoid embarrassment.

That he was well on the way to making the man's daughter into his mistress was a point that did not bear close observation. Nothing must come of that—no more than the extremely pleasant dalliance they had experienced in the hall. Surely she knew it was no more than that.

But he had seen the stricken look in her eyes even through the brandy-soaked haze he'd created to steel his nerves for the announcement. Even if she had done similar things before, she had allowed him to do what he had done because she loved him—or thought she did. He had taunted her with his knowledge of her feelings, cheapening them to hurt her. Then he had publicly pledged himself to someone else minutes after leaving her.

So he was marrying the wrong woman for the right reasons. What of it? The move was very like unto himself. He always seemed to be turning a good idea into a bad one. Though they suited perfectly, Bob and Anne would be parted so that he might advance in society and in business. After her brief visit to the manor he would pack Barbara Lampett back off to the village. She would stay as a virtuous spinster, so long as he kept his hands off her.

He remembered the vague promises he had made to the ghostly coachman of how things would change now that he knew of the problems. But for the life of him, he could not think what he might have done to make any difference. If the visions he had seen the previous evening were true, they would all be the sadder for what had occurred tonight, and he was to blame for that misery.

Too late. Too late.

His valet laid out his things and prepared him for bed. All the while Joseph listened to the ticking of the clock, which seemed to chant the words to him as each second passed. It was a wonder that man had invented such a clear measure of the passage of time—one that could be felt almost to the bone on silent nights like this.

It was not as if he needed a further reminder of his mortality. Lord knew, his father had seen to that in recent nights. And tonight's visitor would be the worst of all. For why would this charade have been needed if the future was a happy one? And it was almost three o'clock.

Too late.

The edges of the room seemed to darken and chill. Though it was well stocked with coal, the fire burned low in the grate. It was the spirit coming for him, he was sure. And he did not wish to see what it foretold.

He had made a mistake. Nothing unusual. He'd made many over the course of twenty-five years. But the mistakes of late were irrevocable. He was marrying a woman he did not love. Toying with one he did. Upending an already fragile community with the arrogant assurance that his plans would set everything right, given time.

But now it seemed that only his own death could call a halt to what had begun. He was unsure whether he was likely to be taken by the night's spirit, or simply driven to make his own end by the grim future that lay ahead.

Too. Late.

His valet withdrew in silence, leaving him alone.

Joseph sat on the edge of the bed, waiting for the end, disgusted with his cowardice. Perhaps his father's real plan had been that he meekly accept judgement on this last night. But there had to be something he could do. There must be some fact he was missing that might explain the village and the women in it, for they were a mystery to him. When Lady Clairemont had announced that they would be staying tonight, rather than fighting the weather, he had asked if it was her intention that Miss Lampett stay as well. He had been greeted with a look of such cold hostility that he could not believe it had risen from a simple indiscretion.

If tonight was to be his end, he would never know the truth. Nor would he know the woman who was sleeping just down the hall from him, in the smallest of the guest bedrooms. He could wait in his own room for the angel of death or the very devil himself to take him. Or he could go to her, demand the truth and love her—just once.

There would never be a better time for it, he was sure. If he was already damned, one more sin was not likely to make things any worse. He dared not miss the chance and leave her thinking he felt nothing.

He stood and threw off the nightshirt, grabbing a dressing gown and wrapping it about his naked body. Then he threw open the door and walked down the hall to seal his fate.

CHAPTER THIRTEEN

IT HAD been a miserable evening, and one that Barbara would repeat in memory for the rest of her life. Each time she saw the happy couple who were lord and lady of Clairemont Manor her stomach would twist as she wondered how much Joseph remembered, and how much Anne knew of it. And if that brief interlude in the alcove had meant anything at all.

Then there was Robert Breton, who had been too cowardly to seize the opportunity when he'd had his chance. She hoped he would fade into obscurity rather than continue to haunt the area. If he stayed, she rather feared that they would become friends and spend long days brooding jealously over the lives they might have had. Perhaps they might marry, and have the same kind of dreary and passionless union that Joseph and Anne shared.

Why could she not just go back to her loneliness of a day ago? It had been so much simpler.

There was a knock at the door.

She sat up in bed and pulled the covers up to her chin. This was not the scratch of a servant, nor the polite tap of Anne, come to share a quiet conversation before bed. This was the firm rapping of the master of the house. He was standing in front of her door, probably one more knock away from calling out to her, which might wake a neighbour or alert a servant. The resultant scene would be almost as bad for him as for her.

She pushed aside the covers, hurried across the room and threw open the door before the night could become any worse. 'What are you doing here?' she whispered, not wanting to draw further attention.

'I have come for answers,' Joseph said, in a voice that was loud and unembarrassed.

'As if you are the one who needs them. Talk to me tomorrow over breakfast, if you must.' Preferably in the presence of chaperones, to ensure that she did not do anything more foolish than she already had.

'I don't have tomorrow.' As usual, he could think of no further than himself.

'Be quiet,' she whispered. 'Someone will hear.'

'If you do not wish to draw attention, you had best let me in,' he said, with a strange tight smile.

She grabbed him by the lapel and pulled him into the room, closing the door quickly, silently, regretting that she had touched him at all, for her hand seemed to burn with the contact. And now he was in front of her, blocking her way into her own room, and she was planted, shoulders to the door panel, in a way that half reminded her of those scandalous moments in the alcove. Except now she was wearing nothing but her chemise—not that there was much of her body he had not seen.

'What do you want?'

She tried not to squirm at the memory, and the traitorous desire to step forwards, to relax and to go to him. But perhaps that was not what he wanted. He did not reach for her. He was frowning, as though deep in thought.

'Tell me what has happened here.'

'I beg your pardon?'

'Here. In this community. Before I arrived. I need to know about the people right now, before I can go another step.'

She laughed, for it was so far outside what she had expected to hear that she could hardly credit it. 'You wish to know now—after moving here, building here and spending untold sums of money to achieve your ends—what the people might think of it?'

'I know what they think of it,' he said dismissively. 'They hate it—as they would hate any change. That is not what I mean and you know it. Tell me about Mary. Tell me about the mill fire. And your father's accident. Help me make sense of it all.'

'Help you to make sense of it?' She pushed past him to return to her bed. 'There is nothing to make sense of.

No blame to assess. Accidents happen. People are hurt. They die. Time passes. The survivors are changed, but they live on. For what else is there to do?' She turned back to face him. 'If that is all you have come here to say, then you are wrong. It *can* wait until morning, and a setting not so completely inappropriate. Goodnight, Mr Stratford.' She climbed into bed, turning away from him and pulling up the covers. He could make his retreat in anger or embarrassment. She did not care. But she should not be forced to watch it.

But he did not leave. She felt the weight of him, sitting on the edge of her bed, not touching, just out of reach of her. 'Tell me.'

'You are selfish and horrible to come and remind me of these things, tonight of all nights.' Even knowing the stupidity of it, after their time in the alcove she had cherished some small fantasy that he would come to her, attempting to continue what they had begun. Perhaps he would speak of love, and even though she would recognise the words for lies, it would be better than nothing.

'Barbara.' He laid his hand on her shoulder, and through the covers the weight of it was warm, heavy and soothing—as was the sound of her name on his lips. 'Tell me the truth. You have held things back from me. I would have no more secrets with you.'

'Like the fact that your engagement to Anne was in place even as you fondled me?' she shot back, the humiliation still fresh. 'Go to her, if you want a bed partner. Let me have some peace.'

'That is not what I mean. Not at all. Or at least that is not all.' He fumbled with his words, as though he could make no sense to her or himself. 'I need to know everything. I need to know about *you*.' He said it with such curious emphasis that for a moment she believed that he really cared. 'Why are the Clairemonts so cold to you? Tell me.'

He stretched out behind her on the mattress, the covers separating them, and the hand that had shaken her shoulder was wrapped about her waist, drawing her close as he buried his face in her hair. He would not leave until she spoke. She was sure of it. If she must give him the truth, it would be easier while lying in his arms, pretending that his strength was her own.

'Because I killed their daughter, six years ago at Christmas time. It is my fault that Mary is dead. They hate me for it, and I do not blame them.'

He did not move away from her, not even to breathe. If anything, his arms held her tighter, and his lips pressed to the back of her throat, close to her ear. 'You said she was ill.'

She sighed. 'And so she was—because of me. My friend Mary Clairemont died of influenza. There is no story. Many of us were sick that season. But none so bad as her,' Barbara admitted. 'We were the best of friends and spent all our time together. When I sickened she brought me broth and calf's-foot jelly. She read to me to pass the time. Her mother came as well. They took the illness back to their own home. Mary died of it.'

'You blamed yourself?'

'Not at first. But Mr Clairemont came and argued with Father. I heard them. He said that I should have been the one to die. It was horrible. After that, we were no longer welcome at the manor.'

'That was unfair,' Joseph said from behind her. 'But from what I have seen of Mr Clairemont it is not so very surprising.'

'Mrs Clairemont was distraught, and still weak from her own illness. It was a cold winter, and she did not recover until nearly spring. Christmas, which had been such a merry time at the manor, was silent.'

'I understand there were parties here?'

'Like this one. But bigger.' She could not help but smile at the memory. 'Not for years, now. Their sadness cut the heart out of them. They could not celebrate without thinking of Mary.'

'Time to move on, then,' Joseph said. His voice was gruff, as though it were possible to reject the softer emotions.

'One cannot just push away grief when everything about the Christmas holiday is a reminder,' she informed him, rolling to face him and leaning on her elbow. 'You must show more compassion for Mrs Clairemont. The family was forced to strip the greenery from the house and use the feasting foods for a funeral. It was a great shock to them.'

'But wrong to blame you for it,' he said, touching her hair with his hand.

'And Mr Clairemont lost his grip on his business. The war took its toll as well. Mr Mackay leased the land from him, but was not able to sell his goods. He bought the new looms to save money at the expense of the workers.'

'If Clairemont had been smart, he would have noticed before things got bad,' Joseph said, reasoning like a machine even while looking at her like a lover and lying near naked at her side. 'He lost a building because of it. A valuable tenant as well. That allowed me to capitalise…'

'Always business,' she said with a sigh. 'Father tried to help him at the last. Despite their differences, he ran to help save the mill with the rest of Mr Clairemont's friends. But he was the one who was struck down by a falling beam. He was unconscious for three days. We were sure he would die. And now…'

'His thoughts are addled,' Joseph finished. 'He blames the mill for it. He blames me as well.'

'But really it is my fault,' Barbara said. 'From the very first. If I had been the one to die, and not Mary…'

Before she could finish the sentence his arms had tightened upon her, drawing her into a breath-taking hug. 'Then things would have been different. But they would have been no better for the majority of people here.' His lips touched her cheek, kissing away a tear that she did not remember shedding. 'I have travelled the country, north and south, and seen what the war has done to trade, and what the new looms have done to tradesmen. It would have been uneasy here no matter what had happened. If your father had not been the one to speak against me then someone else would.'

She wanted to believe that almost as much as she wished that things could have been simpler—young and clean and pleasant, just as they had been a few years ago. 'There are a great many ifs,' she said. 'I think of them often. Sometimes it is only necessary to change the life of one person to set the world upon a different course.'

He stiffened. 'So I have been told. But I do not think that you are that person who must change.'

She laughed softly. 'And so I am put in my place, sir. It is good to know that you think me of so little importance in God's great scheme.'

'On the contrary. You are surprisingly important to…' He paused. 'To many people. But you are also blameless of anything that has happened here. Do not change. You are just right as you are. I would not alter an atom of you. But I owe you an apology. I assumed that the trouble was something quite different. A dispute over a suitor, perhaps.'

'There has never been anyone,' she admitted, then took a breath to gather courage. 'Other than you.'

He lay very still beside her. 'I never would have done what I did had I understood.'

'Did you think I was the village whore, then?' she

asked, struggling to escape his arms. 'It is a wonder you allowed me to associate with your guests.'

'No.' He said the word in a groan, and his arms were no longer gentle but holding her like iron as she fought against him. The lips that had been pressed softly to her cheek were taking her mouth, until she stilled and allowed his kiss, which was as rough and improper as he was. He filled her mouth with his tongue, making the rest of her body feel empty in comparison. The thin blanket that separated them was like a million miles of desert. And suddenly she was fighting not to get away but to be closer to him, praying that in total surrender he might finally admit what he felt for her.

'No,' he whispered, staying her hand and keeping the barrier between them. 'My guests are not worthy of you. Neither am I. I am a villain, a rogue, a debaucher. But I cannot seem to let you go. I only wanted to make things better, I swear. But with each turn I dig deeper. After tonight I will never get free.'

'If it is me you seek to be free from, then I hope you never succeed,' she whispered.

Perhaps it would have been better had he been right. If she had already fallen she would know how to proceed now, to find the thing that would make him happy, would make him stay. She pressed her lips to his earlobe and then his cheek, licking the dark stubble and following it to his jaw. He looked even more tired than he had before. She remembered that he complained he could not sleep. It must be true, for it was well past three and he was still awake and worrying about her.

Whatever he felt for her, he needed a comfort that only she could give him. She nestled her head against his throat and kissed the places that had been covered with his cravat. Then she found his fingers with hers and untangled them from the sheet he held, pushing the covers down so that they could be together.

He sighed and stopped resisting. Then he kicked away the last of the blankets and yanked at the tie of his robe, to be free of that as well. Suddenly she was sharing a bed with a naked man.

Though it was of her own choosing, she found that she was afraid to look on him. So she stared into his eyes, and found them to be infinitely sad, and perhaps a little frightened.

'No matter what happens, no matter how it appears,' he whispered, 'I am yours until I die. Do you understand that? And I am afraid of that. Because I know I will hurt you.'

'You never shall,' she said. It was another lie, of course. But she decided she would believe it, just for tonight. 'Would you help me to remove my chemise, please? For I think I would like to feel...'

His shoulders shook from laughing as he reached for the hem. 'Is that what it is like to make love to a lady? All "please" and "thank you"? I will give you a reason for those words.' He stripped her last garment from her and held her away from him for a moment, so that he could admire her body and kiss each of her peaking nipples.

'Cold?' he asked, smiling against her breast.

'A little,' she admitted, with a delicious shiver as he blew a cooling breath on her damp skin.

'I will take care of you.' He spread his robe over her shoulders and it was still warm with the heat of his body, the quilted silk arousing her body where it touched her. If she had been hoping for some deeper declaration she ought to be disappointed. But it felt good to be cared for, decadent and exciting.

Then he kissed her again. At first his lips pressed innocently to her forehead. Then they slipped down her face in a trail of small kisses on her eyelids and cheeks, coming to rest upon her mouth. It was not precisely chaste. But neither was it as unbridled as it had been a moment ago. His lips had lowered to hers in an almost leisurely fashion, brushing her face before settling, opening, deepening and taking her tongue into his mouth.

She kissed him back, as he had been kissing her, touching each feature of his face with her lips and tongue before settling on his mouth and losing herself in it. Being with Joseph was more than just passion. It was a solution, an answer, the opening of a locked door. It was right, no matter what her head should be telling her.

They parted for breath and he touched her cheek with his finger. 'May I stay with you until dawn?' he whispered. 'We do not have to lie together, if you do not wish…'

It was an odd thing to say. But she did not take the time to wonder at it, for there were far more interesting things to notice. 'It is what I wish,' she admitted. It was yet another point of no return—to say aloud that she wanted him. Before she could lose her nerve, she ran her hand once down the length of him, over his chest to rest near his sex, afraid to do more than that. She took a deep breath, and then spoke what was in her heart. 'Because I want to show you what I feel. Whatever happens tonight, tomorrow or in the distant future, you must know that I love you.'

'You have known me for such a short time that you cannot know the truth of your feelings.'

'I know that as well,' she said. 'And I know that you do not want my love. But I think it is important that you hear the truth. You do not love me. But I love you.'

'You should not,' he said, a little uneasily.

'I cannot help it.' She leaned back into the pillows and closed her eyes. With his body, he followed her, throwing a leg over her hip so that they could lie together, skin to skin.

She felt her body wakening as though it were newly born, every sensation a first. Despite the danger to her reputation, and to her heart, she felt warm and safe, and more sure of her love than ever. She must have been meant for him, and he for her. Why else would their bodies fit so well together? Why else would they respond so quickly? She could feel him, hard between her legs. And her hips gave an answering push against him, wet with invitation. The act of love, which had seemed most unusual when her mother explained it to her, now seemed like the most right and natural thing in the world.

Joseph understood, and gave a little shake of his head. 'Wait. There is more.'

'More?' After what had happened in the alcove this evening, what was left for them but to finish what they had started?

'I wish to know every inch of you.' His hands began to explore, smoothing down her shoulders and spine, and up the backs of her arms. His leg moved against hers, the hairs of it tingling as they brushed her. Then his mouth left hers to kiss her fingertips, her elbows and her ribs. He took one of her nipples into his mouth and gave it the softest of kisses. Then he rubbed his face gently between her breasts, so she could feel the roughness of his cheeks, grating ever so slightly against her skin. Then he turned his head to take the second breast less gently than the first, turning the soft kiss into a series of nips that made her cup his face in her hands, arch her back and press her body into his open mouth.

His fingers stroked her as his eagerness grew, gripping her thighs and parting them, and then giving one single touch of a fingertip in the place where they met. It hovered for a moment, and then slid down, and in.

She gasped. She had thought, after the sample he had

given her by the ballroom, that she understood what it must be like to make love. But though he touched her in the same way she felt different now, as though every part of her body burned.

He slid up her body again, so that he could kiss her on the lips, and the passage of his rougher skin against her body was maddening. She wanted to writhe against him, purring and winding herself about him like a kitten, demanding to be stroked.

'If I can do nothing else, I want to make you feel as you do me, when I look at you.' He smiled. 'I will make you want me to the point of madness. And together we will take the want away with having.'

'You have.' It seemed that now he was nude he was larger. Not just… She looked down and then hurriedly up at his face again. Not just the increase she had expected. It was the whole of him, as though the power and energy which had been hidden beneath his clothing was suddenly released. She was awash in it, tingling from the tips of her toes to the top of her head.

She looked down again, at the pair of them naked and side by side on the bed. For a moment she was more amazed than aroused. It was natural and right to be this way with him, just as it had from the first moment they'd been alone together, when he'd grabbed her by the arm and pulled her to safety. He reached for her now and caught her suddenly under the arms, rolling and pulling her close. Then he was on his back, and she was being pulled down, over and against him, sprawling over his body, covering him like a blanket.

It was his turn to lie back into the pillows, sighing contentedly. Then he pulled her head down to meet his and kissed her, with the tickle of his chest hair against her nipples and the stirrings of his erection between her legs. His hands were busy, adjusting, moulding, positioning, until his body was fitted to hers, his manhood nudging at her maidenhead.

Now she was waiting, fairly sure of what the next step would be, but unsure of how it would come about.

'Relax,' he murmured against her temple. 'We are still strangers, the pair of us. Touch me. Learn my body so that I may better know yours. I want to feel your hands.'

'Where?'

'Anywhere. You will know when it is time for more than that.'

How would she know anything of the sort? Perhaps he still thought she had some experience in the matter. If so, she was likely to embarrass herself soon enough. But all the same she ran her hands over his chest and felt the muscles move in response. She touched his arms and they moved to circle her, to stroke her, to hold her in place against him. She bit his shoulder and he clutched her bottom, grinding his hips into hers as she sucked upon his skin.

And so she dared to sit up, balancing on his thighs, and reached lower to touch the part of him that touched her. His hands slipped between her legs, spreading them wide, probing the opening of her body and taking it while she stroked him. He teased and thrust with his fingertips, leaving little spearings of pleasure that coalesced inside her, urging her to pull his sex, which had grown hard, towards her own. She hung there, on the edge of something, afraid to take the leap that would end in a flight or a fall.

And then she was sure. She wanted it. She wanted him. She wanted to be his, even if it was just for a night. She cried out to him, 'Help me. Please.'

'Barbara. Darling.' The hands that had been slow and gentle before moved lightning-quick, pulling her forwards and onto him. There was a lance of pain. Then he rolled so that she was beneath him.

When she looked up, into his face, the expression she saw was as surprising as anything else had been. It was as though he had changed, in a moment, to a different man. There was no trace of hardness in him, nothing frightening or aloof. The flaws had burned away in a burst of triumphant energy, leaving bliss, peace and desire.

Then he began to move in her. She felt a sense of connection to him that was beyond physical. They were working together towards some common goal, and she smoothed her hands over the muscles of his back, trying to go where he led her, sure that there would be pleasure enough for both of them when they arrived. Everything was alive in her—every inch of skin. The places that touched and rubbed were different from the bare places touched by night air and firelight. The place where their bodies met was the best of all. There was no feeling like this. No words to describe it. It was like springtime, full of promise, melting ice and birdsong, the stirrings of things that had been sleeping inside her.

Inside her body some part of him touched some part of her, and it was as though the whole world had lurched violently to one side and then righted itself. Then it happened again. She seemed to lose all control as her body turned upside down and inside out. And in all that confusion he was with her, holding her, feeling the same thing. He tensed, gasped and stilled.

He was lying on top of her. But it was not as she'd expected. Even though he was a large man, he seemed to weigh nothing, covering her like a shield, keeping her warm and safe. He was a part of her now, and would be even after they parted, as she was sure they must. He drew away from her, but only a little way, reaching towards the foot of the bed to pull the coverlet over the pair of them and then settling back at her side, wrapping his arms about her body and keeping her close.

'I should go,' he whispered.

She did not really wish him to. But it might be better for him to leave now, while they were both happy, than to stay too long, until that feeling changed.

'You should,' she agreed. 'But I do not mean to let you. Not just yet.' She held him close, and he turned her so her back was against his chest, wrapping himself around her in a different way, as though he wanted to know every inch of her body before he released it.

'I will see to it that I am back in my room before the house wakes in the morning. I will listen for the chiming of the clock. It is already well past four. I did not hear it strike at all. Perhaps that is late enough. Nothing has changed.' Then he relaxed, stroking her hair, his hand moving slower and slower as he lost consciousness.

And she dozed as well. But before she was lost to all she wondered what he had been expecting.

CHAPTER FOURTEEN

THE next morning was much as any other visit to the manor had been, even though another man was master. A round of sleepy guests gathered in the breakfast room for steaming plates of eggs, thick slices of ham, toast, marmalade and subdued chatter.

It was all familiar except for their host, who sat at the head of the table looking like death and subsisting on nothing more than black coffee. If he had slept at all, it did not show. His skin was grey and there were hollows in his cheeks that the razor had not touched. Barbara wanted to go to his side and cut the food on his plate, feeding him like an invalid before sending him to bed.

But that was not her job. It was Anne's.

There could be no acknowledgement of what had happened between them—not even to share the fatigue they had felt while lying in each other's arms waiting out the hour between the clock chiming four and five, wondering if each minute would be the last they'd share. She was as tired as he, though she had made an effort to look lively so that no one might ask her about it. But it was a happy exhaustion. She had come to the table and smiled down into her plate, trying not to show the world how wonderful she felt.

Then Joseph had arrived. And the longer she'd sat with him the worse she'd felt. She found herself listening to the ticking clock once more. Eating mechanically and longing for the moment she could escape.

Morning had come and everything had changed—in that it was much the same as it might have been had nothing happened at all. Joseph was there at breakfast, greeting his guests, helping himself to more coffee and making sure that all needs were met. But he showed her no special favour, enquiring politely if she had slept well without a wink or a nod.

She responded in kind. If she seemed awkward, or somewhat chilly, it would be taken for a sign of the estrangement between her family and him. Nothing more, nothing less.

Then he turned his attention to Anne. He could at least manage a smile for her, though it was little better than a death mask. His concern was more pointed. Her plate was heaped full and taken away just as quickly when she did not seem pleased with it.

Barbara felt her own food curdling in her stomach, and reached very deliberately for the teacup in front of her. As she lifted her gaze to stare fixedly across the table she caught the eyes of Robert Breton. His expression was similar. Just as bland and unflappable. He was just as stubbornly uninterested in the proceedings at the end of the table as she was.

But as he looked at her there was the slightest rise at one corner of his lip, and an equally slight salute as he raised his teacup, as though he were toasting their shared misery.

To kindred spirits, she thought, and responded in kind.

'Will you be participating in today's activities, Miss Lampett?' he asked politely. 'I understand that the skating on the pond is quite pleasant. There will be games in the parlour, and the lighting of the Yule Log.'

'I had not given it thought,' she answered. 'When I arrived I was hardly prepared for more than an evening. If there is a way to return to the village...with a servant, perhaps.' Even now she sat at the table wearing her ridiculously unfashionable ballgown, because it was all she had. Today it was just one more thing to single her out from the group as not quite belonging to it.

'Oh, please do stay,' Anne insisted. 'And do not give me any excuses about lack of preparation. Your skates are still here, you know, from when we were young together. Anything else needed you might borrow from me. Or there are Mary's old things...'

There was a sharp intake of breath from Lady Clairemont, who was seated beside Joseph. Anne fell silent again.

'Yes. Please. Stay. I will accept no excuses.' Joseph made the offer mechanically, without even looking up, and Barbara took another hurried sip of tea to stop the words on the tip of her tongue.

What do you mean by that? Are you in any way sincere? Or is that sarcasm I hear? Even if it is a bald-faced lie, could it not be delivered with a smile?

'No,' she said softly. 'I thank you for your gracious offer of hospitality, but I must be getting back to Mother and Father. Perhaps, after Christmas, I might return. It has all been quite lovely and I am very glad that you invited me.'

'Very well, then,' Joseph said, not even bothering with a token resistance. 'I will see that the carriage is brought round—or perhaps there is a sledge.'

A spirited discussion erupted as to the delightful nature of sleigh rides, and what fun it might be to make an outing into the village, which was declared 'quaint' by the visitors from the South. It was a relief when the attention turned to more cheerful topics than the fate of the dowdy young woman at the foot of the table, leaving Barbara to excuse herself unnoticed.

She fled to her bedroom, counting on the privacy of a locked door. There were no belongings to gather before departure. Hiding above stairs would spare her any more awkward conversations. She could sit in the window seat and watch for the carriage that would take her away from the disaster that this visit had become.

But even there she was not alone. When she entered,

she startled the maid who had come to make up the room. The girl was the youngest daughter of the Stock family, who lived a scant quarter-mile from Barbara's home, and she was staring at the tangle of sheets on the bed, and the bloody smudge in the midst of them. She offered a quick curtsey, and muttered an apology for the interruption. Then she smiled, as though she had been presented with a tidbit juicier than any she might see with Christmas dinner, and hurried from the room.

Barbara almost turned to go after her, with a lame story of her restless night and the sudden monthly imposition that would explain the spots of blood. But there was no way gossip could be avoided. To deny it would be as good as admitting the truth: a couple had been sporting here, and the lady involved was the formerly virginal Miss Barbara Lampett.

They had been careful, or so she'd thought. Between kisses Joseph had assured her that the walls were thick, and that no one would see him come or go. She had consoled herself that if she was lucky enough to avoid pregnancy—and she dared not think about any other possibility—the secret would go to her grave.

She had not counted on the maids. While a bit of gossip about Mr Stratford's London guests would be harmless, and gossip about Anne would be avoided for the sake of her family, there was no magical protection that extended to Miss Lampett. She was a lady and should know better.

She gave one last look around the room to remember

that, however briefly, she had been supremely happy here. She had belonged to someone, if only for a few hours. Now she must return to her home and put the happy memory away, as she had so many others. She would not return after Christmas, for she doubted she could bear another visit.

And so she wandered, avoiding the breakfast room, where so many people were still gathered, and the salons and reception rooms, where plans for the day were being made. Instead she went to say goodbye to the portrait gallery, and to the ballroom, stopping to touch the curtain that covered the little alcove and wondering, if she pulled it back suddenly, if she would find the ghost of her younger self hiding there. Or had all those old times been supplanted by memories of Joseph?

With a little smile, she drew aside the curtain—only to hear a gasp, and the rustle of clothing falling back into place as the couple inside sprang apart.

'I'm sorry,' she said, 'I had no idea…' She turned quickly, shielding her eyes.

Anne stumbled forwards into the hall. Mr Breton acted almost as quickly to thrust her back into the recess and step in front of her, as though it were possible to shield her from view. He cursed very softly, and ran his fingers through his hair in an effort to compose himself. Then he bowed. 'I am sorry you were a witness to my disgraceful behaviour, Miss Lampett.' He bowed again to Anne. 'And that you had to experience it, Miss

Clairemont. My actions were totally inappropriate, and no apology can be offered for them other than an excess of alcohol.'

He looked back at Barbara, knowing that she had seen him, sober as a judge, at the breakfast table, less than an hour ago.

He gave a helpless shrug. 'My fate is in your hands, miss, as is the honour of a lady. Though I would not wish what has occurred here to be known, I cannot demand that you keep my secret. Know that I will be leaving Mr Stratford's home early in the New Year and returning to London. There will be no further risk of another incident.' Then he walked hurriedly away from them, down the hall.

The moment he was gone Anne rushed forwards, seizing her hands. The polite pretence of soft, smiling apathy had disappeared. 'Please, Barbara. Please. I beg you. Say nothing to Joseph of this. I know that I have no reason to ask your help. My family has treated you horribly for a thing which was no fault of yours. But, please, say nothing.'

For a moment the frozen woman before her melted into the image of her lost sister, into something much more human than she had been: a woman with desires who was at least capable of making mistakes, if not yet able to admit to them.

There was so much that Barbara was not speaking of already. Why should there not be one more thing? 'I saw nothing, Anne. Nothing at all that I wish to remark upon to anyone. But just for a moment can you not be honest with me? Was this all his doing? Or is there feeling on both sides?'

And Anne, normally so reserved and in control, burst into tears in her arms.

Barbara glanced around, relieved to see that there was no one there to witness the outburst. Then she took a firmer grip on Anne's hands and dragged her back into the alcove, to sit on the bench, pinning back the curtain to allow some light into their sanctuary. 'Come, now. If you cannot get hold of yourself, then at least come where fewer people might see you. Now, tell me. Do you love him or not?'

Anne gave a hesitant nod. 'He is leaving. Even before you discovered us he was threatening. Now he will go for sure.'

Barbara stifled surprise. She had meant to ask about Joseph—the only man whose future mattered. She corrected herself. 'You will lose Mr Breton, if you do not cry off your engagement.'

'How can I?' Anne looked up at her from watery blue eyes. 'I am the only daughter left. Everyone is depending on me to do exactly what is needed. Joseph wishes a lady for the manor. My father wishes to get his foot back in the door. He would rather stay here as a doting father-in-law than learn to be comfortable in new surroundings.' For a moment there was uncharacteristic bitterness in the sweet voice. 'No one is particularly interested in what *I* want. I had thought, since I had no real objections to the character of the man, that it would be enough to be comfortable and back in my own home. But, Barbara. Oh, Barbara.' She smiled. 'That was before I met Robert. I did not know that I could feel like this. And now it will end.'

Then she was crying again, and Barbara could find nothing to do other than offer her shoulder and pat the girl ineffectually on the back. Would it do her any good to be assured that her future husband did not care about her either?

That could not possibly be a comfort. Though she did not seem to expect it of him, Barbara doubted that the girl in her arms wished to know the extent of his uninterest, or that an old friend was a co-conspirator in her betrayal. Love was not her reason for marrying. And there was nothing Barbara could say that would make the Clairemonts' desire to regain the manor any different than it was.

'There, there,' she said, and could not manage to sound the least bit enthusiastic about it. Success for Anne meant failure for her.

There was no way, in good conscience, that she could talk the girl into crying off. 'Would it help,' she asked cautiously, 'if I spoke to Mr Stratford for you? Perhaps if he understood how unhappy you are…'

'No.' Anne gripped her arm. 'You mustn't. He would be furious. So would my father.'

Barbara doubted that would be totally true. Though Lord Clairemont would be angry at having his plans thwarted, she'd seen no evidence that Joseph would be similarly affected at the loss of his impending marriage.

But then, she had seen no evidence to the contrary. In all that little time they'd spent together he'd said nothing about Anne, either positive or negative. She was sure that he'd said not a word about terminating the engagement.

'Very well, then. I will not expose you.'

Anne gave her a watery smile. 'I am sorry again for how my family has treated you. How I have treated you as well. You are good and kind. I will do anything I can to help you in the future if you will keep my secret.'

With secrets of her own, Barbara could feel nothing but sympathy for the sister of her dearest friend. 'I will do nothing to hurt you, I promise. And if I can find a way to help you, I will do so.'

'I can ask for nothing more than that,' Anne said, carefully drying her eyes with a handkerchief.

'Miss Lampett?' Mrs Davy the housekeeper called from the end of the hall. 'The carriage is ready to take you to the village. Dick says you had best leave soon, or the roads will turn to mud.'

Without another word Barbara dropped the curtain into place, pretending that she had been alone. 'Of course. I am ready.' She walked quickly to the front of the house, wondering if she was obligated to say a farewell to her host. She decided against it. He knew very well how she felt, and the reasons for her leave-taking. 'You will give my regards and my regrets to

Mr Stratford, of course,' she said politely to the housekeeper.

'That will not be necessary, miss. He is waiting to see you off.'

'Oh,' she said weakly, forcing her steps not to falter on the way to the door.

He was waiting there, just as the housekeeper had said, looking more like a professional mourner than a party host, a few flakes of snow lying unmelted in his dark hair.

She nodded at him, trying not to show the fear she felt that he would try to stop her. If he revealed even one moment of true feeling she was likely to turn back on her plan and go meekly to the room he had given her.

'I've come to see you off,' he said, without expression. 'I am your host. It is appropriate, I think, to wish you well and see you safely from the premises. People will wonder, otherwise.'

'And it is appropriate for me to thank you for your hospitality,' she answered back. But she said nothing further.

'Well, then. Go.' He said it gruffly, as though he could turn her decision into his own wish.

'There is no reason to stay,' she said firmly.

He sighed, his composure breaking. 'And yet I do not want you to leave.' That was at least said with some tenderness, as though he actually meant it.

'You know I must. There is nothing for me here.'

He reached out and touched her arm. 'There is always tonight.'

'You think that because of last night I will allow you to make a habit of coming to me in secret?'

'There could be no other way. I cannot cry off from Anne without disgracing her.'

There. He had finally said it. He could not hurt Anne, but he thought nothing of what he might do to Barbara Lampett, who had far less protection than the daughter of the most honourable family in the area.

'You are horrible,' she said. Despite how wonderful she had felt, his touch now was torture. It made her want to cry. She pulled her arm from his grasp.

'You said you loved me.' He said it softly, urgently.

'And you have never said the same to me. Not even as a lie. I was foolish to tell you. And foolish to feel it as well. For you are unworthy. Cruel and selfish, just as my father tried to tell me.'

'It is not as you think,' he said.

'But you offer no further explanation to tell me how it might *be*, if it is not exactly as it appears. You are using me, and you will marry another.'

'I did not intend to,' he admitted. 'But I could not sit alone in my room, waiting for the end.'

'The end? That is a tad melodramatic, Mr Stratford. I suppose next you will tell me that you are afraid of the dark.' She laughed scornfully, hoping that it might hurt him just a little, so that he might feel some part of what she felt whenever she looked at him.

His look in response was strange. A little blank, a little panicked. And clearly saying that she had discovered some part of the truth. 'That is it, isn't it? You are afraid to sleep alone in a darkened bedroom. You used me for a night to solve the problem.' She shuddered. 'That is all I was to you. A warmer for your bed and a candle on a dark night.'

'It was more than that,' he said. But still he would not say what.

'I ruined myself in the hope that there was some affection on your part. But I could have been anyone at all.' Without his help, she heaved herself into the body of the carriage and tried to close the door.

'Barbara. Wait.' He was just behind her, his shoulders blocking the entrance.

'I have waited too long already.'

'Do not leave me.' He sounded almost plaintive now, as though he were actually afraid of facing another night alone.

'Tonight you must go to Anne for your comfort. It would make more sense. I am sure you have much to talk about.' She bit her tongue then, to keep back the spiteful revelation that she had been almost ready to share. 'But of course you will not, will you? She is a lady, and deserves better than to be treated as a receptacle for your carnality. And I? I was a lady once. But no longer, now that you are through with me. Now I am through with you. Good day, sir.'

She sat facing carefully forwards, ignoring his presence, until with an oath he slammed the door and signalled for the coachman to drive.

CHAPTER FIFTEEN

How much had the coachman heard? she wondered, huddling beneath the coach robe and pulling her shawl around her shoulders. How much had the grooms guessed? Between the bunch of them they would piece together the bits of her argument with Joseph and their secret would be no secret at all. The tragedy involving Mary had been the talk of the village for a while. Then most had decided that it could not have been helped, and that even if the Lampetts should have known better than to allow company in a sickroom, they'd meant no harm by it.

But now she would be infamous. The people would expect no less of Joseph, for he was a man. He was an outsider, as well, and already reviled. But *she* should have known better, and society would punish her for her lapse in judgement. Women would cut her, and avoid her mother as well. Her father, if he could be made to understand, would be devastated.

She would have to leave. As soon as she was sure that there would be no child she would advertise for a position as a governess, or a lady's companion. Perhaps, if she threw herself on the mercy of the vicar, he would write a letter of reference for her, assuring the world that she was gently brought up and properly educated. Even Lord Clairemont might help, if it was understood that her goal was to get as far away from Fiddleton as she could, so that she could create no further trouble. Her parents would be heartbroken at her leaving, but once she had managed to explain Mother would likely agree.

The carriage had pulled up to her house now, and a groom helped her down, seeming at a loss that there was no package or bag that she might be helped with. She thanked him, and went up the walk alone, without turning back.

Her mother greeted her in the front room, eyes sharp, discerning, not willing to let her pass without a challenge. 'I have sent your father to the bakery to get us bread for supper,' she said. It was an obvious ruse so that they could be alone, for Barbara had seen to the baking only yesterday. 'Did you enjoy your visit to the great house, then?'

'Of course,' she said. 'We stayed the night because of the weather, but I was not feeling quite myself this morning, and thought it best…' She had dropped her head as she spoke, unable to meet her mother's gaze. That was her undoing. She showed her guilt plainly by hiding the expression that she could not let her mother read.

'One of the maids from Clairemont has been to the market and gone already. But on the way she visited her mother, Mrs Stock. The entire family is in service up at the house. And they do like to gossip.'

'I gave them no reason to talk.'

'Do not try to lie to me, Barbara. You cannot trick me with words, like your father and his speeches. The maid says that there was a man in your room last night, sharing your bed. Who was it?'

The plans she had made as she'd ridden towards the village had not included this first, most difficult conversation. If she was to manage any of the scandal it would not do to fight now, against another who would bear the shame of it. She sighed and collapsed onto the bench by the fire, hanging her head in embarrassment. 'It is as bad as you think. Probably worse. I love him.'

'You cannot,' her mother said firmly. 'In my opinion, if you meant to lie with the man before marriage, love is the worst reason for it.'

She stared up at her mother in surprise and wondered just what she might know of such things, and why she was not more shocked than she was.

Her mother gave her a candid look. 'You are not some fainting schoolgirl, Barbara. You are a young lady, well on your way to spinsterhood. Sometimes these things happen. If you were seventeen and in your first season it might ruin your chances. Now there are no opportunities left to spoil.' She sat down beside Barbara and said, more quietly, 'Who was he? I hope it was not some London dandy. If so, his words were likely false ones, and there is little hope that he will stay past the New Year. Was it that nice Mr Breton I have seen occasionally in the village? He might be persuaded to do the right thing for the sake of your reputation. Or we could write his father and demand a settlement.' She sounded almost hopeful at the thought, as though there were a way to make something good come from her daughter's mistake.

'Joseph Stratford,' Barbara said, with a sinking heart.

The older woman slumped beside her, as though her last hope had been dashed. 'I suppose now you will tell me that, while he claims to have feelings for you, he has no intention of crying off from Anne Clairemont.'

'He does not love her.' But that was no defence at all.

'Neither does he love you, or we would not be having this conversation.' Her mother stared down at her hands, which were trembling in her lap. 'Do you understand, even for a moment, the predicament we are in? Your father is failing.' The last words came in a harsh whisper that made them all the more terrible. 'When he is gone, there will be nothing to save us from our fate. My own inheritance is running out. I bore no sons. What little we have from your father will go to his brother. Even a bad marriage is quite out of the question for you once it gets round that you've been bedded by the most hated man in Fiddleton.'

'I thought to leave,' Barbara said hopefully. 'If I take a position, I might send what money I earn back home.'

Her mother said nothing to this for a time. When she finally spoke her voice was even quieter, as though she was afraid that the house itself might hear. 'There is another solution—if you are not too proud to take it.'

'I do not understand.' Until a moment ago Barbara had not thought of herself as hopeless. Now she was not sure what her mother saw as a last salvation.

'Joseph Stratford has no intention of marrying you—not while he can have the lady that belongs in the great house he's bought,' her mother said bitterly. 'He is little better than a child playing with a dolls' house. It does not matter if he cares for her. He will have Anne Clairemont because she belongs there.'

She had not thought of it. But her mother was right. It was a chilling idea that Anne would sit, just as she wanted, in the chair at the end of the great dining table, writing her letters in the morning room, lounging in the salon with the careless grace she had affected with so many years' practice. But she would be little better than an ornament.

'But Stratford has proven himself to be a greedy and licentious man. He cares nothing for the people here.'

'He's not like that,' Barbara said. But, though she believed him to be different, there was ample evidence that her mother was right.

'Of course he is,' her mother said, more firmly. 'And isn't that the argument of every foolish young girl whose head is turned by broad shoulders and a kind word? *"To me, he is different."*'

But to her, he was. It would do no good to repeat what she knew to be true. But she remembered what it had been like, the previous night, as he'd comforted her when she spoke of Mary. He had needed her as much as she had needed him.

'He's had you, and there's little more to it than that, I am sure. He'll do the same again, if you let him.'

And now what had felt so wonderful felt wrong and shameful. Her mother was right. Even as she'd tried to escape him he'd been trying to lure her back. She wanted to bathe herself, scrub at her skin until there was no memory of it left. 'It will not happen again.'

'Oh, yes, it will,' her mother said, with a sad frown. 'If you love him, you will go when he sends for you. You will not be able to help yourself. That is the nature of love, after all. In the face of it, my warnings will mean nothing to you.'

She put an arm around her daughter, drawing her close and untying her bonnet so that that Barbara could lay her head on a comforting shoulder.

Her mother smoothed her hair and whispered, 'We cannot take back the past. I will not stop you if you go to him. But if you do, make sure there is an arrangement. One time and people will call you a fool. Twice and they will call you a whore. If Mr Stratford cares for you at all, make him give you your due. There will be little use for fancy dresses and frippery. But we will have need of a steady income before too much longer.' Her mother choked back a tiny sob, and then said in a firm voice, 'We need to be practical about the future.'

Barbara sank down into a chair, waiting for the room to stop spinning around her. It had all come to that, had it? And so soon. She had wanted to believe there was a respectable future ahead of her, with forged references and a quick trip to a place where no one would know that she'd disgraced herself. But her mother, always the most practical woman, had dismissed that fantasy without another thought. There would be no concealing the truth. She was ruined, and now she must make the best of it.

And she could do that by being honest and admitting that she wished to go back to Joseph. She would be a mistress: a rich man's whore. But she could still love him, and be with him, even if she could not have him for her own.

Joseph would marry Anne, just as he'd planned to do. He would have his great house, and his pretty wife, and his woman, too. Perhaps that was what he'd planned all along. He had silenced the opposition to his mill as well. For she would now be forced to make Father understand how unwise it was to anger the man who put bread upon their table. If Joseph tired of her, for whatever reason…

Barbara's future would be secure and her family

would be safe as long as she pleased him. But when she did not? He would send her away. There were few men like him in this small backwater, but plenty would know her as a great man's cast-off. If she did not arrange for a settlement at the beginning she would have to find another protector.

One that she did not love.

Barbara searched her feelings, trying to remember the conversations they'd shared, the constant rescues, the way she had felt as they had danced, and as he'd held her last night. Perhaps it was not love on his part. But there was nothing to indicate a lack of generosity. If she was to be a fallen woman, she could do much worse than to fall for Joseph Stratford.

As long as she put her heart to one side and thought sensibly there was a way out of this. Her mother was right. But if she meant to survive she must remember that love had no part in it. And as she sat there, ridiculous in an out-of-fashion ballgown, though it was near to noon, she let that part of herself die. There would be no foolish tears over things that could not be changed. She would seize the opportunity that had presented itself, and work it to her best advantage.

Joseph would approve of that, she was sure. Was that not the way he did business as well? If nothing else, she would prove that they were more alike than he knew.

CHAPTER SIXTEEN

CHRISTMAS Eve dinner was excellent, with roast beef fair to melting from the bone, and a Yorkshire pudding to sop up the rich gravy. The Christmas pudding was so soaked in spirits that a man could feel drunk on the richness of it, his own soul licked with the blue flames that danced over the surface of it without consuming it.

To Joseph Stratford every bite tasted like sand.

The Yule Log was crackling in the grate, and beside it were pans of chestnuts. Tables were set with bowls of wine and currants ready for snapdragon. His guests lit the spirits and snatched at the little fruits, shrieking with laughter and shaking their singed fingers.

And yet Joseph was cold.

The music, though not as raucous as it had been the previous evening, was lively enough to satisfy. But all the songs in the world could not have chased the dullness from his own spirit. He had done nothing as the only person who could make a change in him had turned and left. He had not stopped her. And soon he would pay the price for that.

To avoid conversing with others, Joseph danced the better part of the evening with Anne. True to form, she had little to say to him, letting him stride through the patterns in silence. She wore the same serene smile she always did. But there was a slightly panicked look in her eyes, as though she was bearing up no better than he. In encouragement, he squeezed her hand.

She started. Then, her worried eyes darting to his, gave an answering squeeze as if to admit that, while they both might be trapped, there was some comfort in knowing she had his sympathy.

Not trapped for long, my dear, he wanted to say. He had his own suspicions on how this night was likely to end. Try as he might, he could not see a marriage—happy or otherwise—looming on his life's horizon. Though it had been his whole world just a few days ago, the opening of the mill now seemed a distant and unlikely thing that he would have no part in. He wondered if Breton had the nerve to take it on. But that would mean turning his back on his birth and taking on a real position. Perhaps he could find some man of business to run the place. More likely the whole of it would fall to ruin if Joseph was not alive to fight for it.

It made him wonder… Would it have seemed too fatalistic to draw a will? He had no heir. Perhaps the house could revert to the Clairemonts once he was out of the way. It would have been wise to leave some document stating that it was his wish, should the worst occur tonight.

Although he had thought to fear death, now that it was likely upon him he could not seem to care. Barbara was gone, and he felt the emptiness of it as he walked the corridors of the great house before bed. He should have said something to her when he'd had the chance.

But what? How did one find the words for something that came so suddenly, so illogically, so inappropriately into one's life, upsetting plans, breaking vows, subverting all sense and reason? If he had fallen in love with her a few short months ago it might have been difficult. Now that he had formalised the agreement with Anne and her family it was quite impossible.

But then, everything seemed impossible to him. Where once his head had been full of bright and ambitious plans, it was now totally empty. He could not have a future with Barbara Lampett. But neither was he able to imagine one without her.

After his valet left him, he lay in silent dread, waiting for the strike of the clock. His father had been unnecessarily vague about the purpose of these visits. But he had said there would be three of them.

If he had seen the past and the present, then there could be little doubt that next would be the future. What if he had no future? It was quite possible that there was no future to see. If death was coming to take him, then he would be an angry spirit for having been kept waiting a night longer than expected.

If vengeance was due, then it was little more than Joseph deserved. He thought of his recent treatment of those around him, and the way Barbara had turned from him in disgust after only one night. She was right. He had used her, clinging to her like a lifeline in a stormy sea, trying to postpone what he'd known was coming.

If the coming shadow was no more than his death, he had waited too long to tell her what she meant to him. He would go to his grave in silence, and she would never know. He had given her reason enough to hate him. Perhaps that would be easier. Then she would not grieve.

He opened his eyes, aware of a change in the room. There was movement, but none of the light that the other spirits had brought with them. This future, whatever it was, was darkness. And the greatest cold yet. The very air around him was as the touch of the previous spirits, and it froze the breath in his lungs and the soul at his core.

He reached out to the darkness in the corner. Tonight it suited his mood to embrace it. 'Whatever you are, come and be done with it. I deserve all the punishment you wish to deliver. But if this is the end, then I request a boon. Give me one more day to make right what needs mending. Do not take me to judgement, knowing what I have left undone.'

There was no answer.

'Very well, then.' He sighed. 'I suppose that all men facing this have regrets. And if you granted wishes then it would be one more day, and one more, in a never-ending string.'

A deeper silence was his only answer. He could sense nothing: no amusement, condescension or annoyance from the thing in the corner. Only a feeling of waiting.

He studied it. The dark thing was man-shaped, and yet not quite a man. As tall as he. Cloaked, perhaps, for the outline of the head had a hooded quality. But only that. It seemed the harder he tried to look at it the less he could see. This lack of definition made him uneasy, building a fear in him that was worse than anything he might have imagined. If it had simply been some horror, he would have catalogued the deformity and recovered from the shock of it.

But this nameless, faceless thing taunted him with the idea that, if he struggled for a while, he would know it for what it was. It drew the tension in him out like a fine wire, making him wait for the snap of recognition that would cause him to go mad.

He deliberately looked away and stood, walking towards it. 'Come on, then. Take me to wherever it is that you mean to, and let us end this.'

He touched its hand. Or thought he did. For when he looked down there was nothing there. Yet the feeling of cold dry bones in his hands remained. This time they did not fly. They walked slowly—out of the bedroom, down the stairs and into the front hall, marching towards the front door, which swung open before them, engulfing them in a chill mist. He could feel the December wind rattling the leafless trees until they scraped against the windows and rustled curtains. And high on the icy gusts he heard a cry that was not so much a wail as a low moan. It came not from outside, but within.

As they passed the door of the salon he heard voices, and turned to view the tableau. A couple wrestled on the couch in a passionate embrace, near to devouring each other with the intensity of their kisses.

Anne looked as he had never seen her, beautiful but dishevelled. Her hair was free, her bodice loosened and her expression hungry. 'We cannot. We must stop.' Even as she said it she tore at the neckcloth of the man who held her.

'So you have said, for ten long years. Yet we never do.' Robert Breton kissed her again, pushing her hands away to pull at his shirt collar. 'Some day he will discover us. He is not a man who takes lightly the violation of what he considers his.'

Joseph's wife laughed bitterly. 'I doubt he cares. He must know by now. There have been no children. Nor are there likely to be. But he barely even tries any more.'

'Do not speak of your time together. I cannot bear to think of it.' His oldest friend reached up to smooth the hair away from his wife's face. 'You never should have married him.'

'But I did. And now it is too late.'

'You are still young,' he assured her. 'And just as beautiful as the day I fell in love with you, so many Christmases ago. Leave him. Run away with me.'

Do it, you faithless harlot. I do not want you. The words sounded clear in his mind, and in his heart. He wanted to scream at the harshness of them, even if they were true.

'I cannot.' Anne sighed. 'I do not love him, nor does he love me. But without me he would be alone.'

'You know that is not true.'

'I do not wish to think of that,' Anne whispered, with a sad little laugh.

'Then think of his work. He has the mill to occupy him. It is his one true love.'

'He takes no more pleasure in that than he does in me. When he is at home he wanders the halls at night, counting the rooms.'

Had the habit never changed, then? Even ten years later, was he still so unsure of himself that he needed evidence of his wealth?

'He drinks far too much.'

'All the more reason to leave him,' Breton encouraged her.

She shook her head. 'It is likely to be the death of him soon enough. I have looked into his eyes. He is not well. What harm would it do to wait a month? Maybe two? I will be a widow then. None will think it odd that we find each other.'

His old friend's jaw tightened imperceptibly at the

thought of further inaction. 'I will wait, if I must, for the love of you. I know how difficult it would be for you to leave here, and to admit to the world what has been going on between us. But if he does not finish himself soon, then it is not the drink that will end him.'

Anne clung to his arm. 'You mustn't say such things.'

Bob Breton, who was the mildest and most pleasant man that Joseph could name, looked colder than December. 'I think them often enough. I find it difficult to stay silent, with the cancer of it eating me from the inside. I said I understand why you stay, and I cannot fault you for it. He is your husband, and can offer much beyond the legality of your union. But that does not mean that I like it.'

He kissed her again, until she was near to swooning with desire for him. Then he spoke. 'I love you, Anne. But I cannot wait much longer. If he does not let you go with his own timely death I will do what is necessary to achieve the end necessary so that you might be free.'

Joseph waited for the denial, the pleading from his wife that would spare his life. Instead she was silent, but worried. She leaned forwards into Breton's shoulder, as though her only fears were for him. Breton's arm went about her, offering her the support that a husband should have given her.

Strangely, he felt no real jealousy at the sight—only sadness that it had come to this, and that two people so obviously in love had been poisoned to desperation with it.

'Enough of this,' he said to the shadow at his side. 'They hate me. There is nothing more to see. I am a cuckold, but at least I am alive. Take me to the mill, for I wish to see how it fares.'

They continued down the hall and out through the front door, across the lawn and into a mist so thick that the walk might have been one mile or ten for all he knew of it. There was no landmark to show him the way. Nor did he feel the passage of time as he walked.

They were standing at the mill gates now. The silent spectre reached up, resting a wisp of a hand against the gatepost, tracing a divot where a bullet had struck brick.

'There was trouble here, then?' There was no other evidence of it. The mill still stood, even larger than it had been when he'd last seen it, a decade before. He released an awed breath. 'Let me go inside.'

They entered through the dock, to see goods rolled and stacked in neat rows along the wall, ready for delivery. The boilers chugged and rattled, letting off heat and clouds of steam and the stink of sizing and dye. On the factory floor the looms rattled and the shuttles clattered in and out of the warp in a sprightly rhythm—the deafening sound of industry.

Everywhere he looked he saw workers: silent, sullen women and children, operating as surely and mechanically as the machines he'd made for them. From time to time they looked up with quick, rat-like glances at the clock. Then they hurried back to their work with a nervous shudder, as though they did not want to be caught looking anywhere but at their assigned tasks. It was functioning exactly as he'd hoped. And the sight of it filled him with a misery he could not describe.

'Very well, then. All I have worked for, all my dreams, will be like a mouth full of ashes to me in ten years' time. Is there more? Or will you take me home to bed?'

The shadow moved on, out into the fog again. There was nothing he could do but follow.

They walked down the high street of the village, a little way behind a hunched figure that seemed strangely familiar. Joseph quickened his pace to catch the man and end the mystery. But then he watched the villagers look up from their daily doings, stiffen and turn away. 'They see me?' he asked the spirit. If they did, it was not a connection he welcomed. While he had not been well liked in his own time, their glares now held a level of animosity he was not prepared for. What had once been reserve and suspicion had hardened into cold hatred. And it was all the worse because it was mostly the women who stared at him—not just the men who had always been angry.

In fact there seemed to be an unusual number of females.

Then a woman stepped directly into the path of the man in front of him, blocking his way.

The man he was following stopped dead in his tracks. He did not push past the stranger, but neither did he say anything, either in apology or enquiry. It was as though this was a ritual that had occurred before.

'Merry Christmas, Mr Stratford,' she said to the man he followed. 'I hope you are glad of it.' Then she spat on the ground at his feet.

Without a word, this other, older him stepped around her and continued on his way to the edge of the village, past the church and into the little graveyard beside it.

Not so little any more, Joseph noticed. Not huge, by any means, but larger than he would have expected. Had there been an epidemic? Or some other disaster to account for the additional graves? With little warning, the spirit at his side turned in at the gate and walked through the headstones to the last row of stones.

They were all names he recognised, for he had seen the men gathered around him just a few days ago, with hammers and torches, eager to push through the gates and smash the frames on the mill floor. Wilkins, Mutter, Andrews—and the eponymous Weaver, whose family had been at the craft for so long that they shared its name. All dead. All on the same day.

Had he called the militia? Or some other branch of the law? It could have been hanging, or just as easily a pitched battle that the local men were overmatched to fight. But the arrival of troops would explain the crease a bullet had made in the stonework at the mill. No matter what it had been, the rebellion had been stopped. And he had been at the heart of it. Calling in the law to protect his rights, and wiping out families in the process.

'It seems I won the argument in the end,' he said to the spirit. 'But there is no joy in knowing it.'

He looked down at another grave, some way distant from the cluster, and found Jordan—the man whose family he had seen starving just two nights ago. This man's stone was flanked with two smaller ones, topped with stone lambs. Joseph felt a chill, and found he did not have the nerve to look closer, for he was already imagining that table of hungry children, and the likelihood that whatever food was offered there now did not have as far to stretch.

The spectre gestured that it was time to withdraw, but he shook his head. Joseph searched the gravestones for one name in particular, knowing that if these men were here Barbara's father had likely died at their side, a victim of violence. She might have been hurt or killed, and the fault would lie with him.

'Where is Bernard Lampett? He must be dead as well. Why does he not lie with his friends?'

The ghost led him back to a monument worthy of a lord: a marble tomb, with brass fittings and a weeping angel at the top that shone with gilt. It was just the sort of grand thing he'd have ordered, had he the choice. It was garish and horrible next to the sad simplicity he had visited, but at one time he would not have been able to resist this final display of wealth. He fingered the letters carved in the side.

'Lampett. Dead the same day as the rest. And his wife three months later.' Whether she had passed from poverty or grief, he did not know.

There was no sign here of what had happened to Barbara. But he could read the truth in the marble. Whatever had occurred, she had been there to see her father fall and to know that Joseph was to blame for it. The crypt he stood before was the product of his own guilty conscience. He had buried her parents properly, hoping to assuage whatever obligation he had incurred from the deaths.

He would only have done that if Barbara were still alive.

'Take me to her. I need to know what has happened,' he said, not bothering with a name. If the spirit knew to show him this, then it knew everything. He glanced helplessly as it raised a hand in the direction of the village, and they set off down the road together.

They would not be walking if there was nothing to see. He tensed, knowing that if the lessons held to form the spirit had likely saved the worst for last. But he had to know the truth, and so he set an eager pace.

'If you have something to show me, then be quick about it. I think you have managed to teach the lesson you wished. I must change. Although how I will do it I am not sure. There are expectations on me, you know. I cannot throw aside my engagement with the promise that she will be better off. Nor can I let the profits go hang and the equipment be destroyed. I cannot just walk away from it all.'

In response, the spirit said nothing.

'And now you will show me Barbara. What has become of her, then? Has she forgiven me? I seriously doubt it. Does she hate me? What misery am I likely to see? How will you lay it all at my door? Surely these people deserve some credit in their futures?' he said. 'She could just as easily have made a hash of things on her own, without my help. She was well on the way to that when I met her.'

He might as well have been arguing with the fog, for all he heard was the echo of his own empty words. But even he did not believe them. Even if he could convince himself that her misfortunes were her own doing, or her father's, it would pain him to see them.

At least they were going back to the village and not searching the graveyard for another stone. Surely that meant there was hope.

If he could just see her, it would be all right. What he saw—whatever its cause—could be changed for the better, even if he had to move heaven and earth—he glanced at the spectre beside him—or perhaps heaven and hell.

They were stopping at the same cottage she lived in now, as quietly cheerful as it had ever been, despite what he had just seen of her family. It held the same air of peace that he had seen just the other day, with the path swept of snow and the holly bushes by the door carefully trimmed. But it was as if, with the passage of time, the presence of the two others who had lived there had evaporated. If he searched, he would find no pipe ash in the garden, nor papers scattered on the writing desk. And there would be no Christmas dinner big enough for three and whatever guests might stop.

They drifted through the door as though it was nothing more than mist, and he was glad. He was sure that the cold tended to get in with each opening of the door, and it had a way of lingering like an unwanted guest. At least she should be warm and comfortable in her own home.

She was not in the front room, or the little kitchen, and he drifted with the spirit towards the bedrooms, feeling like a voyeur but unable to contain his curiosity.

He was right to be ashamed, for she was not alone. Though it was the middle of the day she was in bed, the sheet pooling around her waist as she stroked the back of the man lying beside her. She was older, as Anne had been, but still as beautiful as he remembered her from the previous night. Her breasts larger, heavier, her waist thickening. He wondered, if he passed through the cloth that hung over the doorframe of the other room, whether he would find a cradle in use, or a row of tiny cots. Were there children playing in the garden behind the cottage?

But there was no sound of laughter in the house or the garden.

He did not like to think that she had made no family for herself. But she was looking up at the man beside her with such warmth that perhaps the future was not so very grim. If he had nothing else, he would know that she was safe.

Then her lover turned, and Joseph saw his older self, rising from the bed.

Without thinking, Joseph ran his hands over his own body, seeking reassurance of sound mind and limbs. Was this really what he would look like? Or did he have some bit of that in him now? Vanity had made him sure that he was handsome, and ladies had done nothing to dissuade him from the belief. But this new him was a strange thing—pale, hair shot with grey, face hardened into a frown, body spider-thin and beginning to stoop.

The other him rose from the bed, not even looking down at the lovely woman who reached for him, pulling on trousers, tugging a shirt back into place and hurriedly tying his neckcloth.

'You cannot stay?' Barbara held out a hand to him, inviting.

'Why would I wish to? You could not even manage to heat the room, though you knew I would be coming.'

If the words hurt her, she gave no sign of it. 'It is warm enough in my bed, is it not?'

'It would be even warmer in a larger bed, with softer sheets. I have given you ample opportunity to move to more hospitable lodgings, and yet you insist on remaining in this hovel.'

'It is my home,' she said simply.

'It forces me to come into the village in the middle of the day. You know how the people treat me. And we both know what they think of you because of my visits.'

She smiled sadly. 'I cannot help how they treat you. What they think of me is no less than the truth. I fail to see, after all this time, how I can change that.'

Joseph felt a hint of dread. How had it come to this? Just this morning she had left him with her pride intact. Lying with her had been a mistake. But he had intended something different by it. Surely it meant more than this?

The older Stratford scowled. 'I do not like it.'

At last he was showing some compassion, and Joseph looked on anxiously.

'It reflects poorly on me. I will build you a house—a fine one—with servants and proper receiving rooms. I will place it closer to the mill so that it will be more convenient.'

Joseph winced, for he could guess the sharp rejoinder he would receive. Barbara would put him in his place, right enough. Then he would apologise for his foolishness.

'But it would not be as convenient for me,' Barbara said softly, with a lying smile that was close to the one he'd seen most often on Anne Clairemont. 'It would cost you nothing if I remained here and you came more often, rather than staying so long at the mill.'

'You know I cannot put aside my work for you.' His

own voice was deeper, rougher and annoyed. 'If I leave the floor even for a minute there is mischief. Thieves and ruffians, the lot of them.'

'You work too hard,' she chided gently. 'And you are hard on those who work for you. Perhaps if you showed compassion…'

'There is no place for compassion in business,' he barked. 'Since you know nothing about it, it would be better if you learned to keep silent, instead of parading your ignorance.'

Her smile faltered. 'Of course. But if I speak it is only because I care too much for you.'

Why do you bother? This man was hardly worthy of her affection. Suddenly, Joseph realised that he was thinking of himself as a stranger, and feeling jealous of and angered by the way that individual had squandered the trust that he was working so hard to earn. Apparently he had not even the courtesy to come to her in the night, to conceal what they did from the eyes of her neighbours.

And Barbara accepted it from him. She allowed him to treat her so after all the things he had done to hurt her, soaking up his cruelty like a sponge.

The other him looked down at her, eyes narrowed in suspicion, as though he had no reason to take her kindness for what it was. 'I give you no reason to care. But thank you.' He reached into his pocket and withdrew a jewel case. 'For you. A tiara to complete your parure.'

'Thank you,' she said, with a misery that the older Joseph Stratford did not seem to notice. She did not bother to open the box, merely set it on a table at the side of the bed.

'You idiot,' he said to his other self. 'I have no taste to speak of. But even I know that she would have no use for a crown. How could you? You are treating her…'

Like a whore.

'You're welcome,' said the other Stratford, and his response was as false as her thanks. 'And good day.' He turned to go.

Barbara's shoulders slumped in defeat, but she did not rise to see him out.

Joseph stepped forwards, unable to stand it any longer. He tried to catch the arm of the man at the door and his fingers passed through it. He swung again, in frustration, with enough force to bruise, and yet felt nothing but the passing of the air.

'Stay with her,' he demanded. 'Hear me, you bastard. I know you can. I am the sound of your own voice in your head. Listen to me.'

There was the slightest flinch in the shoulders of the man, as though he had felt a slap.

'Stay with her, damn you. Or at least take back that jewellery. You cheapen her with such a gift.'

The man he would become twitched again, as though he were throwing off a lead, and strode through the door and out of the cottage, letting the door slam behind him.

Slowly Barbara leaned back into the bed, as though it were an effort to stay upright and maintain the pretence of happiness when he was not there to see it. Without a word, or so much as a whimper, her tears began to fall. He knew the meaning of tears like that, shed in such utter silence. He had cried like that as a boy, when he had been convinced that there was no future for him.

He could bear it no longer, and reached out to touch her. But when his hand touched her face it seemed to glide through, leaving only a momentary warmth on his fingertips. There would be no comfort in this for either of them. He moved to sit on the edge of the bed, so close that he should have been able to feel the warmth of her body against his leg.

Apparently she felt the cold in him, for she shivered. 'It will be all right,' he said softly, hearing the trembling in his own voice. 'I will make it better. It will never come to this. I swear to you. You will not cry, damn me for each tear. You will not cry.'

He leaned closer, letting the shadow of himself fall onto the shadow of her until they were as one body. He felt the fear and pain and confusion that was in her as though it were his own. Worst of all, he felt her despair. She knew with certainty that it would never be better than it was at this moment, and would most likely be worse. He was slipping away a little more with each visit. She could sell the jewellery. She did not need it. She would never know want. But she would never know love. How had it come to this? He had sworn to take care of her.

He felt her own guilt at her weakness, and her shame at betraying her parents' memories each time she touched him. But she had loved him from the first. She still loved him. It had never meant more than money to him, but she had wanted to believe otherwise.

And Joseph realised with a shock that there was no blame here for anyone but him. He had done this to her—had changed every element of her life, had taken her family from her. And what he had put in the empty place was nothing more than cold comfort.

He could feel the increasing impatience of the silent spirit at his back, tugging him free. He fought, trying to stay with her, wishing she could feel some bit of him and take comfort in it, or that he could take away with him some small part of the burden she carried.

But he was gone with a wrench, being dragged back down the street towards the manor. He looked back at the haze of the spirit, feeling tears wet his own cheeks, and he said, 'I can change. Let me change.' He reached out to grab at the hood of the spirit, forcing it to face him as he had been afraid to before.

It turned to him then, reaching a thin, pale hand to uncover its face and stare at him.

It was his own face staring back. Not the one he saw in the mirror each morning, nor even the hardened man that was stalking through this unhappy future. This was him as he would be fifty years hence—still breathing, but near the end. He would be strong and healthy, but nearer to a century than to fifty.

And his eyes. At first he thought them soulless. But there was a flickering of pain, like a tormented thing racing about in his head, and a twitch at the corner of his mouth that he could not seem to control.

Joseph stared at him, into those familiar gray eyes, into the darkest part of his own soul. 'I have seen enough. Take me back. It will be different. As it should be. I promise.'

The ghost's shoulders slumped, as though relieved of a weight. The tension in his mouth relaxed. His eyes closed. And an empty cloak dropped to the floor.

It was a blanket. Nothing more than that. It had slipped from his own bed, in his own room. He had chased it to the rug and was sitting upon the floor and staring at it in the light of Christmas dawn as though he had never seen the thing before.

Joseph gave a nervous laugh and shook it, as though he expected to see some remnant of his vision. 'All over. Merry Christmas.' He said it almost as an oath more than a greeting. 'It is over, and I live to tell the tale.' Not that he could, lest he be thought mad. But he was indeed alive.

To the open and empty air, he said, 'And I will remember it all, whether it be dream or no.'

He reached for the bell-pull and rang for butler as well as valet, thinking it would be easier to rouse the housekeeper through an intermediary rather than directly. It would take more than one hand to set his plan in motion. The whole house might be needed, even though it was just past dawn on Christmas Day.

CHAPTER SEVENTEEN

JOSEPH stumbled down the stairs one step ahead of his valet, who was still holding his coat. The shave Hobson had given him had been haphazard at best. But there was much to do, and he could not wait any longer for the butler to deliver his message.

'Mrs Davy!' He stood in the centre of the main hall and shouted for the housekeeper. It felt as though he were taking his first deep breath in an age, after being deep underwater.

The poor woman hustled into the room, hurriedly tying her apron, a look of alarm on her rosy face.

He gasped again and grinned at her, amazed at the elation that seemed to rush in along with the plan. It made him feel as he had on the day he had first thought of the new loom—full of bright promise. Only this was better.

'Mrs Davy,' he said again. 'My dear Mrs Davy!' And then he laughed at the look on her face.

She took a step back. 'Sir?'

He had worried her now. Though he was not a cruel master, when had he ever taken the time to call anyone dear?

'I have more work for you. I take it the larders are still full, and ready to feed my non-existent guests?'

She gave a hesitant nod. 'There was much more than was needed, sir.'

'Then we need to do something with the bounty. Baskets. Baskets and boxes—and bags. Bowls, if you must. I want you to search the house and fill every container available with the excess. Enough to feed every family in the village. While you are about it make enough for a box for every servant here. Make sure that you and your helpers take enough for yourselves as well. Empty the pantry. I wish to give it away.'

'Sir?'

Had he really become so ungenerous as to cause this look of surprise? If so, it was all the more reason to change his ways—with or without the intervention of ghosts.

'I want,' he said, more slowly and with emphasis, 'everyone in the village to have as happy a New Year as I am likely to. It will not happen for any of us if I sit alone in a house that is barely half full, and they sit in the village with empty cupboards and fears for the future. I have broken a tradition. I mean to mend it now. As quickly as possible.'

'Oh, sir.' She was grinning at him now, as though he had fulfilled her fondest wish by forcing her to labour on Christmas Day.

'If you can fill the baskets, I will take the carriage into the village. And a wagon as well. I will see to it that they are delivered. And with them I will send an invitation for this evening. All who wish to come must dance and drink and be merry.'

'Yes, sir!' She was already bustling back towards the kitchen, disappearing as quickly as she had appeared, as though borne on a cloud of enthusiasm.

'What the devil is going on?' Breton was approaching from the stairs, still wiping the sleep from his eyes. 'Stop making such a racket, Stratford, or you will wake the whole house.'

Joseph grinned at him. Good old Robert. Loyal Bob, who must be sorely conflicted by his feelings of late. 'A Merry Christmas to you, Breton.' He seized the man's hand and shook it vigorously. 'And may I take this moment to say I never had a truer friend, nor a better partner?'

'I might say the same of you,' Breton said, looking quite miserable. Then he took a deep breath. 'That is why I must speak. I know it is not the time or place, but there is something I wish to discuss. I did not get a wink of sleep last night, and I do not think I can stand…'

'Not another word.' Joseph held up his hand to stop

the confession that he suspected was coming. 'I wish nothing more for this Christmas than that you save any difficult revelations for after New Year's Eve. If you feel the same way—'

'I doubt a few days will change my mind on what I wish to tell you,' the man interrupted. 'For I wish—'

'…after I break my engagement with Anne.'

'…to go back to London. I…' They'd spoken on top of each other. And now Breton looked as if he wished to suck his last words back into his mouth. 'I beg your pardon?'

'I am going to speak to Anne. We both know that she does not love me. I am quite sure I will not make her happy. No matter how much business sense it might make, it is wrong to catch her up in it and force a union which might be disagreeable to her.'

'There are certain expectations…' Breton said cautiously.

'And they are all about this house. Well, damn the house. I do not want it,' Joseph said firmly. 'I would be quite content with something smaller. With fewer rooms, and not so many ghosts.' He laughed again. 'Her father can have it off me for a breach of promise settlement. That is what he wants, after all. Unless…' He grinned at Breton. 'Unless you would be willing to take the thing off my hands? I expect you would be troubled endlessly by Clairemont, of course. He seems to have the daft idea that his daughter shall be mistress, no matter what she wants. You'll be in his sights for a husband then, I am sure. You'll likely have to take her with the deal.'

'How dare you speak of her in that way? As though she were property to be traded!' Breton was simmering with rage and quite missing the point.

'I cannot trade a thing I never possessed, Bob.' He gave his friend a significant look. 'I doubt that my leaving will create much heartache for Miss Anne Clairemont. But can there be any doubt that such a lovely girl will be married by spring? I should think there is some gentleman who would wish to fill the void I leave. If I knew of him, I would urge him to act quickly—use the disarray I'm likely to leave in the Clairemont household to good advantage and whatever bait might come to hand to clinch the deal.'

'I see.' But he did not seem to. Breton's face was still wary.

'If there is a man who loves her as she deserves, I would wish him well.' To finish, he gave Bob a hearty clap upon the back, as though to jolt the man out of his lethargy.

'I see. Yes, I think I do.' The grin spread slowly across his friend's face as his plans for the future came clear.

'I think you do.' Joseph grinned back at him. 'And a Merry Christmas to you, sir.'

'I think it shall be.'

'Now, what was it that you wished to say to me earlier? For I do not think I quite heard it.'

'Nothing,' Bob said, waving a hand to scrub the air of his words. 'Nothing at all other than to wish you well.'

'That is good. For this might be a trying day for you. What do you think our London friends are likely to say if I bring the whole of the village back with me for Christmas dinner?'

Breton thought for a moment. 'I expect they will be horrified.'

'Well, apparently, it is the custom in these parts. I cannot keep alienating the workers, or there shall be hell to pay.'

'You might lose some investors,' Breton warned. 'Feathers are likely to be ruffled on your fat pigeons.'

'Then I shall have to win them back another way. Or I shall find others. But let us see, shall we? I mean to visit Anne next. Perhaps I can enlist the aid of her father in smoothing the way with the Londoners. If he does not throw me bodily from his house first.'

Joseph's carriage pulled up to the door of the Clairemonts' new home and he wondered why he had not taken the place for himself. He had deemed it too far from the mill and rejected it out of hand. But, even with the addition of a wife and children, twelve rooms and a modest staff would be much closer to his needs than the monstrosity he now owned. How had he been so foolish?

He was admitted, and waited patiently in the parlour for Miss Anne, who was preparing for church, relieved that their current bond would make his appearance seem somewhat less alarming to the household. How they would feel about him in a quarter-hour was likely to be a different story. He wondered with a smile if he should have instructed his coachman to keep in his seat, whip in hand, for the hasty escape they would need to make.

There was a wild scrambling in the hall, followed by a sudden pause and the sedate entrance of Miss Anne Clairemont. The single curl out of place on her beautiful head and the lopsided bow of her sash were the only evidence that he had caught her unawares. She gave a graceful curtsey, as though allowing him the moment to admire her, and then asked sweetly, 'Did you want me, Mr Stratford?'

'I have come to ask you the same thing, Miss Clairemont.' It was a bold question, but his morning was a busy one, and there was no point in beating around the bush. He watched as her pretty face registered confusion. 'Come, let us sit down and talk awhile.' He sat. Bob would have been horrified, and reminded him that he could not go ordering young ladies about in their own homes, nor sitting when they stood.

But this one did not seem to notice his lapse, and perched nervously on the couch at his side, waiting for him to speak.

He took her hand. 'Before we go another step on life's road, Anne, I must know the truth. Do you want me?'

'I...I don't understand,' Anne said firmly. But the

truth of it was plain on her face—if only he could get her to admit it. 'In what way? Your visit is unexpected, of course, but not unwelcome.'

'I do not mean to ask if you want me now—this instant. I mean as a husband, and for life. Do you desire my company? I wish to know the reason for our upcoming union.'

'You wish to cry off?' Now her face was a mix of hope and dread, and a trembling that was the probable beginning of tears.

'I have asked and you have answered,' he said, as gently as possible. 'And that is how it will remain, if you truly wish it. Do not think I will cry off and leave you.' He paused and looked her clearly in the eye. 'If to have me is the thing that will truly make you happy.'

'Of course I am happy.' Her face fell.

If she persisted in this way he would have no choice but to marry her. Or perhaps he should arrange a match between her and the Aubusson. As she was making her heartfelt declaration she could not seem to take her eyes from the rug at their feet.

'You have honoured me with your proposal. My family stands to gain much by it. It will secure my future. Why would I not be happy?'

That sounded almost as if she asked herself the same question. It gave him reason to hope.

'Then now you must do something for me,' he said. 'Consider it a gift for our first Christmas.'

She looked up, quite terrified. 'I do not think… After

we are married...of course...but now? It is Christmas morning, Mr Stratford. And this is my parents' parlour.'

He laughed at her total misunderstanding of him, and at her obvious horror at the prospect of the conjugal act, wondering about how much she might have already learned from his friend about inappropriate acts of passion. If this was her view of him it was quite beyond a display of maidenly resistance, and much closer to active distaste. 'What I am requesting is nothing like what you expect. If we are to marry, we will be together for a long time. The rest of our lives, perhaps.'

He should not have said *perhaps*. He should have been more definite. That alone should have told him of his own heart. For once they were joined there would be no reprieve.

'And I should think, if we can give each other nothing else, we deserve mutual honesty—to be given without fear of recrimination. I have reason to suspect that you might be happier if you had been able to accept another. And that the primary goal in taking me is to help your family return to the place of social prominence it once held. If that is the truth, there is no shame in it. But would it not be better to state it outright, so that there can be no confusion?'

She blinked at him, unable to speak. But neither did she offer the quick denial that would have corrected a mistake.

'Now, tell me the truth. In one word. Do you love me?'

'It is not really expected, when one is of a certain

class, that one will marry for love,' she said, as though by rote.

'Nor is it expected that they will give a simple answer to a direct question,' he countered, but without any real irritation. 'But am I to assume, from your misdirection, that your answer is no?'

'I respect you, of course. You have many worthy and admirable qualities that would make a woman proud to be your wife.'

He sighed, for she was not making this easy. 'Then I am sure, since you have such respect for me, that you will be happy to hear that this morning I have taken the first step towards selling your old house to Mr Robert Breton.'

There was a moment of blankness on her face, a deliciously unattractive drop of her jaw and a sudden and complete lack of composure. It was the first sign of humanity he had seen in her. Then she spoke—not in the decorous half-whisper that he had grown accustomed to, but a full-throated, unladylike shout.

'Father!' She stood and shouted again. 'Father! Come downstairs immediately. I am about to break my engagement with Mr Stratford.'

Next, the carriage stopped at the first door in the village. His groom made to get down and take a package, but Joseph held up a hand. 'It must be me, I think. At least for the first few houses. Simply hand things to me, and I will be the one to knock.'

The first door was opened by a child. Before she could run for Mama, Joseph thrust the basket into her arms and shouted, 'Merry Christmas!' and then turned away to receive the next hamper and walked the few steps to the next door.

There. Not so bad, he told himself. He had half feared that there would be a punch upon the nose and a slammed door before he could get his gift across the threshold. At the next house he saw a wife. After that he found one of the weavers most vocal in opposition to him still in nightshirt and cap.

Joseph pushed the basket into his arms, with a hurried 'Season's Greetings!'

'I suppose this is to make up for the trouble you've caused?' the man said sceptically.

'It is mince pies,' Joseph answered, lifting the corner of the cloth. 'And a ham. While it lacks the supernatural power to mend our differences, it will at least be good with warm bread. I believe there is some wine as well. More concrete and useful than an apology, I should think. But you can have one of those as well. The rest can wait until Twelfth Night.' He turned away to get another basket.

With the man still standing dumbstruck in the open doorway, Joseph began to walk down the street. From the corner of his eye he saw the man turn as well, shouting back into his house. As Joseph walked he could see the man darting down a side street, and heard a pounding on a back door somewhere ahead of him.

He delivered his next basket, and the good wife who took it accepted it with a hesitant smile and a nod of confirmation—but none of the surprise that he had seen in the first houses. From then on he could almost hear the buzz as the news preceded him down the street with shouts, pounding footsteps and lads panting in kitchens to relay that the old dragon Stratford had gone mad and was giving away his hoard. A crowd was growing behind him as well, for just as the news ran ahead, out through back doors and down alleys, the consequences were trailing him like a parade.

At last he came to the Jordan house, and pushed a particularly large package into the man's hands as the door opened. 'Mr Jordan,' he said happily. 'A Merry Christmas to you. And—' he lifted the corner of the napkin that covered the gift '—a brace of partridge, cheese, oranges, sweets for the children, mince and a bottle of milk with the cream still floating on the top. Children need milk, Mr Jordan. And yours will not want for it once you have accepted the position of foreman at my mill.'

'Mr Stratford?' The man could not manage anything else, not even a thank-you.

'You needn't say more right now,' Joseph assured him. 'But you might help with the distribution of the rest of the packages in the wagon that is following my carriage. I have another important errand to run that will take me away from it. While you are about it, could you be so kind as to invite your neighbours to the manor this evening? The doors will be open, just as they always used to be.'

Jordan managed a weak nod.

'There's a good man. I will see you this evening, shall I?' Joseph looked at his watch.

Then he turned and ran.

The Lampett cottage was on the edge of the village, almost into the country, and set back at the end of a short drive. Joseph could feel the collective eyes of the people on him as he went. It was very near the same crowd as he had seen rioting at the mill. But where he had felt rage and distrust on that occasion he now felt a kind of wary encouragement pressing him forwards. The gifts he had offered had done much to disperse their ill will. But how they felt about him in the future would depend on his reception at this last and most vital of houses.

And none of it mattered, really. Not for the reasons they thought. While he might argue trade and tariffs until the last trump, he would have to agree to disagree with her father, and manage his troubled mind as well. But as long as they could be in agreement on one thing none of it would matter to him.

The winter air was sharp, and he ran until he could feel the pain of it in his lungs, in his side. Then he ran further, as he had when he was a boy and had no money for horses and no use for them either. It was good to be alive—to see the robins flitting in the bare branches of the few small trees in the garden, to kick the hoarfrost from the twigs and see it shower to the ground in a sparkle, and to hear the sound of the Christmas church bells growing louder as he neared the front gate and ran through it and up the drive towards the house. He did not stop even as he reached the door, but banged his body against it, striking knees and palms flat against the wood as he might have when playing tag as a child.

He peeled himself away to knock properly. Then he laughed and hammered on the door with his fists, heedless of the way it must look.

And then the door opened.

CHAPTER EIGHTEEN

FROM her bedroom, Barbara could hear the pounding on the door, and then her father arguing with someone in the parlour.

Why must he act up on Christmas morning? It did not help that she was already feeling quite fragile, nerving herself for the curious glances she was likely to receive in church today. She did not think she could stand a scene from him as well. Mixed in with his rising voice she could hear the chill tones of her mother, who was never able to soothe him.

She looked in the mirror, straightening her brown merino church dress with trembling hands. She could think of only one thing that would cause such strife and anger to both of her parents. But would anyone be cruel enough to tell tales about her on this of all days? If that was the problem, she had best go and face it herself, for neither parent was likely to be up to the task.

When she went into the parlour she saw her father standing in the doorway, his shirt collar open, neckcloth in hand. Mr Joseph Stratford was crumpling the linen of Father's cravat with a vigorous handshake. Her mother stood to the side, looking like nothing so much as an outraged hen when a cat was stalking in the chicken house.

Joseph glanced past her father to her, smiling as though he had not a care in the world. 'Good morning to you, Miss Lampett. And a Merry Christmas.'

'What are you doing here?' she asked, rooted to her spot in the doorway to the hall. Why could she not stop looking at him, cross the room, push him out of the house and shut the door? Why did he have to look so well, so handsome and so much more vital and alive than he had after their night together? Did he mean to show her how well he did without her? Surely he must know that she drank in every detail whenever she looked at him.

Joseph realised that he had not released her father, and let the hand drop suddenly, turning to her mother with a deep bow. 'And to you, Mrs Lampett. A Merry Christmas. I do not think we have been formally introduced.'

'I know just who you are.' Her mother said it in a way that would tell him where he stood with the whole of the family.

He grinned in her direction, as though to say, *Just you wait. Things are about to get interesting.*

Remembering how purposely obtuse he could be when he had a goal in sight, how utterly heedless of others, she gave a warning shake of her head.

'I suppose you are wondering why I have come here in this way, at this hour, on this day.'

'I am wondering if I shall have to put you out,' said her father. 'I assure you that I am quite capable of it, should you make any more trouble.'

Father was no more capable of success in that than in flying to the moon. But this was hardly the time to call attention to it, so Barbara put in, as meekly as possible, 'I certainly hope that will not be necessary.' She shot Joseph an evil glare. 'If I could just talk to you outside for a moment, Mr Stratford? We might settle whatever it is that brings you here, and continue our preparations for church.'

'But I did not come to speak to you, Miss Lampett. At least not just yet. I promise I will be brief.' He gave her the quickest of apologetic smiles, and then returned to her father. And, if she was not mistaken, she saw a twinkle in his eye.

He was making fun of her. After all that had happened he was amusing himself at her expense. She would be sure he was brief, indeed. The first time he stopped speaking to take a breath, she would haul him by the neck from the room.

'Then proceed, sir. Have you have come to threaten me with arrest again?'

Oh, dear. This would be one of the days when Father

was clear of memory and in a foul temper. Barbara's mind worked furiously to come up with a distraction that would separate the pair of them.

'On the contrary, Mr Lampett. I have come to ask for your help.'

This was so shocking a request that it reduced the whole Lampett family to silence.

Mr Stratford used the pause to his advantage. 'You know that I mean to reopen the mill in a few weeks, and that there are likely to be more workers than positions available? This concerns me greatly.'

'It does?' her father said, stupefied at this reversal of positions.

'You know the people better than I, for I am near to a stranger. I can think of no one better qualified to help me find other employment for them. I would compensate you, of course, for it would take a fair amount of your time. Then, if I can persuade Robert Breton to be its patron, we will likely be reopening the school. You would be needed there as well—either as a teacher, or in an advisory capacity.'

'I don't know what to say.' And clearly her father did not. The onslaught of new ideas had stopped his anger in its tracks.

'You need not make a decision now. Think on it for a time. I am opening Clairemont Manor this evening for the annual Tenants' Ball. Perhaps there will be time for us to discuss it then. But feel free to share my ideas with any in the village you might meet. They are in no way secret. I mean to find employment of some kind for all those who are willing to work.'

'I will. I will at that. Margaret!' He gestured to his wife. 'We must go to church immediately. We will see many of the men affected. I will broach the subject to the vicar as well.'

'You will broach it after the last hymn,' her mother said severely.

'Of course.'

But Barbara could see by the look in her father's eye that he was unlikely to hear much of what was preached, and would spend the next hour scribbling pencil notes in the back of his prayer book that would become a stirring and inspiring speech on the subject.

Father grabbed for his hat and opened the door, as though he'd quite forgotten that there was a guest present.

'One more thing before you go, sir.' Stratford touched his arm. 'Might I request your daughter's hand in marriage?'

'Certainly,' her father muttered. 'Margaret, what have I done with my muffler?'

But her mother could manage nothing more than a squeak of surprise.

'It is on your neck, Father,' Barbara said weakly.

'Very good, then. Let us go to church.'

Her mother recovered her composure and shot an exasperated look around the room. 'After we have tied your neckcloth, Bernard.' She struggled with his collar button and the rumpled linen. 'We shall go on ahead—and you, Barbara, shall meet us there. Mr Stratford, if we do not see the pair of you in the family pew before the end of the first hymn… Well, I do not know what we shall do. But I trust you to behave as a gentleman.'

'I do not know why you would, ma'am,' Joseph said with a smile. 'Perhaps you do not know me as well as the rest of your family does. But you can trust me in this, at least. I will take good care of your daughter.' He gave another respectful bow as Barbara's parents withdrew, leaving them alone.

Barbara shot a helpless look after them as the door shut. Then she turned to face Joseph. 'And just *what* is the meaning of this, Mr Stratford?'

'I should think that would be obvious,' he said, with another smile. But there was no mischief in it. He was looking at her as if he had never seen anything so wonderful.

'There is nothing obvious about it. Was it not just two days ago that you made public your betrothal to Anne Clairemont?'

'And this morning I broke it.' He reached out to take her hand, running a weather-roughened finger across the back of her knuckles.

'You did not,' she said, pulling her hand away from him. 'Anne will be heartbroken.'

'She most certainly will not,' he answered back. 'She is utterly besotted with my friend Robert, and thoroughly glad to be rid of me.'

'You knew?' She breathed a little deeper knowing that the dark secret she had uncovered was no secret at all.

'I concur with her. They are very well suited. But to make sure that there is no trouble with her father I am selling Bob the house. Lord Clairemont will have what he wants, and Anne will marry the son of an earl and the man she loves. And no one will be forced to marry into trade.' Then he looked at her more seriously. 'Not even you, if you do not wish to. Marry me, that is.'

'It might be the wisest thing,' she admitted quietly. 'After what happened the other night.'

'You could marry me because it is the wisest thing to do,' he agreed. 'But I would rather you didn't. If it is only out of concern for your reputation I would understand. But I was rather under the impression that you had strong feelings for me.'

Must I confess everything again? Though it is true that I love you, I am tired of being your plaything. She bit back the foolish words that she wanted to say, and fought the desire to throw herself into his arms quickly, before he found a way to ruin it all again. 'I would much rather hear your reason for wanting to marry me. What could I possibly have that you need, Mr Stratford?'

'My heart,' he said simply. 'I think you must have taken it with you when you left yesterday. It is not clockwork, as you said. If it was, I should be able to replace it.'

'You are clever with machines,' she admitted, doing her best to still the fluttering in her own breast.

'It turns out I am flesh and blood, after all. And likely to make quite a mess of things if I am allowed to go on like this. I have given up my fiancée and my manor. I have walked through the village handing over so much food that I am not sure there will be anything left for supper—nor money to buy more, now that I have promised to employ the whole village. And to top it off I will likely frighten my London investors by letting the rabble into the house this evening.' He held out his open arms. 'I am a disaster in the making, Miss Lampett. Someone should take me in hand while I still have a penny left in my pocket.'

'Not me, surely,' she said with a little smile. 'For I would not change a bit of you. It was a wonderful thing you just did for Father.'

'I doubt it will solve all his problems,' Joseph said, taking her hand again. 'But perhaps, if he has a purpose and a different direction for his energies, we might harness a portion of his madness and do some good with it.'

'That is a far cry from threatening him with a one-way trip to Australia,' Barbara noted. 'That was the tune you were singing to me just a few days ago.'

'I find I cannot stomach the idea of a father-in-law who is a convict,' he said, with a wry twist of his mouth. 'I might be in trade, Miss Lampett, but even I have some standards.'

'You seem quite sure I will accept you.'

'Because I will not take no for an answer.' He dropped to one knee then, and gave her hand a squeeze. 'I have seen the future, Barbara. While I cannot claim that I will die if you do not have me, I am quite certain that it would not be worth my living without you.' He dropped his head to plant a kiss on the back of her hand, humbled and at her feet.

'Oh, do get up.' She nudged at him with the toe of her shoe. For she'd had a sudden memory of what had occurred in the little alcove the last time he'd knelt before her. And she was sure her face was burning bright red.

'Not until you say yes.' He looked up hopefully. 'I have no ring to offer you, but you may have whatever you like. And I promise that I will not waste money on a gaudy parure with a tiara that you do not need.'

'That is the most outlandish thing I have ever heard,' she said. 'What sort of man gets down on his knees and swears that he will *not* buy his wife jewellery?'

'One who is so totally undone by love that he is no longer sure what he is saying.'

'You are undone by love?' She was not sure she believed him. But she quite liked the sound of it.

He nodded. 'And running out of time to plead my case. The church bells have stopped. Soon your mother will be coming back to box my ears.'

'Then I had best take you, hadn't I?' She stepped back and tried to tug him to his feet. 'For I rather like your ears just as they are.'

'Do you, now?' He stood and caught her around the waist, pulling her close for a kiss. 'I like yours as well. And your nose. And your eyes. And your fingertips.' He followed each revelation with a brief kiss to the honoured feature, and then put his mouth to her ear and whispered several other things that he appreciated, but that she was quite sure she should not let him see again until the banns had been read.

'It is Christmas,' she reminded him. 'And broad daylight. We are expected elsewhere, and already late.'

He sighed. 'Then put on your bonnet and we will be off.'

'I suppose you've brought your carriage again?' she said, tying up the ribbon on her new hat.

Then he proved to her that he had truly changed. For he reached into his pocket and tugged on his gloves, before setting his hat upon his head. 'Actually, no. It is not far, and such a nice day I did not bring it. We shall have to walk.'

'Together?' she said with a smile.

'I would have it no other way.'

* * * * *